*For my dear s
reading and writing ♡
Always lovingly –
Virginia*

October *2006*

One Was Annie

A Novel

*
Lora K. Reiter

*
*My student whom I hold in
high - esteem !*

PublishAmerica
Baltimore

ISBN: 1-4137-9692-3
PUBLISHED BY PUBLISHAMERICA, LLLP
www.publishamerica.com
Baltimore

Printed in the United States of America

This book is for all my parents,
especially Lora D. and Loren J. Reiter,
and for my brother and sisters

Acknowledgments:

I am deeply grateful to the following for their help to me in making discoveries and finding information that became connective tissue for what I could imagine. In particular I want to thank Susan Case, Rare Books Librarian at the Clendening History of Medicine Library at the University of Kansas Medical Center, who steered me to key consultants and facts; Jack Cooper and Randall Rock, M. Ds., for their assistance with medical details throughout the book; Herb Crawford, Leta Collins, and Della Jones for special help with historical details and some incidents; Marcy Schott, Reference Librarian at the Menninger Foundation in Topeka, Kansas; Sherrie Evans at the Missouri Historical Society; Lori Kravets for helpful suggestions about local museums; personnel at the Treasures of the Arabia Steamboat Museum in Kansas City; Lora Lorenz for assistance with historical materials in St. Louis; John Mark Lambertson and staff at the National Frontier Trails Center in Independence, Missouri; Jan Lee and Jane Ann Nelson at the Meyers Library at Ottawa University in Ottawa, Kansas; Barbara Dew and Hal Bundy at the Ottawa Public Library; Rick Prum, Ph. D., ornithologist at the Kansas University Natural History Museum in Lawrence, Kansas; Elizabeth Parham Robnett, Will and Betty Houston, and Tom Clayton, all of Bledsoe County in Tennessee, who introduced me to Walden's Ridge especially Roaring Hollow, and opened their homes to me to talk about the Sequatchie Valley; Paul Bohning and Irv Kartus who helped me find my strengths; the Faculty Rights and Benefits

Committee at Ottawa University for two research and travel grants; the administration at Ottawa University for a leave of absence to complete the book; all my en route readers who offered insight: Dex Westrum, Neil Harris, Barb Dinneen, Jane Ann Nelson, Peter Sandstrom, Shirley Swayne, Linda Chapman, Margaret, Sherron, and Erma, and most especially Joe Casad; Chris, Cheryl, Barb, Elaine, and the whole Computer Help network for unending technical assistance; Nat Sobel for his encouragement and insight; and above all, my sisters: Dot: for leading me to the topic, believing in my ability to write about it and editing so helpfully; Bev: for her unending enthusiasm, careful reading and support; and Peg: for teaching me about quilts. For the occasional liberties with time, place, and history and for any errors and inadequacies in the book, I alone am responsible.

"To have been
once,
even if only once,
to have been on earth just once—
that is irrevocable—"
                              —Rilke

Part I: The Bargain

"The spirit and body can die independently."
—Frazier

1

Every noise can mean more than itself in wartime. You have to use more than your ears to figure out squeaks and snaps, birdcalls and footfalls. For the men in battle who always have their guns at ready, maybe being afraid is a constant, so they are never surprised by it the way a woman is in her kitchen, peeling potatoes or folding down wash when the footstep or the silence comes.

Mary Sherwood was darning as she just caught the steps of a thin brown mare turning up the way where few now walked. The war had seemed far away for the moment because the day was so peaceful. The April morning was washed, blued, and fresh-dried, and the mocker and bluebird and wren were all loud at their places, the mocker turning flip-flops from the broken-masted east pine, the bluebird warbling from a post where the lot used to be, the wren scolding to the side of the house. Mary didn't even know the president was dead. She had been relaxed until the hooves tapped through the friendly noise and made her heart race. She was instantly afraid—though less for herself than for Annie.

The girl had been warned to hide when any stranger appeared, but she didn't always obey. Her father had liked to tell her that she was fresh as the morning dew, and that hadn't changed, not even through his death or the long days and nights of hiding in the mountain cabin. It wasn't only how she looked with her Irish black hair and skin that belonged on a redhead—as her daddie said to tease her. It was how she thought. She was still not selfish or suspicious. Not all the running and threatening had made her drop her eyes. "I'm not afraid,

Ma," she protested more than once when Mary was pushing her from the window so she couldn't be seen by some soldier stumbling up wounded, tired beyond feeling, or, occasionally, drunk.

But Mary was afraid—and of Union or Confederate alike. She knew anger wouldn't end just because the fighting had. And in this moment, she felt that truth as the acute jab of fear which quickened her breathing. "Nobody's mind is changed by war," she quarreled, though she couldn't have said with whom. "And them that has won can be as mean as them that has lost," she finished as she sat, needle forgotten over the heel of Annie's worn, black stocking. She was as certain of it as she was of her own name. Rising quickly, she dropped her sewing, picked up her scissors, held them like a knife under her apron, then moved to the south window.

The man was dirty, and the horse was lathered under the reins and between her legs. He had been hurrying as if eager—though earlier he had watched the cabin for half an hour, unmoving and nearly as wary as the woman only with much more heaviness in his body. Even his sense of being desperate could not push aside his feeling of being dead weight. He imagined that if he fell in water, not even his hair would float. Yet he was moving—forward, he hoped, though what he was about was so alien to him it did not actually seem to be his own future, a plan which he had consciously elected.

He had reined his horse to a stop above the Sherwood place, just inside the tree line of one of the meadows along Roaring Hollow— which itself descended from Walden's Ridge. Before the war, he had begun to feel some comforted by the charms of the Sequatchie Valley, and this morning, under the clean sky, the knobs above him looked gentle and unthreatening. Their long slopes and sudden drops were like soft dunes in the distance, and the trees there, just assuming summer green, looked familiar and once again welcoming. He didn't want to think that hills very like these—at Murfreesboro, at Lookout Mountain, all over the south—were scarred and darkened by fire and blood. He never wanted to think of it again. But the tightening in his chest and the dizzying vision which could engulf him in an instant— a red swirl of arms and legs and heads and bowels he had tried to piece back together in one field hospital after another—that vision, which menaced him always, commanded him now, bullied him into the sad certainty that he would never be able to escape seeing what had happened. And next, in the hated sequence he could rarely halt, would come the guled images of Narcissa and their baby.

By habit his hand had started to explore his darkened medical bag, but he had managed to stop it, willing himself to focus instead on the memory of a black-haired girl with porcelain skin, her cheeks as red as her scarf, laughing out loud as she rode a big, brown mule around the corner of a shed. That shed was not far from him now in the clearing below.

He had not drunk any whiskey for seven days, and though he was sick, he had forced himself, yet one more time, to leave the bottle in its place. Instead, he had lifted the reins, and the young horse had moved out into the sunlit meadow toward a trail running by the Sherwood's. She was green-broke only, nervous, and he had to help her a good deal. He talked to her, shifted his weight, signaled with his legs, and moved her along, aware before she was of what might make her shy. As he had drawn nearer, he had seen the girl sitting on the stoop. She was as shining and vivid black and white as he remembered, and she made the cabin look mocker-gray. He had felt his stomach pull at his hand again, but he kept it away from the whiskey, smoothed his beard as he could, and trotted the mare on up the path. Their bodies were one over her small, tight gait. His riding made them look like a dancer, elegant, when, in fact, they were a dreary pair.

Annie had seen him coming across the meadow, but she had not gone inside as her mother had commanded her to whenever strangers appeared, especially soldiers. As he approached, she began to wish she had. It wasn't his thigh lean against the side of the lean little mare, the way he gripped her and kept her headed to the cabin, all the time halfway gentle with her while he forced her to what she didn't want. It wasn't their grace—or their individual and rough features in such contrast to it. It was his eyes that held Annie. She thought he looked strange in his eyes, as though he could see your insides as well as your out. It wasn't that he was a surgeon looking at your insides that way. It was something else. And she drew into herself, feeling all of a sudden that he could have power over her if she were to look at him square on and he were to hold her gaze.

Of course she didn't know he was a surgeon as she watched him ride up. He looked like all the other soldiers she had seen. He was scraggly bearded. His uniform was so dirt-gray she could hardly tell it was Union. And he looked exhausted. It showed in his body which seemed to her to yield the way a dog's does when it accepts the beating it knows is coming.

Everybody understood something of that kind of fatigue, how quickly the fighting and the horror could enter into the men, making them all alike in a powerful and ugly way which distanced them from anyone who had not been in battle. When her brother had come back a late October night in '63 after only two months in the army, she hadn't at first known him. Because of all the raiders, she and Mary had left their valley cabin in August after Billy enlisted, and they were halfway up Walden's Ridge in what was left of her grandfather's old place. He had been a shingle maker, and lots of scrap wood still lay around, some good enough to start fires. A few valley neighbors were camped nearby or living in the lean-to against the cabin. That night, Tom Mackey had come up to the door and asked her mother in a voice that sounded like he was struggling with it, "Mary, you couldn't fix up a little meal for a poor, tired soldier, could you?"

They were surviving on the squirrel and rabbit they could snare and some few potatoes they had carted up from the valley cabin. The woman hated to give anything away because she could already look ahead to the day they'd have nothing left. But she couldn't say no, either. "I'll be blamed if I hardly know what to do," she had muttered to Annie, "but what if it was your Pa or Billy at some stranger's door?"

The girl had already lain down for the night to try to sleep and take her mind off sadness and hunger. She watched her mother stir up the fire in the little stove they'd brought and make some water gravy. Mary put in a pea-sized hunk of fat, and Annie knew she was sacrificing for him. Then she had sliced some bread off their loaf and called from the door, "You can come on in here now, if you want. It's mighty little, but you're welcome to it." She returned to the skillet and had her back to him when he entered the tiny, dirt-floored room that was their whole space. He had a hurt leg and was using a crutch, but he wasn't bad off.

The girl had watched him from her cot, and she began to frown, trying to see him better in the light from the kerosene lamp. Then he pulled out the one chair they had brought, took off his cap, and said, "Well, Annie Sherwood! Don't you know your old brother, Billy?"

She and Mary had lit on him at just about the same time, crying and laughing, marveling that he had come to them, even when they were gone from home and after they had felt sure he was dead. The war had already taken Annie's father and grandfather. And they knew Billy had been at Chickamauga where so many were killed. "It's a miracle," they said, over and over, especially after he assured them his leg would soon be as good as ever.

He hadn't even been wounded in battle, he told them, only a camp accident. "Leland just dropped his rifle, and it went off and hit me here in my thigh. It don't amount to a whole lot, but it's got me home a spell. I was lucky to be close enough to try to get here."

But Billy was changed. After they had stopped being hysterical and taken a good look at him, they saw the difference. His eyes were pulled back as though they were trying not to see, and even when he wasn't frowning, his face looked drawn. "I'm so tired, Ma," he said. "I'm not even hungry, I'm so tired." Annie had taken his hand and led him over to her cot. He didn't say another word. He just collapsed. They pulled off his boots, and he didn't move for hours.

Mary had gotten a quilt from her pallet and covered him. She was crying: "Will he ever ever be rested again?"

So the Captain seemed like all the rest to Annie when he rode up to their valley cabin, just more braid, longer whiskers, and deeper lines of weariness around his eyes. But when he got close and looked at her, he was different. No matter what his mouth did, his eyes stayed the same, and they were as gray as ice on the branch in dead of winter. All of a sudden she felt a shiver crawl up her legs and back. She remembered him. He had bought horses from them once—her mule, too, the winter before her brother enlisted. Billy had sold the stock to him, and he had been nice when he had seen how she hated to part with Charlie.

But then when Billy had come home that October, he told them such a story, a story everybody in the valley later came to know—how Captain Will Fairchild had murdered his own brother-in-law, shot him in the back at Chickamauga. Annie knew what had happened next, too, how his wife had bled to death trying to have their little baby, how it died, too, before it even got born, how that bedroom, all fancy with silks and satins, was turned into a blood-covered chamber that she heard looked like hell, itself. Everybody knew the story, and now, as Fairchild himself appeared before her, it made him look like a dangerous man even though he was so thin and grayed by the war and the road she never would have looked at him twice—if it hadn't been for his eyes. She felt herself trembling until she was afraid he'd see it, but his voice was soft and polite as he dismounted, easily for such a tall man and without any fuss over his sword, and asked her, "Miss Annie, is your mother at home?"

"Yes, Sir," she said immediately and started to get up from her stool, but he stopped her.

"Never mind just now. I'll make my way fine," and he walked by her. She was sitting in the morning sun making a small, white-oak basket her mother would sell in town. It seemed to catch his eye. "That's very beautiful weaving," he said, and when she looked up at him, he was smiling a bit. It changed his face, just not his eyes, and that was where she got caught. She felt hooked, like a fish in the river.

She nodded once, sort of like her head jerked, and she mumbled a thank-you. Then her mother came, and he went into their house. She sat there, looking where his back had been, feeling as though the war had finally come to her door.

2

Mary watched the man dismount and heard him speak kindly to Annie, so she felt he intended them no ill. She disarmed herself and hurried to the door. Measuring him against the jamb, she could see that he was taller than her men, but his sword was the only bright thing about him as he took his hat off and said, "Good morning, Mrs. Sherwood. I'm Will Fairchild," just as she was saying, "Hello. Come on in." In the confusion she felt at the moment, she didn't at first recognize him or the name, but then she did, and the whole story was immediately and graphically present to her, though not necessarily as it had occurred.

Much had been made of Evander and Narcissa Parrish's deaths at the hands of a man who had brought no stories with him to the valley, stories which might have softened some people toward him—or cautioned others—the way life does when it is shared. But Fairchild was an outsider, a Kentuckian, they assumed, although they did not, in fact, know anything about him except that he was a good physician and a man fortunate enough to marry into one of the most important families in the area.

Myths have their genesis in the daily affairs of ordinary humans, and Will Fairchild's destruction of George Parrish's family, and of Parrish, himself, was the stuff of legend for people in the Sequatchie Valley. Already stunned by the war which seemed to render neighbors savage, they saw even their image of civility falter and fall.

Doctor Parrish was their steward, a physician who tended them at their birthings and dyings, a good man, they thought, who helped them find courage when no one else could. He was not their hero, not

19

bigger than life to them. Nor did they think him their servant with only their welfare at heart. But they knew him to be kind and decent, and they trusted him.

A fact which they tended not to notice—or which they forgave if they observed and disapproved—was that he had inherited hundreds of acres of good valley land and thirty slaves to work it and to maintain his house, a fine, white, two-storied home near the center of Pikeville. He had also, in a manner of speaking, inherited the white families of the valley, for his father had been a physician, and generations of valley people had come to the office in back of the house where the elder, then the younger Doctor George had ministered to them.

No third-generation physician awaited them, though. Instead, young Evander oversaw the land, and Narcissa, his sister, managed the house. Both of them broke hearts—not because they were fickle or self-involved but because she did not find among the Pikeville youth a boy who could make her trust him with her heart and because he became absorbed in political interests when economics and abolitionists began to threaten what he most loved: the farms.

They were a handsome pair, Doctor Parrish's son and daughter, and perhaps because their mother had died when Narcissa was still a girl, he humored them as he pleased. He dressed them in finery he often sent to Chicago for; he educated them both privately and with tutors in music and art as well as history, the sciences, and literature. He required enough of both of them to help them become responsible children, and he delighted in both of them. Tall and fair, they were much admired and much sought after. But neither married, and to those who saw the gentle, widowed, loving father served so loyally and well by his handsome son and beautiful daughter, the Parrish family seemed a model of graciousness, a small and dear repository of what the South intended itself to be.

Each in the family might know better, but not the people who looked in on them and up to them—without observing that the tensions of the Union were creeping into the Parrish household, too. Though they never said as much, Doctor Parrish and his daughter were increasingly worried about slavery and the divisions it was causing in their community and in their house. Both of them deferred to Evander who was fierce in his condemnation of anti-slavers. The doctor had already put the house-servants' manumission papers in his strongbox, and they knew that—though Evander did not. John, Keelie, and their daughter, Ruth, told the doctor they were not yet ready to go. They liked George Parrish and Narcissa, and they did not have a clear sense of what might befall them if they went elsewhere. They were waiting—though neither they nor Narcissa, with whom Ruth sometimes discussed it as she arranged Narcissa's hair, knew what choices they might soon have to make or what consequences any choice could have.

In the meantime, Doctor Parrish understood himself to be exceedingly careful, maybe even a bit cowardly, about declaring his views openly. Narcissa, too, silenced herself when Evander was present. Her father sometimes wondered if they were both afraid of Evander, yet he didn't think that was fair to his son, and he knew it was a facile excuse for him and Narcissa. He suspected, though he didn't like to admit it, that they didn't want the unpleasantness. Evander could be very argumentative and unkind about political differences. The doctor supposed he and Narcissa simply preferred to avoid the dissention so kept their thoughts to themselves. Occasionally, he allowed himself to glimpse the turbulence and quandaries his conscience might have to move through, and he felt great dread. But for the most part he avoided such thoughts and enjoyed his work, his children, his library, and his sherry.

Then in the spring of 1859, he decided he needed a partner. He knew he could continue as he had been, but Pikeville was growing. People who had made their way as hunters were moving off the mountain to become farmers, carpenters, cartwrights—providing the town the increased services it needed and making more and more demands on the doctor at just the time he wished he had less to do. So he wrote his good friend and classmate, Friedrich Zeller, who trained doctors at his school in Kentucky, and asked for his help in recruiting an able, young physician.

Evander was critical and distant from the moment he knew his father was looking for a partner, and he made it clear that he disapproved. He was certainly opposed to any intimacy with his father's new business associate. "You don't seem that busy to me, father," he had said when Parrish first mentioned needing a partner. Then: "Who is he? How do you know you can trust him with our people? With your patients? What's he like? Why couldn't you get somebody from here in Tennessee as long as you had to have someone?"

Each question had disbelief or anger behind it, but neither of them quite recognized the fear also lying there. Parrish knew Evander was wary of everyone until he discovered where they stood on the slavery issue. Parrish also suspected jealousy in his son. It seemed to him that Evander occasionally thought he had disappointed his father because he had not studied medicine. But that was not the case, as the doctor tried to help him see. Instead, Evander was an excellent farmer and overseer. He liked the crops, the workers, the harvests. He was good with them, and he made money. He had increased their acreage by half. He had also invested in more slaves. This the doctor did not like, but he did not speak of it. Evander felt his father's concern, but because neither pressed the issue, it festered there, below the surface and between them. Parrish feared that war would come and make the division plain, a terrible breach all of them would have to acknowledge and endure. He did not know how they could deal with it. So he did not try to deal with it. He and Evander tried not to talk about politics, and now he managed as well to stop himself from defending a man neither had met. "He is a good doctor, Evander," he would repeat. "That is all that concerns me."

In Kentucky, Friedrich Zeller prepared to send to Parrish a young man whom he knew to be the best physician he had ever trained and whom he had come to love as his own son: Will Fairchild. The decision was painful and difficult for Zeller because he was an honest man who knew young Will was as troubled as he was brilliant. Torn between what he believed he owed both men, Zeller would not say to Parrish all he knew—and feared—about Fairchild, and he agonized over the problems he might cause them by bringing them together.

He thought for days about what he could say or should say as he recommended this young man whom he had known since the boy was four years old. He knew he could write about Will's intelligence and extraordinary diagnostic skills, about his devotion to medicine and his endless work—and he had done so. He also explained that Will was so excellent in animal treatment that men actually seemed to bring more mules than wives for his help, and he spoke of his and Will's worry that they didn't have enough experience with obstetrics.

He described the students' ether frolic which had cost Will an eye.

"It is worse than whiskey for some, you know, and Will, who came upon them bothering a young black woman, was trying to help her. He is, I think, a man of honor, though sometimes he is too much to himself. Maybe it is the eye. I could not save it. The prosthesis is good, but you know how young men are. They called him The Pirate when he was wearing the patch. It is not easy for him, sometimes."

Just the hint at Will's melancholy was all Zeller managed. He found that he could not speak of what he thought was most important: Will's total and unyielding alienation from his own family. It was a separation which Zeller had come to believe defeated Will's every turn toward other people.

From the beginning when Will had stood silent and aching before him seeking admission to his school as the son of a father who had just disowned him, from then through the ten years of their work together—first as teacher and student, then as colleagues at the school and as physicians serving their community together—Friedrich saw that Will was driven by anger he was unable to express or resolve. Though the obedience cost him sorely, he was single-minded in his acceptance of his father's decree. He refused to say even the family name, let alone speak of any person or event from his past.

He had immediately made that clear as he had stood before Zeller that first night, his face tight, not trusting a man he cared for, asking to be enrolled as Will Fairchild, not the Robby Cranach Zeller had always known. "Sir," he had said. "I have come to be your student, if you will permit me. I believe you have a letter and payment for my study here."

Zeller had seen that the boy found a way to speak no names, but Zeller had laughed in pleasure and replied, "Yes, Robby. I am so very glad to see you and to know your desire to become a physician."

"If you please, Sir." He had rushed through it: "As the letter must have explained, I am no longer connected to the family you have known, nor do I now bear that name." Looking sick but not hesitating, he repeated what his father had written. "I am no longer the son of that man," he said. And he sounded so definite Zeller felt as though young Cranach were announcing a formal challenge, as though he were throwing a glove in his old friend's face.

Zeller did not respond in kind, of course. He felt a fatherly affection for many boys at his school, but this one, this Robby-Will— something in him pulled at the doctor's heart. At the same time, he did not like to see the hardness, the obedience turned to stone. Zeller knew that pure law was dangerous, and he looked for Robby's heart, his spirit. He saw only anger in the boy's eyes.

Though Zeller did not know what had caused the estrangement, he thought he understood a part of what must have happened. Cranach's letter had been as cold and unyielding as the man himself had always seemed to Zeller. "I send you this payment for his study there, but I wish to have no word of him, not now or in the future. He must make his own way. I no longer have a son."

"The fool! The absolute, utter fool!" Zeller had spoken aloud as he threw the letter to the floor. It heightened his dislike for this man he had often worked with, even more because it opened freshly his own constant sorrow: he and his wife were childless. "It is *I* who have no son," he said, talking to the letter in the anger he had often wished to direct at Cranach, himself.

Friedrich and his Greta had tried every remedy he knew. When she could no longer drink the concoctions he could think to brew, they prayed to their dear God in Heaven that He should grant them a child. But their God did not answer as they hoped.

Seizing up the letter again, he thought, "But this Cranach. He *does* have a son, a fine, handsome, smart boy. And he throws him away."

Furious and hurt, he sat at his desk and thought of the family he had known for many years: him, her, them. As editor for several medical books Cranach publishers had brought out, Dr. Zeller had often been a guest in their Philadelphia home. But it was not a pleasure for him, as he always complained to his wife. It was not a pleasure for him because of the boy, little Master Robert.

Zeller, himself, found it difficult to talk with the senior Cranach. "He has no interest in what others think," Zeller would tell Greta. "I am surprised that he accepts my *medical* opinion. But the *boy*," he would say. "The boy can say nothing to his father. He comes to my room to ask questions about what I write, what I think. He is a sweet, beautiful boy I wish is ours." They would touch hands and sit in silence.

Zeller had observed well. Young Robert could not talk with his father.

Cranach liked best to tell his son and daughters what they must do to be obedient children and to honor their parents and God. Zeller thought Cranach liked to bully them all he as stood above them in front of the fire and read at them from old texts. He especially admired Cotton Mather: "Child, you have been baptized; you were washed in the name of the great God; now you must not sin against Him; to sin is to do a dirty, a filthy thing. Child, you must renounce the service of Satan; you must not follow the vanities of this world; you must lead a life of serious religion. In your baptism you were bound unto the service of your only Savior. What is your name? You must sooner forget this name that was given you in your baptism than forget that you are a servant of a glorious Christ whose name was put upon you in your baptism."

The girls were young, just four and seven, and they could fidget or fuss without angering him. He would have their mother ring for their nurse to remove them to their beds. But the boy, only nine, must not yawn, must not lean against his mother. Zeller was sometimes so tired and bored when he could not find a way to avoid the evening devotions that his own eyes dropped tears as he stifled yawns. But if young Robert slumped or grew restless, he was frowned at, or worse, and the lessons would stop until he was again dutiful. Zeller knew him to be beaten for falling asleep.

The doctor could see that Robby grew no more dutiful or respectful by such treatment. Instead, Zeller thought he grew stronger in opposition. He saw the boy struggle to hold his eyes wide open until he looked as if he were in a daze. He would hold himself up straight with his arms locked until they shook. He studied to memorize more Bible verses than his father assigned, reciting them quickly after the required ones, not looking at his father who would then have to turn back to him in surprise. The boy always tried to do more than his father demanded. Zeller wasn't convinced that he did so to earn respect. The man's own life and practice gave him examples of such behavior as attempts not to please or astonish but to insist, to prove, maybe to dominate. It was not obedience, then, not duty or respect or love he thought he saw in the boy's extreme efforts. It was argument. It was not to submit but to command. And Zeller hated to see an open-faced child made stern and unconsciously duplicitous by such an exacting father.

That same controlled resolve was what Zeller found in Robby

when he was at the medical school. At first, he had been so happy to see the boy. He had looked for him every day after the letter arrived, and he had hoped to do something good for Robby, something loving, something noble, he sometimes dreamed. But no such intimacy developed between them. All he managed for the decade of their association was to give the young man the best medical education available in the States. From the beginning and without any question about what had occurred in the Cranach family, Zeller agreed to Robby's new name and stayed gentle before his fierce insistence.

"As you wish," he had said, putting his hand on the boy's shoulder. "I am glad you have come. Your name is no matter to me. Your future as doctor is what we will work at now."

And work they did.

At first, Friedrich would say to Greta in delight, "This boy surprises even me, and I was an excellent student, myself." Only later would he see the work as Will's only consolation, his only hold on what did not wound him.

The young man studied every matter in every text available to them. He read all he could find, making tiny, careful notes, especially if texts disagreed or failed to address questions he raised. He visited families after patients began to feel better or after they died, writing his own studies of symptoms, how sicknesses had progressed or spread.

Zeller knew Will slept little. He was always reading, always walking to look for herbs or to study animals, too, always working. Sometimes Zeller would say, "Stop for a glass of wine with me, Will, and we will talk a little." But he soon discovered that his student did not want to talk about anything except his work. So Zeller would read some of Will's notes and do his best to share and encourage the young man's studies.

"Why do you want to be a doctor, Will?" Zeller once asked him.

He was moved to hear: "I think because of you, Sir, the way you studied and had time to. . . .," but Will stopped there, and Zeller was left to picture what Will had edited. He returned to the notes to try to find something in them to speak of.

Fairchild never received a letter while he was in Kentucky. He did not spend time with other students. They drank hard and laughed some as they worked. They made jokes. But not Will. He was always polite to Friedrich and Greta, but he stayed much to himself, too much, Zeller knew. Sometimes Will looked so tired and smelled so of whiskey in the morning that Zeller worried he had drunk his way to sleep. But he always did his work, and far better than anyone else. After he had finished his classes, when he remained to teach and to study and work privately with Zeller, the doctor very much hoped Will would maintain the school after his own death.

Still, when George Parrish wrote him and asked for a young physician to enter his practice, Zeller gave up the dream. He hoped it would be easier for Will to go to someone who did not know of his past. Then, too, Zeller knew George Parrish to be a warm and generous man, a good father who might, in some way, be able to help Will learn to trust again. "He is not free with me," Zeller told himself, understanding that he had never softened the young man's sense of his past. So he wrote Parrish, hopeful for Will but worried about omitting more than details of Will's break with his family and his tendency to drink too much.

He granted that Will was a superb teacher and physician, and he wrote that, while he was not at liberty to speak of Will's family, he knew them to be intelligent and religious people. But he could not write what he believed was most important: Will Fairchild was not yet a man free to enter the future he hoped would deliver him and contain his father's retribution. Zeller was not sure, in fact, that Will even knew this was what he wanted, what he required. For Zeller, Fairchild never grew beyond being the boy bound to the father. Zeller sadly imagined that when Robert Cranach was dead, he would still find a way to say to his son, "You are not a free and able man but only a child who must carry out forever a senseless duty." That, he could not write to George Parrish.

In someone else, Will himself might eventually have come to understand what Zeller saw, that such a hurt become such an anger could make a person adhere to a principle far beyond any legitimacy it ever had. He might have been able to see that a ritual obedience was as enslaving as an actual master and that, after years, such a harness, acquiesced to, even chosen—lived in— could seem one's own nature though it rubbed deep wounds.

But he could not see it in himself. No one, not Friedrich Zeller or, later, George Parrish—both of whom loved him and whom he loved—not Narcissa—who had seemed to him his salvation—no one had been able to free him from his sad, square sense of justice and the profound depression it brought him to.

3

In June of 1859, Doctor Parrish awaited the arrival of his new partner. He was eager to see this man who would be entering their lives. He admitted to mixed feelings, both about giving in to his bodily aches and pains and about bringing into his family circle a man of such sympathies, insofar as he had been able to deduce them from Friedrich's letter. He was somewhat pleased to think, if he was judging correctly, that another liberal thinker might be added to their little group, but he was worried, too, because he knew Evander was tense and troubled about the new doctor's possible views.

When Fairchild rode up, Doctor Parrish noticed first the gray beard and was somewhat surprised. He had inferred that Will was younger. Then he saw what a splendid rider the man was, sitting tall and straight on a flat saddle. The big bay gelding was attentive to him. He only touched the reins, and the horse arched its neck and stopped in its tracks. Fairchild dismounted quickly and lightly, and, giving Amos the reins, patted the horse on the neck and turned toward the house, dusting his coat and walking without hesitation.

The next few days were busy with arranging their office space in back of the house and getting themselves somewhat acquainted in the process. Fairchild refused the offer of an upstairs room. He said he would consider it later, but for the moment he wanted privacy and time to himself, so he would stay in the Pikeville Hotel for a while. "I frequently work late," he explained, "and read until all hours. I don't want to disturb you or your family with my comings and goings." He did agree to come to dinner with the family on Saturday, a few days after he had arrived.

Narcissa, Keelie, and Ruth all worked hard getting the house and meal ready. Somehow he seemed to be a special guest, and they, determined to please him.

Will and Doctor Parrish had not spoken of anything but medicine, patients and the practice during those first days. Parrish didn't know exactly what Fairchild's convictions were, but he was hoping for a political compatriot when Will arrived for dinner.

Parrish had seen his son's eyes take in every detail of Narcissa's table, the Spode and the silver. She was making it a special occasion, and everything looked beautiful—the way it had when her mother was living: yellow roses and fern entwined in the centerpiece, the crystal brilliant in the candlelight. Evander was not happy the moment he walked into the room, and both Narcissa and her father could tell it. Will, of course, was unaware of anything amiss, and he responded much as the doctor had hoped he would:

"This is a lovely table, Miss Parrish, just lovely," he said, and he seemed at his ease.

The two had met briefly, but this was the first time any of them could try to relax and actually come to know one another. It struck Parrish—and he didn't know why he had not thought of it earlier—that Will was a young man without a wife, and Narcissa, though she was twenty-two, had not chosen anyone, either. He sat back a bit and looked at them, and he realized that they might be a match. She was just a little nervous, which was not like her. Perhaps she had already thought about a future with this man. Will was not in any way Parrish could tell abashed or uncertain. He was not lively, but he was attentive and well mannered. He was accustomed to such a house. He did not drink much wine.

They were having what seemed to the doctor a satisfying time until Evander leaned back, wine in hand, and announced, "I'll be going up to Crossville Monday to meet with Governor Harris and some of his supporters there. With Lincoln on the horizon and Bell threatening to drain off Breckenridge voters, we've got to plan some strategies. If we don't, we're likely to lose any voice in what's to become of us." He took a long swallow of wine, all the time keeping his eyes on Will's face.

For a moment Fairchild didn't respond, then he nodded and said carefully, "I'm not from Tennessee, but I know this election will be a very important one for the whole country." Then he looked not at Evander but at Narcissa and asked, "Are you, like your brother, interested in political questions, Miss Parrish?" It was clear to his host that Fairchild hoped to avoid conflict.

Evander reddened and tried to respond for her. "Our women tend not to be politically inclined, Mr. Fairchild. I doubt if Cissa much cares who wins this election as long as she can surround herself with pretty things and has a brother and father to assure that she's secure with them."

In her turn, Narcissa blushed, but her tone was even as she responded to Will's question and herself ignored Evander. "Yes; indeed I am, though I'm not often asked what I think about such matters."

It would have been easier had she stopped there, but Narcissa was stung a bit, and perhaps she sensed an ally. "It seems to me that everything centers on the question of slavery. And although I know I am very uninformed about many aspects of this, I cannot, in my heart, bear to think of how some of the Negroes are treated. I don't think I favor the extension of slavery throughout our nation."

It was a strong statement, and Evander flushed from his collar to his hair. Keelie and Ruth were standing by the serving table. Keelie had nursed Narcissa along with Ruth and watched them grow up side by side. When she heard Narcissa speak, she looked with a sudden frown at Evander and very nearly fled from the room. Narcissa saw also and immediately tried to calm him. They were, in fact, great friends, usually careful with one another, and she had no desire to hurt him, none at all. Still, she was herself a strong-minded young woman, and once committed, she couldn't retreat: "Van, I know you think differently about this, and I dislike opposing you on anything. But I can't help what I feel."

"*Feel*?" He turned his chair toward her. "Feel?" His tone was soft, but he drew the word out like a slow cut. "Well, well, my dear sister. Aren't your delicate feelings just a splendid reason for attacking everything we are? Do you know what we live on, what they're built on, our economy, our whole way of life?"

"I'm not attacking it, Van. I only think that surely there must be ways to keep some people from the inhumane, the inhuman treatment of their slaves. And surely little children should be cared for, not separated from their mothers and fathers."

"You are being foolish and sentimental," he insisted. "I suppose you've got your hands on that Stowe book. You sound like her. You don't have any idea what you are talking about or what is involved. Arguing for laws against extending slavery? For laws dictating how a man shall dispose of his property? What can you be thinking?"

She started to reply, "I admit, Van, that I don't know. . .," but he spoke over her words.

"Have you read what Douglas has said? It's like instructions for how a territory can prevent slavery—regardless of the constitution. Do you even know that a darkie has had his case for freedom argued *before the supreme court of the land* on grounds that he had been domiciled, *domiciled,* in a free state?

"What do you think that bodes for us and our ways, Narcissa?"

She remained calm and started again. "I admit, Van, that I don't know the details of this as you do. But I see people who are hurt and afraid, and I cannot help but feel that enslaving a people because of the color of their skin, then building a society on their bondage and misery can never be appropriate in the eyes of God."

Will's hand had moved to his wine glass, then returned to his lap as Narcissa straightened her back and looked at him. "I am sorry that my brother and I should disrupt dinner, Doctor Fairchild," she tried, then looked down at her plate. "It is not often that we find ourselves in such profound disagreement, I assure you."

But Evander was not ready to stop, and the elder Parrish decided to let it play itself out some. However unfortunate this might be for Fairchild as a first-time guest, the good doctor apparently thought that the words and emotions had been kept back too long, that the discussion was inevitable.

Evander stared at his sister, his mouth curled down, and he made a nearly silent exhalation that moved his head backward. It was an ugly gesture. He had drunk too much and was too full of anger and the uneasiness it covered. "Maybe if you were to try to examine this rationally you would see that everything you have and are depends on this 'ungodly,' as you call it, enterprise." He waved his wine glass in a circle in front of her face as he finished, and his father and Fairchild looked quickly at one another, then Narcissa.

"Do your *feelings*, Narcissa, tell us what we should do to counteract three northern railways that give them industry and power we can't hope to match? Do your *feelings* dictate to us how we are going to live with a president, if Lincoln's elected, who has stated as a fundamental political principle that this nation cannot survive as a house divided? And all that northern strength and all that arrogant, abstract, stupid idealism that you dare to mouth at this table will support him in dismantling everything we have and everything we are. Do your feelings deal with that, Narcissa?"

She had grown pale, and her eyes were moist, but she stood her ground. "I know that I'm not informed, Van, the way you are. After all, I have no voice in this. I cannot even vote, you must remember. But I am not ignorant. I have read some, and I know there is another side to this. I know it is not right by any standard of decency or religious principle that one race of people should serve another, not for any reason, certainly not because of the color of their skin." Her pain and anger strengthened her voice.

"And I'll tell you something else. I'll tell you how I know this."

Evander pushed his chair back and seemed ready to rise from the table, but she put her hand on his, and, for whatever reason, he remained seated.

"Van, from the time I was a little girl, I saw something over and over again that I hated. When Keelie gave Ruth and me some little treat, a piece of cake or a cookie, whatever it was, she would just hand it to Ruth. But for me, she put a white napkin in her hand and laid my treat on that. Always. She would never just hand me a cookie as she did Ruth. At first, perhaps, it made me feel special. Then it made me feel sad that this dear, kind woman, this decent woman who actually nursed me at her breast, this woman would be unable to hand me a cookie.

"Good heavens, Van! Did she think I would think she was unclean? What possible reason could she have from me to be so careful?

"And then when I understood that it wasn't me—it wasn't anything to do with Keelie or me—it was this whole way of life we are part of that made her have to do it and me have to let her do it—when I understood that, I hated it. And I still do."

She had tears on her cheeks by this time, but Evander was unmoved, at least by her story. "Well, would you like it better, my bonnie lassie, if one, two, or three *million* of your fine, kind, decent Negroes, dirty field hands and illiterate *bucks* were free to come and go as you do, to demand pay for their work, to look at you without any fear? Just how would you like that, Missy? Just how long do you think you'd have your fancy dresses and china? Just how in the hell do you think you would live then?"

He had risen and was bent toward her. Their father had to stop it. "Sir!" he said. "Evander. Sit down. You forget that we have a guest. Please calm yourself and sit down. And you, Narcissa. No more talk of abolition tonight."

But Evander did not sit down. He threw his napkin in his plate and slashed out: "I have no appetite for this food or this company." And he left the room.

Parrish apologized to Will. He supposed it was worse for Fairchild than for them, he knowing them so little and being so insulted. But the young man nodded with apparent understanding, then, later, walked out and around the lawns with Narcissa, comforting her and, her father took it, sympathizing with her view.

So it began.

4

Narcissa could not remember leaving the table let alone going out-of-doors with Will Fairchild. But then she was aware of his hand at her elbow. It was very hot and close on the lawn, actually unpleasant, and she was perspiring and extremely warm. Yet she could feel his skin through the stuff of her sleeve, and his palm was warmer, still, than the air or her flesh. She found, much to her surprise, that she was breathless. Her anger with Van disappeared, and she forgot everything except that she was alone with this man she had spent the week thinking of as she never had any other. She found that she was glad to feel his strength and the heat from his body.

They walked slowly along the paths scented by mock-orange and white pine until he finally said, "I do not want to intrude on your thoughts, Miss Narcissa, but I do want you to know that I thought you were courageous and very persuasive in what you said to your brother. I know it is an awful problem, for your family and for all of us, but if it matters to you, I think you are right and did right."

For a moment she thought she would weep in gratitude, but instead she found herself taking his arm in both her hands and moving closer to him. Though he was very much a stranger, she knew with sudden clarity that what he thought was more important to her than anything either her father or brother could say. And that was a shocking realization.

She did not find him especially handsome, though she thought his smooth, firm skin was an appealing contrast to his graying hair and beard. She couldn't really tell how old he was, but in ways he looked settled and wise—except across his eyes. She wasn't particularly preoccupied with his artificial eye, though she had to admit she did keep trying to see which it was. Her father had told them he had lost it trying to help a young woman, and she liked to think that of him. Though the prosthesis was excellent, still there was a definite cast to his eyes, something just askew that made him look sharply attentive, very focused or as though he might shy—like an uncertain horse.

That did not seem to be part of his manner, though. Indeed, he seemed calm and secure with them. And his hand, then his arm, seemed secure and calming to her. She very much liked it that he supported what she said as well as how she stepped. She had had no way to know what his political sentiments were, and she knew that she had risked much. Yet his very presence had seemed to embolden her. Otherwise she would never have found the strength to oppose Van. She hoped that, with Will here, she and her father would discover how to bring what they thought a just order at least into their home. What she couldn't know, of course, was how Will would deal with her brother. Clearly she and the doctor needed a source of strength, and something in her thought Will might supply it to them.

When they came in, he asked if he might speak with her father about calling on her, and she was deeply pleased. She knew her papa would say yes, and, with unexpected joy, she felt in her heart that Will was the man she would grow to love and want to marry.

This was a strange experience for her. She had been courted by several young men and even the father of one of her friends. She was not a girl anymore; in fact, she was one of the last among her friends to be unmarried, and she sometimes wondered if she had been too exclusive, too demanding. She had never found the person who could make her want to explore herself and life together with him. But Will Fairchild did.

Narcissa went to her room and raised the lid of her hope chest, her initials carved deeply into the light cedar. John had made it, and her mother had begun it for her when she was born. After Amanda Parrish became sick, she had filled the chest with the special silks and cottons and linens she could imagine her daughter wanting. On top, wrapped in soft, white paper, was her wedding dress. For the first time in many, many years, Narcissa took it out, held the satin folds in front of her and around her, touched the warm pearls sewn to the high lace collar and the wrist insets, and fantasized leaving their chapel with that white delicacy firmly secured by a black jacket over Will Fairchild's arms and back, his having to walk carefully because the full skirt would be pushing against his legs. She lay down and prayed that she was not being silly, that this could happen, that they might be endlessly happy.

5

Narcissa and her father had not expected to see Van at breakfast after the disastrous dinner, but he entered the breakfast room in much the same temper he had left them the night before. He was still red-faced, and he looked puffy and exhausted. He had not slept, and he had drunk a great deal. His eyes were bloodshot, and when he looked at Narcissa, she had the discomfiting thought that he might have seen or heard Will and her as they walked. Whether or not he had, he certainly wanted to get at Will: "What? No wall-eyed Kentuckian to break our morning bread with?"

"That's uncalled for, Evander," their father replied, and Narcissa kept silent as she handed Van a cup of tea.

"I don't know, Father. You'll have to admit he is one strange-looking fellow!" Then he said directly to Narcissa, "Don't you think so, my dear sister?"

She was immediately nettled, even though she knew that was what he wanted. She replied as she could. "Since you have no respect for my thoughts, I can't imagine that my opinion of Doctor Fairchild would be of interest to you."

It was feeble, and it gave him his opening. He was pleased to be able to return to their difference so easily. He hurt her with his dismissal even though her words had invited it.

"Actually, Cissa, you are right. Your particular political opinion has no interest to me whatsoever. The unfortunate fact is, however, that there are men in power who entertain the same lofty fancies that you and your lady novelists do, and interesting or not, such fancies have to be dealt with. They can be very dangerous, and we can no longer be polite about them."

While she puzzled over what possible politeness Van had extended her, he sat down with his back to her and faced their father. "And you, Sir?" he asked.

"I, what, Evander?"

"Are you prepared to support, here in your own home, the sentimental poppycock Narcissa fed us last night?"

Parrish's hand shook some as he set his cup down, and he was, she saw, very angry. At the same time, she knew he adored Van and had restrained himself many times to avoid this confrontation. Suddenly she wanted to give her brother a more suitable opponent, someone who wouldn't have to fight love to respond to his unkind and unbridled words. "Perhaps you should talk with Doctor Fairchild, Van. Or would you consider his ideas to be sentimental poppycock, too?"

He turned toward her in that slow, lithe movement he had used the night before. It was insinuating and foreign to both of them. "And what do you know of the political persuasions of our Doctor Fairchild?"

Narcissa realized immediately that she had just made these two men dangerous to one another, and for the first time, she understood the insane and completely personal breaches that would characterize this war if it came. She wished she had not mentioned Will, but there was no going back. "Of course, I cannot speak for him, but I sense that he shares some of my feelings, that he is not blindly in favor of continuing slavery as we know it."

"And you think I am blind about it, Cissa?"

She looked directly at him, then, and the years of loving him dearly came into full collision with the months of doubting and fearing his opinions. She did not know how to continue.

Fortunately, their father did. "You asked me, Evander, whether I would support abolitionist sentiments in this house. We have avoided the issues so successfully I think you have no conception of my real thinking about these matters. So I want you to understand very plainly. There will never be a day when differences of opinion will forbidden in my household. Nothing on earth kills the human spirit more quickly than some absolutist position that denies all challenge. I will not have it."

Perhaps surprised by his own emotion, Dr. Parrish continued. "You may find that abstract idealism. For me, some of the greatest thinkers of all times have been abstract idealists who fought tyranny and those who would deny them their voice. In my opinion, many of them are writing now about this dreadful dilemma we find ourselves in. This man, Thoreau, and Lincoln—they are both powerful thinkers to my mind—and Whittier. All of them make me think more and more carefully about what it is we are doing to the Negroes. And like your sister, I have grave doubts."

Evander had risen from the table in the middle of his father's response. He put his cup and saucer down hard. It made the older man flinch, and Narcissa knew she hated what her brother did. Doctor Parrish seemed unable to rise from his chair, and his face looked so sad she wanted to embrace him. But she could not.

Evander stared hard at both of them, then he spoke in an almost normal voice. What he said wounded them. "So. So the lines are drawn, are they?" His mouth was turned down, but more in sadness, it seemed to her, than insolence.

"I am not very surprised, Father, at what you take as an intellectual position. I know your love of philosophy and literature. But I cannot in any way understand how you can arrive at a political position which will destroy the whole fabric of our life. How can you do this?"

He gripped the chair back hard, and they saw tears brighten his eyes. It was a terrible moment for all of them. "You are naive, Father," he said, shocked, himself, at his words. "I never thought I would or could say that to you, but you simply do not know what is happening."

His father's eyes were harsh on him, and Evander was pale and frowning. "You have lived a good life, Father, and you have helped so many. I know that. But you do not understand that all we have, all we love may disappear. Father, they will take everything. Absolutely everything. Governor Harris and Mr. Yancey even foresee that we may have to secede. South Carolina is close to it."

Parrish got up at those words: "Secede?" He had found his own deep voice again. "These are the men you are working with? And this is their program?" He moved around the table to his son. "Evander. You go too far."

But Evander stood quietly and spoke quietly. "Nonetheless, Father." He shook his head just a little, then he said, "Here we are.

Here I am." Then he sighed so deeply Narcissa thought he could have no breath left in him. But he did. Looking directly at their father, he said, "I love you, Sir." But neither of them made a movement toward the other.

Then he turned to her and said the same thing: "And I love you, Narcissa."

When he did that, when he said that, she saw her oldest and best friend, her brother, being torn in two before her eyes. She followed her heart toward him and tried to take his arm, but he moved back. "We all know there is no middle ground in this, don't we?" He was shaking his head from side to side as he spoke. Neither his father nor his sister responded.

"Well. Here we are," he said again, and looking as though he carried a thousand pounds, he moved to the door. There he turned back and looked intently from one of them to the other. "Well." He hesitated, and she didn't know if he was altogether ironic when he said, "May the good Doctor Fairchild comfort you both."

And he left then for the trip to Crossville he had planned for Monday.

6

Theirs was not a storybook wedding—or courtship—Will and Narcissa's. But for the most part, she was happy, and she thought Will was, too. Sometimes they felt they had no right to love and be happy because it was such an awful time for all southerners, and perhaps especially hard for those in Tennessee who seemed forever divided over the slavery question. Certainly the Parrish family continued to be. Whether it was Will's presence or simply the way events developed, Narcissa and her father very soon accepted, though they both wept about it, that their differences with Van were irreconcilable.

As Will settled into the practice with Doctor Parrish and became known in the town and surroundings with people bringing both their animals and their families to him, Van became more and more active in politics, finally moving to Crossville as a strong supporter of William Yancey and Governor Harris. He advocated reopening of the slave trade and secession from the Union, and he was jubilant in October of that first year when the Negroes failed to rally in the abolitionist cause at Harper's Ferry. He saw that as proof that black people would never fight for their own freedom and as evidence that they lacked the intelligence or moral fortitude to aid the north against southern slave owners.

Narcissa and her father often tried to talk with John and his family about it, and though they said little, the Parrishes were persuaded by them that Negroes would seize what opportunities they could if they felt they had some small chance of success. Keelie and John worried openly about what to do. Ruth spoke less about it, but she hugged Narcissa tightly one day, and she, Ruth, when Narcissa reminded her that her freedom papers were in Doctor Parrish's safe and that Narcissa and her father would love Ruth forever no matter what decision she came to make.

Everyone was frightened.

With Lincoln's election and the building of the Confederacy, no one could plead neutrality, and Will was not neutral. He opposed the Confederate Compact and supported Lincoln's determination not to extend slavery. So did Narcissa. In fact, they quietly agreed that they opposed slavery altogether and vowed that they would free all the slaves if they could.

In April of 1861, when the Confederates took Sumter, Will and Narcissa felt they could wait no longer to marry, even though they did not yet have their own house. Doctor Parrish insisted that they share his home, that it would help him if they did. And that was their choice, too. So in June, 1861, just days before Tennessee did secede, Will and Narcissa were married. Evander wouldn't attend, of course, and Doctor Parrish embraced Will as his son—not to replace Van, certainly—no one could do that—but as his compatriot, a man who shared his profession and his beliefs, he thought, a man he was proud to honor as his son.

He gave Will his pocket watch, a wonderful old piece with small diamonds and gold filigree over black enamel on the front, a gold back and chain. It had an extremely gentle and clear chime when the case was opened.

Will couldn't take it at first. "Oh, Sir. You do me too much honor," he said, his head down and his voice blurred.

But George Parrish insisted. "I know what I am doing, Will. I know what I want to do. I love you as my son, and in my heart, this belongs to you. I want you to have it."

Will cradled it in his hand, running his fingers over it. His manner spoke more than his words could have. They saw how he cared for this man who had befriended him and how he struggled with his emotions, swallowing and blinking, not able to speak. Narcissa loved him then more than ever, and she was never more proud of her papa.

They were wed in the Parrish chapel, the little white church Narcissa's great-great grandfather had built. Outside, in front of them as they faced the simple altar, lay generations of her people: her mother, stricken in her thirties with a disease Narcissa's father could not name or halt; her father's father, himself a white-bearded old doctor who created her memory of him by allowing her to pull out his upper lip by its mustache and let it go pop against his teeth. Other grandparents lay there, too, beyond her memory, under huge, curved half-houses of rock, unmortared but weighted forever over the coffins. As children, she and Evander had crawled over them, trying to see into them though terrorized at the prospect—old mausoleums which looked as though the ground had risen around them.

Sometimes during these days, Narcissa felt as though the war was rising around her and would enclose her as surely as those old rocks did the coffins of her forebears. Still she and Will had four months together before he enlisted in October of '61, and she saw him two more times to love him: at Christmas of that year and in January of 1863 when he came to the valley to purchase horses and mules.

Narcissa had wanted to marry him. She needed to marry him. But some part of her hesitated and hesitated, even after they were one. She saw that he was, in every public way, a kind man whose principles were strong and who was willing to fight for them— and in every private way a loving man whose first concern seemed to be her and her happiness. But she also discovered that Will drew a line between parts of his life, and he was absolute about it. He would not, he could not, he said, talk with her about his youth or his family.

"Don't push him, Narcissa," her father cautioned her. "I know it is difficult. I am curious, too. But I'm willing to take Friedrich's word— and to value Will in his own right. I think that's what you should do, too."

And she tried. But she felt more than curiosity. She felt robbed of the laughter and sadness that made Will who he was. Perhaps more, she felt robbed of intimacy, a basis for trust between them.

"Don't romanticize me, Narcissa," he said, pleasantly enough but definitely when she first asked for some hint about his family. "They were good people, but we had differences, and there will be no reconciliation. I've made my own life, now. I beg you to let it rest there."

But he looked so sad she couldn't quite stop, and she pulled his hand into hers and crimped his little finger against itself to tease him some. "Come, Will. Thou shalt tell me all," she laughed to him, trying to imitate Kate.

But he would not play. "It's not a matter to share, Narcissa. I wish I could. I've no desire to make any part of my life seem more or less than it is. But this. It has nothing to do with what you and I have. Please believe that. Please trust me."

There. He had named it, too. Try as she might, she could not arrive at it, the trust he wanted and perhaps deserved. She was accustomed to her father and his clear, open ways. All of her own life was shared with Will as fully as she could. He listened to her stories, asked about details, smoothed her slights and laughed at her humor as dearly as any lover could. But he was not forthcoming in his turn. And that stilled her when she wanted to be everything and all to him.

She felt it most in their love-making. She did not mean to be deliberate about it, withholding from him in a perverse formula of loving, but she nonetheless lay still sometimes when her heart was jumping, and he would turn from her saying, "I don't want to if you can't." Or she would keep her hands still at her sides when she wanted them to be all over him.

His body was strong, and she loved it. And he would tell her she was beautiful and pull her hair over her face and over his and kiss her through it, and she loved that and him. But she did not forget, not ever, that he knew and would not tell her what she did not know and needed to hear. In the daytime, when other people and sights and sounds preoccupied them, it was all right. But in the nighttime, when nothing should have intruded between them, his secrets did. She could feel herself stopped at his boundary, and she felt helpless with it. Sometimes she tried to tell him how far away from him he seemed to her to keep her. He would grow silent and hold her, but he would not speak of it.

He felt awful strain from what was not between him and her, and a part of him wanted to tell her. He wondered, sometimes feeling nearly frantic with it, why he could not simply and calmly tell her about his family and Deborah and the rest of it. He did not think it would have changed what was between them. But the image of his father shouting at him, seizing his name away like some inferior, wrathful god, that scene never blurred or faded. Neither did his own pain and outrage as he agreed in his heart never to say the name again, never to refer to that family, never to think of them again as long as he drew breath.

He had fought for more than twelve years to keep that vow. He willed himself to turn from any thought, even of his mother, from any narrative which could explain her standing quietly at the library door while their world exploded, any explanation which would give him the right to love again at least his sisters without feeling dishonor. He had no way to understand how surprised and helpless and grieved his mother herself had been that day.

7

Perhaps she ought not to have been surprised. Neither she nor her husband was lenient with their children, especially their son. They had, themselves, been taught by the rod, and in their turn they had not spared the boy. Robert, in particular, and often more harshly than she thought necessary, resorted to whipping. Usually she did not watch because her heart misgave her as she saw the boy, at first proud and determined not to cry, begin to weaken as the blows grew harder.

Robert made him bend over a chair, and he brought the thin branch down very hard until the boy's whimpering became moans. Then he would ease and stop. He would tell young Robert that he would be strengthened, that the pain now would keep him from further error, that God's love was not easy to deserve, that fathers must be stern. Esther knew her husband was right, but in her heart she did not want their son to be hurt like that. Afterwards, she would sometimes take Robby a tart or muffin, but often he would simply look at her and it as though they could not be connected, then turn away. She knew that beneath his hose and breeches ran long red slashes that would grieve him for days.

She could not always be certain what occasioned such whippings. It seemed to her that Robby was a good boy. He did well in his studies; he did not talk back; he was responsible for his chores and took good care of his little sisters. If he did err, she could see that he was not always forthright about it, and even that, though it did not actually involve an untruth, was insupportable to his father. Robby had learned very early that no mistake would be tolerated. If he admitted that he broke an egg or spoke in church, he would be punished. If he equivocated or denied, he would be punished. Robert never agreed to discuss such matters or to pose questions about them. He was not prepared to listen. He despised excuses, he said.

Esther had long ago learned to hold her tongue when her husband found discontent with her, but sometimes, as a woman, she could soften Robert's anger or lead him away from his preoccupation, even though she felt false to herself for doing so. But their son had no such means. He could only avoid his father as long as possible, then try to face him, knowing always, she was certain, that he must finally suffer the humiliations of yielding to physical pain and, later, of denying himself even an attempt at self-justification. She often thought that was unfair, but it did not seem critical to her. Robby remained, she thought, spontaneous in his expressions of love and duty to both of them. She was too long in understanding how such love and duty could double back on them. At least so they did on her.

In fact, she had not known how to help her son when he most needed her. His father, face swollen and furious, had closed the dark doors in her face, isolating her away from himself, Robby, and Deborah's father. Esther had had premonitions of the difficulty. She had seen the girl look at Robby, smile up at him. Certainly she was young, just fifteen, but Esther quite believed Robby when he said Deborah was willing. "Why would she not be?" Esther thought. So while she despised her boy's conduct, she could not blame him solely—as her husband seemed to. At seventeen, Robby was splendid, she knew, black-haired, tall, straight and handsome, wealthy, kind: he was a girl's dream, surely. Esther could not believe that Deborah would not let him know that. Still, she knew he was responsible.

What she could not conceive was that her husband would ever be able to act so cruelly. Neither could she imagine a situation in which she would behave with the cowardice that struck her that day. At first she was outside the library doors listening as best she could. She thought she should be in the very room, but Robert had said that she might not be, that this was for men to decide. Later she slapped her own cheek and called herself stupid to have obeyed him until the conversation had gone too far to recall. When she finally braved his anger, the matter was effectively settled.

Robert had called Deborah's father and Robby together. Esther was sure they each knew why. He had planned it very carefully. She supposed he had to, in part because that was the only way he could assure his control, perhaps especially his own self-control. That way, too, there could be no brooking him.

What she remembered most was his calling Deborah a wanton and Robby a willful and indiscreet fool. "I am prepared," he said to the girl's father, and with irony she did not expect from him or think became him, "to make arrangements for this fair child. I am giving you here, sir, five hundred dollars, which I am sure I needn't tell you is a considerable sum of money."

At that point, she dared to open the door a bit, and she saw Robert hand Mr. Huddleston an envelope. The man stepped forward, seemed to bow, then stepped back again. He acted as though he were being honored. Her son was standing with his hands at his sides. His face was pale. He saw her, but she motioned with her hand to her lips, and he nodded weakly, his black hair falling across his brow.

"With this, you can, of course, make certain that your daughter is appropriately cared for until and during her confinement, and it will provide for the child's upbringing and education so it will be able to make its way. But I shall not, you understand, make any other recognition of the child or acknowledge it as an heir, and I expect you to sign this paper accepting those terms." Robert's hand was shaking as he dipped a pen and handed it to the chastened man.

Robby's face was twisting.

Then Robert asked Mr. Huddleston to leave. As he did, Robert saw his wife at the door. For a moment, he flushed deeper, and his eyes were grim and accusing. Then he turned his back and moved again to his desk. He leaned on it for support. She saw that as she walked into the room. Taking another envelope from under the lamp, he extended it to their son. "This is two hundred dollars for you," he said. "She gets more because she has two to look after. You get this. Nothing more. Except. . .," and again he turned to the desk.

Robby let the envelope drop to the floor. "Father, you must listen." He was frantic. "I never forced her. I never. . . ."

"Silence. Be silent." The man looked as though he might fall, that or kill. "I don't want to hear this. I don't want to hear any detail of it.

You knew better. You know better. You have shamed us. I want to know nothing more of it. Do not speak."

Esther could not speak. Her chest was full and painful. She had some trouble breathing, and she was afraid for both of them. They looked dangerous to her, like cornered animals, but they were both pale as death. She did not know whom to go to.

Robert then opened two side drawers, one after the other, and removed a book from the first, and a large, soft, leather pouch from the other. His words slowed, but his voice remained hard. "You once expressed an interest in medicine. At that time, I had Snowden make this for you." And he drew from the beautiful leather cover an even more beautiful cherry wood case with bright, smooth brass hinges and designs. "It is an amputation kit," he said, "one of the finest I ever saw." He handed it to Robby who found the strength to take it and hold it.

He laid the book on a corner of the desk. "This is a first edition of one of our company's finest publications. Every doctor has it. It is *The Universal Formulary*, the best directory available to herbs and medicines. You may want it. You may need it."

After a moment he went on, slowly but without mercy in his manner or voice. He never looked at the boy. "I have sent a letter to Doctor Zeller at his Kentucky Medical School. You know him from his visits here. He will take you as a student and apprentice. I have already paid him for that service. I hope you will not be so foolish as to turn your back on such an opportunity for it is the last assistance you will receive from me.

"As for the kit, I received it only a few days ago. I had no time to have a name engraved on it. That is just as well." He lowered his voice and continued without inflection. He said, "I don't know what you will call yourself, but understand well, Sir, that from this time forward, you are no son of mine. I shall not endeavor to communicate with you in any way about any matter, and I shall expect the same from you. You are to have no contact with any member of this family ever, from this day forward."

Esther cried out then, though she didn't know it until her husband turned to her. As though he had completed the part that required his control, he began to shout: "You mark it well, woman, as well as he. From this day forward, I have no son." Then he sank in his chair with his face in his hands.

50

She ran to Robby, but he could not embrace her. He was looking down at the kit he held flat in front of him. She saw great wet splashes on the dark, burnished wood. Then very quickly he raised his eyes to his father who still refused to look at him. Robby was trembling, but he found strength to make his voice firm.

"As you will, Sir," he said. "I promise you that you shall never again have reason to shout at my mother on my account. You shall never again have reason to curse me. I apologize—I am sorry—I am sorry for the pain I have caused." And he snatched up the book and the leather case and ran out of the doors, up the stairs.

While Robert sat with his head in his hands, Esther picked up the envelope Robby had disregarded. She saw the servant dash to the barn, and she leaned on the banister as Robby ran down the stairs with only a small grip in hand.

"Robby!" she screamed at him. And then he caught her in his arms in such a hug. She struggled to think of one thing to say, but all she could manage was his name which she repeated over and over. She crushed the envelope into his hand. He kissed her hair and her cheeks, then he thrust her from him.

"Goodbye, Mama," he said, and he fled. He vaulted onto a bay gelding Henry had brought saddled from the stable, and he was gone. It was over, just like that.

She had not thrown herself down in front of Robert or under the horse. She had watched her husband disown their son—for her as well as for himself. She saw her boy terrified and hurt and alone. And she stood there and let it happen. In her mind, she betrayed him far more than he betrayed the girl.

She was never certain how her husband managed his grief. He went to his office. He came home. He went to church. He came home. He went to his club. He came home. He published books. He came home. He read, he continued evening devotions, and he occasionally played with his daughters, though he never answered their questions about their brother. Perhaps it changed his life in some way, but she did not know.

For herself, though, she knew in her soul that she lost far more than her son that day. She had not thought she could ever see a life destroyed and do nothing. But she did, and it was her own son's.

She never again mentioned Robby. She never again sang a song. She never again came willingly to her husband's bed. And she accepted that she would die much sooner than she would have had she done what was right that day.

The boy—who chose to rename himself Will Fairchild—had, at seventeen, taken the money, the book, and the kit, and he had left, making his vow of perfect alienation aloud so he could hear it.

He gradually came to a realization of sorts that his oath had wounded him deeper than his father's curse, that it left him without an inner balance he sorely needed. He knew it made him hurt others when he never wanted to. He was very aware that his silence about his past distressed Narcissa. She told him so, that it made her feel distanced from him. But he could not bring himself to say the words which might have eased them both, and she, like Friedrich Zeller and her father, had to learn not to press him any more. She had to accept the rejection of his refusal.

Narcissa also had to learn, early in their relationship, that although Will drank very little with others, he drank a great deal by himself. Of course, that worried her and added to her sense of his private and impenetrable world.

At dinner—or after—he rarely drank, though sometimes he would share a bourbon with her father. He said he didn't care for wines or liqueurs. But late one night—it was after Yancey had left the Charleston convention, and Will was convinced the Union would break—she knew he had stayed to read in her father's study, and she went downstairs. He was sitting at an awkward angle in one of the overstuffed chairs, and he had a glass of whiskey in his hand. He made no response when she entered the room.

"Will?" she called to him, but he didn't answer even though she thought she saw his head move very slightly. She was frightened and didn't know what to think. It seemed to her that he would fall from the chair, he was sitting so strangely—stiff in his back, but leaning forward and to his right where his arm was on the chair arm. Running to him, kneeling in front of him, she called again, very sharply: "Will!" And she tried to take the glass from his hand.

His eyes were half closed, and he looked sick. Actually he looked as though he were in a trance, just not there, not in his body. He gave no indication that he recognized her, and his hand stayed in the curve that had gripped the glass so hard she had to loosen his fingers.

"I'll get Papa, Will," she said because she thought he must be very sick. But then he slowly rolled his head from side to side and made an unintelligible sound. She thought he was saying, "No." And suddenly she began to feel silly. She had never seen anyone drunk like this before, and she even laughed a little at herself for being so naïve and scared.

"Will! You goose!" she giggled. "You frightened me. You truly did. And you're nothing but good and drunk."

He breathed out a little and seemed to try to see her. His head nodded. So she pushed him back in the chair and pulled a footstool over for him. When she lifted his feet, he fell back in the corner of the chair, his head on his shoulder, his eyes shut. She thought, "You're going to have a very stiff neck in the morning to go along with a very bad headache. Just explain to Papa, yourself." And she covered him up, kissed his hair, and went to bed.

But at breakfast when Will joined them, he was much as always. She saw his hands shake a little, but he had his tea, discussed the day's work with Doctor Parrish, was gentle to her, and made not the slightest reference to the night before. She came to believe he didn't remember it at all.

It was some time before Narcissa learned how much a person must drink—and how regularly—before they reach that state and remain able to function the next day. Even so, she loved him. Her father never mentioned that he thought Will drank excessively, and she thought he would know and would tell her if he knew. So she ignored that scene and some other signs, going on to their engagement and their marriage, never reassured about who Will was or what was behind him. She was certain that he loved her and she him. She had had to hope that would be enough.

8

Narcissa's heart beat against her ribs and in her throat until she felt stifled when Will rode up to the house in January of 1863. She had not seen him for thirteen months, and she thought she could not stand it when he dismounted and seemed to her to stumble and nearly shrink into John's arms. He had written to say he would try to be home for Christmas, but he didn't come, and he didn't come, and he didn't come. Still she never stopped looking for him. All her days came to a circle of odds and ends in front of the south bay window with her sewing and letters and reading and bandage rags in piles that began neatly each morning, then by evening radiated out in all directions around her chair and footstool.

Then that blessed day, the afternoon of the eighth, there he was. Because of his special knowledge of animals and the area, he had been sent to buy livestock for the army. He had four days. Then he would join General Rosecrans' divisions.

He was not riding his old Rupert anymore. He was on a much smaller and rather thin gray horse which was not well-groomed. That struck her almost as much as the changes in Will did. As she ran to him, she thought it strange that she should visualize him mourning his horse, knowing full well he had been at the side of a thousand dying men.

His letters had not described the details of it. He wrote that the war was unspeakably cruel, that he couldn't keep up with the wounds, that he didn't have what he needed to treat the men adequately, that what he had learned in medical school seemed unrelated to what he was trying to do in the field hospitals. But he didn't write of the hideous particulars that filled his nightmares and made him wake up sweating and needing whiskey. Now, at home, he was determined not to speak of them. Narcissa had only to look at his face, then to see how he was thinned and grayed by it, to sense what he had not written of, his own unwounded suffering. For the moment he appeared to be older than her father. He looked shattered. John was crying out, "Oh, dear God! Doctor Will!"

Then she seized him away, and they held one another. Or actually he leaned on her, and she held him. Neither of them felt passion, rather the awful mixture of happiness and fear and anguish that comes when you are restored to the living—or someone you love is—though a precious sacrifice of arm or leg or peace of mind had be paid for the return. "I'll be all right, Narcissa," he was saying. "It is just such a long ride—and such a change—from hell to heaven, I guess," and he lifted her face and kissed her forehead.

"You are thin, Will."

"Yes. I know. We have enough to eat." And he left it there. "Let's walk a bit, shall we? Let's walk in the garden. We do still have a garden, don't we? They haven't been here, have they?" He began looking everywhere at once as though he had been gripped by the thought that the war might have marched through the house since he had last heard from them.

But it had not. All the flowerbeds and trees and out-buildings were safe. Many of the hands were gone—most of the stock, too. But nothing was destroyed. Though everything was winter-clad, still the lawns and shrubs were orderly, and neither outside nor inside was much changed.

"God. I am so glad to see you and this place, Narcissa," he said, as he sank onto the first bench they came to and gestured her down beside him. "It is so quiet, so blessedly quiet." And he closed his eyes and pulled her to his chest. His fingers caressed her face—the backs of his fingers on her cheeks and nose. After a while he sighed and asked about her father.

She jumped up and pulled him after her. "Come, Will! He is in back in the office! Oh! How could I have forgotten?"

But Doctor Parrish was smiling at the door, laughing, really, as they ran up the walk. John had called him from the office, and he had been waiting for them, patience and consideration winning over his own great need to see Will. How they did embrace one another—great, huge hugs—patting—pulling back—then hugging again. Parrish shed some tears, then Narcissa did, too. Perhaps that strengthened Will.

"Come, George!" he said. "Cissa! No tears! For heaven's sake, no tears! This is the happiest day of my life, I think. And none of us must cry."

When she could look at him again, his face seemed more in place, more gathered; some lines seemed gone. From somewhere he was summoning the strength to approach a peaceful table and a bed of love. Somehow he was willing himself to leave the bodies and the wounds and smells and sounds of the battlefields to be her husband and her father's son in a civil house. She could not actually imagine what an effort it must take to come from that chaos to the ceremonies of napkins and silver and courtesy. She could not bring herself to think much on what it was like from Will's point of view. She was too full of her own insides pushing all directions at once.

She did notice that he wanted them to talk. He said very little, himself. He asked questions, but he didn't always seem to attend to their responses. His eyes moved around the room, slowly over the fire, over faces, to his own hands, back to their faces. More than once he blinked his eyes, shook his head, and interrupted whatever they were saying with, "I am so happy to be here, to see you once again."

No one spoke of Evander. Narcissa had written that Van had joined the Confederate forces and was at first with General Bragg. They didn't know where he was now. Nothing more could be said.

Keelie and Ruth fixed a simple dinner of pork roast, greens, and baked apples, but, though he made over it, Will ate little. He drank a great deal of bourbon without its having any apparent effect on him—except perhaps to quiet him even more.

Later, when he and Narcissa came together, he was very tender with her, and she felt free with him for the first time. "I wish we could have children, Cissa," he whispered in her hair. "You are so beautiful and so strong. You would be strong enough for both of us. And we need children. So many have died. We must have children."

"I hope you and I do have a child from this loving, Will," she said back to him, not quite granting all he meant. "And maybe we will."

He sighed. "I hope so, too, though I may not be here to help you with it."

She didn't want to hear anything of that sort, so she moved to lie on top of him, something she had not done before, and said straight down to him, "Don't you talk that way. Not ever. I will have your baby, but I won't raise it without you, and don't you ever forget that." She felt him almost chuckle, something he never did, and when they made love again, they rolled over and over one another until they were both caught and filled and emptied.

The next days were a mixture of gentleness and strain. It was as though Will wasn't sure what to do with himself, and they didn't know what to do for him—or around him. If he had been home to stay, everything would have been different. They could have made plans and seen those friends who were left or looked for a place for their house and begun to work. But he was home only for a moment, and that shadowed everything they did or said. Others they met wanted to talk about battles and the wounded, their kin and their fears. So Will and Narcissa stayed in as much as they could and were more awkward than ever before in their lives together.

Narcissa didn't acknowledge that it was easier when Will left, but in a way it was. The stress of worrying about him had become a habit she knew how to deal with by routines of work in the house and at her father's office where she helped as she could—and at the church circle meetings where women rolled bandages and boxed up cookies and scarves and socks and underclothing for the soldiers. With Will at home, every moment was changed and charged with expectations she couldn't name, with longings she couldn't quiet in either of them, and with dread both of saying the wrong thing and of the parting they knew they had to endure.

Will could rarely be still, yet he could do little. He was held in tension between the horror he knew he must return to and the undemanding calm of home. She didn't see how anyone could stand it. She couldn't bear to imagine how it must be for him, and he had no choice but to leave them and return to it. So he drank. He drank most of every day. Though she and her father saw, they did not speak of it—to him or to one another.

When he left, she felt halved again, and only the routine saved her. She looked to it for the fatigue it would bring.

Then in March, she dared to hope, and in April, she knew and could write Will: "My dearest husband. Our fondest wish has been granted. I carry your child. Come home to us without fail and as soon as you can. I love you always, Narcissa."

But he had not come home to them. He had gone from battle to battle, always in gore, the amputation kit with no name on it steeped in blood, the sweet watch sometimes almost able to call him away from the constant dying that constantly confirmed his helplessness.

He had not come home until he had himself destroyed every hope of returning, until he could do nothing but search for graves in the black of night and rain, until his only choice was to flee once more.

9

Chickamauga was the place, the devastated setting which brought Evander and Will together and forced the events about which the Sequatchie Valley people were forever divided. Billy was there, too, a hapless participant in scenes he had no notion of, a boy so confused by it he never actually formed his own opinion of anyone's guilt or innocence. But the valley people took sides. Will, who shared nothing with them except his marrying Narcissa Parrish, who brought nothing of his own with him people could point to to explain him or what he did at Chickamauga, was either a mean-tempered and hard-drinking devil of a man who had killed Evander to become the Parrish heir and who didn't even come home for Narcissa's funeral, or he was a sad figure who had lost his brother, father, wife, son, and fortune fighting against an evil they were all haunted by.

Mary Sherwood's own version also contained what she had been made to feel when she learned from Billy that Fairchild had once held the power of life and death over him. It still scared her to remember what Billy had endured that day, how the Captain thought her boy might be a spy right along with Evander Parrish whom Fairchild had not hesitated to shoot squarely in the back.

In October of '63 while Billy was recuperating from his leg wound, he had told the story over and over again, at least what he could, about Chickamauga and Parrish's execution, as many in the valley came to call it. He couldn't tell everything, of course. He couldn't do that any more than he could tell the neighbors gathered around the cabin about their boys or husbands in battle. It was all too frightening to him still—and too confusing. And some of it, he didn't know.

At first, he couldn't even believe he was safe in his grandfather's cabin with what was left of his family. When he woke up, he thought maybe he had died and been forgiven. It was quiet, nobody moaning, nobody dying, nobody being killed. It smelled clean, coffee and wood smoke. No gun powder. No insides bleeding and smelling like hot metal in the cold air at hog butchering time. But then, after he got up, everybody was asking questions and trying to figure out what was happening where and if he had been with any of their kin or if he knew about any of their kin. Some he did, and some he didn't, but he got so bewildered trying to figure out what truth he could tell he just gradually got quieter and eventually stopped talking altogether. It was hard to go from where he had been to where he was, and he didn't know how to tell about it, friendly, in a circle of people needing to hear what he didn't want to say.

One thing he tried to tell about that nobody believed was once, when it was so loud and awful, a hundred rabbits came out of their nests and tried to hide under the men's coats and legs. "They acted plumb tame," Billy said, "but they was so strange, what they done, that they scared us, and we clubbed them with our rifles to try to make them go away." Some folks laughed a little. Others shifted and stared at him. He knew they didn't want to hear about rabbits.

Mrs. Day leaned against a tree out west of the lean-to, her face nearly as gray as her dress, her arms around her swollen belly, her eyes begging for news of her son. All Billy could see was Jimmy dangling from a broken-off tree branch he ran into his back when he staggered away from a Minie ball that ripped open his stomach. He was just hanging there whispering for Billy to shoot him. Billy was shaking so hard he couldn't reload, but Jimmy watched him and begged him. They had been friends forever, but this wasn't anything they had ever talked about.

"Jesus! Sweet Jesus! Billy! Billy, do it! For Jesus' sweet sake, do it!"

Blood was coming out of Jimmy's nose and mouth and stomach. Billy remembered when the black bear had got their old dog, and Trapper had looked at him the same way Jimmy was. He lifted his gun and remembered the dog's pleading eyes. "May God forgive me," he sobbed, then he shot his friend squarely between the eyes.

Jimmy sank downward and gradually eased off the branch sideways onto his face.

Near the cabin, Billy stared at the woman as though he were dumb or she not asking. He could find nothing to tell her, not about her boy or the rest of it. He could manage to talk about himself some, especially the part about being hauled before Captain Fairchild not three hours after the murder, about how scared he was, about how he nearly peed his own pants. That made some of them relax a little, but he had to steer clear of the worst of it.

His brigade had fought a desperate battle in the late afternoon, just before sunset, and at dark, when it stopped, there had been such a dismal groaning and screaming from all the wounded that Billy was nearly crazy with it. For miles, from Reed's Bridge in the north clear to Viniard's farm, it was a din of torn and dying men and horses. He had wanted them all just to die, right then, and at times he was afraid he might rush out and shoot them one by one. He knew now he could do such a thing.

It was also unseasonably cold for September. Billy had shivered and hugged himself and tried to relax so he wouldn't feel the chill moving toward his bones. Somebody nearby had said, "It'd help some if we could just get up and stomp around." Then he was quiet a minute before he went on, "I wish we could light us a fire. Damn. Wouldn't that feel good?"

And all the time they were freezing there in the woods, they could hear the grieving and dying creatures. One horse called in high, short, flickers of breath, like a killdeer, over and over. They could hear different men moan and cry, then stop, but the moaning and crying never did. The screaming mostly ended, but not the moaning and crying—and occasional calls for help from the unwounded or god. The men couldn't do anything, and god didn't.

What finally got to them beyond anything else was thirst. They had not had any place or time to refill canteens all the day, and now, silent and miserable and scared during the night, they felt as though they were dying for water. The turning point came when Danny Hightower, who used to live in those parts, took his life in his hands, crawled over to Billy, and proposed that they try to get down to Crayfish Springs. "If we can stay west of the big road and some Union fellow don't shoot before he identifies us, I think we can make it and be back here before daybreak."

Billy had hesitated about a second, weighing his fear against his thirst, then he said, "I'll follow you to hell and back if we can get us some water." So the two of them set off into the night, taking several other men's canteens, too, a couple of dry-mouthed boys. But before the next day was over, they would, like bumbling figures entering the stage from out of the darkness, help turn lives upside down and beyond recognition.

When he got home, long after the war, that part was what worried Billy the most: how a person who was completely innocent of any wrongdoing could become a marked man for the rest of his life because he caused a wounded soldier to be taken to a field hospital. He and Danny didn't know who Van Parrish was or even that he was a Confederate. They didn't know that Will Fairchild, Parrish's Union army brother-in-law, was the surgeon at the hospital. All they knew was that they had come across a shot-up man in a blue uniform, and as things turned out, they hadn't had a choice about helping him. They hadn't known anything about anything else. They had just been thirsty beyond the telling and so sick with the shooting and dying they hadn't much cared what became of them, so they had gone for water. The rest just happened.

They had crawled and pulled their way two miles south, sometimes slipping like shadows through bushes with no openings, sometimes edging forward on their bellies through cornfields riddled by bullets into stalks and wisps of leaves. They managed to make their way clear to the Springs where they eased up to the water like a couple of gators, letting the water fill their mouths, sucking it in until they could swallow no more and just letting it run cool over their tongues like pigs too full to drink more but unwilling to leave the trough.

It was on the way back that Billy ran his face into a body that was soft and sticky and smelled like fresh kill. He couldn't help himself. His hackles rose, and he cried out, "Oh, Jesus, Danny! They's a body here." And just like that, three soldiers were on them, knives against their backs, right under their left shoulder blades. The man hunched above Billy said, "You stay where you are, boy, or I'll jab this clean through to your belly button." He talked low, slow, and mean, and Billy didn't see any reason to lie when they asked about his allegiance. He and Danny were more than a little happy to find out that their captors were Union, too.

But the wounded soldier still lay in front of them, and the boys couldn't identify him or prove they weren't all three together. "Let's get him turned over," one of the soldiers said. "Can you tell if he's one of ours? Appears he's wearing Union. Leastawise I think so. Can you feel a pulse?" When they moved him, he groaned, and they didn't wait longer. The big one hoisted him up over a shoulder, and they moved out fairly rapidly due north toward the field hospital. They didn't seem to worry about the Rebels. "They pretty far north, for the most part, now, and east. But pretty soon, all hell's gonna bust loose again."

The wounded soldier was moaning and muttering, now. He was coming conscious. They laid him down for a breather, and the big man put a canteen to his mouth. "Here, mister," he whispered. "We're gonna get you some help. Do you know where you're hit?"

It was what happened next that made them all grow suspicious. As the wounded man came round some, he began to resist going to the hospital. Instead, he said he had to go to headquarters to tell General Rosecrans about a serious break in the Union lines.

"Brannan's battalion has scattered, and if Rosecrans doesn't pull somebody over, there's going to be a gap wide enough for the whole damn Rebel army to get through. I've got to get him that word." But then he fainted again, and Billy and Danny were left to try to explain what they hadn't any notion of. This soldier was talking about their command, but they didn't know him. Billy didn't think the whole battalion was scattered. He knew they had been hit hard, but he thought they had held. Still, in that confusion, who could really tell?

Woods and vines and rocks had made it impossible to see where they were shooting. "I cain't see nothing," somebody had yelled. "Where'n the hell are they?" "Just shoot the direction the bullets is coming from. Maybe you'll get lucky." That had been Eddie Hume. He never seemed to worry and always had a joke for them. Everybody had been shooting—no matter if they could see or not, and they were so outnumbered they were taking ten bullets for every one they fired. Nobody seemed to be giving orders. They were apparently on their own, and pretty soon, after they had run about some, they couldn't even be sure they weren't firing on their own troops. But they hadn't run away, Billy was sure. Even he and Danny were headed back.

"He wasn't with us," the boy finally said. "I don't know who he is. I don't think he's right about Brannon. I know he's wrong about Croxton's brigade—that's the one we're from. We lost a lot of men, but we held. I know we did. Me and Danny need to get back there right now because our boys is waiting for this here water. See? These are their canteens. They'll be ready to fight, believe me."

But the three soldiers weren't convinced. The big one lifted the wounded soldier up over his shoulder again, and in a different, more crouched and cautious stride, the other two walked beside Danny and Billy, their knives in hand. At the door of a very large house turned into a hospital, the boys were given over to a guard. Two orderlies took the wounded man inside, and the other three disappeared into the pre-dawn, heading toward the Glenn house headquarters with the stranger's warning about a gap left in the line.

They had separated Danny and Billy right after they got to the hospital, and Billy had to sit on the side where they disposed of amputated limbs and other body parts. It had been a fine house before the war got to it, he could see, but now it looked and smelled like a shambles. Men wore scarves across their nose and mouth, and Billy wished he had a bandanna. He was sick to his stomach. He was also too nervous to sit still, but the guard wouldn't let him pace. The quiet seemed to grow into a thing, corporeal and sneaking. Even as dawn broke and soldiers started moving around some, no one talked. The silence was broken by moans, but it was bigger and deeper than they were and seemed more ominous to Billy.

Then all of a sudden he heard yelling off to the west. And as though it had been prepared for, all the silence grown to a soft, throbbing accompaniment to the dull moans, a shot rang out, exact, unmistakable, single, and clear, a flat whack against the muted morning. Billy's guard crouched and pointed his gun into the trees instead of at Billy, and Billy hurled himself to the ground. They both figured a battle would commence, and they heard men running toward that shot. Holding their breath and listening with their insides, the two waited for the volley, but nothing happened. Billy felt papery in his lungs, and he imagined a ball burning and crushing his ribs. But nothing happened. Men were running toward the spot where lightning might have struck, but the fighting did not begin.

The sun rose up, and Billy waited without a bit of power in the world to help himself if the Rebs attacked. But there was no attack.

Instead, men began to whisper among themselves about what had just happened. It was the soldier Billy ran his head into. He had gotten loose, somehow. He had been accused of being a traitor, and he had been shot, they said, by the Captain, that same doctor the boys had brought the fellow in to. Billy felt his bowels begin to ache with fear for himself and Danny, and it deepened when he heard whispers of a Cain and Abel situation unfolding right there in front of him. The doctor, it seemed, had executed his own brother-in-law.

"If he was able to do that," Billy would say, still in awe of it as he reported what he could to the neighbors gathered at the cabin, "what was he going to do to a couple of strangers like Danny and me if he was to suspect us? I was so scared I like to peed my own pants." That was when the neighbors would laugh a little—at Billy laughing at himself.

But not Mary. No humiliation or fear or hurt or slight was due her boy. He was fine and good-humored, hard-working and honest. Her hackles had risen in fear of her own, then anger, at thinking anyone could treat him ill or threaten him with anything so outlandish as being a Confederate spy. She had felt no sympathy for anyone who would frighten Billy so, and she allowed herself to be swayed by those who came to call Fairchild a murdering thief.

Annie had remained quiet when Billy told the story. She had no words for it and no clear feelings except unease and grief. She could imagine the fallen soldier, blood streaking his back, and she could imagine Billy falling on top of him or beside him. She could imagine, too, Billy, her father, and her grandfather, all laid out together like white logs in the moonlight, and she stayed very still as though she herself might be the next spied by a predator.

But none of them knew what preceded the shooting, not the years of uneasy intimacy that seemed to impel the men to such a fate, and not the events at the hospital that morning.

10

During the whole night Billy and Danny had crawled toward the Springs, lamps inside the Lee house hospital were kept burning. All through the night in a kitchen turned into a surgery, Captain Will Fairchild had operated. He had worked more than fifteen hours, and he was covered with blood. Occasionally his orderly had tried to wipe the doctor's face, but Fairchild needed him most to help hold down patients. Now a man was losing half a leg, and he was not unconscious.

Months ago Fairchild had stopped being sick that he had nothing adequate to work with, not enough ether, no Saddler's silk, no wax left to pull what thread he had through. He had stopped being sick, but he stayed furious, and now he was sweating and cursing while the blood seeped onto the table and ran down, away from the raised end.

The orderly, Leon Menheusen, had not been on duty long, but he was already feeling wretched. He vowed he would hold on until Fairchild stopped. He wanted to. He had served with other doctors before he was placed with Captain Fairchild, but he never served with one he respected more. This man saved more limbs than anyone else, and Menheusen saw that he was gentle with the wounded. He would lean down to say a word or to touch the arm of a soldier he couldn't help. He didn't just look at them and move on. Neither did he avoid their eyes. He looked at their faces, and he put his hand on their shoulders. The orderly thought that if he were a dying man, he would appreciate such a gesture. He didn't even mind that if he handed the wrong tool or didn't move quickly enough Fairchild would have his ass. He was devoted to this doctor who made him feel as though pity was not dead. Now, confronting the maniacal, as he and another orderly struggled to hold the patient down while the Captain hurried to sew up what he could, two other orderlies brought a young man through the kitchen door. It was the soldier Billy had run his head into.

One of the men said, "Sir, the sergeant says this here fellow has got to be given some special attention because he may have information about our men to the north."

Menheusen looked from the soldier to the doctor and waited for the explosion. He knew the Captain was always definite about whom he'd work on and in what order. He made all those decisions himself, and the orderly was not surprised when Fairchild straightened up looking murderous. What he was not prepared to see was the color draining from the doctor's face. He seemed to lose his balance some, and he caught himself on the table. He stared at the man hanging between the two orderlies, and as the fellow tried to raise his head and look back at Fairchild, the doctor whispered, "Van! My god! What has happened?"

Menheusen could plainly see that the man posed some threat to the doctor, and he tried to think of a way to intervene. But he had no time. "Menheusen," Fairchild rasped, "take that man to the side room. Cut his shirt off and give him whiskey. I'll finish here and get to him."

Evander tried to talk, but he couldn't raise his head. He hurt so badly in his body and his mind that he wasn't even able to take pleasure in Fairchild's distress. "That Yankee son-of-a-bitch," he managed to think, his feet dragging as the orderlies half-carried him into what had been a pantry. But he could hardly focus his eyes as he hung there between two Union soldiers in a stinking side room and remembered Fairchild's sudden pallor. He remembered, too, having watched him ride in from Kentucky on a big bay gelding, the horse arching his neck to a touch of the bit, the man tall and elegant on the flat saddle. He remembered Fairchild at ease at their table, raising a glass of wine to his father. And before he lost consciousness again, he remembered him walking on their lawn, Narcissa on his arm, their heads bent toward one another.

When he came to, he was back in the pantry on a bed of sorts, his head raised on dirty pillows. The stench of ether and cauterized flesh lingered on him, and Fairchild was standing by his side. Worlds were between them. The Captain poured a glass of whiskey, then he spoke: "You know I've got to get you to Rosecrans now. Is there any way on earth we can handle this without treason?"

Young Parrish tried to laugh, but it made him cough, and Will gave him a drink. "You see the uniform I'm in. You know blue is not my color. You'd best take me on to Rosecrans. If I've had any luck at all, those fools that picked me up gave him my message hours ago." He managed to look at Will, and he found himself wondering again whether Will looked pitiless or helpless. "Strange," he mumbled. Then: "I don't have anything else to say—to you or to him. Just get me out of here."

Fairchild studied Van's face a moment, searching against certainty for some reprieve. Then he downed the rest of the whiskey, breathed hard, and said he would have his orderly get a cart ready, wash up, and go along. "It's an awful time for me to leave, even for an hour, but I don't want any mistakes between here and there."

Will didn't actually make a mistake, but he did allow the orderly to escort Parrish to a privy out west of the house. When Van opened the door, he swung around to the left as hard as he could with all the motion of opening the door added to his blow. He caught Menheusen by complete surprise and hit him so hard with the door that he went down with hardly a sound. But then the door banged shut, and Fairchild heard it and saw.

"Van! Van, God damn it! Don't you do this!"

But Parrish was stumbling up the hill and into the woods much faster than he had thought he would be able to. Again the doctor called: "Stop there, mister! I'll have to shoot! You know I will. Don't make me do this, Van!"

Parrish didn't think he would. He didn't see how he could. Not him. Not Cissa's brother. But he did. Parrish actually felt the ball hit him before he heard the sound. And he didn't care. He was laughing, he thought, while the Captain ranted: "God damn you for this, Parrish. God damn you!"

When Menheusen came to, he was lying flat on his back by the toilet, his nose sideways and blood all over him. He couldn't see anything, but he heard men running up the hill—then nothing. Gradually it all came back to him, and he tried to sit up and get up.

Then several soldiers went running by him, and before long they all came back down carrying the soldier who had hit him with the privy door. The man's good arm was dangling without any hint of muscle or bone, and Menheusen knew that he was dead. Fairchild was following behind, his face another kind of story. The orderly had never seen anyone look more like a sick dog. The doctor was staggering more than walking, and Menheusen moved to him as fast as he could to take his arm. It was the only intimacy the Captain ever permitted him.

The next hours were frantic with the General interviewing first the Captain, then the orderly, then the Captain summoning Billy and Danny. Menheusen was the one who was finally able to assure Rosecrans that his Captain and Evander Parrish were not conspiring together. Menheusen knew Fairchild had nothing to do with the Rebel's plan. He had heard them talking in that pantry, and he remembered what the Captain had said about having to take the prisoner to the General. Confronted by Rosecrans who barked questions at him so fast he could hardly think, Menheusen had some trouble explaining his part in the humiliating business, how the fellow had hoodwinked him. The General was not a calm man. All kinds of bad news were coming in, and he was eyeing the orderly the way a snake does a toad, making him feel as though he had done something to die for when all he had done was, as he put it, "be a god-blamed fool for some wily Confederate."

Mid-morning, when they finally marched Billy into the house through a side door, Fairchild was standing in the middle of the room staring straight at the boy. To Billy, he looked like a cross between sick and dead, and it didn't help to hear his voice. "He sounded like a rattler, dry and mean," Billy would say. "He told me I'd better tell him how I come to be with that wounded man, or they'd be hell to pay. I figured that meant I'd be at the wrong end of a firing squad—if he didn't do it hisself like he done that Rebel."

Billy didn't actually want to talk about the questioning, but he could make a little fun of himself, and that would sometimes satisfy the neighbors gathered at the cabin. They could feel his fear, get angry, then be relieved that at least this part of the war turned out right. Billy wanted that for them. So he would tell them how he was shaking and talking harder and faster than he ever had before.

"Fairchild just stood there staring at me," he would say. "He was a strange looking man across the eyes. I'd noticed it before. But that day when he was deciding what was to become of me, he was scary strange, and I was sweating even though I was as loyal a man as he was."

At first Fairchild couldn't place him, Billy recalled. "He knew me, but he didn't know how he knew me, and he had a notion maybe he'd seen me with that wounded man. It wasn't until I mentioned Annie that he started to calm down some."

And that had been the case. Billy was talking at sixes and sevens about how Fairchild had come by their place down near Pikeville in the Sequatchie Valley, how it had been cold that January, how he had bought two mares and a gelding—and Annie's mule. "Charlie, Sir. You remember, Sir?" Then Billy could see the change. Fairchild started nodding a little, and Billy redoubled his efforts: "Remember, Sir? Annie was riding our big mule in from the back pasture when you come. Big Charlie, Sir. And you took him. You said Annie was a pretty girl. Annie is my sister. I'm Billy Sherwood, Sir. Remember?"

Annie liked to hear that part, but it didn't lessen her dislike of the man any. He had shot his own brother in the back. That was all she needed to know. It branded him a coward. She was convinced no man in her family would ever have done such a thing, and the rest of the story did nothing to change her mind.

Billy said he couldn't get himself slowed down. While the Captain paced and occasionally nodded, his own mouth ran: "And then, Sir, you come to the house and spoke with my Ma and asked where our sympathies was and why I was still not enlisted, a big, strappin' lad like me, you said. And I told you I was signin' up after our crops was harvested, if we managed to save any." Billy had gone on and on about how he did enlist, how Fairchild had spoken kindly to Mary, especially when he had learned that both her husband and father were already dead in the cause, about how he had given them a good price for the stock, then an extra dollar for Annie. Then everything came to a stop, he said, when the Captain finally interrupted him. He couldn't hardly stay quiet, he said, yet the Captain wasn't looking at him any more, and it all seemed finished, like the bottom had fallen out of things.

"Mister," Fairchild said, "I remember clearly now." At those words, Billy said he could feel his own muscles again. He managed to stand up straight, and that seemed to make the Captain refocus and look back at him. At first, he just shook his head and said he was sorry it had all happened. But then he went on, and even though Billy wasn't sure he understood what Fairchild was saying, he remembered the words. Even more he remembered the gouged-out tone of the words. But he could only repeat them, not it, so he never quite got all of it right as he tried to tell about it.

"Before I got to the door, he called my name, and he said, 'Billy Sherwood, I'm truly sorry for all this,' and he made a kind of half-circle with his arm. He wasn't altogether steady, and he said, kind of like he was choking, 'We should have taken better care of our boys, all of them.'

"I wasn't for sure what he meant," Billy would conclude, "but I knew I was a free man under no suspicion of wrongdoing."

What Billy liked most to tell Mary were the Captain's last words. He would say, "After I thought he was finished, he said something else. It was real nice, Ma. He said, 'Please give my compliments to your mother.'"

Billy could see by Mary's face that she had never before been given compliments by a gentleman. But then her frown told him that the very idea would take her some days to come to grips with.

11

As she stepped back to let Fairchild come in the cabin, Mary Sherwood looked carefully at the face of this man who, whatever view people took of him, had beyond any doubt been part of scenes it pained her to imagine. One point everybody agreed on was that no family had suffered worse than the Parrish family. She saw how wiry and rough-bearded he was, dark from the sun and road-dirty. He looked to her as though he would do what he had to.

But then she saw his hair curling around his ears and over his forehead which was much whiter than the rest of his face. She saw the furrow his hat had made in his hair, and she thought how thick and pretty it was, even peppery now instead of the black it must once have been. She was partial to black-haired men. She saw that his gaze was steady. His eyes weren't quite right, but to her that made him seem a little scared and needful.

Altogether the effect he had on her was such as to make her interested, not defensive. And to be sociable, she said, "I've seen you before." She was speaking over his words, again, at just the time he said, "Thank you, ma'am," and stepped inside.

"It's a good things we ain't dancin' because we're not in step," she laughed, and he smiled and nodded. She pulled out a chair for him at the table where she had been sitting.

She did not often feel awkward at being a poor woman, but in that instant, she did. It was his sword, the only one that had ever been in her house. It looked like something from another country to her, and it imposed its rank and tradition. Her table and chairs were

72

from her father's cabin, made by him and by Sherwood, and though they fit her well—her feet could touch the floor when she sat in them—she knew they were not polished or dark and shining the way some store-bought furniture was. And she coveted some of that furniture now when this tall, strange man was going to have to be seated opposite her.

But then when he did sit down on the little, round-legged, white-oak chair she offered him, his knees were too high for him to rest his arms on comfortably, and he looked to her somehow like a toy soldier. She found the courage to continue the conversation. "You were here a couple years or so ago and bought some stock," she said.

He had undertaken the same task at the same time: "I was here some time ago and bought some stock." They heard themselves midway through the sentences and finished up by punctuating the last words with small nods of their heads.

Mary laughed out loud: "Reckon we'd best make arrangements to take turns," she said, feeling suddenly confident that the good she had heard about him outweighed the bad. She shifted on her chair and wondered why he had come. In fact, she had a terrible curiosity about it and came as close to asking as she thought polite: "We got nothing left, Doctor Fairchild. I don't see as how we can give another mite. Besides, why would they need more stock, now?"

Not quite ready to begin what he knew would be a difficult negotiation, Fairchild slowed the conversation. "No, ma'am. I haven't come for the army this time. As a matter of fact, I was mustered out a few days ago—down in Chattanooga."

"How could they do that?" she asked, thinking about his being such a fine doctor and considering the need there would still be for what he could do.

"Well." He hesitated and looked at the tarnished, frayed braid on his cap. "They told me I had done my duty, ma'am, and they discharged me."

She stayed quiet a moment, but she was drawing her breath to start again when he continued: "Actually, Mrs. Sherwood, they probably would have kept me longer—even with the fighting effectively over—but I had been having some trouble."

He stopped and looked around the cabin. Nothing there allowed him to pause over it. The room opened into a parlor of sorts, but it, too, was square and spare and rough, the only color added by a large, round, mostly green and red, hand-hooked rug.

She could see that he wasn't nervous about talking to her. He didn't shift in the chair. But he sat stooped, his shoulders rounded, looking, once again, at his hat. And she thought, "This man carries a heavy load." For the first time, she felt free from the notion that he was a bad person. This was no murdering devil sitting in front of her.

"They mustered me out because I was drinking so much I couldn't do my work as required." He stopped a moment, then straightened some and went on. "I was discharged honorably, but I was discharged early. They. . . they seemed to think," and here he stumbled. "They seemed to think the circumstances of. . .of my wife's death. . . could explain my depression and what I had been doing. I left without permission that winter after she died, but they didn't do anything to me about it. And I drank a lot—from then on."

He did not admit, even to himself, that he had been drinking a lot for years. He was speaking slowly, trying to get out to her what he knew she needed to understand. Everything depended on that.

On the stoop, Annie had not hesitated to plant herself under the window. She knew that army officers, Union or Confederate, never called on her mother, and she listened to every word they said, at first not making any sense of it. Why should he be telling his business to her mother? Why would he think they would care? She was certain she did not. Just his being there worried her. And even though she could not see him, his halting and sad voice told her he was not finding it easy to talk about himself. So what in the world was he doing it for?

He could hardly focus on what he needed to say, and he tried to read his ability to make sense in the way the woman across from him sat or held her head. Behind what he wanted to make honest and gentle words were the treacherous images and terrors he knew could seize and pull him under. He had to split his concentration between that past and this present, and Mary could plainly feel the pain and intensity Annie heard.

Having mentioned leaving without permission the winter after Narcissa's death, he could not stop the rest of the story from flooding his mind, sometimes making him stop talking altogether and sigh so deeply Mary's sympathy for him secured and deepened.

74

He had not been able to accompany Evander's body back to Pikeville. None of the Union soldiers got that sort of treatment. But because of who Fairchild was and the ironic and terrible nature of the event, General Rosecrans was moved to allow a small detail to try to get young Parrish back to his home. Will had decided to write George and Narcissa two letters, one to go ahead of the body and soften the news as much as possible, the second, to confess to the circumstances of Evander's death. He had hunched in his tent over words that defied him, asking himself what difference anything he could write would ever make.

Later he had called Menheusen in and, after a glance at him, tried first to fix his nose. The orderly had wiggled it round some, himself, before it swelled up so bad. Fairchild told him he'd got it back about as well as anybody could and that he'd just have to breathe through his mouth for a while. Considering the detail he thought he might be going on, Menheusen figured a nose injury wasn't the worst that could have happened to him.

The Captain looked awful, and Menheusen felt more pity for him than for the men who had lost legs or arms. Fairchild seemed to have nothing left inside to prop himself up or even to explain himself.

"I want you and Billy Sherwood to ride with. . . with," he tried. Then: "I want you to take Billy Sherwood with you to Pikeville. He's one of the boys they brought in with. . . with the Confederate soldier." He could hardly say the words. "He knows the territory and can maybe get you through to Pikeville where I. . . where my. . . ."

When Fairchild came to a stop, shaking his head, Menheusen undertook to speak for him. "You want me and Billy to go along with the, with the body, and. . . ."

But he had to stop, too. "Be damned if *I* could say it," he would faithfully report on himself. "I thought I'd bust out myself. My chin was a-tremblin'."

Finally, in silence, he took the two letters addressed to Doctor George Parrish and another which Fairchild wrote for Menheusen and Billy to use as a pass should they need one to get through Union lines. Neither of them mentioned what might happen should the detail encounter Confederate troops.

Like Billy, Leon Menheusen could talk and laugh a little about his own fears or weaknesses, but, again like Billy, he couldn't share some stories. For one, he never told about the end of that conversation. He didn't mind if people knew two grown men wept together. Something in him said they had cause enough. But he couldn't speak of the watch.

Menheusen knew it had been a present from Fairchild's father-in-law, but he knew no other details. He had never managed to learn anything of the doctor's own story; therefore he had no reason to understand that the watch could suggest more than the affection and respect one might expect between a man and his new son. The orderly knew only that Fairchild prized the watch as much as he did his amputation kit and that he took it out in any quiet moment to look at it and listen to it. Menheusen was not an imaginative man, and it did not occur to him that the simple, civilized chime could bring the Captain in the charnel house visions of order and peace his soul needed. He only knew the doctor loved the watch.

So when the orderly was tucking the two letters and the pass inside his shirt and saw Fairchild take out the little timepiece, he understood the pain of the son's separation from the father, and he even understood the catastrophe of a killing within a family. Still, as he watched the doctor open the case and listened with him to the crystal "four o'clock," he was unprepared to see the doctor react as though he had himself been pierced by a sword. He seemed cruelly forced down into his chair, his head fallen, his eyes shut.

Menheusen backed out of the tent saluting his Captain, and he walked away taking the greatest care to be silent.

12

Nothing of this could Fairchild explain to the tiny woman perched like a big doll in the chair opposite him at her kitchen table. Everything depended on his ability to convince her of his trustworthiness and good intentions, so he skipped the killing and the letters, the whole day, going on from where he thought he'd got to—his unauthorized trip to Pikeville after Narcissa's death. He tried to continue with some sense of direction though he was very unsure of his way.

"They didn't penalize me for that or for any of it—which they could have. They said I had done my duty, and they gave me an honorable discharge."

He looked straight at Mary when he said that, and she felt his hurt as her own. In his turn, he felt her sympathy come into him, and for a moment he thought he would break.

It is easier to stay tight and alone inside yourself than to let another's understanding be a support. To give only a little may be to lose everything, and he struggled to keep control over his lips, his eyes, his stomach. He could not, though, keep from remembering his journey that December to what had been his home.

Of course it was all changed, utterly changed—as he had known it would have to be when he had brought down the fleeing soldier, when he had written the letters for Menheusen to deliver—nearly three months before he fled home, leaving without permission, unable to stay away any longer.

Fairchild *was* an imaginative man, and he had seen Evander's homecoming a hundred times before it happened, visualizing it while he struggled with the letters he knew he had to write. Even he, though, had not adequately conceived of the consequences. Even he, filled with his guilt and grief, did not foresee how the awful day would end.

John and Keelie had watched the orderly approach the house on a road-filthy horse. The second rider had stayed at the gate holding the lead-rope of another horse. It was laden with a body secured over its back like a sack of cotton.

Within the hour, George Parrish had gathered everyone in the yard back of the big house, called there by the bell they rarely heard except at mealtime. They knew, though, that its summons could be to the terrible, and as it rang and as everyone still there hurried to the lawn, the field hands were frightened. A few had stayed after the '63 emancipation, and now they feared that the Johnny Rebs had taken the town and that they would be conscripted to fight—or that something worse might await them.

But when Doctor George told them that Mister Evander was dead and that their work would therefore be stopped that day and the next, their manner changed. None of them hated Evander; he was not a cruel master. But they didn't like him. So they made a polite moan for the father whose face looked like the suffering Christ on the Cross in their Bibles, then they went to their own work or to their own houses to be with their own families.

Evander's funeral the next day was mercifully quick, and the preacher did not try to explain away his death or to reconcile the people there to one another's views. Rebel and Union supporters stood together around the grave, most of them with cloths over their nose and mouth. A son and a brother and neighbor was laid decently to rest, and while the war was in everyone's heart, they did not show it that day.

The day before, Menheusen had told John that he and Billy had to leave immediately to get back to their duties but that he should give Doctor Parrish and Mrs. Fairchild the second letter after the funeral. He did, just after George and Narcissa had finally eaten a bite and after the last few friends had left.

The doctor and his daughter had not been much surprised at the first letter—which had simply told them about the sad burden the two soldiers had brought to their door. They were stricken, but they had known for a long time that unless the Confederates won the war, which they did not believe would happen, Evander would not return.

"We lost him a long time ago, didn't we, Papa?" she said to him as they sat together, she petting his hand. They had gone about like sick or wounded people, hands on door frames, supporting themselves on the furniture, she bursting into tears she as quickly stopped as she did this or that, then went back and did it again. But they made the preparations for his burial.

More than once that day they shared their surprise that Evander and Will should have been together at the end. They hoped the gray and blue had been reconciled then, at least in their own family, with brother somehow able to comfort brother against the forces that had made them enemies. They clung to that vision the next morning, and it strengthened them through the funeral.

But then came the second letter, the one which went beyond telling that Evander had been killed in the line of duty. Doctor Parrish turned the brown envelope over and over before he opened it. "It's the other letter Will promised," he said. "I don't want to read it."

But he was, as John and Ruth understood while they watched the two of them, a brave man, a good white man, and he did what was necessary. He began to read aloud. But in a moment, he went silent. In another, he stopped reading altogether, raised his eyes to Narcissa's, got up from his chair, and simply handed her the letter. He could not speak, and he knew she had to know.

The truth came over Narcissa as Ruth supposed it must have come over Eve, that all was lost.

It was one kind of pity for a brother and a son to die. It was something altogether different for a husband to kill a brother or a son to kill a son. Something in the blood rose against it. And this father and daughter, understanding—accepting, as they did—that their son-brother could, even must, die for what he believed, could not accept in their hearts what they could understand in their minds, that their son-husband should be the killer.

Without any comfort, they fell into a grief they could not express or endure. It sent him wandering into the evening and night, John following him—only to bring him back when Keelie's screams reached them. It sent Narcissa into labor, a labor she could not keep from starting, a labor she could not cause to end. Ruth and Keelie held her, and Keelie wept while the woman screamed and strained and sank into her own darkness.

Ruth, raised with Narcissa, schooled with her, friends with her, was rigid but not stunned by what was happening. Feeling alternately frozen and feverish, she had a somewhat formal sense that Narcissa, who was not her sister although they had once pretended so, was dying in an effort to bear a son for a man who had tried to save sons by the hundreds. Narcissa could not have this child, and he could not save this child, his own son. Ruth watched her scream in the most extreme misery for her husband then rant against him as a murderer and a thief. She hemorrhaged until they put a pan on the floor under the mattress to catch the stream, Keelie now wailing in a corner of the room.

Her father could not save her or the child. He had no knowledge of how to take the child, to save it or her. The placenta was in the wrong place, he said, first, before the baby. He finally took the dead boy with forceps, and Narcissa Fairchild died in anguish before a father who adored her. They heard him scream at her and for her, then watched him go silent, and in the silence, listen to the slowing drops of blood.

Ruth was sorry for all of them, and she had her own grief. But beside her grief, her clear thought was: "I did not and I will not take their name."

Will could not get permission to return; neither could he steel himself to leave without it, not until December, more than eight weeks after Narcissa was buried. By that time, everyone left in the valley knew what had happened, and many Sequatchie Valley men were returning home during the winter. For the Rebel sympathizers, the cause was lost, but some of them seized upon the Parrish "murder," as they called it, as a kind of rallying point. They vowed to avenge Evander's death, and they detailed how they would mutilate Fairchild before they slow-killed him.

Ruth planned to go north. She knew she had no place in the south as a Negro woman who could read and write and think and who had no desire to hide those facts. To her, the white men seemed meaner and more dangerous than before the war. Then, they would have used her, she thought. Now, she believed they might kill her. She knew they would hurt Fairchild. Some of them talked about it freely in front of their former slaves who were, they thought, incapable of the honor or courage it would require to defy them or frustrate their plans.

For her, then, it was a profound moment of conscience when her father and mother came to her bedside in the middle of that December night to tell her Will Fairchild was in the kitchen. It had rained hard, and it was threatening rain again. The night was unsettled with lightning showing the clouds heavy and purple-gray from horizon to horizon over the numbed valley and Walden's Ridge. The trees were brown, still and nervous. Everything seemed suspended and much too close.

"It be Doctor Will, Ruth," John said from behind the candle. His hair looked like a halo, she thought. "He say we got to take him to Miss Narcissa's grave right now. He lookin' wild, Ruth. And he be drinkin'."

Ruth could see that her father was frightened, and she knew he had cause. To get to the Parrish Cemetery, they would have to go by two houses of Confederate sympathizers. Dogs and guineas could call attention to them, and if straggling Rebel soldiers or certain others caught anyone with Fairchild, nothing but evil could result. Ruth had seen him drunk often enough to know he could be unpredictable and unresponsive to anything around him.

"Does Doctor George know?" she asked.

"Oh, no. No. My goodness, no," Keelie stammered. "He say we the only ones he can trust. Oh, Ruthie, he look so bad."

"Let me dress," Ruth said, "and I'll see if I can reason with him somehow."

But of course she could not. He was mud from head to foot, and that, coupled with his gray beard, made him nearly unrecognizable to her. She had not known a man could age so fast. And he was drunk enough to be unreachable. He just stared at Ruth when she talked to him about the dangers.

"Doctor Will," she began, careful to make her voice calm and as white as she could. "You know it will be death for you—and probably Papa—if the wrong people catch you here. And Doctor Will, we still don't always know who we can trust and who we can't."

Perhaps he didn't hear her. He made no response, at least not to what she was saying. "I'm going to the cemetery, Ruth, and someone has got to show me where Narcissa is." His voice broke over the last words, but he went on. "I've already been there, but I don't know where she is. There are so many new graves, and they're not marked yet. God, Ruth. I can't find her."

He looked straight at the young, black woman whose antelope eyes were soft but without tears. "I can't find her, Ruth. Somebody has got to help me find her."

It was a powerful plea, and she knew they should not resist it, even if they could. If you don't learn anything else as a slave, you do learn that people who are hurt in their souls have to be comforted. Ruth knew it had nothing to do with skin or family or how nice a person was. She had learned that it has to do with your own insides and coming to see—not as some shimmering truth but as a gray rock certainty—that if you don't respond to such a need, if you don't try to do something, then mercy and hope and justice are only words floating around in the universe, not as real as the clouds crowding over the house. They're either in you and come out in what you do, or they just plain aren't.

"We will help you, Doctor Will," Ruth answered for all of them.

John seemed to understand. "Yes, Sir, Doctor Will. We going to help you. *I* going to help you." And the strength he was feeling came in the accent of his words.

Keelie began to moan softly, but even she seemed willing. "God bless you, Sir. And you, John. You be careful."

"I be careful, Keelie," he said as he embraced her. "And I be back directly."

He was. In about two hours he came back, alone, shaking and nearly beside himself with fatigue and pity.

"We ain't have no real trouble," he told them. "The rain be a protection for us. But it be so wet and dark and muddy in there. I be troubled to find the grave, myself. They only put little rocks by so many, you know, and he be like a crazy man, pantin' right behind me as I think and study the plots and try to see through the rain. Finely I remember that Mister Evander, he right on east of old Master George, and Miss Narcissa and the baby, they just on east of Mister Evander.

"When I show him, he kneel down there in the rain and mud, and mercy, sweet Jesus have mercy on his soul, that man done wept. Keelie, he be a man of sorrows, a man of sorrows.

"I leave him there and hide under the chapel porch. And after a while he go over to the fence and come back with a tree. He have a little cedar 'bout your size, Ruthie. He be 'termined to plant that tree on her grave. He have a little soldier-shovel he try to dig with, but the rain keep fillin' up the hole. He be diggin' in that mud like a crazy man, and the rain keep fillin' up the hole. Finely I tell him that if he can just get it to stand up, I be back in the daylight with Daniel and a spade and make sure the tree be plant deep and straight.

"He look up at me then, and he say, 'John, may there be another life and may you be rewarded in it.' And he take my hand and put something in it. Here—I ain't look at it yet."

It was ten dollars, more money than the three of them had ever seen before, at least that was theirs. John laughed and laughed. "Praise the Lord, Ruthie. And praise Doctor Will. You goin' north now just as soon as you please."

Fairchild also gave John a small box for George Parrish. When he opened it, there, without any message, was the watch he had given, with his love, as a gift to honor the marriage of his second son.

The old man sat forward at the table, his arms resting on it, holding the watch in both his hands, a look on his face as far away as history.

13

"Let me get you some water, Doctor Fairchild."

For a moment, he did not recognize the voice. It was Mary Sherwood's bringing him out of the cemetery and back into her little house. She was heading for the bucket.

Watching him go silent and pale as he had started to speak about returning to Pikeville that December, she realized that he could not and probably should not tell her about such matters. She was curious, but another part of her didn't want to know.

"You don't have to explain anything to me," she said.

He said, "Thank you, ma'am. You are very kind to me," as she finished: "I know all about what wars can do," and they both managed a smile.

"Reckon we'll have to number off," she said as she handed him a gourd of water. And he nodded before he drank.

Feeling much more relaxed because of his willingness to talk personally to her and because of their tendency to talk at the same time, she decided to try to help him get to the point of this visit.

"Well, Sir," she said, "I know you haven't come here to go over old wounds with me. So what is it I can do for you?"

"I appreciate your kindness, Mrs. Sherwood, and I'll be direct with you—though this will be something strange to hear, I think."

Certainly it *was* strange to hear. She didn't interrupt hardly at all, though more than once she frowned and shook her head as though she disbelieved her ears.

What he wanted was Annie.

"I know I'm a lot older than she is, ma'am, and I'm not much to look at for such a pretty girl." He began to make his way through it. "But the fact of the matter is that I do think she is pretty. And during all these terrible months since"—he hesitated only briefly—"since the tragedies in my family, I've had one vision in my mind's eye that could lift my spirits somehow. It was my picture of that girl riding that brown mule in from the meadow that January I was here—which seems a lifetime ago, now.

"She had a red scarf on, and her cheeks were red, too, and all the rest of the world looked winter-dead beside her.

"I had spent four days at home and had just said good-bye to my wife, and I was sad." He repeated that: "I was sad," and stopped on it a minute, but he went on. "Annie was bossing that mule around and laughing at him until Billy told her they'd have to give him up. Then she just slid over his shoulder, looked at Billy and me, and let the rope drop. She didn't look back at us when she came up here to the house, either. She didn't like it, but she didn't cry about it. There was something sensible and strong about her—full of life. I felt glad to see such a girl, but I hated to take her mule."

"You give her an extra dollar, I call to mind."

"Yes. And I wanted to give her more. Maybe that is part of this, too, Mrs. Sherwood." He was leaning toward her some, and his voice was more lively. "I'm not drinking now, and I'm going west—to Nebraska or Kansas—to try to start again. The war is over, but I don't want to stay here. Part of it is the memories that everything in the valley makes me have. But part of it is because too many people here think what I did was wrong, that…"

Here, she did interrupt him, both because she had already made up her mind about him and the degree of guilt he ought to assume and because she very much wanted to get to the heart of this proposition he was making.

"I have heard, Doctor Fairchild," she said, "of the threats against you. In fact, I'd think you'd be worried about being out and around right now." In her concentration on what he was saying, she had almost forgotten rumors that several men in the valley had vowed to shoot him on sight or something much worse if he ever came back. It called back her uneasiness about having him there. And it made his taking Annie seem suddenly dangerous as well as strange.

"Well, sometimes I am a little worried. But I don't imagine anyone will try to bushwhack me in broad daylight. I don't imagine that's their style. Besides," and his voice grew husky as he added, "no one knows I'm here except a man and his family who helped me get some of my things last night. He risked his life to take me to the cemetery after my wife died, and they'll tell no one I'm here now."

His voice returned to what seemed normal. "I'm camping up on the Ridge. Almost no one's around there now. I'll keep close guard.

"Anyway, what I want to say is that that picture of your daughter has comforted me when nothing else could. I could see her fresh face in the middle of such darkness, and sometimes I would summon it to mind to keep from thinking everything in the world was spoiled and dead."

He wasn't looking at Mary or anything else when he said that. His eyes took on space, and for the second time, he didn't appear quite to remember where he was.

"I don't know what it is that pulls me here and to her," he finally went on. "It is not that I lust for her because I don't. Sometimes I think that part of me is dead. But I want to be near her and to see her. And this is what seems strongest to me."

Here, he seemed to come back to the room and to the straight little woman whose hair was blacker than his and who was looking at him with a mixture of amazement and dread. He spoke directly to her.

"I want to do for Annie. I'm a doctor, Mrs. Sherwood, and a good one. I'll make money. I will be able to give Annie a home, a very nice one, and pretty things, if she wants them. I can get her another mule—or any horse she wants. I can teach her to read and write."

Here Mary interrupted very definitely: "Annie *can* read and write," she said. "Print her letters real fine, anyway. She was a good scholar until this blamed war stopped her schoolin'."

He heard her defense of all of them. "I didn't mean any criticism, Mrs. Sherwood," he said. "I only mean that I can give Annie an education, a real one, so she can read all books—or write them herself, if she would like to. I'll be able to give her everything."

He stopped again, and she studied him with no effort to be polite. He flushed a little and answered the question she didn't ask.

"I'm thirty-three years old, Mrs. Sherwood, and so far, nothing in my life has turned out the way it should have."

86

Almost in time with his heart, old scenes pulsed behind his eyes: his father, crimson with anger hurling a book at him, taking his name from him while his mother stood and watched; his colleagues at medical school mocking him as the Pirate after they had cut his eye, cursing him that the black girl had escaped; Evander Parrish furious at dinner because an abolitionist had entered the house, then dead on the ground in front of him; Narcissa dead; his son dead. He stiffened in the chair, trying to force the pictures to stop, struggling to continue.

But Mary stayed at "thirty-three" a spell. He could have said "fifty-three," and she wouldn't have been surprised. But thirty-three she found hard to believe.

"You look older," she said, and immediately wished she could take it back. Her husband had always said she talked before she thought. But the man opposite her didn't seem offended. In fact, he looked relieved at what she had said.

"I know, ma'am. But I can't do much about that, I don't suppose. But what I want to say is that I want a fresh start. I want to try again. In my heart, I don't feel that I was born to be like this, tired and finished. I am not a lazy man, and I'm not a bad man. I intend to rebuild my own life and to help build a new country, not tear one to pieces and leave it strewn stinking over the hills.

"But I know myself well enough now to understand that I need some help. I need someone to work with, work for. I have to have a future to look toward. I don't want to be alone in a strange part of the country ever again."

He had pretty much brought her up short, and he could tell it. "I know you must have many questions, ma'am, and I'll try to answer them. But just try to hear me out. You can tell I've been thinking about this, and I've tried hard to sort out my intentions and your reactions—and Annie's.

"It has been more than a year since my wife's death. I know I am far from over those awful feelings, but I have to try. I am still alive, and I can't just go back there and lie on her grave. Believe me, that's what I tried to do. But it didn't kill me, and it doesn't appear that it's going to."

He frowned and spoke softly when he said that, but he didn't falter. He wanted to rise and walk while he talked, but the room was too little for him. So he cupped his hands over his knees, too high in front of him, and went on.

"I know I'm in danger here in the valley, and I've decided that I don't want to die yet. I want to get out of the south altogether and go some place where nobody knows me or cares about anything except my skill as a doctor. I want to start again."

She was silent, her eyes intense and as blue as Annie's.

"And you know, it's not all a bad bargain for your daughter. I'm no girl's fancy, I know that. But there aren't many such around even in the best of times—which of course this isn't. In fact, this country is going to be short on young men for years to come. And I'll be a good husband. I'm the kind of man who likes to do for a woman, and I'll be able to, once we get settled."

She focused on that next. "Yes! But where would that be? You mentioned Nebraska. Lord, have mercy. That's a thousand miles away. I'd never see Annie again. And she is only fifteen years old. Oh, Glory! I can't bear that." And she began to cry.

Throwing her apron up over her face, she rocked back and forth and felt as though she were mourning the dead. Even though nothing was settled, something in her said that what he said was what would come to pass, and she felt torn in pieces. Part of her was honored that this gentleman had chosen her Annie. But part of her was scared for the girl, his being so much older and having the past he did. Even if she didn't mistrust him, which she didn't, men were hunting him and aimed to kill him.

And part of her was scared for herself. Here, like a lightning bolt on a cloudless day, this stranger was proposing to take her only daughter away from her, clear away, so far away she would never see her again. That nearly ruined her.

"No, Mrs. Sherwood! No, ma'am. It won't be like that. Annie can come to see you. It's a long way, I know, but we'll be getting railroads and better routes here very soon after the war. Travel won't always be so hard, you'll see. You can already go from St. Louis to Kansas Town in ten days or so by steamboat. And don't forget that I'm a doctor. I'll be able to send you money, too, for fare to come there. And I will!"

He believed everything he said. It was a plan based on what he was convinced was the future of the country.

"People are flocking west, Mrs. Sherwood. They're building towns. They will need what I have to give, what Annie has to give. It's a good place, ma'am. We should do well there. They need new lives."

For the moment he was speaking so confidently and with such animation she was convinced, too—and eased.

"She is young," Mary said. "She's never been with any man."

"I know that," he said, more quietly again, "and I will honor it."

"Still, some girls are married younger than she is," Mary replied.

"Yes, many are," he agreed. "Still, Annie is young. That's partly what calls me to her. She is unspoiled and fresh. I don't mean as a girl with men. I'm not thinking that way. I mean as a person who hasn't been broken down by this war and these times."

"She's had plenty of sadness." Mary's desire to spar with him arose again. For her, it was as though he had just ridden in there, got it all settled with him having what he wanted and her not being sure but knowing she'd feel awful, and with Annie not even being consulted. "She's lost her daddie and her grandpa. She's cared for the sick and wounded. She's buried men torn to bits—without a casket. She's had to help support herself and me. She's had her griefs the same as all of us."

He nodded and honestly smiled. "Yes. I didn't mean to suggest that Annie hasn't been hurt by all our troubles. I know she has. But it's her spirit I'm talking about. Something in her seems to have stayed strong and hopeful, I think. That's what I mean. She seems. . .," and he paused before he finished: "healthy."

That, Mary understood. There never was anyone like Annie for being cheerful and trying hard. That never failed in her, and her mother recognized that he had seen the girl's strength. She nodded and looked at him. "It mislikes me still to think of her going so far, but you do seem to me to talk sense. She is a fine girl, so full of life, and so much here is already wasted."

She studied him. "He's not an ugly man," she thought. "Cleaned up. . . . Well, anyway."

"If she's willing," she finally said. "If she's willing. It all depends on that."

"Yes, ma'am," he replied. "If Annie's willing, I intend to come for her in two days.

"Tell her to bring only a little. We'll have one pack mule between us. We'll have to buy what we need as we go." Then he stood up and brushed at his clothes. "I'll try to be more presentable."

They paused a minute, looking at one another, then he asked, "You'll speak with her?" while she said, "I'll talk to her," and they laughed again, almost friendly.

As he walked off the stoop, she saw him look around for Annie, but the girl had disappeared. He patted the mare as he raised the reins over her head and checked the girth. Mary watched him step in the iron and ease himself up, and she thought, "I'd of liked him, I think, if I'd ever of had the chance."

14

Annie did not believe what she was hearing. She shut her eyes and gritted her teeth and shook her head against all of it. She knew of cases where boys and girls had been married without knowing one another very long. But she always figured their families were acquainted or that the people were ignorant. She could not imagine her mother's ever considering such a proposal and from such a man.

"Will Fairchild!" she argued inside, angry at the world and hunkered over into herself. "Everybody knows about him." And her mind flew over the facts as she had heard them. She imagined demanding of her mother, "Who could ever trust a man who would shoot his brother in the back?" She pictured Mary having to look down, acknowledging her terrible mistake.

Worst of all was just him, how he looked. He was old. There was no other word for it. He had said he was thirty-three. That meant he was nearly as old as her father. Fairchild had been eighteen years old when she was born. She couldn't stand to think of it, and she shivered from head to foot.

But then, when she heard her mother say she would talk to Annie about it, Annie not only believed what she was hearing, some part of her believed it would happen. She remembered how caught she had felt on the stoop, and how she had stopped breathing when she had realized who he was. Now her body more than her head dealt with what was happening. As she heard him getting ready to leave, she headed for the Hollow, springing like an animal, a rabbit or squirrel, in and among the trees surrounding the meadow, stopping immobilized to see if he was where he could spy her, finally coming out on the trail road that ran up the mountain beside the branch.

She knew the Hollow as well as she knew her front yard. Her grandfather, then her family, had lived high on the Ridge. She and Billy had always played there. Up until the war, her family had still visited with those few whose cabins looked out over the branch. And she and her mother had lived up there again for most of the winter of '63-'64. Earlier her parents, like most others, had moved down from the Ridge. There was no end to the need for workers in Pikeville, and Sherwood—he was always called by his last name—and Mary lived with more comfort in the valley. He made barrels and wagon wheels, and she sometimes cleaned the homes and cared for the sick of families who had never owned slaves or, more recently, of those whose slaves were gone. Mostly, though, she wove baskets she sold up and down the valley.

But Annie preferred the Ridge and Hollow. She especially loved to play in the waters of the branch, and particularly up by the Hudson cabin where the water descended a series of curving, wide, flat rocks that looked like the natural model for an elegant staircase. The rocks were never more than a foot high, though they were perhaps fifteen feet across and six to eight feet deep.

Annie liked to walk up and down them, the water cold on her bare feet. Then she would turn to her tree dance, as she thought of it, granting that the rocks were too slick to walk on safely. She raised her arms above her head and swayed her body, extending the motion up her neck and arms and out her fingers, careful to keep her feet as still as she imagined tree roots to be. She was a pretty girl, and she was graceful, though she was not tall, which she longed to be. Her hair turned blue and silver when the sunlight touched it, and her body was muscular. She turned in the sun and moved her arms in a kind of disciplined, repeated motion until she achieved a rhythm her hands released against the pine and hickory and oaks whose colors danced as the sunlight passed through them. Annie would close her eyes, smile, and cherish the sense of harmony she felt with the solid, whispering trees, the warm sun, the smooth rocks and the cold, insistent water that sounded like a tree full of red-winged blackbirds.

When she tired of that, she would sometimes sit smack in the middle of the rock steps or even lie flat on the largest, her side to the flow, her arms and legs spread wide, and shiver with the chill she partially dammed, then felt slip around her as she looked up into the leaves flowing over her head like the water flowing under it.

The sides of the stream were cluttered with rounded rocks of all sizes. Annie often thought of them as she felt the water pushing at her head and arms and body. She imagined the water smoothing at her until it got to her bones and made them white and round, then pushed them down the branch, mixing them with the rocks which people would find and choose and take home for door stops—or just because they were pretty.

When she couldn't stand that any more, she would run round, then climb up on a big, flat rock she always considered her own. All her life, the branch and this rock had been her place for thinking, and her granite stone, suddenly rising twenty feet above the water—but approachable from the forest side—was like a crow's nest on a ship. Annie could look up and down the branch from curve to curve as a sailor might look from horizon to horizon, and she had a sense of immensity and height even though the world her stone dominated was, in truth, intimate and small. Still, even when the waters were high—which really meant widened and fast—even when the trees and rushing stream combined, thundering like a waterfall, to give Roaring Hollow its name, especially then the rock provided height and stability which made it Annie's philosopher's seat. There, she sensed her own scope.

What she had long ago come to see was that she was tiny in a world that she would have very slight impact on. The water could wear her down and roll her away, she knew, as it did the rocks and as it had little Hurly Guipre when she fell off the tree bridge upstream during high water.

Yet Annie loved it, the place and the world she knew. She loved to be in it, and she felt, even as a very young girl, that it was a good place even though it was so powerful and mysterious to her she couldn't say why she thought that.

On this day, as she hugged her knees and sat in the sun on her rock, she had a new sense of the branch and of herself. She came to know that she was in motion, like the water, and although it frightened her a little, she felt some persistence, some push that she didn't altogether want to oppose.

"In the long run," she thought, "I have to marry somebody, and maybe he is better than most."

She thought of the horse she might get. It would be a chestnut with long, blond mane and tail, and she would ride it on forest paths and through streams and across meadows, her hair streaming behind her as she sometimes used to imagine it did when she could coerce Charlie into a gallop.

Then she thought of taking her clothes off in front of this man, and a shudder ran the length of her body. Nothing in the rocks or trees could explain that to her as even possible, let alone pleasurable. She had imagined kissing Riley, her teacher's son, whose verbs and subjects agreed. And she liked thinking about that. But this man had whiskers! And he was gray-haired.

So her thoughts went on for more than two hours until the sun grew hot on her head, and her body was stiff. She thought about it every way she knew how, including being able to buy her mother pretty dresses and her brother good mules. And she concluded, as she pushed herself up from the rock the way an old woman might, gone in the joints, that the way was definite even if it wasn't clear.

She was not rooted to this ground, and she would not be rolled to the branch bank, clean and round and permanent. She would go, if her mother thought it best. She would go like the water over the rocks, from somewhere at the top of the Ridge down the Hollow to the valley, to the Sequatchie, then stay in the river until it took her wherever it was going.

15

He did not himself know how they would go or where they would arrive. It was generally north and west, and he assumed Nashville was a first safe haven, a place where he was not likely to be recognized and where they could make connections upriver. He would tell Annie and her mother that Nashville was where they would end the first stage of their trip. They would marry, visit the city some, make provisions for the next stages, and send word back to Mary. Those were his intentions.

Because he did not want to risk travelling by coach yet, and because he knew Annie was a good rider, he decided that they would head first to Sparta on the old Higginbotham Trace, and he selected from a man he knew well three mules for that trip, big red-brown mules with long shoulder stripes, mules that were very much like Annie's Charlie. He hoped that would please her—although the mules and saddles and equipment, like yesterday's mare, would soon be traded or sold for whatever the next day's journey would require. He also knew the mules would have the endurance to make the trip with little rest and that they could manage the mountain terrain if he and Annie had to leave the trail.

He shaved his face clean for the first time in ten years, leaving only a small mustache. He immediately wished that he had not. Attention went straight to his eyes, he thought—his eye. And his face was too white and red-speckled from the unaccustomed shave. But he did look different, and that was what he wanted.

John and Keelie had helped him retrieve some savings and clothes. Although they were now too big for him, he raised his shoulders in pleasure as the soft cotton of a civilian shirt relaxed around him. The boots, cordovan and polished, calf-high and specially made for him, eased on as they always had, and with a slight smile, he threw his army boots, stiff and ill-fitting, as far into the bushes as he could. He buried his uniform in much the same temper, but he kept his sword and its maroon sash. Those he would give to Mary. He had seen her eyes rove over them, and he imagined she admired them.

In her turn, Annie prepared to leave. The only object she longed to take was her father's guitar, but she knew her mother treasured it even though only Annie could play it. She had very little of her own, but she made sure that what she had was clean and smoothed out in her mother's old carpetbag. On the very bottom was a white nightshirt Mary had made her last winter. She put it in quickly along with some small rags she folded carefully, then stuck in as fast as she could and covered with underwear, two long skirts of yellow and brown, and two waists, both white, some stockings and winter boots, her coat, her red scarf, and her mother's comb and brush. They were made of celluloid, the color of light stone—or a chestnut's mane and tail, Annie's favorite color in the world.

"I'll get another, child," Mary had said, giving them to Annie, and the girl had taken her mother's face between her hands and turned it back and forth while tears streamed down both their faces.

Later, when they sat waiting for him to come, Mary worried about what she should say about men and women, and Annie hoped her mother would not try to talk about men and women. Finally Mary asked, "Annie, do you have any questions?"

And Annie, long ready for the subject, exploded, "No!"

Her mother, sighing a little, said, "Well, don't worry none. You're a nice, healthy girl, and it ain't as bad as some pretend. Could even be you'll like it."

They sat a moment longer, and Mary finished: "It's nature's way, you know. And though it's awkward as all get out sometimes, it's natural. Sometimes it's mighty nice."

"It's all right, Ma," Annie managed, her cheeks blazing. "Me and Billy, we know about it." And she wished Billy was home right then, back from the Crossville sawmill where he had begun to work. She needed him, and she wanted so to tell him goodbye.

Much relieved, Mary sat silent a few minutes, then went on to something else. "My mother, rest her soul; I wish you could of known her, Annie. She told me once that if I ever run into people or situations where I didn't know what to do, I should just be kind. 'That'll pretty nearly always be all right,' she said, 'even if you ain't sure how to act.' I thought that was good advice."

And again they were silent, each trying to conceive what Annie was going to, each heartsick at what she was leaving, neither with words to say it.

When he came, they were all three subdued. The two women listened to his plans. Mary saw that he did indeed look more presentable. His clothes were loose and wrinkled, but they were well made, and his boots were shining. Annie saw that, too, and pulled her skirts forward to hide her scuffed, black, single-last shoes as best she could.

She was trembling for her life, but she bit her lip and ducked her head when he boosted her up on the third mule where, except for the saddle, she felt somewhat at home. She scooted forward, then bunched her skirts under her and around her legs a little before she sat back.

"His name is Rumble," Will told her, and he smiled a little when she looked at him. "If we go quickly, Annie, it will be easier," he said, and she, looking at her mother who was gripping Will's sword in front of her like a fence rail, nodded yes.

"Heeah, mule," he said, suddenly loud, and he put the lead animal instantly into a fast trot.

Annie's mule followed the pack mule too closely, and she had to give him her attention. She could not look back in time to see her mother's face clearly.

Gradually she stopped crying and became aware of herself. Her skirts protected her, but she was not comfortable and wished she was riding bareback. Still, when he saw someone approaching, on foot or horseback or in a wagon, he pulled off the road and deep enough into the trees that they wouldn't be seen. Then she was glad for the stirrups that helped her balance as Rumble moved over the rocky and uneven ground.

It seemed to her they had ridden for hours without speaking. She tried very hard to think of something to say. For some reason she began to think that she should try to make it pleasant, to talk with him—

though she had no such desire. She did not see anything around her to comment on. The rhododendron and mountain laurel were not out yet. Maybe he didn't like flowers anyway. She watched the sun shadow and highlight Rumble's shoulders as he moved, and she thought that was pretty. She wondered again where donkeys got the stripe they gave mules. But why would a doctor running for his life want to talk about a mule's stripe? What came out before she knew she was going to say it was: "Is it true you shot your brother-in-law in the back?"

As soon as she said it, she wished she had not, but she also knew it was one of the worst stories about him, what she hated even more than that he hadn't come to his wife's funeral. And she realized that, whether she intended to ask it or not, it was the one question he would have to answer before she could figure out how to get along with him.

A minute must have passed before he turned back toward her, his hand on the cantle, and said, "Ride on up here, Annie, and I'll tell you about it. You deserve to know."

She took a deep breath and edged Rumble around the pack mule. It laid its ears back, but it didn't kick, and she felt a little rush of courage, both that she had asked a question he agreed to respond to and that she had got the mules out of order without their resisting it.

"You're right to ask, Annie," he said. "It's hard for me to talk about. What happened was awful." He looked over at her. "Do you know that you are the first person who ever did ask me about it point blank?" He wasn't talking easily. She thought he sounded as though he had been running, as though he didn't have much breath left in him. "I'm glad you care whether I would do such a thing—and that you give me a chance to explain."

She felt he was saying that she was brave or right-minded, somehow, to inquire into what happened, and she dared to look at him. He had on a light brown hat that didn't have sweat creeping up the sides. She thought it was pretty shaped, the brim about four inches wide, curled up at the edge. It had a leather band around the crown. His eyes were shadowed, but the rest of his face was smooth and regular. He wasn't mean looking. With only a mustache, he didn't look so old, either, just a little two-toned.

"There are two answers to the question, Annie," he began, a deep frown pulling his eyes into darker shadow. "The first is, 'Yes. I did it.' He was running from me; he was unarmed; and I shot him."

When he got that out, he was quiet longer than she expected, and she wondered if he had gotten lost in remembering it. But then he went on, maybe a little stronger. "If we leave it at that, we have the truth, but it's not the whole truth, so it's not right.

"The second answer is that I shot him because he disobeyed my direct order to stop. He was a Confederate spy, Annie, and he had given incorrect information to the Union commanders so the rebels would have the advantage at Chickamauga—which they certainly did, as you well know. In that situation, his being my brother-in-law had no relevance to my duty. I did not want to shoot any man. I surely did not want to shoot my wife's brother."

He could not finish without stammering and panting, it sounded like. Annie was able to imagine the awful choice, and she knew he was making a powerful effort to tell her about it.

"Did you aim at him to kill him?" the hunter in her asked.

He made a sharp, harsh sound and shook his head. "I don't think I even aimed, Annie. I'm not a very good shot, you know. I'm a doctor, not a rifleman, and it was the only time I fired a gun the whole war. I was surprised to hit him at all. And I'll be sorry for it until the day I die."

After a moment she was able to say, honestly, "I'm sorry it happened."

She spoke so directly and easily he looked at her in surprise. "Oh," he half-moaned, "so am I. So am I." Then he asked, "Do you believe me?"

"Yes, Sir. I do," she answered promptly, and he felt his first affection for her.

They rode on quietly, letting the mountain sounds come to them. A downy woodpecker in a distant oak silenced as they approached, then, like a squirrel, moved sideways and around the trunk, keeping the tree between itself and them. The mules' hooves crunched leaves in a pleasant, complicated rhythm. Finally reaching over to pat her hand, he asked,

"Would you be comfortable calling me Will?"

She thought about it a minute and said, "I'm not sure, but I'll try to if you want me to."

Riding side by side, they both thought over the conversation, both feeling some relief. Then Annie came to her next question. "Would you shoot somebody else if they disobeyed you?"

He hadn't heard himself laugh for a long time, but now he did. He was beginning to sense how very young she was and how much he would need to help her with all sorts of matters.

"No! No, Annie, Never again. We were at war, you know. As it turned out, more than thirty thousand men were wounded or killed at Chickamauga. Your brother knows. He was there. It was a terrible time, a terrible battle. All of us were desperate."

Again she saw and felt how particular and dreadful this was for him. He did not move steadily through it. His voice shook and faded, but he found it again and again to go on with what he needed to say.

"At times like that, orders are absolute. Everything depends on them. They have to be obeyed or you have complete chaos. I had to shoot.

"But outside the military, nobody can expect that kind of obedience, not ever and not from anyone." For an instant, his father's red face appeared to him, but he managed to close his mind to it and to continue. "That makes slaves, and we've just fought a war to end slavery."

He found a way to smile at her and took her question the direction he figured she intended in the first place: "I want a helpmate and friend, Annie, not a slave."

She liked the way he talked. He sounded like her teacher.

When they wanted to eat, he found a clearing where he felt protected — not far from the road. He hobbled the mules and loosened their girths, then spread out a thick gray blanket to sit on. He had brought hard-boiled eggs and bread, apples and spring water for their lunch. She wished he had brought an onion, too, but she didn't say so.

Later he suggested that she might want to refresh herself while he walked a bit. She appreciated the way he said it, and she felt herself relaxing some.

When he came back, she was stretched out on the blanket, fast asleep, and he watched her for several minutes before he went to the animals, making sure he was noisy with them so she could awaken without embarrassment.

The afternoon passed much as the morning had except that Annie was so tired she could barely stay awake. Rumble's gait was very smooth, nearly a rack, and she wasn't the least stiff. She was just tired.

The strain of the last days was partly over, and because she didn't have to struggle so, she could let herself go a little. But then exhaustion struck. She didn't want to try to talk. She only wanted to sleep. Every hour or so they stopped to rest and attend to their needs. When they found water, they let the mules drink. She didn't think she could go on. When he finally said they would make camp, she nearly fell off Rumble.

"Would you rather sleep than eat, Annie?" he asked as he helped her, careful about snakes, to a seat on a fallen tree.

"Oh, Glory! Yes! Please," she said, and he saw the fatigue on her face.

"It won't be this hard much longer, Annie, I promise." He kicked and pushed leaves together into a long mound and put the blanket down for her. "Here," he said, tucking the gray wool around her. "I'll bring you a saddle blanket for a pillow in just a minute." She thought he sounded very kind. She was aware of his hands smoothing the blanket close to her, but she was too tired to be nervous. When he came back with the saddle blanket, she was already asleep, her head on her arm, her mouth open.

He shook his head a little and wondered if he was, in fact, in his right mind. Then he wrapped himself in another blanket, sat down, leaned against the log, and slept, himself, a relatively dreamless sleep until about four in the morning.

Talking about Evander for the first time with anyone had seemed, at the moment, to be helpful. He had felt more relieved about it than ever before. But when he awakened at his wolf hour, unable to go back to sleep, he fell into the pains and thoughts which took him inexorably to Narcissa and the baby, then to still older agonies.

Night struggles had nothing to stop them, and he knew he was in trouble. More than once at such a time he had sat with a pistol muzzle against his temple—if he hadn't had enough whiskey to stop the rush of images and terrors that swirled around him, finally so fast and mocking he seemed able sometimes only to catch their shrill and rising cry. It was always an attack of scenes he had gone through or had not been able to stop imagining: Narcissa moving under him in love, then screaming for him as their son drowned in her blood, watching him shoot Evander in the back when he should have fired in the air. Her face became parched skin over skull or a caul over a black mouth gaping for breath.

It went on and on, finally so loud and fast it made him whine and shake like a dreaming dog. But he would not be asleep. It was all uncontrolled in his waking head, ready to swirl at any instant into tall speed until he had to work to exhaustion or drink to stupor to stop it. He would fill with pain. His father's accusations would become phrases jerking before his eyes like lines ripped from a book. He couldn't hear them. He had to read them. "You are a wanton, willful fool. You bring shame. You are despicable in the eyes of God. You are nameless and diseased. You infect others with your pride, your sickness. You were better never to have been born." And finally all would chase all like dogs gone mad, and what he could hear was their howl which he knew was his own had he been able.

Now, watching the girl and weeping, he imagined the whiskey burning down his throat and belly, eventually stilling his brain. He wanted it frantically and felt himself sweating with the strain. But he could see Annie silver in the moonlight. He didn't think she had moved since she lay down. He knew he didn't want to frighten or hurt her. He knew she was his last, best chance. And he fought his demon, begging some distant non-entity to let her awaken and talk with him or a bear to spook the mules or a storm to force them to break camp.

Of course nothing of the sort happened, and gradually the night passed. When dawn broke, he was staring wide-eyed at the girl, wishing with awful fatigue that they were sleeping in one another's arms, both as innocent as she looked.

In the morning, they went on with the routine he had begun for them, he, excusing himself to give Annie time and privacy, she, grateful to him, but increasingly aware that this was not the way they would continue and increasingly anxious about it.

They ate a good breakfast of dried venison, bread and coffee he risked making a fire for, and he again took out apples for them to eat as they went along. This day, her question was about his wife and why he wasn't at her funeral, and she found that it was much more difficult for him, not explaining his absence at the funeral—he was able to say that Narcissa had died just after her brother's funeral, that he hadn't known about it for several days, that he wouldn't have been given permission to go anyway—but speaking with any detail or coherence about their life together. He knew Annie would be sympathetic, and he even thought she should know. But he did not feel able or willing to share much of it with her. He did try. He managed to say he was sorry it was so hard for him. But he could not tell her about Narcissa and their marriage or his feelings at her death.

In fact, he didn't know some of them. The hurt was plain—to him and ultimately to Annie—but below that was a morass he could not wade through. He had fled Philadelphia, then left Kentucky after years of study and work. Now he was leaving Tennessee, having dared to love and marry, having lost everything a second time. All that—yet still the old haunting, and his silence before it, continued and weakened him. He felt himself flushing, not at Annie's question but in persistent anger at that stubborn and self-righteous man who had crumpled their world and forged a chain of suffering no one seemed able to break. Try as he might, he could not explain, not to Annie and not to himself.

Seeing his struggle—as she interpreted it: his being caught between the grief of losing his wife, son, and family, and his inability to think of anything else—Annie rescued him. She was actually contented within herself to believe that without any doubt he had loved and still loved his wife. That was the reality she needed to uncover. "It's all right. It's all right, Will." She used his name. "I don't need to know anything else. Mostly I just needed to know you hadn't forsaken her, that you loved her."

He groaned, and she didn't want him to try to talk about it any more. "It's all right. Please. Just let it be."

Once again he found himself looking at her with relief and gratitude. This time she smiled at him.

In the second night outside of Sparta, he was struck again by the waking nightmares. Battling not to get the whiskey, he gazed at the girl sleeping near him, and to his surprise, he began to want her. Desire had deserted him for months, but as he watched Annie breathe and listened to her small sleep sounds, he imagined their being together, the relief it would give him, perhaps the pleasure for her. He thought of her natural kindness and interest in him, how she wanted to please him. He could see that. And he thought that if she were to understand his need, she would want to help him.

He went over again this whole, strange undertaking they were about. She was to be his wife. He was responsible for her. She was his.

Beginning to ache, he watched her. She was so lovely and fresh. He wanted to be tender with her. His promises rushed through his mind.

Then she turned over toward him and opened her eyes. Going quickly to her, he whispered her name. She was instantly alert, and although her first instinct was to cry out, she lay quiet and still. "What is it?" she asked, and she heard her mother's voice: "It's nature's way." Then she heard her own: "We're not married yet, Will."

"I know, Annie. I know. But we will be. Just a few more days."

He was breathing hard, and she thought he looked miserable. She put her hand out to him and said, "It's all right," not actually certain what she meant.

Moving beside her, he said, "It's not what we planned, Annie, but I feel so awful over there." He was working at her clothes and his. "I need you."

She lay very still. Then she could feel him between her legs, warm and hard, his hands touching her, finger inside her, then lifting her behind a little. "Don't be afraid, Annie," he said, but he was breathing fast, and she was afraid. "I won't hurt you. I wouldn't ever hurt you."

He did not kiss her. It was the one thing she knew about and expected, but it didn't happen. He moved his penis around and over her sex briefly, then shallowly in and out of her. She felt a surge and some light specks in her thighs and down there, then he came into her, and she felt a sharp pain. After that, she didn't feel much of anything of her own as he moved slowly then fiercely over her. Then he moaned and shook and finally lay on top of her a moment before he eased off to her side breathing unevenly. After a while, he asked, "Are you all right?"

She supposed she was and said so, but just as quickly she began to worry. Ruined women were a pet subject of her mother, and Annie knew all the songs about fatherless children and cruel wanderings. "What if he doesn't marry me?" began running through her mind in a jangled melody, and she felt tears leaving cool traces in front of her ears.

When he became aware, he turned toward her and said, "Please don't cry, Annie." He seemed to understand. "I will marry you, and I will provide for you.

"I know you can't feel anything for me yet. I'm sorry this

happened. I wanted to make it good for you, too. I didn't want us still to be strangers when we made love. I just felt so bad. But don't cry. Don't cry." With great gentleness, he ran his hand up her cheek to dry the tears, and she shook, both at his touch and with her fears.

"Let me hold you," he said, and with something more than obedience, she did turn to him.

His arms felt strong. They comforted her some.

She was so tiny that he knew—all over again—how young she was, what dread she must have, how miserable and hopeless he had the power to make her. Resting his chin in her hair, he stroked away the tears that kept coming and said over and over, "It's all right, Annie. I'll make it all right."

She didn't know what to say and again felt inadequate that she couldn't talk and couldn't stop crying. Pretty soon he said, "I'll make it better for you next time, too." But then he slept, and she had no idea when the next time would be. She lay awake the rest of the night expecting it. About dawn, he got up and went to the mules. She could hear the bits and chains hitting together, the mules shifting as he approached them.

The blanket wool was prickly against her rump. Her skirts were bunched up at her waist, and she felt wet and some bruised. She raised the blanket a little and tried to pull her clothes down. She could smell herself and him. She worried about blood on the blanket. But she couldn't raise herself enough to manage her skirts. She would have to stand up. She wanted to wash, but standing up to go to the water would make him notice her and be aware she was awake, and she didn't want that yet.

In fact, she hadn't slept since he came to her, but she could tell from the way he had moved so carefully away from her and gotten up that he had thought she was sleeping. She wasn't afraid of his starting it over again if he knew she was awake. Indeed, if the ground hadn't been so hard and her self so sore, she might well have been willing to try again. She thought it was possible she could be one of those her mother said might like it.

Mostly, though, she wanted to wash. She wanted a moment to arrange herself, to be fresh before they came together again, in any way. And she wished he had waited until they were married.

16

He spoke very little at their breakfast, and Annie saw that he moved more quickly than usual. He dropped the canteen, and he put his hand to his mouth and hair unnecessarily and often. Not expecting him to be uncertain of himself, she was especially careful to thank him for the fruit and cheese. She was never sure what he would bring out of the willow food basket—which she thought loosely woven—but she always enjoyed it and realized that he had planned carefully for them.

Except for last night. She did not think he had planned to come to her last night, and she thought that was why he was nervous. It made her feel better to think that he hadn't deceived her, that he really had intended to wait. So she said that the best way she knew how: "It's all right, Will. I don't hurt much. And I know it's nature's way."

He dropped his head and closed his eyes a second. "I don't know what to say, Annie. It surprised me, too. I hope you really are all right and not saying it only for my sake."

She didn't look at him.

Leaning to touch her hand, he said, "You were a great comfort to me."

Still not looking at him, but not moving her hand, either, she said, "I'm glad for that."

She wanted to ask him about what had been so awful for him, but she supposed she already knew. She figured that making him talk any more about his marriage and the baby would be like filleting a fish before it was dead. Besides, she knew all she wanted

106

to, she thought. He had to have more time. He said he needed her, and that was all right, too. She could see that he was clean and decent. He had possibilities. So did love-making. It was all right for the moment.

They rode hard that day, stopping in Sparta only for more food, some crackers, tins of sardines, which she had never eaten, and salt, which he had forgotten. For their midday meal, he opened the sardines which she liked very much. "These little fish are good," she said to him, delicately moving backbones and threadlike entrails off to the side of her plate. "The tin says they've come from Norway. I wonder how on earth they got clear out here?"

"The world's getting smaller, Annie. Ships cross the Atlantic all the time, now, bringing us all sorts of merchandise."

"Do we send them anything?"

He stretched his legs by the little fire while he thought about it. "It seems to me I ought to know that, but I honestly don't. With the war and so many settlers like us moving west, I don't know whether producers or manufacturers have much left for export.

"I suppose under other conditions we'd be sending over cotton, tobacco."

"Have you ever been on a ship?"

"No. Not an ocean-going one, I haven't."

"Have you ever seen the ocean?"

He hesitated a moment because, in fact, he had, but as a boy with his father, and the thought changed his mood. He suddenly wanted to get up and walk away, but he steadied himself. He tried to see their conversation as the innocent and insignificant exchange it was, and for the first time in years, he allowed himself to refer to an experience with his father. He felt rigid, but he spoke of it. "Yes. I saw the ocean in Philadelphia. Well—the bay there that leads to the sea. I used to play on the docks as a boy.

"And I saw it in New York City. My father took me to watch the tall ships." He sounded abrupt to himself, but apparently not to Annie. She continued her own thoughts, not aware of the effort he had just made or even much aware of what he'd said.

"I miss my father," she said, picking up on that. "It's hard for me to think that he is dead." She scraped sardine bones into the fire and watched them hiss and smoke. "It's hard for me to think that I'm here right now with you." She looked over at him soberly. "Do you ever feel a little confused about just where you are and what's real?"

He was struck by her question and where it would take him if he answered truthfully. He knew he could say nothing of that kind of reality to this girl. She was sitting opposite him, a life-sized doll, it seemed to him. "And I am hoping for strength from her," he thought with a kind of bemusement.

He heard himself laughing, and he dropped his head to his chest. Then he heard his father's voice and tried to close his ears against "Shameful! Irresponsible!"

"Yes, I do, sometimes. I do," he answered, but he didn't know how to go on.

"I thought maybe it was just me that felt that way," she said, slicing into her apple crosswise. The first day, she had explained: "They're harder to eat this way, but they're prettier because you can find the blossom instead of just the seeds in the core." He'd never before seen the petals at the heart of the apple.

Now she went on. "It's a little like being lost, I think. I can't make it come together and make any sense. Like us here—who we are and where we're going." She ate her apple rings thoroughly. "This tastes so good, too." After a moment she continued. "I know what you said to Ma about helping to build a country and all, but I can't begin to understand that. It's all so far away from me. It's too big. I can't even see how the country looks there or how we'll look in such a place. I can't connect it up. And I can't connect us up, either. I don't understand the two of us together or how you see us turning out.

"Sometimes, if I pretend I'm high up in the sky watching all this, it looks like the wrong side of something you're sewing. You can't tell what the picture is. I don't see anything but this right now, like me eating this apple and you watching me, and I can't tell what we're really doing.

"When I was thinking about this, up in Roarin' Holler, I thought it would be like water flowing, little brooks into streams and streams into rivers. It would all be in a direction you could see. But now that we're going, nothing leads to anything, as far as I can tell, and that scares me a little."

She fell silent, and he tried to think of some way to comfort or explain. He took refuge in the obvious. "I think—I hope—that we'll both feel better about it all as we get comfortable, you and me—as we learn to feel safer with one another. Then the rest of it will fall into place, don't you think?"

"I don't know. That could be. But I don't see how that's to come about, either. You're a smart and educated man, and I never even got to finish the fifth grade. I've never been off the mountain, and you've been to the ocean. You've been married. You had all those terrible things happen to you. I can see it in your face, how it's hurt you, and I. . . I. . . . I don't know what to do with all that." She had talked herself into bewilderment.

"Annie!" he knelt in front of her. "Annie! Don't think about dealing with all that's passed before we met. Don't worry about that. It's because you are so young and strong that I'm drawn to you.

"With you, I have a sense that I can make things good again. With you, it feels as though I have some time, and I have energy, and I have someone to build with—to build for—after I thought it was all gone.

"You're a second spring to me, Annie. That's what I need from you."

She raised her eyes to his face and saw how much he meant what he said. Leaning forward, she brushed her lips across his in her first kiss, then she sat back and looked at the yellowing apple blossoms in her hand. "I hope you're right, Will." In a moment, she stood and ambled around their camp. Finally she said, "Even so, though, I wonder if we could plant these blossoms? If they grow, it would maybe be a sign someday to somebody that we had passed this way, wouldn't it?"

He stared at her a moment then jumped up and went to the edge of the timber where the sun brightened the grass. "Bring 'em here, Annie," he called. He intended his voice to be cheerful, but it cracked some. "Planting a tree to show where someone is—or where they have been—that's a good thing to do."

And together they dug a small hole, wet it down with water from their canteen, planted one blossom, then covered it and put a little circle of rocks around it.

"What about the other two?" he asked.

"No. I don't think so," she answered, closing her hand around them in her pocket. "I'll save them for a day we don't eat apples."

By nightfall, they were nearing the old Tennessee Trail where Will thought they could make stage connections into Nashville. That night, he did not sleep apart from her, and she accepted it because he seemed to want it, because she thought she might, too, and because she knew no other way. Although she was worried, he had promised again, and she believed they would marry in Nashville. This night, she was moved to let her hands rove over him some, catching in his hair. She was not much pleased because again he waited too long until he was rushed by need and could not properly make love to her.

It was as though he didn't want it to happen and perhaps believed it would not. He, too, thought, for her sake and because he had promised and because he was afraid of spoiling her life with his, that they should wait until they were married—or, more deeply, that they should never marry at all, that he should never have started such a bizarre affair. He wished he could undo it, that he'd never seen her.

But when his breathing changed and he felt hers change, too, when he had waited as long as he could, he turned to her and saw her awake, just looking at him, no protest in her eyes.

17

At the first way station on the Trail, Will traded the mules and equipment for tickets and some two hundred dollars. It was more than he had paid for them. The manager knew farmer after farmer who would need them, he said, and mail riders would want the saddles.

Annie had more questions as the days went on, but the stagecoach and way stations, totally new to her, absorbed much of her interest. Her eyes were everywhere, over the horses and the faded, chipped red paint on the stage door, and especially the thoroughbraces on which this particular old coach rode. When they stepped out for air or to try to regain some sense of their original bones or muscles after bouncing and rolling the ten or fifteen miles between stops, his inclination was to lean his back against a solid tree to see if he could stand still and upright. But Annie, after some initial unsteadiness, explored the stagecoach, her first concern being to see what was under the contraption and why she didn't just jar over bumps as she did in a wagon. He could see her interest as she found and touched the tough, black layers of leather and pushed and pulled on them to discover that they were rigid, in fact as strong as they looked. He began to see that how things worked fascinated her, and he realized freshly how little he knew about her.

She watched the other passengers, too, two men who sat behind the driver's seat facing them. One had the face of a drunken angel, flaming and peacefully, seamlessly round. His boots were filthy with manure, and his pants were too tight. The other man, much abused by his seat partner, was very pale and narrow-faced. He was thin, which was lucky for both of them. He nodded only slightly to Annie and Will, then stared out the window, holding tightly to the leather side strap and the edge of the seat to keep himself generally upright, looking sicker every mile. He coughed until he gagged.

"Could you help him?" Annie asked Will at the first stop after the men had boarded.

"No. He's too far gone for help, but if I had some foxglove, I might be able to ease his cough."

He shook his head, frowning. "I'll have to make new medicines when we arrive. . . or buy some. I've used nearly everything I had."

Annie thought about that for a moment. How in the world would he make new medicines? Would she be able to help him? She had seen him examine his large grip to check on his medical bag and another stained leather case he said was part of his equipment. He had shown her some books, too, which he said he hated to take with them—they were so heavy—but which he had to have for his practice. She liked thinking of strange things like that riding under the boot. It might be interesting to be a doctor's wife, to watch him prepare his instruments, to help him mix the medicines, to welcome people when they came for help.

And she was getting used to his face. She still hadn't asked him about his eye, nor did she have any sense of what he was like as a boy or where his own family was. She remembered that he'd mentioned Philadelphia, but found no way to ask those questions yet. Most of all, she remembered that nobody in the valley knew about his past. She thought that, when they were married, it might be different, easier between them. Then she would ask. It didn't seem to matter a great deal just now.

But marrying did. She wanted the marriage very much, partly because she was sure Will felt guilty about their love-making and would be eased when it was with benefit of clergy, as her mother used to say, and partly because, the farther they got from her home, the more she knew she had to rely on him. If she should also find herself with child, she would be lost without him, she thought, and the old stories and songs of husbandless, wandering women and fatherless, hungering children intruded again into her quiet moments. She did not think he would abandon her, but she knew she had no claim upon him beyond his word, and her concern grew each morning.

After days in a variety of coaches and one or two taverns, arriving in Nashville and leaving stagecoaches behind forever was a welcome thought to both of them. They were stiff and dirty and sometimes hungry, and they were sick of it. But neither of them complained, and he did not drink.

Annie finally seemed to realize that they were nearing the large city, and the thought renewed her and excited her. She remembered Mr. Clayton's telling them about the capital building and about President Jackson's fine home there that had burned down and been built back up. She wanted to see them. The day before they arrived she could not contain her excitement, and she asked a hundred questions: Where would they stay? What would they need for the steamboat? What river would they be on? Did he know about steamboats? Would this one be safe? How would they contact her mother? Where would they be married?

Will didn't know the answers to many of her questions, but that didn't matter because they became occasions for talking with other passengers, which Annie was eager to do. She was far better at it than he was, and he could see people warm to her quick smile and observations. He recognized his own reticence, but he didn't much mind. In fact, he was relieved to discover that Annie made people comfortable, and she created a place for him with them even if he had little to say.

But when they were alone and she asked about their marriage, he felt sick. His mind fled over the years of flight and failure and his terrible efforts before meeting Narcissa, before the war, nights in Kentucky when, so tired he could no longer read, he drank to allay his loneliness and anger and sadness. Sometimes he had felt so ancient and worn with it that he found it hard to rise from a chair. He had used whiskey because he had read studies of opium and laudanum addiction, and he held himself back from them with a brutal effort of will. But it was nearly impossible to blur the faces of those whom he loved and who seemed to stare at him from all directions. He had to pass out before he could silence his father.

When he remembered this and could not stop his mind from scurrying rat-like over his whole sorry life, he was consumed by doubts. Repeatedly he heard his father accusing him of shameful irresponsibility, of tricking this girl as he had Deborah, of covering his lust with some grandiose notion of saving her and living into an epic where he would build a new and better world for her. Such thoughts assured him that he was a wrecked, thin-blooded fool who could not hope to care for anyone. Then he knew that he should not go on with this, that Annie would be better off with her mother than with him. He shrank in fear at marrying her, forcing her to share his stupidity and endless need. He wished he had never seen her, that he could simply go to sleep forever.

Annie could feel his growing tension, and when she was able, at rest stops, she urged him to walk with her. "Come on, Will," she would say. "We need the exercise. We've been sitting too long. I'm scared of the boats, but at least we'll be able to move around on them. Come on. Walk with me."

It had been over two weeks since he had drunk whiskey. He counted the days but with no sense of victory, for he was never free from wanting it, needing it. Sometimes the bottle in his medical bag at the back of the coach was all he thought of during a whole afternoon of travel. Sometimes he tapped his heel so hard and fast Annie would put her hand on his knee to steady him. Sometimes passengers were uncertain about making eye contact with him, he looked so fierce. Sometimes Annie was scared, too. She remembered that he'd been discharged for excessive drinking, that he had told her mother he had stopped. But she knew her Uncle Joe and other mountain men who spent long days drinking and long nights carousing. Their women were thin, tired, and silent.

At night, she would get up with him or try to hold him and talk with him. She felt she should not question him, yet her good instincts told her that he should talk, if not about what he was feeling, then about something else. Anything. She did her best. "Are you sick, Will? Do you have any medicines that could help you?"

Sometimes he just sat and shook, wrapped in blankets. Sometimes he tried to talk, to ease her. "I'll be all right, Annie. I will. These dreams and feelings—I have to fight them, but I'll be all right. Try not to worry."

"I'll try not to, Will. But I know it must hurt something awful."

He did not want to hear that. He had no resources left to deal with her sympathy or her misunderstanding.

The night before they arrived in Nashville was especially hard for

114

them, and he finally stood up abruptly and turned away. "No more, Annie. I don't want to talk about it," he said. "I don't want to talk about it. Not now." Then, in a dry, exhausted voice, he asked her what he knew would wound her: "Could we just get on north as fast as possible? I think if we can just get on up the river, get there so I can concentrate on something, so I can work, I'll be better."

"You mean not stop in Nashville? Not get married there?"

He heard her voice wilt, but he couldn't summon what she most wanted. "Yes. Let's just go on—on the first boat north. It'll only be a few more days, Annie. We'll have time in St. Louis. I promise. St. Louis."

Her heart fell, but she didn't think she had a choice.

So in haste they made their way to the Nashville wharves where he bought tickets for them on the first packet up the Cumberland, a little transient steamer so loaded with cotton and cattle her freeboard was barely above water. They would change boats at Paducah on the Ohio, thence to Cairo, and finally up the Mississippi to St. Louis.

18

Annie was afraid of steamboats, and the "Ivy Linda," a dirty little batwing with only one main engine, did nothing to calm her. School had given her one view of steamboat travel, but her parents had provided another, and Annie had long ago sided with them.

As one of Hickory Grove's best students, Annie had received many awards for "diligence and good behavior." These were certificates prepared by railroad and steamboat companies which were in head-to-head competition with one another.

Those distributed by the steamer companies had pictures of majestic side-wheelers, the flag and the smoke from their stacks waving in elegant, regular parallels which were also in precise harmony with the water's ripples. Ribbons of rhyme enclosed the pretty picture:

> Remember thy Creator,
> Child with the glad, glad heart,
> And joy shall be thy portion,
> When thou with life shall part.

Contrary to every purpose the companies had for their advertisements, Annie connected the verse and its promise of heaven to other pictures, some Sherwood and Mary had. These were broadside versions of steamboat wrecks and fires, and they were more persuasive to Annie than either the depictions on her awards or the assurances in her schoolbooks that steamboat travel was opening the west and north to rapid settlement.

Two pictures that scared her about equally were "The Pittsburgh Broadside" and "The Helen McGregor." The first was, it said, of "the great conflagration" in 1845. In this view, the wharf fire was glaring at its height, burning violently and destroying steamboats and bridges. Eventually, Annie had read with awe and horror, it had leveled more than a thousand buildings. Here, the blaze turned impenetrably black as it sucked up debris—and probably people, Annie thought.

Even more poignant was the explosion on the "Helen McGregor" right at the Memphis wharf. Annie marveled at the wheelcase bearing the ship's name and heading skyward—along with flailing gentlemen and ladies, skirts still decorous inverted tulips, a smokestack, and an extraordinarily long American flag. Survivors already in the water raised their arms above their heads in perfect Us. Annie imagined she could hear their pleas as they confronted an enormous, obviously hungry crocodile.

Sherwood and Mary had more than once spoken with outrage and pity of the sudden, dreadful, and undeserved fate steamboat travelers met, and Annie was instructed by their faces, grim above the pictures. She had no trouble deciding, at seven, that she would learn to swim and that she would never set foot on a steamboat.

But now, still not being able to keep her head above water, here she was, marching onto the deck of a decrepit and stinking boat that was belching ashes and some live cinders onto cotton bales. Anxious-looking black men stood with buckets of water at hand, but she knew it would never be enough if a fire actually started.

Annie and Will were among the last aboard, and they were just aboard when the gangplank was raised, the moorings cast off, and the boat guided, creaking and complaining, into a slow, slow northward journey.

The "Ivy Linda" immediately drove from their minds any preconceptions about "floating palaces." It did offer separate cabins for men and women, with tiers of curtained berths from floor to ceiling. But they were cramped and dirty, the old mattresses stained and lumpy, and with nothing to serve as sheet or pillow.

There weren't many other passengers, and one group of four was an immigrant family who seemed to speak no English—except for the daughter, about six. Looking at Annie with huge and solemn brown eyes, she said, "Ve go Amereekah."

Annie felt her heart grabbed, and she smiled for the first time in hours.

"Yes, you pretty little thing. We go America, too!" And the two of them, then the whole family, and finally, even Will, nodded vigorously and repeated together with smiles that gradually broke into laughter: "We go America! We go America!"

So Annie and Will and the Zajics found themselves allied for the duration. That was helpful to all of them because three or four passengers were rough and obscene, making everyone else feel vulnerable and afraid. With four adults, they could take turns watching the children and the baggage while some slept, went for food, or walked as they could for exercise.

Annie, despite her fears—multiplied at learning that Will could not swim, either—took pleasure in helping the mother and daughter learn some words and sentences. Sometimes she and Will could hear them practicing or helping the father and son in their turn. Once when Annie was helping them distinguish father, husband, son, and brother, the mother looked at her and Will and asked, "Father?"

Flushing both at what they were understanding and what she knew, she said, "No. Husband." And Will put his hand very gently on her shoulder.

"You are good with people, Annie," he praised her later as they stood together on the deck catching what breeze they could, trying not to hear the miserable livestock or the struggling engine.

"I used to think it would be nice to be a schoolteacher—like Mr. Clayton," she answered. Then, seeing his question, she added, "He taught Billy and me over at Hickory Grove. Except he didn't teach Billy so much. Sometimes those big boys would be so discouraging the way they would bother everybody and make fun. Sometimes they were downright mean." And she finished, "Don't suppose I'd much have liked teaching them, would I?"

He took her hand, and she let him hold it, holding his a little, too.

He had been more relaxed after they boarded the steamer. He was often busy, and that clearly helped him. Just staying in control of their belongings was hard, and making the accommodations bearable was nearly impossible. They put the bedding on the rail during the day and slept in their clothes. They organized watches to protect themselves against the passengers who seemed to regard them as plums ready for the picking.

Then there were Annie's fears: what *would* happen if lightning struck the cotton? What would they do if someone fell overboard? What would happen if the engine *did* explode? Will found himself patrolling the boat, trying to see how it worked, what its weaknesses were, what they might, in fact, do to save lives should one of Annie's disasters strike.

But what helped Will most was that the "Ivy Linda" crew and cargo seemed beset with accidents, and Will had revealed himself to be a physician who also knew a lot about animal medicine. The Captain carried a full cabinet of medical supplies, had for years, but most were untouched because he rarely had a doctor on board and himself knew nothing about the medicines, some of which were in crumbling cartons or dusty bottles. Will's face had come alive when he opened that cabinet door and found such a treasure of quinine, ether, blue mass, laudanum, chalk. . . . He had been nearby when one of the crew feeding cattle caught his arm on a hay hook. Will saw that it was a deep, bad wound, and he had wrapped his belt about it the best he could and run to the Captain to see if the boat carried any medical supplies. That had been the start of it.

Since then, he had sewn up all sorts of cuts, splinted broken arms, taken ashes out of eyes, wrapped burns in egg white, treated ringworm and colic, delivered a baby by Caesarean surgery for a woman who would otherwise have died, deloused, and lanced two boils. He had also advised the Captain to shoot and butcher one cow Will was convinced had swallowed some object. They were afraid she was sick and would infect the other animals, but Will said to shoot her. He would cut in to try to find the object. If he did, they could eat her. If he didn't, they could shove her overboard. When he found the nail, the whole crew cheered, and that night everyone on the boat had fresh meat, the best meal of the whole trip.

Annie saw his skill and patience. She also saw that he would, indeed, be a good provider. Though he asked nothing for his services, people gave him what they could, and it was a lot, Annie thought. Some gave him money. The woman tried to give him her watch. It had been her mother's, she said, and she wanted Will to have it. But he put it back in her hand and closed her fingers over it. "I don't want your watch," he said, with particularly strong emotion, Annie thought. "You keep it for your daughter."

And best of all, the Captain gave him at least half of all the supplies in the cabinet. "When will *I* ever know how to use them?" he had asked and happily turned Will loose with them.

Annie liked to watch Will work with the people. He was very specific with them, but he was also careful, and she was soothed and glad to see that.

"You're good with people, too, Will," she said back to him, laying her other hand on his. "Black, white, human or animal, you are good to help. You *are* a good doctor, aren't you?"

And they smiled at each other, almost contented for this moment to be where they were.

19

They changed steamships at both Paducah and Cairo, and each was, to Will's pleasure and Annie's growing confidence, more comfortable than the last. The "A. J. Conner," running between New Orleans and St. Louis for the Eagle Packet Company, was no small transient. When they later toured the ship, they were told that she weighed 371 tons and had two enormous engines. Though neither of them quite understood what they were seeing, both Will and Annie were properly amazed by the cylinders that were twenty inches across with six-and-a-half foot piston strokes. For Annie, the "Conner's" only serious flaw was that it did not have "low pressure" under its name on the wheel housing—as her father had said all safer boats had. Otherwise the steamer resembled the majesties on her merit certificates, and her heart jumped as she and Will joined dozens of others waiting to walk up and onto the guards around the cabin deck, already lighted for this evening boarding of the great vessel which looked, for all the world, to be a fairy ship.

This steamer was spotless. Even the tall twin black chimneys were shining clear to their petaled tops. The rails around the three decks were white gingerbread trimmed in blue and gold. The ship, itself, was white, but its name was bright red and outlined in gold against a sunburst of a dozen colors. Annie had no words for what she was seeing, and when they were shown to their cabin by a broad-shouldered, handsome, young black man dressed in a white and gold uniform, she openly stared.

Their stateroom actually had a full-sized bed with a pale green satin spread. The floor was covered with heavy dark green carpeting. Two ivory overstuffed armchairs sat by a small, round, walnut table in front of a large armoire. Annie ran her fingertips over the shining pink, green, and white floral insets across the doors. Behind a tall dressing screen decorated with strolling peacocks, their tails spread in glorious show, were a handsome little commode inside a wooden cabinet with a lid that closed and a wash stand with a Royal Doulton pitcher and bowl. To Annie's amazement, above the wash basin were a golden pipe and faucet out of which came water.

"Merciful heaven, Will!" she cried out. "I never was any place as fine as this." And she threw herself into one of the chairs and let her eyes rove while her fingers stroked the upholstery and her shoes pushed into the rug.

Discreet signs with directions to passengers spoke of baths to be had, barber shops, and a salon for eating and conversation. They also suggested that passengers might wish to remove their boots before retiring and refrain from whittling on the furniture. "Why I wouldn't *ever* harm *this* furniture," Annie insisted, as though the signs might be directed at her personally. "I could *sleep* in this chair," and she sank back against the cushions, closed her eyes, and giggled at the outrageous pleasure of such a thing.

The décor was basically green and ivory, and the walls were actually papered. Annie could see them tremble a little as the engines throbbed. It was a vibration she had become accustomed to, and it no longer aggravated her or kept her nervous as it had on the "Ivy Linda." Here, she didn't care that the wood-work was flimsy; the paper over it looked like silk that should be dancing.

For the moment, Will was relaxed and happy with Annie's eagerness, and he suggested that they freshen up right away so they could have dinner in the salon. They had shopped some in Cairo, so they would both be presentable in the big city, as Will put it. Annie had been too shy to say much about what she liked or didn't like, and, in truth, she hadn't even known what she ought to have. But Will had turned her over to a saleswoman in a store which had almost everything but shoes, and Annie emerged redressed, very nearly reborn, she felt, from head to stockings—in her first store-bought dress, a soft, periwinkle which set off her eyes until even the saleswoman had had to comment. "You're a very pretty girl, Miss," she said. "Such eyes and hair." Then she added, "Your papa must be very proud of you."

So Annie had to face it again. "He is my husband," she said, and she tried to level her gaze back at the quieted woman.

Annie had left the store carrying boxes with two other dresses, one for daytime and one for dinner, the woman had said. She had petticoats and stockings and stays. She had two hats and a parasol she hadn't any idea how to use. She had handkerchiefs and a reticule. She did not have a hooped underskirt.

"Why, I could never ride a mule with *that* on," Annie had said, first seriously, then laughing with the saleswoman who had gone from disbelief to pleasure in helping the girl.

Her shoes they bought from a cobbler who had two pairs he had made for a woman who died, he said very quickly when he caught Annie looking at them, before her husband could pick them up. Will strongly suspected that, because Annie had tiny feet, the woman was going to have to wait a bit for her order. Annie, who had never before had shoes made differently for the right and left feet, couldn't stop looking down at what she was wearing. They were soft white leather with delicate white buttons. The other pair was identical, only black.

Will had recostumed himself, too, and when he had come back to the dress shop to pay for Annie's clothes, he looked very handsome, she thought. He was wearing a dark gray suit with a deep green and black striped vest and black tie. He had new, soft, black boots, too. So Annie was more than willing to show off her fashions when Will suggested that they go into the salon.

As he opened their stateroom door, the explosion of crimson and filigree drew her the way warmth does a cat.

The rugs were Belgian, and Annie felt as though she was waltzing as she stepped on that soft, deep, blood-red pile in her high-buttoned, wide-heeled shoes. She thought it was like walking on water might be. And, of course, with the undulations the steamship was now making as it began its way upstream, and with the engines vibrating throughout every inch of the woodwork, her image was a good one. She immediately took Will's arm to steady herself, and he was happy to assist her.

What she wanted to do was sink down to the floor and pull her fingers through the red, the way she might her own hair. But she was aware of many other people in the long, slim room, and only her fundamental delight in the colors and textures around her—and her confidence that Will would know what was appropriate and what wasn't—enabled her to put one foot in front of the other as she walked by women whose hair was high in sleek and shiny wings and rolls, whose skirts were as full and delicate as hollyhocks, and whose shoes were, she knew, polished and soft. She was endlessly grateful to Will for her new clothes.

Will felt her tension and patted her hand on his arm. "You're the prettiest one here, Annie," he said. "And I'll bet not a one of them could shoot a squirrel at twenty paces!"

She laughed up at him. What he said was funny, and it felt good to her. She found herself raising her head, taking in the room and the ceiling. Dozens of crystal chandeliers hung the length of the salon, and the ceiling was intricately arched over each. Gold roses in low relief against the white ceiling wove around the lamp bases, and under each sat a leather topped table and two chairs, mostly crimson and ivory.

On both sides of the tables, the stateroom doors were painted ivory with gold trim. Each upper panel framed a different landscape or hunting scene. Though none was signed, Will found them skillfully painted, and Annie, who disliked such scenes of animal death, could nevertheless hardly resist touching the horses and hounds, they looked so real.

They strolled the length of the salon, and Annie began pulling them toward what was, for her, the most wonderful treasure there: a piano, the only one she had ever seen outside of her Hickory Grove school.

But this was no ordinary piano. It was a magnificent, cabinet grand Steinway, and Annie went smiling to it, running her hand over its gatherings of mahogany flowers, the arabesque of its music rack, its cool keys.

"Can you play, Miss?" A tall man dressed formally in black was speaking to her. He was leaning back in one of the chairs between the piano and the last table next to the texas. He looked frankly from Annie to Will, then said to her, "You can play it if you'd like."

Annie caught her breath and exclaimed, "Oh, I can't play the piano, only the guitar. But how I wish I could!"

The exchange caught Will off guard. In the first place, he looked at Annie through another man's eyes, which he had not done before. And he saw that she was, in fact, an extremely pretty girl. Her hair was long, black, and sleek. It had no curl, and she just let it fall. It was very different from both the elegant, high-piled styles of some of the women and the combed-back and secured make-dos of most. It was a surprise to see, and the face it surrounded looked framed and set off by the shining black. Annie's nose was too short and her mouth too small for her to be beautiful. But her blue eyes, bird-wing brows, and porcelain skin made her very, very attractive. She was coming into her young womanhood, and her slim, compact body, her pert breasts, and her springing, muscular walk, all made demure and sweet by the blue dress, helped her give the impression of being strong as well as young-woman lovely.

To Will's surprise, he felt himself sizing up the man who spoke, and he stepped closer to Annie. At the same time, he realized again that he knew almost nothing of Annie's preferences or abilities. He assumed she was smart. She spoke well and was curious and reflective. He knew she was sensitive to him. But he had not gone beyond that to think in any specific way about her as a person. He realized that he was always more focused on himself and on getting through a night than he was on what might be special about Annie. Certainly he had never thought of her as being musical—or even liking music, though he was glad she did.

"Could you play for us?" he asked the man, understanding from what the fellow had said that he must have some responsibility for the piano.

"Be glad to," he replied. "I'm one of the musicians, and we'll be playing a lot for you as the days go by." He moved to the piano. "What would you like to hear?"

Will didn't know much about any music, actually, so he didn't know what to suggest. "You choose for us, Sir," he said.

But Annie was asking for "I Dream of Jeannie," and the piano player smiled at her and nodded as he began the simple, wistful melody. He was a good pianist, and he improvised some around the tune once he had played it through plainly. Annie had never heard the song on a piano, nor had she ever thought of doing anything around or between the notes of what she sang—for sing she always had.

Annie's family were all musical, she, the best singer by far. Music was in her bones. As a little girl, she had worn out four sets of rockers on the chair her grandpa made her as she sang and hummed, smiling and chanting before she could properly say the words. Then she sang by the hour, first with Sherwood accompanying her, then, up on her flat rock or with the family on the front stoop, chording for herself when she was old enough to manage her father's big guitar. She sang songs from the Ireland of Mary's mother and songs from the England of Sherwood's father; songs from the war of the revolution, and songs from the people of the valley. She sang the hymns and patriotic songs from her schoolbooks. She sang songs from the fields, songs from the mountain, and whatever popular songs she could learn—especially Stephen Foster's. So she was delighted with the pianist, and she felt suddenly comfortable, placed by the familiar sounds back in a world she loved.

"What did you think of that?" he asked, mostly of Annie, although Will, too, was listening closely.

"It was wonderful, Sir," Annie replied. "I never heard it played nicer." She paused a moment then added, "I never heard all those notes before. Are they in the song? Or are they in you?"

It was a sweet question sweetly asked, and he began to talk some about variations and embellishments and key changes. Annie listened, but what she really wanted was more music, so when he paused, she ignored all he'd said and asked, "Could you play 'Gentle Annie'?"

He caught her intensity. Most people paid a little attention, then started talking or meandered away. But Annie was far more concentrated. It was a sort of insistence, and he responded immediately. Without a word, he began the song, at first using only one finger from each hand to tell the sad, sad tale. Before he reached the second line, he could hear Annie humming with him, a low, pure sound. "Sing it," he said, and continued playing.

But Annie grew wide-eyed at the suggestion and, for a moment, drew back.

"Do you know the words, Annie?" Will asked, and she nodded. "Then sing 'em! No one will mind!"

They did mind—though not as Will had intended. When Annie began, "You'll come no more, gentle Annie" very softly, with that round, sure voice people in the Hollow said was the saddest in the world, many in the salon quieted and turned toward her. Then some were slowly drawn in the direction of the piano and the girl.

The song, itself, was as plaintive as Foster ever wrote. Combined with Annie's bell voice and her earnest, open manner, it reduced half the listeners to tears. Will felt his throat tighten as he watched and heard Annie move through the song, her own heart clear in the words and notes she warmed and left unchanged.

No one could have sung more simply. It is unlikely anyone could have sung more beautifully. When she finished, people applauded, softly at first, then louder and louder, and they cheered for her. "Bravo! Bravo!" they called. "That was mighty fine."

"Sing us another one, little lady!"

But Annie was overcome, herself, more by the song and the sense of love and loss it evoked than by the response. She looked to Will for help, and he jumped up, gave her a hug in front of everyone, and escorted her back to their room after she said a hasty "Thank you!" to the pianist.

It was the first time Will had wanted her because of her self rather than because of his own need, but she was crying hard, and he did not intrude on her. He did try to comfort her. "Tell me, Annie."

But she could not. He was no part of the world she had suddenly gone back to, where her father and she would sit together, singing, singing. He was, instead, the reason she would come no more to her home—he and the war, death and time, itself, had shattered what she knew, and it was gone as certainly as she was gone from it, as certainly as Annie in the song was gone from those who wept for her.

Pain and fear merged as she drew away from his hand and his voice. "I can't tell you. I don't know. Please. Just leave me alone for a while."

He rose from the bed where she lay and moved to the door.

She felt even worse when he closed it behind him.

20

When Annie awakened, she was still crosswise on the bed, and she thought she was alone. But as she rubbed her eyes and became more alert, she grew aware of a presence in one of the chairs, and she smelled whiskey. "Will," she called, but he did not answer, and she was instantly afraid. Although her eyes had not yet adjusted to the darkness, she could make out a man's figure at the table. She was sure it was Will, but she felt a terrible anxiety rising and merging with the sharp physical sense of fear that struck her when she first awakened. This felt as though she was sick, as she had when word came that her father was dead. Without at all understanding, she felt more threatened than ever before in her life.

Rising slowly but taking in the whole of the very dim stateroom, she stood in front of the door trying to think of one thing she could do. Vague and flickering light from the guard made its way through the crack between the curtains, and it caught on some objects in the room—the tiny insets of pearl and quartz on the armoire, the smooth surfaces of the fleur-de-lis designs in the wallpaper, the lamps she knew she would not be able to light, a bottle, and Will's glass eye. She felt pinned by it—standing there unable to move. Even more, she was certain his other eye was fixed on her—that he was not asleep, that he was deliberately not responding to her—intending to frighten her.

"Will!" she said sharply. "You're scaring me. What is it? Why won't you answer me?"

He had begun to drink about an hour after he left Annie in the stateroom. He had never intended to start. But there it was, bottles, glasses, the smell, the glittering. He was struck by it, his senses literally assaulted by the liquor and by the anguish. It was like a blow to his head and stomach. And once he started, he offered no resistance. He let himself into it quickly, the burning almost instantly gone, the warmth slow to start. His turmoil was always like ulcers and fresh grief until he drank enough to push it back and shut it in. Before that stupor, he would sit quietly, drinking steadily as much as he could, letting the fury inside him have its way except that he was gradually surrounding it, backing it up, forcing it into submission as he lost consciousness.

Usually he had been able to find privacy when he did this kind of battle. In the army, Menheusen had learned to recognize the signs and had tried to stand guard for him, always saying he was exhausted and too weak to operate more without rest. The orderly had not wanted, after the first time, to interrupt the Captain's concentration on his demon. The man had been too well taught by the rage that emerged out of what had seemed blankness when he had urged Will to lie down, to try to sleep. But he had excused it as an outburst from someone whose soul was aching from the filth of blood-letting, sawing, and death.

Annie had nothing to explain what she sensed. She knew she needed light; she needed to leave the room; she needed help. But she did the wrong thing. She interrupted him before he had drowned his beast, and he changed his focus to her. "Will," she said again, and put her hand on the doorknob. "Please talk to me. I don't know what to do."

He had been looking at her, though not always seeing her, given his thoughts and the darkness, for over two hours after he had returned from the salon with a bottle of whiskey. He would have stayed there longer except that the piano player had sat across the room, and Will had felt his eyes, knowing and accusing, though he had never turned to be sure. He had bought the fresh bottle and returned to their room.

He had not been prepared for the agony that hit him when Annie asked him to leave her. Anger and despair were simultaneous. He had been feeling pride in her, a little jealousy, desire, almost forgetting at the moment, the rest of it. He had wanted her and felt she would want him, but she had turned from him and entered a place he couldn't go. He understood, and he did not blame her. But he could not bear it, either, that she would reject him. As he drank, she became one of the faces staring at him, accusing him along with his father and, sometimes, now, his mother, Narcissa, George. He was not conscious of turning against her, of having to control her in order to balance himself, but he felt that she had slipped somehow into his past, dragging at him instead of pulling him forward as she had been, as he had, in his mind, made her promise to do.

He could not see her well, but he heard her through some distorting distance, and he knew she was afraid. Had they been alone, he might have let her leave. But just outside the door was the world, a huge room full of people who might already suspect—and would certainly know—if she merely opened the door. And the piano player would see it—all of it. Wanting most of all to hit that man, to make his face go blank, Will lunged at her so fast and hard Annie had no time to react.

Flung to the bed by the same motion that seized her from the door, she did not fight. Stunned without being struck, she felt him rip off her dress and petticoat, then pull her to the edge of the bed. He threw her on her stomach and tried to take her from behind, panting and cursing, gripping her wrists over her head in one hand. She remained silent and made no resistance. She had the sense that he would kill her if she screamed, but she was also aware that she was not afraid of what he was doing to her body. She despised it, but she was not in much pain. What she feared more was the voiceless man who had been sitting in the chair and who she thought would reappear when this act was finished.

Instinctively she understood that it was her motion at the door that made him leap at her, that and her fear. It was no different from what her father had taught her about dogs and panthers: don't let them know you are afraid. Don't run. So while she willfully relaxed her body and tried to position herself for his ease, while he struggled over her, finally collapsing to the floor without finishing, she considered how she should quiet him.

She remained still, at first half on the bed, aware of his hand around her ankle, then, after a time, of his deep and regular breathing. She slipped to her knees and knelt there for a long time until the rug finally began to cut into them. Then, her back aching, she pulled her foot loose and crawled to a chair.

He slept, unmoving, until late the next morning. Annie sat still, trying to understand what was happening. This was a deepening of what she was beginning to see in him: underneath the gentle and generous front he showed to the world—and to her most of the time—was a very different man, someone driven by what he could not stand and face. Perhaps he had had no father to tell him about panthers and dogs, how to confront what could devour you if you didn't know what to do.

She thought, as always, that he was in the grips of guilt and pain, still, at what had happened to his wife and her family. Maybe he couldn't bear it that he was alive and they were dead. Maybe thoughts of marrying her were causing the old wounds to bleed freely again. Maybe it was such old rages, irrelevant to her, that hurt him. Maybe if she were very calm and very kind, he would understand she made no claims on that part of him. Maybe if she stayed very quiet and asked for very little, he would come to trust her, like the wolf that will finally allow a human touch. Maybe if she asked no questions and cast no blame, he would have no cause to hurt her, ever again.

When he awakened on the floor, Annie rigid in a chair watching him, he felt his stomach lurch. Just as quickly he wanted to turn from her eyes, to spin her chair around. He couldn't stand to see her look at him.

"Get out," he muttered. "Go on. Get out of here."

But of course there was no place she could go. She did understand that she must not touch him, and she had some sense that she should not speak directly about what had happened. What she said was, remembering for some reason how grateful to him she had been for the privacy he had once created for her, "Let me move the screen, Will. Then you can rest or change as you please."

He heard, and he understood, and it helped him. But at the same time, it was very close to focusing him on her as being kind, very close to causing him anger for what he appreciated.

She rose slowly, moved to the large, folded screen, and spread it between him and her so that he had most of the suite to himself, including the bed, sink, and commode. "I'll just sit here." She kept her voice calm, but her head seemed to swell and pulse as she waited for what he might do or say.

Gradually and slowly, he pulled himself up to the side of the bed, then on it.

After a long time, she heard him get up and begin washing, then dressing. Finally shaking, she felt that at least the immediate danger was past.

When he opened the screen and came to her, he was rational again. He knelt in front of her. Taking both of her hands in his and bending his forehead to them, he asked, "Can you ever forgive me?"

At the same time, he was clearly aware of how she sat, how straight her back was and how cold and still her hands were. He knew she was cornered and afraid. "Please forgive me," he repeated, and he knew that she would say she did. He thought she might well mean what she said. He knew even better than she did how she depended on him and how careful she would be with him. It was not what he wanted. He wanted for none of this to have happened, to be happening. With a slight sense of strategy he felt repulsed by, he allowed himself to suggest a cue: "It was that man, Annie, that piano player. He made me. . . . I didn't like. . . ."

He didn't need to say more.

"It's all right, Will. I didn't want to talk to him. It's all right." She kept her hands as quiet as her voice, though, and felt nothing in her heart or stomach that went with the words. They didn't even make sense to her.

She, in her turn, bathed and changed, and together they returned to the salon where tables laden with eggs, ham, turkey, fruit, fresh venison, pancakes, coffee, tea, wine, bread and rolls greeted them as though they were honored guests. Annie felt starved, and she returned to the table three times.

No one paid them the slightest notice.

21

When they docked in the huge St. Louis wharf, they had been travelling for almost five weeks, and every day for the past two, Annie had thought of the small rags, folded untouched in the bottom of her mother's carpetbag. Will had said nothing, and she was very afraid when she considered that he might think of it. She did not want to be with child. She could not begin to predict his reaction if she were, but she feared it, and by now, really and actually lost between rivers and woods and among people she no longer felt free to talk with, she had no idea what she could do if he hurt her or left her.

The only person she could think of who might be sympathetic or helpful was the piano player, and she knew very well that he had to remain a presence only, one she was not to notice or respond to. Other men and women had occasionally approached them, the first day or two, especially to tell Annie how much they liked her singing or to ask if she would be singing again. But she kept her eyes down and simply thanked them. In fact, she and Will did not often stay in the evening to hear the music, and they never danced or sang.

Will gradually found his place on the "Conner" much as he had on the other steamers. This time he had booked passage as a medical doctor, and within hours his skills were needed. From then on, night and day, the Captain had him called, and, as before, the work, the challenge of people needing him, and the respect they gave him steadied him and helped him, once again, keep the whiskey at bay. Annie's tensions fell with his, but her guard did not. Some people greeted him occasionally as the ship's doctor, but they rarely tried to talk with him. Gradually the two of them were left alone to sit or stroll along the guard, gazing over the rail at the brown water which hid a thousand snags and at the dark shoreline which rarely opened onto anything and relentlessly closed behind to herd them forward.

Because St. Louis was busy, loud, full and inviting, it interested them both, at least for a while. Will hadn't been in such a city for half a lifetime, and he felt buoyed and hopeful again. He also knew what they would need, and he wanted to buy some supplies here before they went on to Kansas Town—or maybe Logan, Nebraska. He hadn't yet decided which. Annie had never seen such a place, and she regained some of her own cheer and curiosity as they walked among shops that seemed like magnets to her.

It had taken them hours to get their legs back. Then they left their hotel and meandered for hours—days, actually—across Front Street and up Market, down the old *Rue de l'Eglise*, now become Second Street, to the Cathedral off Walnut where Annie marveled most at three languages engraved in the shining stone of the portico. She tried to read: *In Honorem S. Ludovici. Deo Uni et Trini Dicatum. A. MDCCCXXXIV.* She remembered some Roman numerals, but the Ds and Ms escaped her, and she had to have Will translate both the Latin and the 1834.

She loved the church, especially the little side chapel dedicated to St. Patrick whom she revered without knowing why. And to think that some remnant of the crib of Jesus Christ was inside one of the tall reliquaries on the main altar made her sit soberly and thoughtfully in the front pew. She knew the story of the birth in the stable, and she liked it very much. She was always comforted to imagine a god who would come into the world where animals stood around him. She felt that if god trusted them that much, she was right to surround herself with them, too, and she did—dogs, cats, rabbits, any animal she could find, save. She liked to smell dogs' feet and puppies' mouths and horses' breasts. She loved the brook sounds of cattle eating hay, even the smell of horse manure. She wondered if the crib remnant preserved and elevated in front of this altar would maybe be manger wood rubbed golden by a cow's neck.

But she had little sense of the suffering and dying Christ, the man she saw falling beneath his cross in the scenes along the nave, the man she now studied hanging agonized on a huge, gold, glowing cross above her.

She saw his sad power quieted there, and she felt tears start as she thought of the baby become a man, a gentle martyr, as she understood it. She wished she, like the women kneeling in front of the communion rail, might also light a candle—a candle for her mother, for herself, for the child she feared grew within her, for the Christ himself.

Will, however, was ready to go on, and he guided Annie back up Walnut to Barnum's Hotel where he suggested she wait while he get a shave and hair-cut. They then stopped at the Ladies Bazaar of Fancy and Simple Dry Goods where he picked out, first, another blue dress and cotton skirts. Then, while she tried them on, he stopped before a mannequin dressed in a black skirt, fitted to the hips, slightly flared to the hem, and a black sateen blouse with a high, fluted collar, long sleeves puffed above the elbows, with covered buttons and more fluting at the cuffs. It was an elegant ensemble, and he imagined that Annie would like it, that he would like to see her in it. As a surprise for her, he chose it and a second crimson blouse made much like the black. As the clerk wrapped them, Will was pleased to think of giving Annie such gifts. He hoped she would like them, that they would help her forget what he wanted to forget.

The next day they visited the Courthouse with its struggling display. A huge cenotaph to commemorate Lincoln confronted decorations celebrating Lee's surrender. Red, white, and blue bunting was interwoven with shining black streamers, and a bust of the fallen president was grimly poised on top of a tomb-like structure. That in turn rested on an enormous platform draped in black crepe and supported by tall columns. A fringed, black canopy completed the dismal arrangement. Gas lamps surrounded it, and solemn Missouri soldiers guarded all of it.

Will had not expected to encounter soldiers or any reminders of the war in the Courthouse. He stopped, shocked at the bizarre scene, realizing that, in fact, he should still be in uniform. He had also never mourned for this man he so admired. His face was stricken.

"What *is* this?" Annie felt accosted, and she stepped close to Will, taking his arm.

"My God, Annie. It's a memorial for Abraham Lincoln. They haven't taken it down yet."

"Was he such a great man, do you think?"

He couldn't respond. She was too young. He pressed her arm

against his side, wanting to share, but he could not speak. He could only nod, and she felt him tremble. They stood silent, he before the dreadful fact, she, before his sadness.

Later, they both marveled at the tremendous spiraling iron stairway that rose from the center of the rotunda and branched in two directions to the lower gallery. Annie grasped the oak railing where the stairs divided and bent her head back to look high into the cupola. It was too big and dizzying for her. She couldn't figure out how it could ever have been made, and Will couldn't explain, either, how such a dome could rise over such a space.

Enormous painted figures leaned over her and toward the central skylight, catching the day from it and the windows. At another, lower level she could better see, great oval paintings filled her with foreboding—though they seemed unnatural to her, more gilded than she would ever really see. In one, she could make out covered wagons and a man and horse in armor beside what seemed to be a large lake or river. In another, black bison seemed to be looking at a train pass below tall orange bluffs under a glowering red sky. Tiny stick figures on top of the bluffs watched everything. Annie was taken aback by a directory to the paintings which said they represented the discovery of the west. She did not want to think that such animals and such scenes, apparently with Indians, too, awaited Will and her. Unconsciously she laid her hands on her stomach, breathed very deeply, and made her way back down the stairs.

That night Will gave Annie her presents. When she opened the boxes of soft shining black, she could think only of the crepe decorating the cenotaph. The material seemed aggressive to her, and the shapes, themselves, were not even familiar.

"Put them on, Annie," he urged, eager to see her in them, to see her happy with something so well made and handsome.

Feeling that, she tried. But she was short, not tall, as these garments required. Her breasts and hips were not yet full. And she did not have the undergarments or shoes she needed. Her hair fell over the collar, hiding it and her neck. She managed, in every way, to destroy the lines of the clothing. Worse, she had known she could not wear them before she began to put them on.

His eagerness disappeared, and she felt that she had failed him.

She knew she was not the woman these clothes were made for—not the woman he must want her to be.

"I'm sorry, Will," she began. "They are very beautiful, but. . . ."

"No matter," he interrupted, more roughly than he intended. "It doesn't matter."

"Perhaps we could take them back?"

"No."

That seemed to irritate him. "No. Just pack them away. It's no matter. Maybe you'll grow into them."

As he said that, he remembered that she was only fifteen. Of course she couldn't wear such clothes. She should not wear them. He thought of her blue dress, her young self, and, for the moment, how she must feel. He was ashamed without being angered by it.

Moving to her, he took her hands, but, feeling her stiffen, he let them go and, instead, pulled her hair back from her face. Her eyes looked tired.

"Annie, it truly is all right. I wasn't thinking." Tipping her chin up, he said, "Just pack them away. Who knows what use you'll have for them in ten years, when you've had children and a chance to finish growing. I wager they'll fit you fine, then. Don't worry. It's all right."

She felt hot with anxiety, but her instincts told her she should not show him. She had not been able—and he would not—to speak of the marriage they were supposed to enter into here in this city. But this seemed the moment. Quietly she asked, "Do you want us to have children, Will? We've never talked about that."

"Yes, I do." He answered strongly and without any hesitation. She was sure he meant it, at least at this time, and her insides settled a bit.

"I do. I like children very much, and God knows we'll need a family to help us in the new territory." He stopped a moment and sat on the edge of the bed. "Yes, I want children, a whole passel of them."

She sat down beside him and took his hand in both of hers. "What if I was in the family way now, Will?"

There was silence. He had not thought seriously about such a possibility, and the days and weeks had, in one sense, gone by very quickly. What if she were? He half smiled. "Well, now. That would be something, wouldn't it?" He realized that he was feeling glad, renewed, something like the way he had felt when he left the valley with Annie. It was as though the future opened to him one more time, as though yesterday, if not cancelled, was obscured. He was smiling. She could feel him relax.

"I'd like it, Annie. I've seen so much death and destruction I feel the need to hold new life in my hands. I think it would be just fine. It would make me very happy." He turned to her. "Do you think you are?"

"I don't know." She was surprised that she could talk about it without embarrassment. "I'm a little late."

"It could be the excitement—all the change. But still. . . . Are you usually regular?"

She nodded, and he put his arm around her shoulders. "Well, perhaps you are then. Actually, I hope so. It'll be fine." And he went on. "I'm experienced with obstetrics. . . with babies, Annie. I know what to do. We'll do it together, Annie, if you are."

Again she knew he meant what he said, and once again she tried to believe in that part of him which dared to hope and tried to share. "Maybe this time," she thought, and she leaned against him.

"Will, would people have to be Catholic to get married in that church we saw?"

She felt him holding his breath. When he spoke again, his words seemed separated by days. "Yes. Yes, they would, I think." He stopped. He could see no retreat, no way around it.

Then, feeling just a little dizzy as though he had fallen to the depths of his spirit and risen too quickly, he saw that he did not need to go around it, that he did not want to go around it. This was what he had promised. This was what he had brought them to. And if she was with child—that led them to a totally different life. He made the choice and stood up to look down in her face.

"But I don't know for sure. Maybe they would make some exception for a couple of travelers, especially if she's got a baby needing its daddie's name."

She didn't laugh, and she didn't cry. She stood, herself, and very quietly stepped into his arms.

The moment did not seem threatening or ambiguous to him. In fact, he felt better and stronger than he had since Narcissa's letter had told him of their child.

After a little ceremony performed by a justice of the peace—the young priest politely refused their request—they sent a telegram to Mary: "Married in St. Louis. All's well. Heading for Kansas Town. Love. Annie and Will."

That's how Annie found out where they were going.

Part II: Into Kansas

"...only connect...."
—Forster

22

Annie was surprised at everything he wanted to buy. They went to store after store where he purchased all sorts of tools and supplies. "I won't just be a doctor," he explained, "at least not right away. It will take time. I'll probably end up doing more with animals than people, at first. We'll need a garden, and we'll break some prairie, too. And we'll have to build us some kind of house. It'll take us a while to get started."

Annie felt her spirits rise and her courage falter. Nothing was clear to her about what lay ahead. She still could not imagine what anything would look like, not the countryside, not a home or settlement. Only the courthouse paintings could come to her mind, and she feared what they promised. "Kansas" was just a word to her. It evoked nothing the way "Tennessee" did. She couldn't conceive of what she would be doing, and it seemed to get more and more complicated. She could understand "garden," and the thought of weaving some baskets also helped her steady herself a little against what seemed to be sweeping her along—as in fact all the waters had since she left the Hollow.

Over and over she relived her decision to go with the creeks and rivers, to go with him, wherever he and they would lead. He was telling her now that they would buy the wagon and mules and horses in Kansas Town and head on northwest into Kansas with the first wagon train they could join. It was nothing she could envision, but she knew, sometimes with the dry, tired certainty following turmoil, that she could not turn back. She tried to surrender herself to the flow.

But the opposed feelings didn't soften or recede. Instead, they grew stronger as the last steamer churned its slow way up the Missouri. It seemed to her that these passengers were more tense and more thoughtful—and that's how she felt, herself. It wasn't only that the "Lady Arabella" and her travelers were as a whole rougher than the "A. J. Conner" and her St. Louis-bound group. This steamer had no Belgian carpets or grand salon. It was loaded deep and wide with everything from huge kegs of nails and carpenters' tools to Limoges china, pearl buttons—and plenty of single-last boots—much of it intruding onto decks where passengers might otherwise have walked. This was a cargo boat laden with what traders and settlers would need—and over-laden with the settlers, themselves. It was also that more people seemed to be watching the river and shoreline, and they usually talked of only two matters: how dangerous the Missouri was and what they might encounter once they got off it to go find their places.

Annie had long since numbered sawyers with engine explosions as her worst fears. Snags were everywhere in the brown river, muddy in the channels its swift current swiftly changed. The huge, jagged stumps of trees—once cut as engine fuel for the very ships they now threatened, loosened and washed out by the fast-flowing water—hurled themselves to the surface like long, ancient fish rising for air or floated by, silent as crocodiles, projectile end weighted up by the skeletal roots. Annie could sometimes hear them—and always visualize them—bump, bump, bumping against and under the ship, and she felt as though she were a hostage surrounded by mocking enemies. Will was watchful, too, especially because he had spent a good deal of money on his own cargo.

They couldn't escape the stories of hundreds of wrecks: "They's a sunk boat in ever bend, doncha know?" "These steamers don't run mor'n four or five years at best. You can't hardly get insurance on them."

"You hit a big one, you got maybe ten minutes—unless you're lucky and in the shallows."

"If they keel over, you're as like to be knocked out by a box or a chair as you are to get drowned."

"Wish we could find us a barrel or two of that Kentucky whiskey that went down with the 'Arabie.' Guess they was a thousand of 'em. Wouldn't that be dandy?"

They also couldn't escape stories of Indian massacres, tornadoes, floods, and prairie fires raging through grass that was fifteen feet tall, tall enough to get a man and horse lost in if they didn't get burned up in it—or people killed by rattlesnakes on the hilltops or water moccasins in the creeks.

Nobody on the steamer had been west yet. Some women had letters from their men who had been gone for months—or years—and who had sent for them in the letters—now months old—saying that they could come. The men would write that the sod house was finished or the cabin chinked or ten acres of prairie turned or that the settlement now had a store or that the train had finally come within fifty miles.

These women seemed to Annie to be in the worst possible situation. They had to go alone, hoping that their partners were still alive and still willing. She saw them occasionally pull their children under their arms in unconscious gestures of defense while their eyes searched the unyielding river. She thought of her silly bantam hen who'd cluck to her chicks and gather them under her wings on the flat, trampled dirt between the cabin and the branch, right where run-off water would be sure to drown them all unless Annie ran to save them.

Yet by mid-June, the "Lady Arabella" steamed into the wharves of Kansas Town, and no one had died or even seen an Indian. Within two days, Will had already bought mules and arranged for a wagon, one of the smallest, but big enough for Annie and him, given that they had no household goods and would need the wagon only for supplies and shelter during the trip. Now he was buying their horses.

"Separate them out for me," Will told the men maneuvering their cutting horses in and among the hundreds of animals milling in the rough, new-hewn corrals. Major's overland freighting business had thousands of wagons of all kinds and thousands of oxen, mules, and horses to go with them. It had outfitted settlers by the thousands. Some locals talked about plans to build a bridge across the Missouri, and that would, they said, bring the railroad. But for the moment, wagons forged the trails west, and migrants far outnumbered those who stayed by the river.

Will was considering two horses. The four mules he had already chosen were in a holding pen, and he figured he would be able to complete preparations within the next two to three days. Getting the horses and loading the wagon were what remained. A dozen or so men had begun to follow him as he looked over the stock and selected those he wanted to examine. Few of the men knew about livestock, and word had spread that a fellow with very particular knowledge of mules and horses was down in the lots. Several men had hurried to find him.

"Where are these from?" Will asked. He didn't want animals that had been grained regularly. "They have to be able to fend mostly for themselves. Otherwise they won't make it," he told the man at his elbow. "We can't carry a lot of grain. If they know about the open range, they'll do for us." Most of the animals looked healthy, and Will didn't expect to see any sick or seriously lamed ones. But he had insisted on isolating those he was interested in, and he took plenty of time inspecting them, especially their legs and hooves.

He listened to their breathing and pressed down beside their spines the length of their backs looking for tenderness. He ran his hand around the thigh and forward over the stifle, back over the hock, gently massaging, searching for any soreness or protuberance. Quiet but insisting, he talked to the animals: "Easy boy. All right, girl." Leaning into them and lifting their feet by the pasterns, he examined foot after foot, tapping the hooves, looking for splits or bruises or old shoeing problems, sensing the animal's temperament. "No feet, no horse," he remarked to the men.

One after another they asked him to help them, and he did so, very willingly. He liked examining the animals, and the attention from the travelers increased his sense of well-being. He felt productive and useful. He craved such feelings, and he went out of his way to serve the men well. He pointed out an abscessed tooth to one, incipient curb to another, and apparent kidney pain to a third. He helped one young man avoid buying a fifteen-year-old mare being sold as six.

They found out that he could also treat horses and mules and that he had definite ideas about which would serve best in long hauls or short. He was honest that he knew less about oxen, and they appreciated that.

At one point, Major asked him to stay in the town to assist the agency with injured animals and to help sell. The travelers began to urge him to join their messes for the trip. Then, when they found out that he was a doctor, they began to offer him money or other inducements to go with them. He was the only physician among all those gathered to head west.

"Come with us, Fairchild, and we'll keep you in food the whole way."

"We have several women with young children, Sir. Come with us and we'll help you build your house when we get there."

"Come with us."

"Come with us."

"Come with us." He could see their fear and hear their need.

Will was gratified, even excited by the attention and the offers. "Annie," he said, "it's going to be even better than I thought. People will do all they can for us because they're so desperate to have a doctor with them. They know I can help them. We'll have a rough trip, no matter what. But people are going to give us special attention, and that's good. We don't have much to take with us, and with you in the family way—and me not much of a bullwhacker," he laughed as he said the word, "we can use the help."

He had been feeling better since they left St. Louis. And he was helped by sensing Annie's greater ease as he relaxed. They could even talk some about it.

"I was so afraid I'd lose you somehow, Will. And I didn't know what I would do. I couldn't go backwards or forwards without you." They were curled under light blankets in their wagon, the canvas top rounded above them, voices from other wagons close beside them.

He whispered back, "I'm not going to leave you, Annie. I'll be all right now. There is too much to do to give in to old worries. Maybe I can leave them behind forever, now." He knew the demons were not gone, but since the marriage, since he had used about all the courage he had to turn his back against the mocking faces linking Annie and Deborah and his perpetual disgrace, he had not felt so sick for whiskey. He was up at dawn, but it didn't always feel like an escape.

During the days, Annie was especially glad that he appeared not to mind her talking with the women who gathered in the Emporium where they priced dry goods, food stuffs, and utensils. They talked, too, often urgently but quietly, about what faced them. Annie discovered that she had been very lonesome, and she felt much soothed to be able to share the days with other women. She was also not bashful about admitting her ignorance.

"How do we know what we need?" she asked.

Then many others nodded in agreement. It was their question, too. They'd just been too scared or shy to admit they didn't know. "I guess we just have to ask our guides. They should know, shouldn't they?"

"Who is our guide?"

"Where are we going?"

Then they would laugh at themselves.

"I feel kind of like a sheep," Annie said. "I reckon I'll just follow along wherever somebody leads me!"

"Will the clerk know? He has surely dealt with enough of us. Let's see what he says."

Later, with husbands by their sides, they bought a fortune's worth of provisions which they worked long hours to pack carefully, according to the instructions of guides and some men who had made such journeys before.

Box by box, barrel by barrel, the big wagons absorbed the common loads: bacon surrounded by bran to take up the fat then wrapped in strong burlap sacks and laid in the bottom of the wagons, the coolest place; flour stored in double canvas sacks; butter soldered in tin canisters; cones of sugar wrapped in gutta-percha sacks to stay dry; "dessicated vegetables" from the Chollet Company in Paris, hard as rocks, an ounce of which, boiled in water, would swell to become a meal; dried fruits; pemmican; coffee; tea; "cold flour" of parched cornmeal with cinnamon and sugar—to make a sweet, sturdy drink.

Some had barrels of crackers or biscuits. Some had tins of sardines or even oysters. But everyone had pork, flour, salt and coffee. Everyone had whiskey, too, but for medicine, only, everyone said.

They also bought the same woolen goods—rather than cotton or linen which, they were told, wouldn't protect them as well against sun or rain.

They found out that trousers would need reinforcements on the inside, and women began sewing in buckskin patches, the first time most of them had worked with leather. As a result, most families who could added to their sewing boxes awls, buckskin, and buckskin strings in preparation for the heavy mending they now realized they would have to do.

Those who were going through the Rockies bought extra woolen socks and boots made of buffalo skin with the hair turned inside.

Everyone bought gutta percha ponchos, and Will bought extra supplies of the water repellent material—to go along with the extra wagon wheels, tongue, and open chain links he was concerned to have.

Those without household goods bought blankets, two per person, a comforter, pillows, and gutta percha or painted canvas cloth to spread under and over their bedding.

Each mess of five or six wagons bought a large iron camp kettle to boil water or meat and a Dutch oven to bake in. They bought coffee pots and heavy tin cups with riveted handles, tin plates, iron frying pans, and one mess pan of tin to mix food in. They bought knives, forks, and spoons, a tin or gutta percha bucket for water; an axe, hatchet, knife, and mallet. They bought a spade and carried matches in a tightly corked bottle. They carried quinine and calomel. They loaded extra wagon parts—bows, Ss, tongues, coupling poles, kingbolts, hounds. They took extra doubletrees and lead bars.

Each wagon had to become its family's own tiny emporium, their own life-source, their private oasis in the midst of what was not named. Each family prayed that they had thought of everything, that they had bought wisely and that they had not been misled.

Their chief horror, even above facing sickness and Indians, was to be caught without essential provisions, to be unable to continue. Even though the wagon masters helped them decide on the rules they would live by as they headed out; even though everyone understood how their little democracy operated: what punishments would be meted out for what offenses, what individuals could expect to give or receive from the community, and what appeals they could make if they thought they were harmed somehow—all that so no one need fear being left beside the trail unless, of course, they disobeyed the rules or died—even so, the fear remained. Faced with hundreds, even thousands of miles of the unknown; shrinking, already, from the terrors they did know, the travelers wanted nothing more than to band together, to be bonded, to feel something as certain as the ties of a family which would move heaven and earth before it would abandon them.

And to be buried beside the trail was as awful to contemplate. Strong men grew tight lipped in imagining their eternal, nameless separation after some poor, mumbling fellow, holding his hat in his hands, would speak to the silent group that must immediately go on: "Trouble yourselves not about those that sleep."

The women helped one another as much as they could. When they learned that Annie was the doctor's wife, they began to pay her special attention, too, and to beg her to join them. They already liked her, and they all vied for her to be part of their groups. Discovering that she was pregnant, they were particularly kind to her, wondering, when they returned to their tents or dark, smelly hotel rooms, or, nearer departure, their laden wagons, both how such a girl came to be with such a man and how it would be—for her and for them and for their daughters—to bear a child in a wagon on a trail going no place they could conceive of.

Will decided to buy two mares, both supposedly settled. One was a dark chestnut, her lovely tan coat set off by long, nearly white mane and tail. It was the merest coincidence. He did not know Annie's preference in horses any more than he had known about her love of music. But when he brought her to see the horses and to try out her new saddle on the prancing little chestnut, she never once thought that.

She was still young enough to feel that here before her was the most beautiful animal in the world. It was her dream. And Will had bought it for her, just for her. She granted him purpose and was delighted with him. "Oh, Will! Will! Will!" she screamed, laughing and crying at once. "Is she really for me?" And she simply could not believe he had done a thing so wonderful. "You doll! You doll!" she crooned to the mare. All who could see her felt happiness. The moment was like a good omen for everyone.

Doll, as Annie quickly named her, was gentle, and as Annie scratched its neck, the little mare stretched her head high and sideways, her under lip quivering loose, her ears turned to the girl. Under saddle, Doll was alert and curious, but easily handled. Annie adored her, was confident with her, and much more comfortable on her, it turned out, than in the swaying bouncing wagon. Will did not think riding would be unsafe for the baby, so, day after day, both he and Annie rode beside their wagon—driven by a boy who could handle the mules much better than Will could and who was glad to help them—Will on his sorrel Belle, Annie on her Doll.

150

They did not know where they would go. They had decided they would break off from the main train somewhere in central Kansas, but they had no real sense yet of the area or its possibilities. For the first days, sometimes four miles a day, very infrequently ten, they rode west with the big train, more than ninety wagons, west, just west into territory which, a hundred yards beyond the trail, yielded no sign of people like them, no sign that people like them had ever before passed this way.

After supper, when she had apple blossoms, Annie planted them beside the trail and marked the spots faithfully with circles of tiny stones.

23

They all needed one another, and they all felt that. It wasn't that they were lonesome or scared. Mostly they weren't either of those, it didn't seem. Nearly everyone had their most loved ones with them, and they were blessed not to run into bad troubles. But something about being separated from what you know makes you want to talk about it.

Annie hadn't thought much about such a feeling before. She hadn't noticed it so much on the boats—when she had been preoccupied with her fears—or in town where they could see other people going about their lives. But out here, away from any hint of settlement, where you were all there was, everyone seemed to need to talk. Annie saw that they were a bunch of strangers thrown together and trying to get close to one another, even if they didn't know that's what they were doing.

She didn't think it was for protection—and perhaps not even for company. It seemed as though it was for something inside that would weaken and might die if they didn't let others know about it. They had to find some way to tell about what was inside them to people who would listen and maybe come to care. They needed that from one another or else they felt lost in a way that had nothing to do with where they were. At least that was how she thought about it. She figured that was why dinnertime got everyone in the messes quieted down listening to stories, especially about their families or what they remembered best about home and growing up. She, herself, loved these moments.

"My uncle Harry wrestled a bullsnake one time. Said he just wanted to know how strong it was."

"How strong was it?"

"Well. Doncha know he said it was so dang strong he finally had to stand on its tail and kind of peel it off his arm."

Allen took about five minutes to tell that half-minute story, but nobody hurried him any. He was laughing all the time until, at the end, he had his eyes clear shut with tears running down his face. He was shaking his head back and forth and holding his belly. They knew he was seeing his uncle tell the story. They were all laughing, too, more at Allen than what he said because they started laughing when he did, and some didn't even think the story was funny.

"My grandma had her a little copper coil in the shed out back, and one afternoon when the church ladies came to call, my sister and I brought them some hard cider. Granny didn't know we'd made the switch, for we gave her the soft, you see. 'My lands! This is just the loveliest apple cider,' one of the ladies said. When she got up to leave, she took one step, and her legs must of just twined round each other, for she made a kind of half circle and just sat down facing that chair she'd just rose up out of! Her hat fell clear down over one eye!"

"My grandfather played an awful joke on my grandmother. It seems there was a terrible blizzard and deep, deep drifts, so deep the big ravine north of their house was filled in level. Early that next morning, my grandfather got the children's sled and walked up north a ways. Then he let that sled run down the hill, clear across the ravine and way up the slope on the opposite side. Then he walked clear west around the house and south down the valley some until he could head back northeast to get that sled—and he came all the way back again. He did that a couple more times, then finally he went to grandma and said, 'Addie, you'll have to come out here and take a sled ride. It's the finest you'll ever have, I can tell you.'

"Well, he took her up there where he'd pushed that sled off from, you see, and he said, 'See? You can go from clear up here to clear over there half-way up that side hill.' She didn't hardly believe him, but the sled tracks were there as proof, so she finally agreed to have a ride. He pushed her a little ways until she got going real good, then he settled back to watch her. She was just laughing and flying over the snow. Then, of course, when she shot over the edge of the ravine, she just disappeared! The bottom dropped out, and so did she! I guess grandpa had to dig quite a spell before he could rescue her!"

They would seem to draw closer to one another as they listened, usually coming closer to the fire, too, as the darkness deepened, all except the guards—and Will. He remained behind the circle, near the horses. The guards were different night to night, but Will was always back with them.

"Will, couldn't you just come and sit with us sometimes?" Annie would invite him. "It feels so warm and friendly up by the fire."

"I know it does, Annie. But someone needs to stand guard by the livestock."

"But can't you change off, take turns at it?"

"I feel more useful there, Annie. Besides, you know I'm not much of a talker. It's better for me."

She knew more than to persist, but she felt his reticence quiet her as well, and several times she clamped her jaws to avoid speaking about what it would have pleased her to share. She realized that she yearned to talk about her mother and the mountain, about her brother and father.

She thought of how their Trapper pup would perk his ears and try to look in her mouth to smell his words when she said them: "Water?" "Supper?" "Go for a walk?" She figured the words were the things themselves to him at least until he learned better and began to dance in joy at what the words came to signify. Now she found she wanted to feel the names and memories she had made with her dear ones come out over her tongue and out of her own mouth so she could bring them into this time, this place, this moment of her life, so she could smell and taste them in the telling.

But Will's reluctance made her feel withdrawn, too. If he wasn't going to talk with people, she sensed that she should be careful about what she said. She knew she could not talk about his past, so she felt awkward trying to say anything about how they'd met or got together. That meant she felt awkward, too, talking about her mother or home. She was certain she should not sing. Altogether she became uneasy when what she most wanted was to relax with everyone else and give something of herself to them.

Gradually the stories changed. Everybody would seem to start out happy, telling what you could see they'd told at home a hundred times, probably in the same way, him or her chiming in at just this point or that as you knew they always did—so they could share in the telling.

"Remember the time your dad asked your mother for something for his chapped lips?"

"Oh, mercy yes! Papa thought Mama knew everything. She was a schoolteacher, you know, and she *was* awfully smart. Well, one time she was mad at him for some reason; I don't remember just what."

"He shot that coyote pup she wanted to try to raise, doncha know?"

"Oh, that's right. Well, he and Uncle Willie had been out cutting ice on the river, and their lips were chapped something awful. 'Jose,' he asked, 'isn't there anything a man can do for these chapped lips? They hurt bad,' he said. 'Well, of course, there is,' she answered him, 'if you're man enough to do it.'

"Well, of course, she had him hooked right then, doncha know? He straightway assured her that they were men enough to do what it took, so she went in the kitchen and got her lemon extract! 'Here,' she said. 'Just pour a little of this out in your hand, then put your lips right down in it. It'll sting a little, but it's a sure cure for chapped lips!'

"Well, of course, they believed her, and they did just what she directed. I guess you never saw two grown men cut such didos as they did. Mama said they acted just like they'd been hokey-pokied. And I expect that's just how they felt. You can imagine how that lemon would feel in those cracks. But Mama didn't have any pity on them. 'That'll teach you to go kill some helpless little creature,' she told them. Uncle Willie cried out, 'But Josie! I didn't shoot your pup!' But Mama just said, 'Well, you would have if you'd have thought of it!' And that was that! She was a smart woman, Mama was...."

And then you knew she was dead.

So stories started being about hard labors or babies born with the marks of snakes or birds, twins that never separated, babies so ugly you looked away from them that turned out more beautiful than painted angels; dyings so gentle you knew they were saints or so foaming-at-the-mouth mad you had to tie them down so they wouldn't bite you; cemeteries with eleven little stones around the mother's; parents walking around and around in their smoke-filled kitchens, patting the backs of their children dying from diphtheria; all that passed between borning and dying as man, woman and child told what they knew themselves by.

What began with laughter almost always tapered off into tears and silence as all of them looked back and within themselves and saw by that where they were now, who they had become, and what they needed from those who listened.

But not Will.

If anyone asked him to tell about himself, how he came to be a doctor, where he grew up, he'd say, "That was another lifetime." It sounded so solemn and definite nobody went on with it, and soon they didn't ask any more.

Annie tried lots of times, but he wouldn't or couldn't tell her either. "How did you come to be a doctor, Will?" she once asked. "You are so smart, I know you could do anything. But why a doctor? What led you to it?"

And he tried, too. Some of it he could manage. But it was mostly so caught up with what he could not bring himself to utter that he could never satisfy her.

"I knew a man once, a doctor, and I admired him."

"What was his name?"

"Zeller. Friedrich Zeller. He was a German man, a physician who was a...he used to...." And he stopped.

She could feel his ambivalence, and she did not know what questions would help him.

"He had a school in Kentucky. That is where I studied to become a doctor. I was lucky to be his student."

"Was that near your home?"

"No. No, it was far from my home."

"How did you get to know him?"

That brought him to it, and he could feel himself begin to huddle inside.

She felt it nearly as soon as he did. "I don't mean to meddle, Will. I guess I'm like Ma. My papa used to say she could ask more questions than any three women ought to."

He didn't want her spirits to come down. "No. It isn't that, Annie. It's that...I don't think I *can* explain. It's part of all that...."

He looked so dejected she wished she hadn't asked, and she said so. But he didn't want it that way. "It's nothing to do with you, Annie, you must believe me." He hesitated and tried again. "I don't even know why it's still hard for me. But it is. It's that my family and I are separated, Annie. That isn't going to change. I just can't talk about it. Nobody's been maimed or killed. There's no crime. But please, just don't ask me about it. Maybe someday...."

She never did ask again, not intentionally. But sometimes it slipped out. Once when they'd gone back to the wagon after some hymn singing, it came to her—before she thought—to ask if his family was religious.

"They were," he answered. "They were the most religious people you could ever know."

She hoped he would go on, but he didn't. "They must have been good people," she said. She always tried to find something pleasant to say. That seemed to her to be her duty. She meant it, too. She sometimes worried about her family. They were not very religious, it seemed to her. At least, they didn't go to church regularly. Still she thought they were good people. But she guessed they probably weren't as good as his, if they'd been very religious.

He looked toward her, then, for just a moment, and she wished she could see his face. "I don't know if they were good people," he said, his voice husky. "You can't always see what's in a person's heart."

"What do you mean, Will?" But he didn't say anything, and she remembered the boundary she had just forgotten. She wanted to ask what was in his heart. She thought they needed to talk like that, the way other people did, or at least the way she thought other people did. But they did not. He didn't know about her rock or her papa's guitar or her old Trapper dog the bear mauled. She didn't know if he had a brother. She didn't even know his mother's name.

In the shadows, she could see him, stiff and silent. Finally he shook his head slowly and said, "You go on to bed, now. I'll sit up a while longer."

The stars were high and cold when he finally lay beside her.

24

Coming from the intimate, tree-covered knobs of Tennessee onto the wide and open hills of the Kansas prairie was like a revelation to Annie. Nothing vertical, not a tree, not a fence post, not a human figure, broke the powerful green horizontals which repeated over long blue shadows until they became the absolute horizon. Annie felt the infinite in them and in herself as they lifted her upward.

It seemed to both her and Will that they were on the world's summit, but they weren't sure how they got there because, from the east, as they had approached, the hills, which rose very suddenly, had not seemed particularly high. They were not at all like mountains which, though they might occasionally put you into a cloud, usually cast your vision into another mountain, all of them asserting the vertical. Instead, these waves of green raised you above a vast, wrinkled space which extended in front of you forever without any intervening object by which to gauge their range or height. You could assume valleys under the indigo shadows, but you could see only the one immediately before you. From the next hill on, you could see the shadows or rose-touched mists or sun-lit tops—depending on the time of the day or the height of the hill. But what you were conscious of was distance. The sky above, perhaps cloudless, arched into deeper and deeper blue over the land.

Annie thought of the courthouse dome she had been dizzied by. It was nothing, she now knew. Nothing.

"Indians say God slumbers in the rock," the guide told them.

Annie liked that sense of a mighty power at its greatest ease. It seemed to her the likely spirit of the place. She straightened her back and breathed to her very toes. "I'd like to stay right here," she said to Kitturah—whose wagon and five others had turned off with the Fairchild's onto the Smoky Hill Trail. "It seems to me like I never saw so much so clear."

"Doesn't it make you feel tiny and exposed somehow?"

"No, it doesn't," Annie started to reply. But then she thought a moment. "Well, maybe it does. You sure don't have any place to hide!" She frowned a little and patted Doll's neck. "But at the same time, it feels like such a strong place. I think some of that rubs off on me. It makes me feel strong, myself, I guess, just to be here taking it in. Sometimes I feel like I could run forever. Maybe it makes me feel free."

She pulled her hair back with both hands, letting the reins fall in front of the saddle. "It makes me feel like a bird, like a hawk, like I can swoop over it and see everything. I love it here, Kitty. I'd stay if you would."

Kitturah giggled a little at the idea, but it actually seemed serious to her, and she was more scared of these hills than Annie had been of steamboats. "Oh! Annie! This would be a terrible place to live. There's no water for miles. And look at the outcroppings. We couldn't farm any at all on this land. Cattle, we could raise, but they would stray 'til we'd never find them. And we could be seen! Indians would always be bothering us. There's no other people, and this grass is so tall. Imagine a fire!"

She was prepared to go on, so Annie smiled over at her and interrupted: "I know. I know. It's not a good place for us. But I wish it was for I love it better than any other place I have ever seen." And they continued, talking for the hundredth time about what their homes might be like and what they would do first.

These families had decided to break from the larger train because the Smoky Hill Trail was well traveled, especially with the big Butterfield stages running to Denver. Then, too, several forts along the way, built to protect settlers and railroad workers from Indians— in their turn, protecting their hunting grounds—seemed to offer at least some security although the travelers had no idea where they were relative to the forts.

Most of all, the Bakers, one of the families in their original mess, had people settled near Brittsville in the north central region. They had written that the place was almost as good as the boomer literature had made everywhere out to be. Reed's cousin had written that two major rivers joined nearby, and several creeks emptied into them, so water and timber were no problem. In fact, they were already building a mill. And wells were not terribly deep at forty-five feet. The river bottomland was flat and rich, and plenty of pasture was available. "We're lucky that the Kansas Pacific Railroad branch is under construction to the east," he wrote. "It will be open in a couple of years, and you know how much easier that will make it to be settled out here."

So the site had many attractions for several families, not the least of which was that someone already there would welcome them and help them begin. Nearly everyone needed that sense of connection.

"It's like there's a string pulling us along," Annie said. "I think if a person doesn't have someone looking for them"—she hesitated and interrupted her own thought—"or waiting for word to know they're all right"—then went on: "they must be the loneliest person in the world."

She thought first of Will and understood more clearly than ever how the separation he lived with might feel. Then she thought of her mother waiting for word of them, word which, day after day, did not come, and she had her first adult sense of what a mother is. That night she sat a long time on the tailgate of their wagon writing—in the lantern light—a letter to Mary.

"Dearest mother."

It sounded formal. She'd always called Mary "Ma." But written down, it seemed all right to her. "I wish I could see you right this minute, for I love you so much. But we are awful far away Ma in Kansas now. Can you believe that? We didn't go to Nebraska. We have come so far. I don't think I can write about it. But we will talk about it for sure. The railroad is coming right to where we're going to be. It's a place called Brittsville. It's all just like Will said. I can come home or you can come to see us. It will get easier and easier. So you think about that because it will happen real soon. Will bought me a fine chestnut mare. Her name is Doll. We are doing fine. People come to him all the time. He is a good doctor. How is Billy? How are you Ma? Do you have plenty to eat? How are your wrists? I'll write more when I can and try to tell you more about the trip. I like Kansas best

160

of all. I'm going to have a little baby. Your loving daughter Annie."

It was the first letter Annie had ever written. She sat quietly, holding it respectfully but thinking at the same time how little it did what she wished it would. Two crumpled pages braided the lantern's light. She had tried very hard. She knew what her mother would like to read about—a gentle, devoted husband and happy friends sharing an adventure to a new world. But Annie couldn't smooth it over that much. She thought back over the trip, itself: the funny round man on the stagecoach, the steamboats and the sweet little girl going to America, now the wagon train and these hills. She couldn't find the way to build it, to help her mother see and understand. Then there were Will and his moods and changes. She didn't want Mary to know about them.

Around her spread the hills. Over the hills hung the sky, deep and still. Its stars, a thousand-fold, like breathing candles, testified to the ancient, giant energy she felt. She could hear coyotes shrieking like maddened ghosts over their kill. The train dogs growled without barking. Annie felt no fear. Without even trying to explain it to herself, she felt increased by the absolute insistence, by the silent, dimly-lighted universe in which the wild ones stalked and ate, in which she, too, now breathed.

She could say none of that to her mother, so she skipped it, all of it, all the past and all the present, hurrying quickly to the little future she still hoped would finally connect the pieces, preserve and explain them, pull itself towards itself to stop the loneliness of the past and the isolation of the present.

She hoped it for Will as much as for herself, but a part of her saw that peace for him might not lie in the connections her heart begged for. He seemed unable to stop, to linger over anything, to look back at anything that eased or comforted him. He didn't look up the way she did, either. The space and distance that surrounded them had started to make him crawl into himself.

"I don't much like them either, Annie," he had told her when she was laughing about Kitty's sense of the hills. "It's a raw place, just animals and time out here. It makes me want to keep moving—and faster!"

"Oh, Will!" She shook her head. "They put me in touch with what I didn't even know was part of me! I'd like to run naked through them."

He grinned at her. "Well, that might be nice to watch."

She dropped her head. "Well, I don't mean really, I don't suppose. But I love them."

Within the week, they encountered some Shawnee who were returning to Westport from hunting and trapping. In exchange for a good meal, a place by the campfire, and two bars of soap, the men agreed to take Annie's letter with them and see that it got sent on to Tennessee.

Annie watched the Indian, small, wiry, looking sunburned, fold the letter decorously, then push it into a little scratched and beaten leather pouch hanging at his waist. She wondered if he understood what it was; if he cared the least about it if he did understand; if he would forget it; if he would be honorable when he would later discover it and remember.

25

Once past the great hills east of Fort Funston, they found the journey much easier physically. Although their route was also called "The Starvation Trail," the seven wagons inching their way nearly straight west did not suffer any shortage of food or water. In fact, other than the fatigue of the traveling, itself, and of their anxiety about what could happen, they fared very well. They crossed streams without having to switch teams—and they never had to dismantle the wagons. They bartered with groups of Pawnee who frightened them without threatening them until they learned that food, not scalps, was what the Indians wanted. Although they were generally poor shooters, they managed to kill enough game—antelope, rabbits, and turkey—to vary their meat supplies pleasantly.

On some hunting forays, often on Sundays, they found watercress, its delicate leaves making wonderfully fresh salads. Gooseberries ripened like small jade marbles along most creeks and rivers. Their long thorns and the long, striped snakes frequently cooling along their branches taught the children patience in gathering them. But baked into pies in the Dutch ovens, they urged greed and laughter in everyone—especially when some fresh, water-cooled milk was available. The women found sweet flags, their young, deep stems, opened to the air, spicy to chew on, if not as sweet as the candy some made from the stalks if the women had time on Sundays to boil them and boil them and boil them.

"I wonder if we'll have berries and nuts in Brittsville?" Annie asked.

"Oh, yes!" Lucy Baker assured her. "Reed's cousin says they have plums and strawberries and black walnuts and chokecherries—all kinds of natural things to eat and use."

"It's a good place, isn't it, Lucy?" Annie asked.

"Yes. It is. We'll like it." Then, more slowly, thinking while she spoke, Lucy added: "It will come to be home, Annie."

So they made their way without pain or disaster. Thunderstorms menaced them, boiling over the trail in clouds that seethed to the heavens or sliding into their view like a smooth, relentless flood of indigo waters threatening to break their bounds and roll over the circled wagons. Once past, they displayed their tremendous power in the huge, perfect curves of their anvils. Hail clouds mumbled and coughed overhead like sick monsters barely able to move, their clustered tumors hanging green or mauve in the suddenly chilled air. But while the travelers were often drenched, they were not flooded, drowned, or blown away. Their livestock were not scattered to the winds. Lightning killed no oxen in the yoke. No one stepped on a rattler or developed any illness worse than a cold—which Will promptly soothed with eucalyptus or peppermint drops.

They saw graves beside the trail, two with crooked wooden crosses, one marked with a rock, "RC" scratched deeply into it, and two simply mounded with stones near some stump or outcropping which was probably supposed to call attention to them. But no one in their train died.

Between Will and Reed Baker, who had skill both as a carpenter and blacksmith, the animals stayed healthy and the wagons avoided breakdown. They had a good guide, they were sensible about breaking and making camp, and they sometimes drove more than seventeen miles a day—except for Sundays which were their days not only for spiritual renewal but for physical ease and care. On Sundays they hunted and gathered. They cooked and washed and mended. They baked, soaked wheels, and repaired harness, aired the bedding, and repacked the wagons. They ate a good meal together community style among the seven wagons.

Sometimes they sang, Annie's voice clear among them but very carefully controlled to blend and support, never to lead. Sometimes she borrowed Nathan Holbrook's guitar to chord for the group, but she didn't sing by herself.

Early on, Annie was occasionally uncomfortable in the mornings, but she was not much incommoded by her pregnancy, and she worked as hard as anyone else did. In fact, it was Annie who shot this little group's first turkey. The women and girls had gone together to a creek bend south of camp to bathe and wash clothes. Annie knew how to use a rifle, so she was the one to carry it. This day they made their way through the cockleburrs, pigweed, and foxtail bordering the trees, then into the bushes and the trees, themselves, which were very near the water. The creek here was shallow and wide with no banks to speak of, so they could walk right up to it and into it. They began to laugh and squeal at the cold, fresh, delicious water.

Just opposite them, five large turkeys, brown and black and rust like the banks and rocks and roots, ran to the left and tried to take flight, their big wings beating violently in the still, heavy air. The women screamed as the birds flew, but Annie, who took her guard role seriously and had been looking around for any problems, recovered, cocked her rifle, and fired, almost without aiming.

"Why! She didn't even hardly look at that bird!" Kitty bragged. "She threw that old rifle up faster than you could say, 'Scat!' and 'Bang!'— that turkey fell straight into the creek. You should have seen her, Will!"

It seemed to be all right with Will that Annie drew the attention of the women. He laughed with Kitty and joined in teasing Annie about being a dead-eye—Daniel Boone's half-sister. All the adults in the train were older than Annie, and he could feel their sense of her as a girl. She was not, of course, proud or vain. They could praise her and indulge her without having to feel threatened or jealous. Will liked to see her, be with her, watch others be with her. In fact, as the weeks passed, he was able to say to himself all over again that she was what he had seen in her as she rode in from the meadow: fresh, strong, and very, very dear.

Sometimes he told her that. At night, the wagons in a circle, guards posted around the outside—often with mules which Will thought were excellent sentinels—they would lie spooned in their wagon, sometimes coming slowly to love-making which often made her laugh and sigh.

"So this is what bodies are for," she said one night.

Will hugged her close, his chin on her head, his mind isolating far to one side visions of entrails spilling down to boot tops and blood running off the table.

"Yes, Annie," he gasped into her hair. "This is what bodies are for."

26

"There they come! God have mercy! There they come!"

Claire Wilson was screaming it out to the whole settlement. She was a heavy set woman whose legs seemed to move faster than the rest of her did, and right now she was running east from town yelling to the world: "There they come!" She could see them on the east hill before the turn: One wagon, two, three. Five. No! Seven! Seven wagons full of people!

Her heart turned over to see so many—and because she was running her fastest. "Now if we can just convince them to stay," she thought. They had a good place, yet so many just passed on through. They needed people, and she aimed to make this bunch feel welcome.

"Jimmy!" she yelled at her middle boy, already far ahead of her. "You go back and tell everybody the wagons are coming. Hurry now! And go ring the bell. Ring the bell! Ring it hard, Jimmy!"

Claire's neighbors, the Bakers, had been planning for weeks for their folks. They'd even fixed up their old soddie for Lucy and Reed and the three children. Later everyone would pitch in to help them once they'd got their feet on the ground and made plans. But the rest? Claire just prayed they'd stay. She snatched off her apron and waved it like a flag, yelling at the top of her lungs: "Hello! Hello! Oh! We're so glad to see you! Welcome! Welcome to Brittsville!"

Della and Michael Baker high-tailed it past Claire and led the wagons on in. Lucy and Della couldn't hug enough, and Michael and Reed, who were the real cousins, walked together as the wagons rolled in. They had their arms on each others' shoulders and every once in a while, they cuffed one another or slapped backs.

Claire knew what they were feeling. She had felt it, too, when they first came, only there weren't so many to greet Claude and her. She remembered her light-headed relief at actually arriving, at actually being where they had been headed for months. For her, it was like your insides open up, unclinch and spread wide because you don't have to be stiff and on guard any more. Your shoulders can just come on down, and you can shed tears—at least if you are a woman, you can. She didn't think they were purely the tears of happiness people speak of. As she saw it, a person was all at once too tired and too aware of new things to do to be what she would call plain happy. But happy was a good part of it, she knew. And so was laughing. Almost everybody laughs.

And so it was as these seven dusty, weaving wagons rumbled and rattled into her little town. There they were, and there was everyone else within hearing of the pounding bell, and finally Jimmy, too, sweat streaked and full of himself. They were all laughing and crying and hugging and squealing, the train dogs circling and sniffing the town dogs, the train kids, the most sober faced of all, meeting the town kids who couldn't keep from grinning, the mules' ears flapping back and forth, and the horses become all of a sudden light-footed high-steppers.

The men in the fields were the last to arrive. They unhitched their teams and left plows in the ground, riding one mule or horse in and leading the other, for they intended no more work that day. Everyone was so relieved and happy and glad to see one another. It immediately became the holiday the town folks had been planning ever since they learned a wagon train was coming. Of course, no one knew when that would be, but they all knew what they would do when it happened. And by evening they had a feast they figured was fit for kings.

Women baked fresh bread, the loaves looking a little like brown, covered wagons. Boys lifted fresh butter and milk, cooled, from the wells. The roast beef was so tender they could cut it with their forks. Blue windmills appeared on huge platters as dozens of crisp pieces of chicken disappeared. Mountains of mashed potatoes had butter slavering down the sides. The potato salad even had paprika, and huge chunks of ham swam in crocks of green beans. They had cucumbers and onions in vinegar. They had baked apples smelling cleaner than rain. They had apple pie, gooseberry pie, cherry pie, squash pie, and chocolate cakes three tiers high.

Nothing was fancy, but it was good, and it showed the newcomers right away that the settlers weren't starving, that they hadn't forgotten how to cook up a meal and be civil. The food was piled so high on long boards set up by the town well they couldn't begin to eat it all, and the dogs and an occasional foolhardy cat made out just fine, too.

Claire was everywhere, saying over and over, "Oh, it is so good to have new people." She couldn't help crying a little, and she wanted to hug every person there.

Some of the older town boys guarded the wagons, though it was more a game than a necessity, and helped the new arrivals drive their stock into the pens back of the livery stable. Then the town's people who could put up the travelers in their houses so they could have soft fresh beds and just be taken care of for a spell. It was their pleasure. Because Claude and Claire had so many young ones, they couldn't take in a family, but they opened their home to the Fairchilds and gave them their own bed.

Though the Wilsons didn't have anything fancy, Annie was wide-eyed, and she walked around as though she were asleep, touching chairs and curtains.

"You'd think she'd never been in a house before," Claire observed to her husband once they'd managed to get to bed—in their daughters' room. "He's a calm one, ain't he? And ain't she the sweetest little thing?"

Claire went on a long time about how lucky they would be to have a doctor in Brittsville, how much older Will was than Annie, how strong the Baker family resemblance was. Only Claude's snore quieted her. But she lay on her back for hours, bright eyes open, and she made a hundred plans for Annie and Will before she finally turned on her side and slept.

While they were having breakfast early the next morning, a quick, hard knock came at the door. It was young Johnny Johnson from over east a mile. He was looking for Doctor Fairchild. "My ma wonders if you can help us, Mister. My little sister, she's named Molly, and she's awful sick. That's why we couldn't come last night. But we heard there was a doctor here. And my ma said, 'For God's sake, ask him to come.'"

Claire was trying to hush the boy, at least to slow him down, but he looked as scared as he was fast-talking, and Will rose from the table without hesitation. Claire knew the Johnson girl had been sickly off and on, and everyone was worried about her.

"Excuse me, ma'am, sir," Will said. Claire smiled with pleasure at his politeness, but she also felt that he had suddenly taken over. Everything changed the moment he spoke. "We're very grateful, but we must go." Then he turned to Annie. "Come, Annie. I'll need you. We must hurry. Every minute may matter."

They fairly ran, he asking the boy about where Molly hurt, Annie rushing ahead, shouting back, "I'll get the horses saddled and meet you at the wagon."

If anything could have won Brittsville hearts and made the people work together every way they could think of to get the Fairchilds to stay, it was what Will and Annie did for Molly Johnson. Of course, Claire wasn't there, but once she had a version of it, so did everyone else. As she told it, the child was feverish and too sore in her side to bear any touch. When the doctor said it was appendicitis, the Johnsons knew it was a death sentence.

"But Doctor Fairchild, he wouldn't hear of that," Claire said Rebecca said. Claire told it as though it wasn't second-hand. She was confident she had every detail. She explained how Will had said Molly had one chance, just one chance, and he had to operate immediately. Rebecca and John were scared to death, she explained, but they knew they didn't have much choice. "If he didn't operate right then, dangerous as it was, their Molly wouldn't make it."

As it turned out, Will did save the child's life.

With everyone's help, especially Annie's, they prepared the kitchen for the surgery—the children killing flies which Will thought were dirty, John putting wooden blocks under the table legs at one narrow end, Rebecca boiling water in which Will dropped his scalpels and scissors, Annie covering the table with oil cloths which Rebecca scrubbed, then Will disappearing into Molly's room. In a moment they could smell ether, and finally John carried Molly to the table.

"That young wife of his hadn't ever helped before," Claire reported with amazement and pride. "He told her, he said, 'If it makes you feel sick, don't look at anything but me, and listen to exactly what I say.' He told her, 'You can do this. You're as smart and steady as any orderly that's helped me. Now concentrate.' Rebecca said that was the first inklin' she and John had that the girl hadn't done this before.

"That give her some pause, Annie bein' such a little old slip of a thing, herself, and there she was, helpin' him cut into Molly.

"I swear to God, I couldn't have done it," Claire insisted, but she wondered if that was right. Maybe she could be that strong if she had to be. "You never know," she thought, "the strength the Lord can give you." Then she went on to tell how John and Rebecca couldn't bear to look, even, how they stayed by the window, praying, their eyes closed. "The long and short of it was," she concluded, "that that girl come out of it feelin' just fine—a little sore, but just fine. He saved her life. Without any doubt, he did." Claire was breathless from telling it.

What was almost as remarkable as the operation was that Will asked for no payment, and the Johnsons made certain people knew that. "He never said a word about money or payment of no kind," Rebecca said. "He just raised up his hand like he didn't want to talk about it. I tell you, it made me cry. I cried to think he'd saved my Molly. Then to think he wasn't...." She would cry again, remembering it.

The truth of the matter was that Will showed himself that morning to be a man they were proud to know and more than a little grateful to have live among them. Annie, too. Most of them knew, in their honest places, that they could not have stood there watching that razor-sharp knife cutting into that frail white skin without losing more than their nerve. Annie had shown her pluck, and they all fell in love with her.

What was more, neither Annie nor Will said a word about it to anyone. That astonished Claire. Annie might talk about how Molly was doing, and she would praise her husband as a fine doctor and surgeon, but she didn't give any details.

"I don't quite understand all that's involved," she said to Claire, who asked many times about parts of it she could imagine as especially gruesome, "but Will says doctors aren't really supposed to tell about their patients. He says that only the patients or their families should talk about it."

Claire figured she was very lucky Rebecca and John weren't reluctant to fill her in on all they knew.

27

Martin Britt was the son of the town's founder, and he ran the land office while he and hired men worked to clear or plant more than three hundred acres of land. Like everyone else, he was glad to have Will Fairchild in Brittsville, and he hoped the couple would settle there. He saw immediately that Will was intelligent and gifted. The surgery on the Johnson girl was remarkable—courageous and fine work. Britt saw Will become everyone's hero overnight, and he thought the doctor might well deserve the honor.

But there was a lot he couldn't figure out about the couple—why a doctor would be moving west with strangers; why he had a wife half his age; why together they had nothing except some livestock and new farming equipment. The rest of the wagons were loaded heavily with whatever the settlers could bring from both sides of their families. Not everyone had a lot, but everyone except the Fairchilds had something. And some of them had fine tables and chairs, armoires and beds, even pianos and trunks of china. They all looked as though they were moving from one place to another, bringing their past with them, laboring to preserve what they already loved.

But the Fairchilds did not. They had nothing. Of all the settlers, Britt expected a doctor to have possessions. Of course, he didn't ask any direct questions when Fairchild came in to apply for his hundred and sixty acres under the Homestead Act, but Britt did try a conversation. He discovered that, while the doctor answered questions, he didn't volunteer much.

"Will you be able to improve the land, Doctor? Do you have experience as a farmer?"

"I'm not a farmer, Mr. Britt. But I'm strong, and I am ready to turn the prairie. I have good animals, as you know, and with a little advice, I think we'll catch on all right."

"I take it that doctoring has been your full-time profession in the past?"

"Yes. Yes, it has."

"Were you in the service?"

"Yes." He didn't seem unwilling to speak of it, just sober. "Yes. I was a surgeon in the Union army—in Tennessee. After the war, it was…it was…all was changed. It was all gone."

Britt could tell those were hard memories.

"So you see me at the beginning of—well," and he laughed a little. "A new chapter, I guess. We have to start over."

"I see," Britt said, and he hoped he did. But he was reasonably sure Fairchild's pretty little wife had not shared his losses in the war. She was young enough to be his daughter, he saw. Still there it was. Fairchild had the $24 for the land, and Britt suggested that he look at the acreage about a mile-and-a-half south of town, just bordering the Wilson property.

Given the terms of the town's settlement, the Fairchilds were also eligible for a town lot, and because of his skill and the whole area's need for a doctor, Britt gave him his choice from three or four of the best. Britt also told him he could take his time and talk it over with his wife, but Will said they'd been staying with the Wilsons and that he knew she'd prefer a place near them—to the south of town. It was about a quarter mile from the Wilson's house.

For the moment, Britt had forgotten that particular arrangement. The townspeople had taken in everyone. They all wanted the new families to stay in Brittsville. Every newcomer increased chances to build a community that would last. They had a good start, but they needed more services and more people to serve. Britt decided for the moment that even if Fairchild was running from something, he seemed to be a real doctor, and Martin was also glad for Will's land application and his apparent pleasure at having the Wilsons for neighbors. Everyone knew them to be good, hard-working people.

Neither Britt nor his wife had spoken with the Wilsons about it, but they, too, were part of the general effort to help the wagon train families. The first chosen to be helped—on everybody's list—were the Fairchilds. The Wilson's old cabin was already being cleaned and strengthened for them. Word was out that they had no furniture, and people were rounding up everything they could think of for Annie and Will to use. Later, when they decided where their house would be, the townspeople would help build it. And something in Britt also said that the town would donate the labor for the house—and its furnishings—if need be, in order to persuade Fairchild to stay, and that, whether or not he turned out to be a good farmer.

The thought made him consider the particular kinds of help Fairchild might need with his farm, and just as quickly he decided to make a suggestion.

"By the way, Will," he said, as they finished the paperwork for his homestead. "Judging from the way you've started out here—and the need this whole place has for a doctor—you are going to be a very busy man. Let me recommend to you a fellow who might be helpful to you in a dozen ways. He's a pretty hard-working man, in his own way. That is, he'll give you the proverbial honest day's labor. He used to be a cowpuncher, but he's more of a handyman now, and he does good work whether it's well-digging or house-building. He stays over at McCleary's Boarding House most of the time. His name is Julie Winkler."

28

Julie had watched the wagons come in, too, but over a cool beer in front of McCleary's. He wasn't out there waving his neckerchief and hugging strangers. "Too damn hot for that," he thought. He was not a man who took root, not a man who cared about settling a town, and he certainly didn't care to exert himself in order to see a bunch of wagons and cattle coming down a trail.

He must have followed ten thousand of them up a trail—eating their dust. He had brought stock north from Texas a dozen times, out to Fort Leavenworth and Kansas Town, up to Abilene, Fort Harker. But the herds were getting bigger every year, bigger and tougher to handle. Then the law started keeping Texas cattle out during the summer—unless the cowboys ran them through dip—and that was a thankless job, one they didn't get paid extra for. Sometimes they would run the cattle past the law, but Julie didn't want to do that. He liked cattle all right, and he didn't much want to see any stock die because somebody had brought in a fevered critter. The other choice was a spring drive, and Julie thought they were the purest hell. You had to bring the cattle up through storms that always spooked them, and you had to try to bring the stock along slowly enough to fatten them as they moved. It was stupid and endless, he thought. So cattle driving got to be a losing proposition for him—no more fun. And he quit.

He and his brother trailed a little herd out to Brittsville from Abilene once for Martin Britt, and when they had finished their business, he said, "That's it for me." His brother pestered him some about it, but he was done with it. He said it and he meant it. He made more money at odd jobs, anyway, and given how the town was growing, he figured he would have all the work he wanted. More, really.

So in the fall of '65, after he'd worked for Fairchild during the summer, when the doctor asked him if he would hire on full time, he wasn't keen on it. Along with everyone else, Julie came to know that Fairchild had been an officer in the war, and it seemed to him that the doctor was very comfortable suggesting things for other people to do. Whether it was chinking the cabin at the very beginning or later trying to turn some prairie out on Fairchild's south land, Julie felt like he was obeying more orders than he quite wanted to. What he most liked — next to being at Ellie's down in Abilene, anyway — was a good card game and a good cold beer with some good old boys that knew how to play easy like, who were ready for a joke or two, and who didn't get all bent out of shape if they lost a dollar or two.

Julie, his brother, and another man they ran with had managed to stay out of the war. As he and his brother always said, "It don't make no damn difference how it goes." They figured a man could get killed as easily on one side as the other, and that's all that mattered to them. They certainly weren't concerned about preserving the union or helping Yankees free slaves or maintaining tobacco plantations. All that was the same to Julie. But he was plenty fond of his neck, and he wasn't going to risk it in the fighting if he could help it. He didn't, either. The three of them lay low and kept their noses clean, as he said, and the Yankees and Rebs got along fine without them.

But now, here was this doctor-officer who didn't look to Julie as though he could ever loosen up enough to drink a beer or laugh at a joke. Julie figured Fairchild had some definite ideas about who should fight who and who should do what when, and he wasn't much interested in trying to get along with such a person on an every day basis. Julie was willing to help with one odd job or another, especially when lots of other people were doing the same — for instance, digging the well. But he didn't think he wanted to work one on one with Fairchild.

The doctor seemed pleasant enough. Like most people he had been interested in Julie's name right away. "Julie," he had said, looking skeptical, Julie thought. "How did you get a name that's usually for women?"

"Usually?" Julie laughed like he always did. "Hell! They ain't no *usually* to it, is they? I'm the only man I ever heard of with that name."

But he liked to explain it. Julie always did think his mother had her quite a sense of humor. "See. What happened was that my ma plain run out of names. They was thirteen of us, and she finely took to callin' us for the months we was born in. I got sisters called April, May, and June. I was next, and she up and called me July. Most people kind of slough it off to Julie. Hell! I don't care. It don't make no damn, does it? I even got me a brother called August! Good thing we wasn't born in November, wasn't it?"

Fairchild seemed to like Julie's story all right. He even asked where the Winkler family was.

"I ain't seen 'em for years, Doc. We was from down in Missouri, and I ain't never been back. I wrote 'em a letter once, but I never heard back. I got a brother down in Abilene, though."

"Is that August?" Julie saw the doctor grin a little.

"Yeah. That's August."

"Well, would he want to help out, too? There is going to be plenty to do."

"I don't know. Mostly Auggie likes to punch cows."

The doctor didn't miss a beat, Julie saw. "Well, I'm going to buy some cattle. I'm thinking about trying to run some Herefords out there."

Julie was struck by that. He had never seen that breed, and he wondered what they would be like.

"What I want to do is to get a bunkhouse built out south there in the vicinity of the saddle-back hill. I want a well and some cattle pens there, too. Next spring, if all goes well, I want to start the herd. I'll need men full time. They'll bunk out there for a while, at least, but take their noon meal at the house here.

"Why don't you talk to August and see if he's interested?"

Julie wasn't sure either one of them wanted to hire on, but eating regular meals at the Fairchild house—that was a different kind of proposition, and not because they'd have some home cooking. Julie thought Annie Fairchild was just about the prettiest thing he'd ever laid eyes on. She was so fresh and friendly—all of them just liked to look at her. She was nice, too. She'd carry cool water out to all of them when they were working at the house.

Of course, all the women did that. They always brought tea or water or sandwiches. But when Annie brought something, Julie felt as though he could ride a bucking horse without a rope. She always had a smile even if she didn't say much. He did his best to make her smile big. He'd ask her, "Got anything for Miss Julie, ma'am?" He could see her eyes twinkle, and sometimes she'd laugh out loud.

He couldn't stop thinking about her. It was enough to make him consider becoming Fairchild's full-time hired man. "I'll let you know," Julie told him, looking at him straight on and wondering how Annie ever got hooked up with such a funny looking old fart. It was clear to him that they were hooked up, though. He tried not to think about the two of them together. But there it was. She was showing with their child. Julie knew Fairchild had her whenever he wanted, and there was nothing to be done about it.

Still, he thought, if he hired on, he could maybe be around her some. He could maybe get close enough to touch her, sort of accidentally. Or smell her. That would be something, he thought. "I'll think about it," he told the doctor. "I'll talk to Auggie and see what he thinks. I'll let you know."

29

Annie didn't mind the little cabin. Claire fretted herself dizzy that they were going to have to spend the winter there, but it wasn't a bad place, Annie didn't think. It had a wood floor—which some others didn't. The lean-to kitchen was a little awkward for Annie, but any kitchen would have been, her never having cooked much anyway. So many people brought them food they never lacked, not even in bad weather. And the men chinked the cracks so well no snow at all would blow through.

Inside, women hung blankets and quilts, and when Annie put up a little whatnot shelf of the Bakers along with some pictures of Washington and a yard of roses someone else loaned them, it looked very pretty, Annie thought. The windows were isinglass, but they let in plenty of light and kept flying insects out. It was a good deal better than what some folks had—who still lived in tents or even their wagons. It reminded Annie a little of her Grandpa's cabin up on Walden's Ridge. Only she and her mother didn't have as much to do with as she and Will did, not even in the valley cabin. And she was sure they never had anything so pretty.

The Wilsons lived in a frame house spilling over with children and curtains and comforters. When the Fairchilds first stayed with them, Annie could hardly see anything because there was so much. Later, when they moved into the cabin, Claire was as busy with it as she was with her own house. Annie was grateful, too, for she didn't know what to do about much of anything, the stove, the mice, the bedding or the bedbugs.

Will put up their little Warm Morning stove, but they lacked nearly everything else—table, chairs, even a bed. Claire set Claude to building those, and she made cheesecloth curtains which she tea-dyed a soft tan. She loaned them a small table with knobs and ledges and curlicues everywhere. It was the first perfectly useless furniture Annie had ever had, and she loved it. Claire covered it with a pulled-thread cloth and set a clear glass kerosene lamp on it. Then, best of all, she loaned them an Old Man Winter rocker. Annie didn't much like to think of the ugly face always at her back, but the chair rocked so smoothly it delighted her. "You'll need that when the baby gets here," Claire told her.

Annie thought it possible Claire might be more eager than she was for the baby to come.

Often Annie was scared, but Will comforted her, and actually she wanted the baby very much. She thought she could feel it move sometimes, and she tried to keep perfectly still, then, herself, for long moments to be sure.

"Mercy! We've already replaced those rockers I don't know how many times raisin' our brood," Claire chattered.

"Looks as though we might be finished, now. Lord! I hope so—though maybe you can't have too many children...."

She got their straw mattress started—and big pillows, too. She seemed to take such pleasure in helping them even if she did worry Annie some, rushing herself breathless all the time. Claire looked older than she was—probably because she was heavy, and her hair had grayed early. But she didn't act older. She never walked, even though she herself never seemed to go as fast as her feet did. She took tiny steps, but lots of them, and, like a pigeon's, her head and shoulders moved after the rest of her did. Sometimes her face turned red from the effort she put into talking. Her eyes were big and green and shining. She made everything seem exciting.

But Will and Annie couldn't keep all that busyness and good cheer in their cabin when they closed the door behind them. For most of the settlers, staying in wagons so long made their cabins—or even the lean-tos they built against their wagon beds—seem mercifully welcome. In comparison, the cabins seemed huge at first, and any shelter that wasn't to be packed up the next morning was a solace because it seemed permanent. But their cabin didn't feel that way to Will, therefore not to Annie, either.

Their wagon had carried nothing of them that was personal. It was merely a cover from sun and rain. Usually they weren't even in it until they were too tired to care where they were. It was just a short respite in the midst of endless motion. In fact, sometimes they would dream they were still moving across the prairie, and they would wake up tired, with the persistent sense of weaving along the trail. The cabin, though, was rock solid. Planted and heavy, it made them come to a full stop. They had finally arrived where they had been headed since they had known one another.

It was not sudden. It was planned and even longed for. But it was definite, and Will discovered, almost as soon as he entered the door, that he was more nervous than he had been for weeks. Even though he could see the work ahead of him: a house to plan and build, land to turn, gardens to plant, a baby coming, people to care for; even so, he felt face-to-face with what had for nearly four months been comfortingly ahead of him. His stomach went sick as the cramped space cornered and stooped him.

The cabin was just one room, and the roof was pitched from the back to the front where it was only a few inches higher than the door. Will had to bend his shoulders and lower his head to enter, and he couldn't even stand up unless he was near the back wall. There wasn't any room for either of them to walk in a straight line unless it was beside the bed.

Even the first night, he was anxious and brooding. He could explain it to Annie only in terms of space. "I feel claustrophobic in here," he said, then seeing her question, went on: "It's too close in here. I'll have to fix a window so it will open. It's too close."

She immediately opened the door and moved a chair to it. "Sit here, Will. Maybe that will help."

But it wasn't the space. It was the stasis. He wished they had gone on. California would have been better, he thought.

One night, after a week of sleeplessness during which both of them struggled to find house things to keep him busy—grinding roots for medicines, sanding wood for a cradle he was trying to make, attempting to read, drawing plans for the house—the vicious shapes and words began to gather, jumping and gaining color behind his eyes. He felt so sad and tired he didn't want to move, let alone make the effort to throw them back. But they were terrifying, and he did try to focus and defend himself. He knew they would soon lurch into the gaping mouths of his father or Narcissa or cut out tongues or blackening limbs that he could not keep from seeing. They would circle him, screaming at him, pulling him into the red, whirling whine like a rifle bullet through the brain.

He stood bent by the table, then sat down hard in one of the chairs and lowered his head into his hands. He was shaking.

Annie saw and was instantly afraid. She remembered the screen she had stretched between them on the steamer, and she wanted one now—to hide herself from him, to conceal him from her. What she had wished, when they first came into the cabin together, was that they might just fall down onto their bed and laugh and love as she thought her mother and father would have, as she knew Claire and Claude would have, as she knew they expected her and Will to. Instead, it had come to this: he was cowering in front of her and she had no place to turn her eyes. Though it was after eight o'clock, it was still hot in the cabin, and Annie could feel sweat running from her hair down her face and back.

But he looked pale and cold.

"Can I go make you some tea, Will?"

Her voice came to him through the building chaos, but he knew it was not tea he had to have. He shook his head no, and looking at her, then past her, he said, "Bring me my bag."

"Oh, Will, no!" she cried out. "Let me help. Let me get Claire. You're sick."

He rose quickly at those words and went, himself, to the back of the cabin where he kept his medical bag and medicines. "Don't bring the Wilsons into this," he told her, then added, "I'm not sick. I don't know what it is." With a painful wrench of honesty, he mustered, "It's going too fast again. It feels like I'm crazy."

She felt as trapped as he did, but she didn't shrink. "No, you're not, Will," she said, stepping close to him and touching his arm though she also thought she ought not to. "That doesn't make any sense. Look at you, who you are, what you've done for all of us on this long crossing, how these people believe in you. Will, you've been wonderful. We couldn't have made it without you. We can't make it now without you. Surely you know that."

She had to let his arm go as he pulled from her. But in a steady, warm voice, she asked, "What has happened to discourage you so?"

He opened the bottle and drank a fifth of it without stopping.

She moved back away from him, then, toward the table, and her voice quieted. "Think of what we have come here for, Will, what you hope for—what you've worked so hard for."

He looked at her again, steadily, his eyebrows pulled together. The whiskey had hit his stomach and jolted the demons back some.

She had thought to sit, but the other chair was between them, and he saw that clearest of all, some defense against him. He wanted only to be alone, to get on with this bout he couldn't avoid. But there she was, too, every line in her face and body showing her fear of him, seeming to him accusations. He lifted the bottle again and drank the fiery liquor as though it were water.

"I don't think you are crazy, Will," she said, taking care not to look directly at him but at his mouth or his hair. "I think the army was right." She said it without thinking enough. "It has to be all the pain and misery of losing Narcissa and your little boy. I don't hardly see how anybody could survive that."

Of course, she meant it kindly, and a part of him recognized that. But his miserable and aching self translated what she said into another of the gathering voices shouting his guilt and helplessness, and he felt himself need to bring her down, make her yield, take her pity away from her. He had enough control to warn her.

"You need to leave me. Get out of here."

It was enough, he thought, but she didn't get up.

"Where shall I go, Will?"

It was too reasonable, too calm, too slow to fit with his flying thoughts. He kicked the chair aside, seized her arm, lifting her and shaking her some, shoving her toward the door. He saw Menheusen in the V of the tent opening. "God damn you! Get out of here." He didn't sound human to her.

With her foot, she felt behind her for the doorsill. Staring at his feet to mark his position, she backed out and slipped into the growing dusk. Her arm hurt where he had grasped it, and she knew she would be bruised the next day. Fearing to be seen, she quickly edged around the side of the cabin to the lean-to kitchen where firewood was stacked against an old stove and beside barrels and cartons from their wagon.

Though the evening was still warm, she knew she would need some wrap in the cool of the deep night. She tried to remember if any of the boxes contained rags or clothing, but she didn't think so. She did find part of a gunny sack that had held potatoes, and she located one worn saddle blanket. As the darkness gathered and dampened, she drew these around her shoulders, and the smells of earth and horse rose to ease her some. She was worried about night creatures, especially mice and rats and the bullsnakes and rattlers that hunted them. So every slight sound made her stiffen and try to pierce the darkness with her own inadequate vision. She made small noises, herself, and moved frequently to alert any animal away from her. But she stayed low and quiet, too, to avoid calling attention to herself from any neighbor or their dogs.

She could not hear Will at all, nor would she be able to see him if she went around to the window. She could tell that he had not lit the lamp, and she supposed he was sitting at the table—or maybe on the bed or on the floor beside the bed. She didn't know if he had other bottles of whiskey. She didn't know if he would drink himself unconscious as he had on the steamer. She was certain, though, that he was compelled by something terrible. Once again she realized how delicate must be the balance with which he walked, therefore with which she must walk. She felt pity for him mingle with the respect and affection she now bore him, but all were cornered by the fear he had again raised in her.

She was suddenly exhausted, and she began to cry as she realized that she had no idea of any kind what she could do. She sank down in the dirt in the middle of the lean-to, afraid to place her back against any structure where a snake might rest or crawl. Arms around her knees, she felt her belly press against her thighs, and as she so often had since she left Tennessee, she ached to be home.

While her mind's eye watched mockers turn cartwheels in tree tops above her big rock, she thought over and over, "Poor little baby." Then she listened to an inner voice sing to her growing child. Rocking slowly back and forth, she comforted the both of them:

> Hush, little baby. Don't say a word.
> Mama's gonna buy you a mockingbird.
> And if that mockingbird don't sing,
> Mama's gonna buy you a diamond ring.

30

When he awakened early the next morning, he couldn't bear his own stench, so he stumbled outside to the wash bench near the door and poured a bowl of water over his head. Sputtering and shivering, he shook the water off like a dog, then stood, trembling from the drinking and supporting himself with his arms straight down to the bench. He didn't look in his small shaving mirror hanging on the cabin wall. It was shadowed until he could have seen only a blurred face, anyway. He didn't know where Annie was, and he felt uneasy that he was going to have to go through it again with her. At the same time, he felt anger beginning at the thought that she might have gone to the Wilson's, that others would know what had happened. He turned to look in the direction of their house when he heard Annie calling his name from beside the cabin. She had heard him and decided to take the risk. Peering into the still dark place under the pole and canvas roof, he could just make out her shape huddled on the ground. Instantly he hated what he had done. At the same time, he was relieved to see that she had not left to seek help.

"Oh, God, Annie!" he groaned. "Did I hurt you?"

She knew he was asking if he had hit her or abused her, and she wanted to reassure him, but instead, she felt sobs rising in her chest, and she could not speak.

He was beside himself with remorse and knelt beside her. He wanted to hold her and comfort her, but she could not make her body soften and curve to his even though she willed it to, and he felt the rejection. He realized that she could not do otherwise, but he also knew his own helplessness, and he felt harsh toward her that she did not forgive him before he asked.

He did ask. Over and over he apologized and promised, much as he had before. "Forgive me, Annie. I never meant to hurt you." He went on with it, telling her how he needed her strength, how he would fight against the moods, the liquor, how sorry he was. And in her turn, she found the words he needed, words she wanted to be true the same way she wanted to believe what he said. But neither of them was renewed by what the other said or by what they, themselves, said.

She heard herself: "It's all right Will. You have not hurt me, and I do forgive you," but she knew better. She did hurt. She did not need a third instance to show her how meaningless, even despised she was when he was struck by this. She did believe that he was sorry, that he did not want to hurt her, but she knew as well that his promise meant nothing. She knew that she meant nothing when the sickness was on him. A presentiment that weakened her said that their child might mean nothing when he would fall into one of these spells. And she knew she had no way to prevent him, no protection from him when they hit.

"Will," she tried. "Is there anything we can do—anything I can do—to help me understand what is happening? Can we talk about this? Is there any way we can keep it from happening?" She did not look at him as she spoke, but she did relax some and stretched her legs out to lean against him.

It was her motion, not her words, that helped him stop mounting his defenses and concentrate instead on what was vulnerable between them. "I can feel the baby move, Will," she told him. "We have to think of it, too, now, don't we?" She raised her head toward him.

He stood up and pulled her from the ground. "Yes, we do, Annie. And I've made a poor show of it." He seemed more calm and within himself again as he led her inside to the bed which he had not slept in. "Come now. You haven't slept all night, I know. Come. Let me help you."

"Will, can we talk about it?"

He nodded yes, but he did not look at her. "If I can, Annie. I don't know if I can. Sometimes it builds and goes so fast. I can't control it. It makes me want to run, only it's faster than I am. It's been worse since we moved in here. Sometimes I think it might have been better to go on to California."

She flinched unmistakably, and he shook his head.

"We'll stay here, Annie. You're a gift to me. You make me want to stay.

"Try to rest now.

"You see if you can get some sleep, and I'll try my hand at some biscuits and coffee after while."

31

Brittsville had the advantage of being laid out in the Solomon valley, surrounded by bottomland along the good-sized river which flowed into the big Saline. The water, wood, and rich earth available there under the Homestead Act coupled with the three hundred and twenty acres the Britts and their co-investors were ready to divide into lots made the place very attractive to settlers. Still, it was remote, not yet a railroad stop, and it had, in 1865, only twenty-two permanent families. Outliers and passers-through used the services gathered there and made the population seem larger, but probably not more than seventy people, including children, were trying to put down their roots in this little respite on the frontier. California and Oregon looked more attractive to most of those who came, so most went on.

In truth, the hasty eye could not find much to rest on. The model windmill for the agricultural implement company didn't arrive until the mid-eighties, so nothing yet rose above the single-storied buildings—except, on a couple of them, a false front built five feet high or so above the actual roof line. The Hardware and Stove Store, the General Mercantile, and Britt's Land Agency had slanted porch roofs supported by poles, but horses as well as people could get under them.

Two east-west streets intersected the larger north-south one, but most businesses faced each other across the main street. It was too wide to give much of a sense of communication, but it was just about right to let blowing dust get up a good headway, so even the painted buildings were graying. And none of them had walks in front, so the planked floors of all the interiors were sod gray.

Nothing in particular caught your eye unless it was the large bronze bell suspended between enormous sawhorses out in the middle of about ten lots around the town well and watering trough. Ever since the Britts arrived, with one small wagon in their train specially reinforced to carry the German-cast E-toned beauty, plans had called for a church and a school there in what they hoped would be the town square, but the town hadn't yet decided which would come first or which would get the bell. So there it sat, a long rope tied to the tongue so it could announce emergencies or celebrations, school and church. Both of the latter were held in the Britt's old cabin nearby.

Several houses bordered the town but did not seem to be part of the business area. The Wilsons and Britts were two of the founders, and their large, white, frame houses were at opposite ends. Some soddies were still being used, and many cabins were homes even into the next century. Wagons, some with lean-tos built against the boxes, sheltered a few newcomers, and in three or four places, amber wood testified to the good fortune of families building new houses.

The land around was flat. The hills were several miles distant, small, and relatively treeless with long slopes. Everything beyond the river and some occasional creeks flowing toward it contributed to the sense of unbroken sky and earth with nothing leading into or out of it. The general impression of the town was of a scattered, squat, basically gray and white outpost, everything seemingly defenseless because nothing was clearly connected to anything else in the huge, hovering space. The buildings didn't have enough size or order to appear alert or protective, even though Indians still raided in the area. The structures weren't in any way handsome. At best, they looked functional, ready for the moment, perhaps, but not for any future that might be long in coming. Brittsville needed people.

So when it was clear that the seven wagonloads arriving in July were going to stay, that twenty-nine new citizens, seven dogs, dozens of oxen and horses and mules, guineas, chickens and several new trees were going to become part of the town, the town was ready to celebrate. Any occasion was an opportunity to bring gifts, talk, eat, laugh, weep—be together in those gestures of the heart which, far more than buildings, provide the foundations of community. Unspoken loneliness, maybe fear, maybe boredom, had to give way to the festive spirit that entered Brittsville along with all the new life.

"We thought we was doin' fine," Claire told Annie, "but when you all come, we learned better. We was needin' some reasons for singing something besides hymns!"

Welcoming the wagons was only a start. Every time a new family settled into their home—whether it was soddie, cabin, or a new house—the whole town threw a housewarming party. Sometimes it was a pot-luck pig roast or a beef barbecue lasting all day and well into the night. Sometimes it was a box supper where all the women packed a meal into boxes or containers they decorated—fancy or funny—and sold to the highest bidder—usually a sweetheart for single girls or husbands for married women. The money went to the community treasury intended to finance the school or church, when they would decide which they wanted first.

The celebrations were usually around the town well, starting with the cooking, which filled the countryside with luscious smells, and ending with a dance on wide boards spread out on the buffalo grass, scratchy in any season. Travelers and cowboys staying at McCleary's usually mosied over for the dancing, though they were also welcome for the suppers. And about that time, too, some of the men who didn't dance much would bring out jugs and bottles of liquor which they drank from, not often to drunkenness but always to stories and laughter.

Because the Fairchilds were the most favored among this group of arrivals, their housewarming was the first. By mid-September, wheat and oats were stacked, hay was in its slow growth, and corn was yellowing and waiting, so Claire, Lizzie Britt, and Della Baker got plans underway for the party. No surprise was attached to it, so for days Will could feel his tension growing. Along with it was displeasure, a kind of low-grade anger that he could not get out of what he did not want to do.

Annie sensed his unease and tried to help him with it. She could only say the obvious. "These are our friends, Will. They're trying to please us and show us they're glad we're here."

He knew that was the case, at least in one sense. But there was always another sense for him, the reserve that made him silent while others talked, the need to keep a cover over that part of his life which he thought they were curious about. It seemed to him that the darkened part grew larger as he got older or moved farther from its beginning. It was as though the secrets increased as he had more people to keep them from. At first, it had been the other students at medical school who started calling him the Prince because he seemed arrogant and unsocial to them. Later, when they had put out his eye and he'd had to wear a patch for some months, they'd changed it to The Pirate or Blackbeard, and they had nearly all shunned him. It had not felt much different from his father's accusations and beatings. Then it was Narcissa and George who were never able to confront him or call him anything in anger. He thought he knew what they would say if they could, and he still doubled over in pain at imagining it.

Now it was Annie. He recognized the confusion and hurt he was putting her through. He saw it most clearly when she curtailed herself, lowering her voice along with her enthusiasm any time she thought he might be critical. He could also see it when she talked most brightly, with determination, he could tell, to distract him to what was pleasant or, more often, to some future moment that promised peace or dearness—especially to the birth of their child.

He needed that help, but every time she gave it, he felt a kind of intrusion from her into his territory, territory forbidden to everybody else. And then he needed to oppose her, to insist on doing his battle alone. It was as though he would step backward into what he knew would surround him and suck him up in it, even though he did not want that, even though he wanted to go with her into the friendly world of people who care for one another, who forgive trespasses, who bear and nurture children.

Even worse, her kindness could seem obedience, a gesture born of fear which offended him because it showed him what he did not want to be part of himself. Or it could seem pity, which he found worst of all, condescension masquerading as sweetness. He despised it because it said he had nothing and was nothing. At his most vulnerable, all the dark patches lay over him at once, and his descent into his personal hell would begin.

Neither of them could explain it, but they did intuit some aspects of it. He did not like crowds of people; that was plain. And he did not like the cramped space of the cabin. But they did not translate those into a fear of talking, of disclosure. They did see that he should not be pressed. Annie remembered that he didn't like the openness, either, that the pure space of Kansas hills and sky made him uncomfortable with its infinity of directions—or absolute lack of any.

"Too close. Too open. Too fast. Too slow," she would say to herself in frustration. He was a mass of contradictions that kept her puzzled and on guard.

But she countered those feelings with others: he was loving and generous far more than he was hurtful, and his harshness came, she felt certain, from his unending grief and guilt. "He will heal and be better," she told herself—and him—even though she was aware that the efforts they both made to steady him were constantly jeopardized. Now it was this party. Everything was for them, focused on them. He couldn't send an excuse or convey to Annie that she should not go. They were both filled with dread. He hoped for a long, difficult delivery back in the hills, and she wondered how she would shield him from these neighbors who were preparing to offer friendship and gratitude.

At the party, she tried to stay with him, to be beside him or very near him, laughing for them both, including him with her eyes and what she said. But when the dancing began and Annie sat down to watch, Will moved toward the edge of the group. Claude was there. So was Martin, so Annie judged he would be all right. So did Will.

Claude and Martin were drinking some Kentucky bourbon Martin had brought, and though Will knew well he should not because he wanted it so much, he accepted Martin's offer of a small cup. The first swallow caused such a wave of need to sweep over him that he could barely stop himself from drinking all of it at once. Feeling his hand start to shake, he laughed deliberately and exaggerated the tremor. "Look at that! It's been too long since I've tasted the real thing!"

"Drink it up, Will. You've earned it." Both the men were glad to see him relax and joke a little.

"Yes, sir! This night's for you and Annie," Claude added. "Drink up and enjoy yourself. We're damned glad you're with us, Will."

And as quickly as he could without gulping it down, Will drank that cup and the next.

He did not, though, become more expansive, as they had hoped he might. Instead, he grew tight-faced and increasingly quiet. After an uncomfortable time, they guided him to another small group and made their way separately to their families, freshly aware that their Doctor Fairchild was not cut from their cloth.

Will roamed. Frequently he stopped for other drinks offered him, but he managed not to yield to his desire to seize bottles away from the unsuspecting who seemed more and more foolish to him. He found their talk infuriating and impossible. He wanted only to drink and to be by himself. He began to concentrate on Annie and moved closer to the dancers. She was not among them, but she was also not where he had left her, with Kitty and Hannah.

For a terrible moment, he felt completely alone, abandoned, and helpless. It was as though she had disappeared, and he was slipping without a hold on any place in the universe. Until he heard her laugh and saw her to one side with Claire, Claude, and a small group of jabbering people, he was gasping for breath. Just as quickly, he was angry with her. He could see that she was at ease. The group was physically close. Sometimes one person would touch another's shoulder or laugh and grab an arm or elbow. They were friends having fun. He felt slapped, and he wanted to hit them all, but especially her. It took every bit of his strength to gather himself and move slowly toward her.

Annie was not long seeing that he was in trouble, so she immediately began creating a way for them to leave. "Mercy!" she laughed. "I didn't know your own party could be so exhausting!" Going to Will and trying to take his arm, she adjusted to his stiffness. Her voice calmed and lowered.

He felt deeper anger.

"Or maybe it's this baby." She touched her stomach. "I do get tireder these days." Looking at his clinched face, she asked in a playful way for the others to hear, "Do you suppose, Doctor Fairchild, you could escort me to our new home? I think it's time to leave the party to the young ones."

She was far from irony, but everyone laughed. At sixteen, she was one of the young ones. He felt them laughing at him.

"Yes, you old-timers go on home, now," they called back to her. "You have to get your rest!" It was the meaningless, easy, goodbye talk of people who were comfortable with one another.

"Thank you so much, everyone," Annie said. "It was a wonderful party."

Will managed a nod as people said good night to them, but he was rigid, allowing himself to be offended at the reference to ages, using that to cover his misery at the whole evening. The alienation it forced him to see and hear was another version of his ineptness. Annie's ease showed him his distance. He was anguished and enraged, all at once, and without much understanding of anything.

That night he drank himself to senselessness but not before he punished her. More frightened that those outside would somehow know than she was of him, at least when it started, she made no effort to talk much with him or, later, to defend herself. It was the first time he hit her—on her sides, her upper ribs. She believed that he knew what he was doing until he passed out.

32

They had no way to discuss what happened that night—or others like it. Everything had already been said between them. All they knew to do was to go on. They were both caught up in it some way neither of them knew how to stop.

She sometimes thought it would have been better between them if she could have found a way to make him think he was always helping her. He needed, more than anything, it seemed to her, to be useful and to feel generous even if he couldn't actually credit himself when he was. Everyone relied on him, and he helped them. He never said much that wasn't necessary, but when he did talk, about doctoring or animals or planting, he was clear and definite, and people listened to him, trusted him. He fed on that. The more they needed him, the more he gave them. That was a good circle.

She thought that if she could have been struck dumb so she couldn't remember what had happened and couldn't say it, even to herself, if he could just have started over again, with her not knowing the truth, he could have been easier with her. He always seemed to want that. It was always, "I'm sorry, Annie. It'll be better.

"You are my future, what I live for." He was always going to stop the drinking, change. It was always going to happen.

But it didn't happen. He didn't change, and she didn't get struck dumb. She granted that perhaps she didn't know all she should have, but she also knew she wasn't how he liked to picture her—fresh and innocent riding in on her Charlie mule. Sometimes she felt much older than she was. He had seen to that, it seemed to her. She knew

195

enough to prefer that he be able to spend some time drinking with the other men rather than by himself watching her. That didn't happen often, but it didn't have to. Once had been enough to teach her how to sit very still, how to say nothing if she could manage, how to say only what was kind if she had to say something, how to keep from crying out—or even crying—when he decided to have her or hit her, how to be her own comfort by thinking of home—the soft green stairway under the water, her quiet old rock. Annie tried not to think of her mother then. She just tried to get through it, the bad sex and the beating.

Later, she wouldn't be able to stop herself from trying to figure it out. She would worry at it until she felt as though she was drowning in it, but she never got beyond where she started: he was so full of loss and guilt he had no room left for the rest of them. Maybe no matter how much he wanted to let them in, she thought, and was nice to them for that, he still had to keep everyone away from him or punish them, himself and her, anyway, just for being alive and together when what he most loved was gone. She never knew more than that.

She kept thinking, though, that her mother would be able to sort through it, and she wanted to see Mary so badly she could taste blood in her throat even though she knew she would never tell the truth. Her stomach, even her bowels, ached sometimes to see her mother, even if she wouldn't say one word out loud. Annie could feel her cheek on Mary's heart and Mary's arms around her, and she was not ashamed to see that she had cried until the front of her dress was wet.

When she told Will how much she missed her mother, he seemed to understand and to want them to be able to visit. He always said that it wouldn't be long before they would go to Tennessee or bring Mary for a visit. "Within a year, I should think," he would say.

Annie didn't actually see how her mother could ever make the trip by herself. She thought perhaps she could go and bring Mary back for a stay.

"Once the baby is here and we get in the new house, we'll talk more about it," Will answered. "She'll be able to come most of the way by train when the Hannibal Bridge is completed. That will be easier for her."

But still Annie was so far away from Mary she couldn't visualize the journey for her mother—even though she could remember coming every step of the way herself. Everything looked so hard to her sometimes. She was so far from home. She was going to have a baby. And she had to try to tend to this man who confused her more and more. Despite the harsh hours between them, despite his struggles inside, he was so good to her other women were envious.

Will seemed to know before Annie did what might make her work easier or what would please her, and he didn't hesitate to provide it. Supply wagons coming out from Kansas Town or down from Logan, Nebraska, nearly always had something for them, something for Annie. Most of the other men ordered only new machinery or tools for themselves, but not Will. He bought her a sewing machine before she had a place for one. She thought it must have looked funny to see her out in front of the cabin sitting at her new Singer treadle machine with the sky and half the women of the town as a backdrop.

Actually she didn't have any notion how to run it. Claire and Kitty and Della and Lucy did, though, and day in and out, they kept it at a steady hum making everything from curtains to shirts. They tried to teach Annie how to sew a straight seam. She got so she could do that fairly well, but she always preferred to sew by hand. As it turned out, the other women were willing to make most of what Will and Annie needed in return for using the machine to sew for their own families.

Annie appreciated all he did. She told him so, too. She knew he was, at heart, a generous man. That didn't go together with what could make him so distant and cruel. But there it was. And there she was.

Sometimes she would think of what she might be doing if she hadn't come with Will. She thought it would have been peaceful at home and far easier to live with Mary. But then she'd think that if she had not joined with him, she wouldn't have her baby, and however scared she was, she wanted her baby. And if she hadn't come with him, she wouldn't have her Doll, the house he was planning—which was the grandest she ever saw. She wouldn't know her Claire or Kitty. She wouldn't know about the hills. She wouldn't have Will in his gentle times or in her bed.

Marriage was for better or for worse, she knew. She just hadn't expected so much of both so soon. She also knew that Will tried hard, and he was considerate most of the time—unless he was drinking. It was just that, as time went on, he didn't get better. Instead, he was drinking more and more.

33

Annie and Will loved their baby until it blocked out all the rest of the world for weeks. Those days of Edward's infancy were, Annie was convinced, what a man and woman should share.

She named the boy Edward William, Edward for her grandfather and William for Will, she assumed. He said he didn't care what name she picked. All that mattered was that their son was well.

And he was. He was black-haired with a cowlick right in front that spun his hair in a circle and made him look surprised all his life. His eyes were so big she called him Hootie Owl. He looked forever as though he could see everything at once. His fingers and toes were perfect and long, like Will's, and he was as fair as Annie, "fairer than the morning dew," she crooned to him. He was a perfect, beautiful, little boy, and Will was as happy with him as she was.

Edward was born in January of that first year in Brittsville, and their cabin was so snug and warm she could sometimes think he was lucky to have those long, quiet weeks to be introduced to the world. Will rocked him and changed him and knelt beside her while she nursed him. They could smell his own little body there in the warm air of the cabin made moist by the kettle of water they kept on top of the stove.

Annie couldn't get enough of that baby. She kissed him everywhere, in the fat little folds of his legs, the blessed little star just above his little buttocks, behind his ears, on his palms and the soles of his feet. When he was at her breast, she felt such a wonder and such an ache. He was flesh of her flesh. At the same time, she thought of

Roaring Hollow, the Kansas hills they had come through, and the coyotes screaming on the trail, and she knew that this baby and she were part of that which had gone on forever, which was as ancient as they were new.

Most of all she knew, without any words for it, that, however much this tiny one needed her, had to have her, that was how much she needed him and had to have him. However small she knew them both to be, she felt a power in her she had never before known. She was certain she could face any danger because of him. He made her feel wise. He gave her such a blessing of courage and place and meaning. He was the one, definite, undeniable, precious gift of her life.

Edward also let her see, over and over, how Will could be when he forgot himself. From the beginning he had wanted the baby, lived for him, she sometimes thought. He had laughed out loud when he held Edward up for her to see right after the baby was born. "It's a boy, Annie!" he shouted. She believed Will loved Edward exactly as she did.

Of course, she had to learn that. At first she didn't want to give him the baby to hold. She had some fear, some anxiety, when she saw the baby's head in Will's hand, not at all filling it, the long fingers curved around the tiny skull. She didn't know what she expected, but much between Will and her had caused her to worry about how he would actually respond to their child. She was not prepared for the unrestrained tenderness she saw in him as soon as he was with his baby.

He nuzzled Edward just as she did and looked so long into his eyes. She knew Will was seeing himself in those lovely little mirrors just as she did and thinking that the baby could see himself in Will's— even if he couldn't. It was such a precious thing—Will's gaze, without suspicion or defense, just a steady look into another person's soul. He laid his cheek against Edward's little head, and with the backs of his fingers, he touched Edward's soft, soft hair, just petting him. She thought it the sweetest gesture—as though the palms of his hands might be too rough, even though they were barely callused.

And soon she came to know that Will could handle the baby every bit as well as she could. Not only that. It gave him some kind of peace nothing else ever did, so far as she knew. For weeks after Edward's birth, Will did not drink, and he was unfailingly gentle with Annie, too. Much of the time, he seemed very nearly healed.

He was no more willing to talk about himself or to let her ask about grandparents and what they might think of this boy. But he did talk with Edward. He sang to him. He played baby games with him. Sometimes she could have wept to see the love in his face when he was simply relaxed with his son.

He was the same with each of their four children he was blessed to know.

34

They weren't in the cabin long, not quite a year. Will's acute need for more space made him begin drawing plans for their house well before Edward was born, and Annie encouraged him every way she could. She liked the small, warm cabin for herself and the baby, and when Will was out, she felt comfortable, a kind of sweet peace if she kept her mind on Edward. But when Will came in the door, stooped and brooding unless he was with the baby, the discord, even silent, was oppressive to them both. She became fearful, feeling awkward, too, the more she feared.

His plans looked like a fantasy to her, but what he wanted was what they got: a square, two-storied sandstone—a soft, dark stone native to an area just northwest of Brittsville. He wanted three bedrooms upstairs in addition to two small rooms downstairs behind the parlor and kitchen. These were for his practice, he said, and he was very particular about that when he talked to Martin Britt who would be financing the loan.

"I hope I don't have to operate very often," he said, "but when I do, I need a special, separate room for that procedure and for medications. The other room will be an examination and consultation room which I'll use much more than the other. But if there is ever an emergency—and there will be—all of us will be glad we went the extra mile and built the surgery."

He wanted all that at the back of the house with its own special entrance. "Annie and I will have young children," he said. "We don't want them bothering sick folks, or *vice versa.*"

He wanted the pump in the kitchen and a big range next to the surgery door. "Clean, hot water is essential," he said, "and you need it as close as you can get it." Will said lots of doctors weren't as concerned about flies and cleanliness as he was, but he had some ideas about diseases passing between and among people, and he wanted the whole area for his practice to be spotless.

Actually, he gave Martin Britt considerable confidence in him because he was so specific and had planned so carefully, even if the expense and labor, which would be mostly volunteer, did seem excessive. Britt knew well that a doctor in the town would be the best magnet they could have for new settlers. So did others. So he didn't hesitate to arrange the finances, and everyone else did all they could to make the Fairchilds happy. They were an investment, in a manner of speaking.

Though he worked hard for Will and Annie, Britt still had his reservations about helping build and furnish such a house—the first like it in the area. But he didn't voice them. He did his best to be fair to the doctor, and he couldn't explain to himself why he continued to feel cautious about allowing the man his respect and support.

He knew Fairchild was making his own considerable investment in the town. Will had bought his homestead, then another eighty. He had spoken with Britt early on about starting a bank, and after some years in town, he was, in fact, one of ten men from the Brittsville and Salina-Abilene area to found the Central Kansas Farmers' Bank. His and Annie's four children in ten years were perhaps the biggest investment of all. Everyone could see that Will was a good father and a hard-working, excellent doctor who tended his family, his practice, his land, and his livestock carefully.

That kind of word spread, and people came some distance to have him look at their sick child—or horse. They trusted him. And when they came, they could also see the town and maybe make some purchases. Several families who might otherwise have passed through decided to stay as much because of a doctor in the region as because the soil was rich. Those who couldn't pay seemed to receive the same attention and help as those who could. In their turn, they would bring Will potatoes, seed, chickens, a pig, linens, a ring, anything they could. Between them and the town's efforts to settle the Fairchilds in nicely, Annie and Will soon had a bigger variety of livestock and furnishings than most.

Martin saw the doctor's work and the town's response, but he couldn't accept the man the way he could Claude Wilson or John Johnson—or any of the others. He couldn't understand the marriage, either, and more than once he had to tell himself to stop thinking about it—which he knew meant that he wanted to. He found Annie lovely, and while he tried to name his desire to help her a matter of friendship or even leadership of the sort he wanted to accord everyone, he recognized that she gave him a special pleasure he didn't want to name. He found that he disliked the fact that the Fairchilds were begetting a large family, but he could not bring himself to admit to jealousy. He tried to admit only that Annie and Will were a puzzling match. Of course, no one had yet had their curiosity satisfied about the couple, and Martin, like Claire, had to let it go.

Claire had come much closer to asking because she felt such love for Annie and because she couldn't always control herself. The house at first provided opportunities for them to spend more time together than they had since the Fairchilds lived at the Wilson's. Claire had long ago decided that, however dear she was, Annie was inept as a home-maker.

As she put it to Claude, "Annie acts like she's in a foreign country. Whether it's scaldin' off the dishes or dustin' the furniture, she's at a loss!" She remembered when Annie had told her that the Wilson home was the first real house she had set foot in, how her eyes were everywhere at once, how she had shared that she and her ma had just a little cabin back in Tennessee. Claire had been immediately disposed to like Annie, and she straightway assumed responsibility for helping her learn to take care of hearth and home. Her efforts never quite "took," she was quick to see, but that never dampened her enthusiasm for trying.

Later, she also liked to see what it was the doctor could think to buy, for he bought a lot. Other folks occasionally sent to Logan for a clock or plow, but Will Fairchild seemed to have an order for every supply wagon that left Brittsville. Claire was especially taken with the range he bought. None of them had anything to compare to it. It was a six-burner, blue-steel model so shiny it looked like glass. Nickel designs flowered over the oven doors and water reservoir. Claire told Claude she'd never seen a Mexican saddle as pretty as that range, and he grew sober at the thought. She could tell Annie had no more notion of how to clean the range than she had how to run the sewing machine. So Claire redoubled her efforts to teach the girl. Annie was always willing, much more than Esther, Claire's daughter who was just a year younger. But she didn't seem to have a knack for it or for getting the household organized.

Claire didn't think it was only that Annie was so young. "It's more like she ain't been broke right," Claire told Claude. Claire could see their Esther married and mothering, even at fifteen. She seemed ready, and Claire was positive she was willing. But Annie seemed sack-whipped more than settled. That was the only way Claire knew how to say it: tied up and buffaloed, she thought. She noticed it most when they first went through the new house together. What often struck her was that she was more excited than Annie about all the Fairchilds had. Claire couldn't account for it. She remembered how delighted Annie had been about the Wilson's house where they talked forever and laughed together easily. But in her own house, she seemed dispirited somehow and pale—a little peaked looking, Claire thought.

She didn't know if it was all too much for Annie and she was worried about taking proper care of it or if maybe it was the baby. Annie was such a little, old thing, and she had that big boy to nurse. And Claire also knew Annie was homesick. She had talked about her mother and Roaring Hollow so much Claire began to feel as though she could see them, too.

"We'll have Ma come up—or we'll go down to Pikeville—just as soon as the railroad comes on through. That bridge in Kansas Town is supposed to open in a few years, too, so we wouldn't have to go so far by boat. I know Ma would hate steamboat travel. I sure did. So did Will. We can't any of us swim. Ma and my Pa were scared to death of steamers. She wouldn't mind coming up on the train, though, I don't think, though it is such a long way for her to be alone."

Annie was sure Claire and Mary would get on well together. "You'd like her, Claire. Ma is a good woman."

"I'm sure I would, Annie," Claire would say. "I hope to meet her real soon," but she figured it would be a long time coming if it came at all. She couldn't see herself making such a trip, and she didn't suppose any other woman could, either. Annie might dream, but Claire was sure a beggar would get horses to ride before Mary Sherwood would arrive in Brittsville.

One morning Annie looked especially tired, and Claire decided she'd take a chance. "Annie, you look a little peaked to me," she said. "Are you feelin' all right? Is that big old boy getting' you down?"

Annie felt strength leaving her knees, and she grabbed for the table to support herself.

Claire thought she looked scared out of her wits, and, honestly concerned for Annie, she was immediately sorry she'd asked. She apologized quickly and could see Annie working at her feelings. Claire didn't know whether Annie was fighting against the sympathy she wanted the way we do sometimes when it will make us crumble or whether she thought her friend was too much the busybody lots of people thought her or whether Annie had something bad wrong she didn't want Claire to know about. Clearly Annie was struggling. "I'm sorry, Annie," Claire said again. "I didn't mean to pry." And she went to Annie, putting her hands on the girl's shoulders.

Annie was thinner than Claire had thought, and tears were running down her cheeks.

Claire decided Annie wasn't mad at her, but she wasn't reassured when, after Annie turned away, she said, very softly, "Don't you worry, Claire. I'm all right. I'm not sick."

"Then what *is* it," Claire couldn't keep from asking.

Annie shook her head and looked down. "No, Claire," she said. "There's nothing to be done, I don't think." Then she looked back at Claire quickly: "Just don't mention anything about this to anyone, all right? Not even to Claude?"

Of course, Claire said she would not, and she didn't. It nearly killed her more than once. But she didn't tell. It seemed to her that she just could not fail Annie—even a couple of times when she thought she ought to. It was the first secret Claire ever properly kept. But she couldn't keep herself from thinking about it, looking for explanations, and gradually, as months and years passed, it seemed to clarify for her.

Everybody always said that marriage troubles began in bed, Claire thought, and nothing she had ever heard or witnessed convinced her of any error in that way of thinking. And Will and Annie? The more she thought the more she remembered how little they talked, how they never spoke about old days or letters from his family. They didn't hold hands or pet. They didn't even look at one another most of the time.

That especially bothered Claire. She loved looking at her Claude. Lots of times that was how she could tell what he needed from her but would be too considerate to ask. And she never stopped having strong feelings for him rise in her when she would discover he was watching her with little crinkles at the corners of his eyes.

But Annie seemed to Claire to back up or sidle away from Will, and sometimes she seemed to be in pain as she tried to rise from a chair or pick up one of the babies. Claire knew, too, that since the birth of Edward, Annie had not often left the house.

"I depend on you for the news, Claire," she once said, "for with the baby, I don't seem to get out much."

Claire thought it was strange that a person in such a small town could be so little seen. Other women had babies—and much less to do with than Annie did—much less help, too, once Will had hired Melva, Brittsville's only black woman, to assist in the house. But Annie stayed in. If Claire or Kitty or Lucy wanted to see her, they had to go to her house. And all but Claire did so less and less frequently.

After that one time, though, Claire never again asked Annie if she was well. Neither did she try to explain anything to the other women who at first commented on how little they saw of Annie, then came to wonder if she preferred her big new house to their company.

Claire kept the secret, but a part of her knew Will was hurting his wife. She would have kept the secret for Esther, too, and she would have asked the same of her own mother. Some problems are private, she concluded, and there was nothing anybody could do about them, at least nothing the law or holy book would allow.

35

One morning when Annie was carrying her fourth child and Edward was about seven, he was hoeing in the garden with Julie Winkler. Will extended both the vegetable and herb gardens some each year, and while Julie disliked the work, he still liked the chance to be near Annie. Edward enjoyed gardening with his mother or being with her when she was stirring up a batch of Nuremburg plaster. But he didn't like it so much when he had to work with Julie. He didn't like the way their hand talked. It wasn't any different this morning.

"You like dirt farmin', do you, boy?" he asked.

"I don't know about dirt farming," Edward replied.

"Like this, here. Workin' in the dirt."

"But we're making an herb garden for Papa's medicines."

"Same difference. Just turnin' it over to plant seeds. Herbs or oats, it don't make no damn difference. It's all the same."

"Papa says there's no other garden like this in the whole area, maybe the whole state."

"Oh, he does, does he? Well! He's the doctor, ain't he? An' course he knows more than all the rest of us put together, don't he?"

It seemed to Edward that Julie was always saying things to make him halfway mad, but then Julie would laugh, friendly-like, and Edward couldn't be sure getting mad was what he should do. Like now.

Julie said, "Well, it'll be a real fine garden, all right." Then: "Say, Mister Edward. Do you know what *is* a herb, anyway?"

That made the boy feel important because Julie seemed so honest and interested all of a sudden, not like he was laughing at Edward and—by extension—his father whose work they were assisting.

The boy knew lots of the herbs. They planted new ones every year, and his father had taught him how to make a map, as he called it, of every plot. He showed Edward what to look for when the seeds sprouted or the buds started. He helped him make notes on how the herbs grew, which ones died and under what conditions, as he said. Edward did the maps very neatly, and he was immensely proud when Will told him he might grow up to be a botanist. He began to draw the plants, too, at different stages, trying to make them perfect. Will told him, nearly honestly, that they were as good as illustrations in a schoolbook.

Will was also teaching Edward the plants' Latin names, and Edward was gaining some sense of what language is. Will frequently talked with him about other places, other times. He knew Edward was an intelligent boy, and he wanted him to have a sense of the world beyond them.

"When you're older, you'll travel to Kansas Town and St. Louis, maybe New York City. You may even go to Paris. I've never been to Paris. You'll need to know about people who live differently, maybe even speak another language."

Savoring the feeling of having special knowledge, Edward answered Julie's question. "Well, Julie, an herb is a plant that you grow so you can get medicines out of it. Sometimes you dry them and grind them into a powder people can take when they get sick. Or sometimes you squeeze the oil out of them and use that. Or you can just eat them, I think."

"Do you get to salt 'em any?" Julie laughed.

Edward wished he wouldn't always try to make a joke.

"Name me one herb you plant here."

The boy didn't know whether he should give the regular name or the Latin name, and he hesitated just long enough for Julie to think he was ignorant about it.

"You can't do 'er, can you?" He had a smirk on his face, Edward thought, and it didn't feel like he was teasing, but Edward couldn't quite tell.

"Yes, I can, too. I just don't know what kind of name I should give you."

"*Kind* of name?"

"Yes. Regular or Latin."

"Regular or *Latin*? What the hell are you talkin' about? Regular or Latin?"

"Well, Papa says that most herbs have two kinds of names, the ones regular people use, then the one scientists use."

"*Scientists?*"

Julie wasn't hoeing any more. He was just standing there shaking his head at Edward.

"Yes! Scientists! Like my Papa!"

"Your *papa*!" He sounded disgusted.

"But it's true, Julie. Take the foxglove, for instance. Papa says it's one of the most important plants for medicine in the whole world. It's a heart medicine. But it's got another name, too. Scientists call it *digitalis pur ...digitalis purpa. . .*—or something like that. It's got two names."

"Well. *Why* has it got two names? Ain't they sure what to call it, them scientists?"

Edward knew Julie liked to keep a person on edge. That was one reason he didn't like to work with him. Now, Julie was grinning big, his teeth even and white in his square, brown face. He was a handsome man, handsomer than his father, Edward knew. And he wasn't stupid. He was just ornery.

"How does *your papa* know which herbs'll even grow around here?"

Julie exaggerated "your papa," and Edward thought he was like a bully looking for a fight.

"We never know for sure." Edward had decided to put himself right alongside his father. "Papa always says some likely won't make it here. The soil and climate won't be right, he says. We just have to try and see. We just have to experiment."

"Experiment, huh? Just like a real scientist."

"My papa *is* a real scientist," Edward said as strongly as he could, but he didn't look at Julie, and he knew Julie knew he wasn't sure.

What most upset Edward, though, was how Julie talked about his mother. "She ain't gonna have another youngun', is she? They keepin' busy in the bedroom, ain't they?"

Edward knew his mother was in the family way again, and he also knew the three of them were pretty little. But he realized that it wasn't any of Julie's affair. Lots of people had lots of babies. And he felt compelled to defend his parents. "They want lots of children," he muttered. It was hard to talk about, and he didn't think they should be saying anything of the sort.

"He's gonna make her fat and lookin' old as him, I reckon."

"Mama ain't fat, and Papa ain't old," Edward blurted out even though he didn't want to.

"Course he is," Julie said right back. "Look at 'em. She's young enough to be your sister instead of your mama, boy. *Look* at 'em."

"You just shut up, Julie," Edward fairly shouted, feeling himself nearing tears. "You shut up, or I'll tell Papa what you say."

He was worried because he wasn't supposed to say such thing even to his little sisters, let alone a grown man. And he knew he didn't want to repeat any such conversation to his father. But his words did seem to have an effect. For a minute Julie stared at Edward—who didn't make eye contact but swung the hoe down repeatedly and quickly. Then Julie started working again.

But he always managed to upset Edward, and one day the boy did tell Will how the hired hand talked.

It was just before Lydia came, and Annie was big and awkward.

"She was such a pretty little thing before he started gettin' to her," Julie had said.

The boy was old enough to understand what he meant, and Edward suddenly hated him for butting into their life with his comments that felt close and stinging. He was also on edge because he had become aware that his mother and father were not always comfortable with one another. He felt their tension. He knew Will drank when Annie didn't want him to. She would make the children go to the girls' room when he started. "Take care of your baby sisters," she would tell Edward. "Be very quiet and very good."

So he would, and usually he'd fall asleep across the bottom of the girls' bed. Maybe he wouldn't remember anything about it the next day. But sometimes Annie would look sick in the morning, or she would hold her side or her back, or she would limp when she walked.

"It's all right, Edward," she would always tell him and pull him close to her. "Do not worry, my darling. I'm all right. It's just something your Papa and I have to deal with. Try not to worry."

But of course he did worry, and he didn't understand. He later supposed that was why he made such a mistake as to tell his father what Julie said, how he talked.

They were grinding some cranesbill root into powder with Will's little mortar and pestle—out in the surgery—while, in the kitchen, Annie was stirring some red lead and cloves and the other ingredients for Nuremburg plaster. All of them loved the smell. It was better than pickling or canning time. So Edward was enjoying that and feeling happy being there working with both of them, all of them making medicines. Will had explained that he wanted to compare the cranesbill and the plaster as astringents to see which would draw better, so he wanted a fresh batch of both. He also had a notion that a cranesbill poultice might help the swollen knee of a mare he was trying to doctor.

Edward thought he understood what his father meant, and he always liked Will to talk with him about what they did. The boy tried to use the words his father did. Sometimes he dreamed a little about the possibility of being a veterinarian himself. He didn't want to help women have babies, he didn't much think.

Tennessee was entertaining Emily with a whirly-gig. They were sitting on a quilt back by the kitchen table behind Annie. Tennie had the button impossibly wound around the string, but the girls were laughing. The whole family was together, and it felt good to Edward. He trusted the moment enough to say what had been bothering him.

"Papa, why does Julie talk all the time about you and Mama?" He didn't catch on right away to how straight Will got because he kept pounding the cranesbill root.

"What does he say, Edward?" His voice had dropped, so Edward quickly raised his eyes. He saw that Will's face had hardened as it did during the bad times. The boy wanted to take back what he had asked, then, but he knew it was too late.

"What does he say, I asked you?" Will grabbed him by the shoulders, pulling him to his feet, knocking the pestle to the floor. It was the first time Edward realized that his father might hurt him the way he suspected Will sometimes hurt his mother. He knew he would not be able to get out of this. He was certain he should never have gotten into it.

"He says…. He says you're too old for Mama. He says you give her too many babies and that she's the prettiest girl in these parts but that you're making her old and ugly." When Edward said Julie's words to his father, they sounded a thousand times worse than when Julie said them, himself, and Edward hated every one of them.

Will didn't say anything more to the boy. Instead, he turned to the kitchen, and with three quick steps, he was through the door and at Annie by the range. Edward saw her face come apart before he heard her shout, "Will! No!"

Then Will grabbed her by the arm and started pulling her up the stairs. She couldn't go as fast as he could, and Edward saw her fall and him dragging her.

"Watch the babies, Edward! Watch your sisters!"

Then he could hear his father's boots and his mother's high voice, but not what they said.

Edward thought he had better move the plaster off to the boiler top. Then he lay down on the quilt beside Tennessee and Emily so they could crawl over him and think it was a game while he knew it was how he could best keep an eye on both of them and help them all three be quiet.

He wasn't sure about it, but he believed what he said made his father very angry with Julie because, the next day, Will made the hired man go away, and Annie told Edward that Julie would not be coming back. Edward wasn't sorry about that, but he felt sick to see his mother hold her side and gasp as she walked. For days after that, she could not lift even little Emily.

36

Annie played with the children more than she worked in the house, it seemed to Claire. She was forever using Will's newspapers for animals and make-believe critters for the children.

"Oh, it's fun, Claire," Annie would say, "and they like me to spend time with them. What you do is stir up lots of flour paste, then soak the paper into a kind of pulp, then mix them. When you figure out the right proportions, you can shape the paper into whatever you want, and after it dries, you can paint it up nice and pretty."

Claire could see Annie had a knack for this kind of nonsense even if she couldn't take care of her house. The children had dolls and toy soldiers and pull horses, but they liked Annie to make special "orders" for them. If a book had a picture of an elephant or a fancy horse, Annie could usually fashion it for them, and they would play with it until it broke or, more often, until it dissolved in the rain when they left it outdoors.

One day Melva saw Annie making trousers for a little boy doll she'd fixed for Tennessee. "You can make most anything, can't you, Mrs. Annie?" she said.

Annie worried about Melva. Hers was the only Negro family in or around Brittsville.

"They was six of us families come out from St. Louis," she had once told Annie. "But it seems as how we can't take no hold here any more than we could there. We can't make no go of the land, and my man, he's so discouraged he don't rightly know what to do next. Long as I can do a little cleanin' and cookin' for you, we can get along, I guess.

But we ain't gonna make it here, Mrs. Annie, no more than the others done. An' they long gone."

Annie had never heard anyone say a bad word about Melva or any of the others, but she knew that not many Negroes came through, and none of them had managed to stay. Melva had got word of some black people trying to build a settlement called Nicodemus somewhere farther west, but she didn't know where it was, and she was determined that north was better for her family than west was.

Annie hadn't thought anything about particular hardships different kinds of people might face. When she did think about it, she realized that everyone in Brittsville was alike. That seemed to mean white-skinned and Christian. The only Jewish person any of them knew was old Mr. Lerner who made his way around the territory with a little peddler's wagon. He sold buttons and potions, a single needle or some scraps of material, usually a little cheaper than the Mercantile did and right at your door. Once in a while he would have some fruit or the most wonderful soft, white cheese any of them had ever tasted. They didn't know where he got his supplies or how he made the cheese or even if he made it himself, but they always bought it when he had it. He never stayed in Brittsville, though, and Annie didn't know where he went. It had never occurred to her to wonder about it, but she did, now, when Melva told her they were going to have to leave.

Annie wondered if it was, in fact, religion and color that bound people together or made some successful and forced others to move along. As soon as she wondered, she developed a specific and deep anger at that kind of thinking. Melva and Mr. Lerner were the first people who had made such prejudice real in her own home and heart, and Annie tried to help Melva all she could. Will paid her, but Annie would look for food and clothes for her and her husband—and occasionally some old toys for her girl and boy.

"You know what I'd appreciate more than anything, Mrs. Annie, if you was a mind to do it?"

Melva never asked for anything, so Annie had no idea what she might do to please.

"If you was a mind, my little girl ain't never had herself a dolly that looks like her, a brown dolly, you know. I tried with some old black rags I had, but I swear, Mrs. Annie, it didn't have no life to it no more

214

than the rags did before I pieced 'em together. It was just dreadful. She ain't never had no baby doll like herself she could love. If I was to work something extra for you, do you think you could arrive at makin' her a dolly?"

Annie started to shake her head no because she thought she couldn't even begin to do such a thing. But Melva's face was so happy and alive as she thought about Ellen's brown doll, Annie found that she could not refuse. "Well!" she said, "I never did such a thing before, but I'll try."

And try she did. She made the head first, just about the size of a little cabbage, and she worked as hard as she ever had to make a little cap of the curliest hair she could manage. She knew it would end up hard, but she wanted it to look soft. When she finished, she knew you'd have to touch it to know it wasn't.

Annie asked Melva to watch while she tried to shape the face. She'd never paid that much attention to how Negro lashes curled up or how their noses were different from hers. Melva finally said, "Why don't you look at Ellen herself and see if that'll help you. Growed-up womens is different than little girls." So she brought her daughter the next day, and Annie tried her best to copy Ellen's face in the gray pulp. Ellen let Annie feel her face because it seemed that Annie's fingers were more certain than her eyes were.

When she could finally use black paint on the hair and, for the face, a mixture of some brown and white Will had saved from painting part of the woodwork, the doll began to look like a real Negro baby. Annie shaped the hands and feet, then attached them to stuffed cloth arms and legs. She fixed up a stuffed cloth body which she worked into the paper she used to fashion the neck. She painted the eyeballs creamy white and the eyes, themselves, the very dark brown. Annie never managed a nice pink for the lips and nails, but Melva said it would be all right to paint them a creamy brown. Finally, Annie made a pretty little dress so you couldn't see what the body was made from. The head and feet and hands were all that was visible.

Of course, Tennessee and Edward watched every step of the process, which took about a week, and Tennessee and Emily both wanted brown dollies for themselves. Then Tennessee and Edward wanted to make something for Ellen, too. Annie helped Tennessee fashion a frog which she could do by grabbing a big handful of the paper, scooping out a mouth from one side to the other, attaching two paper knobs with a hole in each for eyes, and pushing in just a little extra paper for legs by the sides of the mouth. They painted it a bright green, and all of them laughed in pleasure at the awkward, big-mouthed creature that was exactly right.

Edward was considerably more ambitious and considerably less successful at first because he wanted to make Abraham Lincoln. "He was a great president and friend to Negroes," Edward insisted. "Without him, they'd still be slaves, papa says." That was true, but it didn't help them make the figure. They came up with a rigid, stick-like thing with an exaggerated beard and hat, but it didn't look nearly friendly enough for a gift.

Actually, Will came to their rescue. He had checked on their projects several times. To Annie's pleasure and confusion, he was never upset to see her helping the children draw or read. And he seemed to admire the Negro doll.

"You're clever, Annie," he said. "I wish you had some clay to work with."

Although she was happy with what he said, she sometimes wondered if he liked to see her playing with toys and the children because he liked to think of her as a child. It all seemed so sweet— which it was, she supposed. But what she did was for the children, games for them. It didn't have anything to do with what was inside her, herself. And she never forgot that.

When he saw Edward's Lincoln and understood the problem, he thought for a moment then said, "Edward, a lady always likes to receive flowers! You draw plants better than anybody else. Why don't you try to draw some for Ellen?"

That is what he did. He isolated himself in the parlor for hours, and the wallpaper roses in there inspired him to a very generous if somewhat lopsided bouquet. Then they rummaged through his clothes and toys for a couple gifts for little Henry. So when Melva and her children came the next day, the children were able to join Annie in their first thoughtful act for someone outside the family.

Ellen grabbed her black doll to her little chest. Henry seemed to like the frog as much as she did, and they left the house with happiness all over their faces.

It was not a week, though, before Melva told Annie that the family was leaving Brittsville for Chicago. "Up north, it's better for us," she said, her immense, beautiful eyes filling. "We just can't stay, Mrs. Annie. It's too hard here for folks that got no way to buy land or tend it. We have to go."

In time, Annie made Negro dolls for her girls, but her heart wasn't in them the same way, and she never made another as nice as the one for Melva's Ellen.

37

Annie knew the day she conceived their fifth baby. Though she had come to love the Kansas sky, she never saw it look like that before.

She knew well, by then, how to read the clouds. She thought most people could, if they were attentive, but, still, it seemed to Annie that she had a special sense of how the heat and dampness built into signs she seemed able to interpret, and she heeded the messages. Maybe that was because she wasn't raised in the mid-west, and she had had to learn what to look for in the way of storms as she had had to learn about snakes in Tennessee. But she was sometimes convinced she had a special gift about it—gift or curse, maybe.

Annie was not naturally a moody woman, but on some days before a storm, she would be. Her body seemed to register something the hours before in ways she couldn't explain and wasn't grateful for. All of a sudden she would become aware that she was hurried and anxious, and she would not know why. She would feel fierce and stubborn and on alert as though she had to be on guard about everything and in all places at once. Sometimes she would be unnaturally harsh with the children, and they would run complaining to their father. Or she couldn't bear to have them out of her sight. And she wouldn't be able to tell why no matter which way it was. It took her several years to figure out what was affecting her and then to learn to help herself stay at least reasonable.

On this day, she came to be certain a bad storm was brewing. She had gotten so nervous with the children she had finally saved Edward from herself by sending him to the creek to mark white oak, and she made the babies nap when it was much too early. Then by the time she realized what she was upset about, she wanted Edward home and the girls right beside her.

But she knew in her head that Edward would be home before the storm broke. He was smart about the sky, too. And, of course, the girls were right upstairs. She checked them more than once, her blessed little Tennessee lying in the middle of her and Will's big bed with Emily on one arm and baby Lydia on the other, three little girls with just about two years between each of them.

Annie knew some people said they had had too many children too quickly, but Annie didn't think so. Without them, she would not have survived, she didn't believe, and she was sure Will would not have.

Like Edward, their three girls were their life. Claire had said one time that you can't have too many children, and Annie found that true of Will and her. The babies filled them back up with love when they seemed to drain one another with anger and confusion. They gave Will a direction and meaning when he seemed without rudder or hope. And they gave Annie—how could she ever say it, she thought—they gave her joy and sweetness and the strength to see her life as it was. She believed that without her children she would not have cared to go on, herself. Too many times, when Will was sick, she had only them and their need for her to sustain her.

Sometimes she thought of leaving, of trying to go home, for her heart was always pulled to her mother and the mountains of Tennessee. Will knew how she felt, and when he was feeling mean and punishing, he would mock her by telling her she could go back anytime she pleased, only none of the children could go with her. That made her see squarely that her children were more than all the rest of the world to her, that she would never leave them. The cruelty of what he said was also clear to her, but most of all it showed her how much she loved the children.

She couldn't tell if that feeling was more than it would have been had Will and she been all right together. But as it was, what he did demonstrated to her as nothing else ever did how closely happiness is tied to unhappiness or love to hate. At those times, the pain he made her feel by taking away her hopes of ever seeing home again became, in a strange way, a kind of measure of the necessity and joy her children were to her.

And the terrible sense of himself he could cause in her forced her to understand that you can be bound to someone in powerful and opposite ways. He could not have hurt her so if he hadn't been as able to please her, she didn't think. He made her wish she didn't care. But the truth was that she did.

And because the babies always needed her, she couldn't slip off into the solitude or bewilderment Will forced on her. So she needed them the same way. They made her see how close love and need are and how much you have to give to find out what you have. When Melva had helped Annie, she could spend much of her time with the children, playing, singing to them. It had been such a pleasure for her to hold their tiny hands in hers and to rock as big as a swing would go while they stood in her lap and bounced and tried to sing with her.

She had managed to make some little gowns and booties for them so Claire—or her mother—would not think her a complete failure, but what she wanted most was what let her touch the children or share with them.

As soon as they were able, she and they would feed the chickens and gather eggs. Tennessee never seemed afraid to reach under the hens though Edward and Annie might both hesitate at the ruffled feathers and quick, angry squawks. And Tennessee had her own little flock of bantams when she was only four. She would sit with the chicks by the hour.

"They talk to me," she said, grinning because the chicks were hiding under her hair. And they would follow her as readily as they would the hen.

Somehow she and Edward taught the hound—Beauty Bugle Topsy Trail, Edward had named him for reasons of his own—to circle and guard all the chickens so they would not stray. Will liked to see Tennie stand on her tip-toes to open the gate to the coop so the chickens could feed "abroad on the land," he said. With Bugle's help, she never lost a one.

Will was as gentle with the girls as he had been with Edward although Annie thought she could see that he distanced himself from Edward as soon as he realized that Edward had some sense of their problems. Edward seemed to worry about his mother or to be aware when she was feeling poorly. "Let me carry her, Mama," and he'd reach up for Emily or Lydia. "She's too heavy for you," he would say, and he was still very small, himself.

Later, as Will lost more control, without Annie's saying a word, Edward would take the girls off to tend to them by himself, teaching Tennessee to help him. Annie understood that he had learned to read danger signals the way she did. And he learned to help her on mornings when she hurt too much to carry out wash or hang it on the line. They would carry it together in one of the clothesbaskets she had woven, and he would wrestle the pieces out and flap them straight so Annie could pin them up.

He asked only once, "Did Papa hurt you?"

She told him yes, that he had, but not on purpose. She said that accidents could happen between grown-ups the same as they could between children. She didn't know if he believed her, but it was all she knew to say. Her worst fear was that Will would find some reason to turn against Edward. They had always been such friends, Will reading to him, teaching him to read, teaching him about the medicines and herbs, helping him become such a fine gardener. They were close. She didn't know if Will could feel Edward turning more often to her, but it frightened her.

On this day, in the midst of the unease she felt from the air, she felt anger and need and dismay at all the rest of it and all at the same time. She had never seen the sky look so extraordinary. It wasn't just the turbulence and fire. It was the shape within the clouds. The color was bold, magnificent, she thought. The clouds were dark gray, nearly black, but the sun was low, and it made the undersides look golden. The clouds were rushing and crashing into one another in tall towers except in one place just a bit to the north.

There, in a very strange formation, the gold seemed to roll upward in a smooth, rounded line as though you'd made a deep, long curve with a knife, as you sometimes do in cake icings. It was like an ocean wave but spilling up instead of down.

That motion disappeared into the black then spilled back down through gray into gold again, still in that long, straight sweep. Annie could actually see the far western end of the curve like a steady tip of gold and gray against the rush.

She was on the step watching it when she decided she had better tell Will what the sky was promising. He was in his consultation room. She assumed he was reading. But when she opened the door, she saw that he had fallen asleep on the couch there, his head thrown back against the cushions, his arm resting on the couch arm, his hand relaxed.

He had taken off his jacket and rolled his sleeves high, and she could see the line where his skin stopped tanning. It was so white and perfect, as perfect as Lydia's. She looked at his beautiful hands, the long fingers so cleanly formed. She loved his hands. And she felt longing for him come over her as it never had before. She thought she had to feel his mouth on her breast.

Tearing open her waist, she leaned over and drew her nipple, already tight, across his lips. He moved, then wakened, looked at her a moment, then took her breast into his hands and mouth. They stayed like that, she pulling his hair and gasping until she could stand it no longer. She sank to her knees, and he slipped off the couch to his, then raised his mouth to hers. Their tongues were strong against each other until his slid over hers and hers curled around his and nursed as though she were starving.

Somehow they got their clothes off, enough, anyway, and in a moment he came into her in that motion which feels so full you can't move or breathe and don't want to. She grasped his hips and pulled him deeper into her. He caught his breath and arched his back and carried her far, far away.

38

About two months later and in the face of what looked to be another bad storm, Miles Bassford came for Will. Hermione was trying to have their baby. Will couldn't ride Belle because she had a stone bruise. He didn't want to ride Doll because her foal was too young to go along on such a night as this promised to be, and separating them was a different kind of risk, especially for the filly. So he rode Belle's two-year old filly, Pet. That worried Annie because he hadn't finished training her, and he had said, more than once, that she was flighty, a horse he wasn't sure would ever be trustworthy. But Pet it was.

There was no question of waiting until the storm passed or of not going at all. Will had been concerned about this baby during the entire pregnancy, trying to make Hermione stay in bed most of it to avoid the problems he feared if she did not. So when Miles galloped to their door, almost appearing to be chased by a smooth, ice green cloud which threatened a deluge and powerful winds, Will grabbed his bag and headed for the barn without a moment's hesitation, shouting at them as he ran, "I may not be back tonight. Watch the clouds. It looks bad."

Annie didn't know if he heard Tennessee call, "Be careful, Papa." Their oldest daughter, she was like Annie in so many ways—one of which was picking up on the signals of the sky and trees. She came under her mother's arm as they stood in the south doorway, watching Will ride away west into what looked like the mouth of hell.

Miles had started back when Will went to saddle Pet, and Tennessee and Annie could see him in the distance, a tiny man and horse, his red shirt marking their progress like a drop of blood blowing across the blue-green underside of that cloud.

The air was completely still, but the cloud hunkered over constant lightning that forked across the ground. Thunder met itself returning from the horizon. It never stopped. Above, the cloud looked like ice cut from the river except that it was rounded like a creamy, satin-glass bowl turned upside down or like the crown of an old man's head, the hair all flowing forward over a stricken, bruised face. Black slashes like bear paws streaked through the smooth, white fringe and reached out of it.

Annie watched Will ride under it, and she shuddered as she turned to the children and prepared to take them to the storm cave. Edward helped her with Lydia, and Tennessee gathered little Emily and her favorite doll, black Melva. Annie caught up blankets, matches, and the lantern, and they went as quickly as they could. Stinging drops of rain hurried them.

Annie worried about the animals. The horses were in the corral and could go in their barn if they wanted. The cattle were in the south pasture, no place to be seen. Neither was Bugle. She gave in to necessity, accepting that she could do nothing even if something should occur to her. But she felt very afraid, and she pressed the blankets over the child she knew she carried as she went before her children down the rock steps, lighting the lantern, checking carefully for snakes and toads, which Tennessee especially feared, then calling the children down.

Once they had crept down the stairs, she settled the little girls on the benches which she and Edward shoved together for an uneven bed, and she felt gratitude to Will for his foresight. Not everyone had such a safe place, she knew full well, and on such a night, she wished they did.

Annie tried not to think of Will and Miles, now almost surely in the midst of what could blind them, kill them—if the hail was large—and craze their horses. She tried to remember that Will was as good a rider as any man she'd ever seen.

Above them, wind was beginning to whistle through the vent pipe. Rain splattered against it and the strong, wooden door, and repeated, terrible thunder cracks told her that the lightning was very close.

It was such a violent storm it would not last long, she thought, and that was the case. Yet before it finally moved on, leaving hours of steady but unthreatening rain in its wake, water on the cave floor was ankle deep. That had never happened before. Annie sat on the table beside the lantern, her feet on the corner of a bench. She watched the soft light give her children golden, shadowed, angel faces. Lydia frowned over her thumb, Tennessee curved around Emily, and Edward slept with his head on his arm, like his father.

It was calm, now, the thunder receding east into the distance, water trickling or dripping clearly here and there, no longer rushing, the peepers calling. She thought of Roaring Hollow, and she wished again that she could see its green stairs and its sweet, sweet laurel, like pink and white dotted Swiss, that she could feel its peace. She did not want to wake the children. It seemed to her that they were safer there and then than they had ever been or would ever again be. Not until dawn funneled a pink glow down the pipe did she stir to go up into the world.

She left the children sleeping and pushed the heavy, soaked, oak door open. Grass was down in every low-lying patch, and new small ditches in the yard were criss-crossed by the trails of worms driven above ground. It had rained a great deal and very hard, but they had no damage. The sky was shining clear, the morning was fresh, and when Doll saw Annie, she nickered hello from the corral.

As Annie turned toward her, she saw Pet, her head down, her left forefoot resting unnaturally straight in front of her, one rein dangling, the other gone.

39

Miles found Will on the town-side of the creek, twisted very near the water but not in it, below a steep embankment which dropped from a small, protected bend where deer frequently bedded. Perhaps Will had mistaken the crossing as he returned in the rain. Perhaps he had tried to urge Pet where she could not go. The embankment appeared to have caved in, but Miles couldn't tell, because of water and mud, if that had been natural or caused by a struggling horse. Perhaps deer had spooked the horse, and she had bolted and fallen, throwing Will over the embankment. Her leg was badly strained, and the broken rein was still in Will's hand. They couldn't account for where he was, and they were never to know.

What they did know was that the fall was violent, breaking Will's neck and leg, nearly burying him in mud. "I don't imagine he even knew what happened, Annie," Miles said as he sat in the kitchen, his big hand, gray with mud, over his eyes.

He and Claude, who had met them coming, had laid Will in the surgery. She was glad they had not taken him to the funeral parlor. There was time for that.

Now, she had to reassure Miles. He was, himself, nearly unrecognizable with mud caking his clothes to his body. He had crawled down the bank to drag Will away from the water, then walked in the mud beside his own horse to bring Will home. Shaking until he could not hold the coffee Annie gave him, he moaned, partly in horror, she supposed, at what he had just done. Not many can easily bear the touch of the dead, and he and Claude had fairly had to embrace Will as they brought him into the surgery and straightened him on the operating table. "If the baby just hadn't of come last night, Annie. If it would just of waited. I feel so bad that I had to come for him on such a night."

Though she understood what he was feeling and his need to say it, Annie herself felt some impatience with it—though not with Miles. As a matter of fact, she didn't want him to say much of anything, not to her or about Will. She interrupted with what she knew to be true: "Will loved children more than anything, Miles. It would have taken an army to stop him from going with you last night. He would never begrudge you, and neither do I."

Facing his grief, she knew she was much calmer than he would expect when he would finally recover himself enough to observe or think. Two hours lay between her seeing Pet and watching Will's little procession slowly enter her range of vision. She had known beyond any doubt that Will was hurt, and she suspected the worst. She knew he was far too strong and determined a man to let the horse escape him unless he was very badly hurt or unconscious. And she had not been able, not all through the night, to lose the feelings of dread that had washed over her when he had ridden into that cloud. So when she had found Pet, hurt and feverish, her sense of helplessness and oppression had only deepened.

Her stomach had coiled. She had been afraid. She knew that, but she had felt no panic. She didn't know what they would do if Will was dead. He and she were a part of the little town, the community, though certainly that was mostly a matter of Will's services. She knew her own friendships had lapsed in ways she couldn't control. She did feel some security in remembering how people respected Will and depended on him. Martin and Claude would advise her. They would help her know what was best to do.

But the children—the children....

Before Annie had gone to awaken them, she had ridden Doll— without saddle or bridle, the filly sashaying around them all the way—to Claire's and told her what was happening.

"Oh, my God, child," Claire had cried out. Then in the same breath, she was yelling, "Claude! Claude! Get down here! Come this minute! The Fairchilds have got trouble!"

She turned her red, round, Swedish face to Annie, tears rushing down her cheeks, and began to take over. "Send the children here, Annie. Send them right over. No matter what, you'll need some time and space. Edward can bring them."

"But Lydia...," Annie started to say.

Claire interrupted. "Liddie's just fine for me and Edward. Don't you worry. We'll do fine. Bring them right over, now." And she was pushing Annie out the door while she was pulling Claude down the stairs.

When Annie had awakened the babies, they were stiff and a little cranky. Lydia started crying the instant Annie slipped her arms under her, and she wouldn't let her mother help the others at all. Screaming and purple, she started the day as she always did, only this morning, Annie didn't try to quiet her. Somehow it seemed fitting. In the house, with Edward spooning her soft egg to her, she bent her head to the side like an imp and smiled at him, tears still silvering her long, black lashes.

He grinned over at their mother with good humor. "Liddy is really beautiful, ain't she, Mama?"

And Annie had used that as her way to begin. "Yes, she is, Edward. She looks very much like you did when you were two years old. Can you believe that?"

He liked to hear it. Despite Lydia's tantrums and really dreadful temper, he adored her and could handle her better than either Will or Annie.

"She is going to need you special today, sweetheart." Annie went on with it, knowing Tennessee would listen and help her brother. "I think your Papa had an accident last night. Pet was at the barn this morning, and he is late."

Edward and Tennessee straightened and turned toward her, frowning and holding their breath. Emily was quiet, but she didn't understand. Annie did the best she knew how. "I think instead of doing the chores this morning you children should run over to Mrs. Wilson's house. She is expecting you. That way I'll be free to help your Papa when he comes."

"Is he all right, Mama?" they asked together.

She didn't look at them. They were only eight and ten years old. What should she say? "I don't know. I truly do not know. But I am worried. You are a big boy and girl, now, and you must be strong for both your Papa and me."

Tennessee's eyes were filling, but Annie did not go to her. She thought that might make it harder.

"Remember how much he loves you. Think of that. I promise that I will come to tell you as soon as I can. What will be best is for you to help Mrs. Wilson. Try to play nicely with Lydia and Emily. I'll come for you as soon as I can."

They did as she asked. Very quietly, walking in the wet grass, they had made their way with Edward carrying Lydia on his shoulders, Tennessee and Emily holding hands.

So when Claude had headed west to look for Will, Annie had time to prepare the kitchen and surgery for what she dreaded. She built up the fire and heated as much water as she could. She made bandages of several sizes and got towels down. She readied fresh clothes for Will. She found herself hesitating to get out his black suit, but she did—and his black boots. She did not hurry, but she seemed to think of a hundred things to do. She cleaned his hair brush, and she polished his boots, only once crying as she found herself buffing one toe so hard and long her arm ached as her mind pictured—without her willing it—how his brown ones had looked that day he'd ridden up to the cabin for her. After she had prepared for every possibility she could think of, she made coffee, then paced between the table and the door to watch for Claude—or Will—or anyone to come over the west horizon.

As it had turned out, Miles had left his house around six to check on Will. He told Annie later that Will had insisted on returning home after the baby was born—without any complications at all, a big, healthy boy. By that time, the worst of the storm was long past, and only the rain continued. Pet had done much better than Will expected on the way there, he had told Miles, and he did not worry about riding home in the aftermath of the storm. He had left around midnight. Just after dawn, walking beside Will's body slung across his horse, Miles had met Claude about two miles west of town.

After they had brought Will in, Claude left to go to the undertaker, then to return home to Claire and all the children. Miles had stayed with Annie. Now she wished him to be gone. She appreciated his care, but she knew she had only a little time before the news would spread, before people would be coming by, before the children would need her.

Perhaps sensing that, Miles staggered to his feet like a sick man as Annie tried to thank him. He did not mount his horse while she was watching. Instead, he walked, half stumbling in the mud, still leading the horse behind him.

40

In the still time between their bringing him and coming for him, Annie was with Will. It did not seem to her that he was, in death, much more distant from her than he had often been.

At first, guided by that, she did what she thought was necessary. Not wanting anyone else to see him dirty, she began by wrapping a soft, wet towel around his head to moisten the mud, especially in his beard and hair. But then she sudsed her own hands to rub his. She loved to wash the children's hands that way—as her mother had washed her "paddies." It was the softest touch she knew, and it was what she was suddenly pleased to do for him.

From the beginning, she had admired his hands with their long, elegant fingers, slim, unwrinkled, clean. She had come to love their touch, and as she lifted them now, stiff and unresponsive, what she felt as anger rose in her throat. Nonetheless, she rubbed them gently, unbuttoning his cuffs and pushing his jacket sleeves up so she could wash above his wrists, running her fingers down his and over his palms which were less callused than her own. Very carefully she cleaned his nails, seeing more clearly than ever that they were still perfect, none deformed or split like her father's, all curved precisely and smoothly like delicate stones in flowing water. She laid her cheek on his left hand but only for an instant. Indeed, the chill against her face did not seem unfamiliar.

When she washed his face, she was aware of how she had trained herself not to look directly at him, of how little she knew the lines there which formed the scowls or smiles her life was directed by.

Unlike his hands, his forehead was deeply creased, and those and the frown lines between his eyes were unforgiving, even in death.

While his left eye was closed, his right was open to show the glass eye he had not lost in the fall. It, too, was muddy, and of all that she did, only trying to clean that eye made her tremble. She attempted to close the lid, but when she removed her hand, it instantly slipped open again. She tightened her lips and persisted, finally trying to hold the lid shut with a dampened, folded towel.

Having washed his hands and face and combed his hair and beard, she found that she was unwilling to leave him in his muddy clothes. They, more than his stillness, made him seem foreign to her, and she set about, with some haste, now, removing them. She tried, at first, to unbutton his shirt and trousers, but the material was damp and stubborn. Shivering a little, she discovered that she was slightly afraid. Never before had she undressed her husband. With another flash of pain and anger, she pulled hard at the material under the buttons, but they did not give. Without hesitation, she seized a scalpel. Using that and surgical scissors, she disrobed him, cutting the clothes and pulling them away, leaving, finally, only the backs on which he lay, those and his boots which she made no attempt to remove.

She pulled his arms across his chest as she washed him, still heating water as she needed it, changing cloths as they darkened. His broken leg she could not straighten. The fracture was compound, the bone protruding below the knee, jagged and split. There was little blood. Grim and silent, she bathed him, his chest and arms, his thighs, relaxed but hard, his sex, curled white and innocent in its dark nest.

Having finally done all she could, she stood by him, her hands quiet on his, wondering for the thousandth time how she could have made it better—not this ritual but their life. Her answer was always the same. No matter what she did, she knew it was always Narcissa, Narcissa he needed; Narcissa he wanted; Narcissa he loved as he fought against herself, frightening her away from him over and over and over.

At last she cried to him, "Oh, Will. You should have been my joy. You should have been my joy." For a moment, she lowered her head to his neck, pushing her face hard beneath his chin.

"My joy." Her voice had lowered to accusation as she straightened herself and looked at him, wiping her own face with the cloth in her hand. Then she covered him and went to sit in the kitchen.

41

The Brittsville cemetery was still small, perhaps twenty graves, most with soft limestone markers, some already weathering gray. A low fence around it kept cattle from grazing among them. Annie chose a little hilltop from which she could look north over meandering prairie and south over the river valley and far hills, one white road now weaving among them into the distance. Flutes and checks and gurgles of meadowlarks, dickcissels and red-winged blackbirds turned the silence into a busy, friendly accompaniment to swift flickers of red, yellow, black, and brown. All became parts of the mosaic of grass the southwest wind constantly rearranged against the tall, wide sky.

Most of the town was there, everyone who could walk. They touched the children's heads, patted Annie's shoulders. Kittie and Lucy embraced her, but they found few words. The people created a circle of tangible pity she and the children stood within. Even Lydia was good for the moment, interested, it seemed, by all the faces, all the eyes focused on her. She held Edward's hand or looked back over his shoulder when he carried her, singing her small, favorite threat to the world: "I bweaken de window, I weeal," which brought smiles to some faces now when it had usually brought her mother flying to remove rock or spoon from her as she pounded at any window she could reach.

All four children were handsome, Lydia, extraordinarily so. And Annie, startling in black, her hair caught up loosely, made them remember freshly how lovely and how young they had always thought her. Emily, tall for her age, graceful and brown as a thrush, stood by Tennessee who, rarely blinking, stared in anguish at the black casket.

"What a terrible, terrible shame," some said in profound sympathy. "Whatever will they do now?"

Many wept at the sad story, itself, others at the sight of the family, and some at the loss of a man they liked and depended on. Martin Britt looked grim. His wife on his arm, his children gathered around him, he stared at Annie, his heart aching for her.

Annie herself felt clear-headed. She was extremely focused on Will. While the preacher spoke of sacrifice and service to the community, she thought of the obsessions which kept him selfish, at least with her, his endless need to conceal what he was and what he felt most deeply, his refined ability to wear one face to them and another to her. Who would ever believe her if she told them?

At the same time, she acknowledged, as always she had, that the pain he caused her had very little to do with her. She still believed he had been honest in what he tried, that he had not lied to her mother.

"I know you wanted to build, Will, not destroy," she said to him while the preacher described Will's death as a dedication to life.

"He died because he would not refuse the cries of an unborn child," the Salina minister was saying.

Never having met Will, he had talked with neighbors and with Annie and was now doing the best he could. Most of the people there were moved by what he said.

"He loved the children. He will not be numbered among the unnumbered. He will not be among those who have perished as though they have not lived. He is not without a child to succeed him. He died because he was courageous enough to face a cyclone in order to bring a little baby into this world, a fine boy.

"He has four beautiful children of his own to spread knowledge of him. Here they stand, beloved of Jesus who said, 'Suffer the little children....'"

Annie wasn't actually listening. She was responding to the truth of what the preacher said. She was connecting it to the truth she knew and he could not—the reason why, as she had in misery framed it for eleven years, Will was as he was: "His first baby died because he shot a man in the back—his wife, his baby, his only love."

She caught her breath audibly, and Claire looked at her, expecting to see her weeping. She was not. Her face was calm.

"He loved her so much he never had room for any other woman," she thought. "Never—not even when he wanted to."

Old scenes tried to run through her mind, but she was able to ignore them, what he forced on her, her fear of his fists, his eye, the loneliness. She ignored it all and imagined, instead, his rocking Edward, loving his boy, then his girls, Tennessee, Emily and Lydia. She willed the pain away and, with the simplest act of heart, she forgave it.

"You couldn't help yourself any more than I could, Will," she said to him, lying stiff in his coffin. "I know that even if you never did."

She imagined him in the small, dark space. "And it is all right. It is all right. She must have been a fine woman, Will, for you to love her so much. I make you a promise. If this baby I carry is a girl child, I will name her for your love. I don't mind. I will call her Narcissa."

Part III: A Second Chance

"My life had stood a loaded gun."
—Dickinson

42

In the days following Will's funeral, Annie realized more surely than when he was alive how controlled by him and how afraid of him she had been. It was not that she did not grieve for him. A part of her did. She mourned for that good in him she had always believed in and looked for and often found. He was a part of her, and she felt maimed. She sat, holding herself, rocking back and forth in physical distress.

She felt even worse for the children, the two oldest, especially, as they sat stunned and silent or shaking and weeping. She found Tennessee huddled in Will's coat in front of his armoire. "It smells like Papa," she sobbed into the collar, and Annie could only kneel by her and stroke her hair. She had also felt an appalling helplessness looking at the papers in his desk and realizing that she hadn't the slightest notion of his business, his finances, not even what he actually owned. She could hardly bear to talk about it with Martin Britt and Claude—who were trying to help her sort it out.

But all that was balanced by a strange sense of lightness. She felt such relief sometimes that she had to sit down, as though the muscle and bone and weight had disappeared from her body. She would be hurrying at this or that, listening for his step, waiting for his shape to come into her sight, when she would realize that this would not happen. Her children were all with her. She was alone with them in the house. That was all and that would be all unless she decided differently. At the thought, she would sink in gratitude and ease. She did not have to be on guard. She did not have to be afraid. And that realization would become a wave of release that flowed from her heart through her arms and legs clear to her hands, her fingers, and her toes. She felt straighter and calmer and stronger than she ever before had. But she could hardly stand.

It was in the midst of one of those feelings when she heard a knock at the kitchen door. She managed to get to it, feeling weak but whole, and when she opened it, there stood July Winkler.

Julie had wasted no time returning to Brittsville once he got word of Will Fairchild's death. He had been surprised the morning Will had told him he'd be shot on sight if he ever set foot back in Brittsville. Julie knew he could outshoot Will anytime, but he had faced upset husbands before, and it wasn't his favorite pastime, so he had gone on back to Abilene. One town was pretty much like another to Julie, so he hadn't been much discommoded—except for Annie.

Annie was in Brittsville, and that did make a difference to him. She had mattered to him for years in ways he didn't like to dwell on. He was never willing to call it love, and sometimes he thought he couldn't get her off his mind just because he couldn't get her mind on him. But he couldn't deny he'd lost sleep over her. And he'd done all he knew to make her pay him attention. He would accidentally brush against her arm over by the pump where he'd help fill up the water glasses, and she'd move aside like it hadn't happened or didn't amount to enough to say, "Excuse me."

When he found out she liked prairie flowers, he'd gather some for her, and she'd say, "Those are beautiful, Julie. Do you know what they are?" And she'd put them in a glass on the kitchen table where the hired hands ate. It was as though they were interesting but not personal.

Of course, he didn't know what they were, and he didn't care what they were. All he wanted was for her to notice him or give him some sign that he wasn't just a bug—the way Fairchild made him feel at first. But there was never a moment when she gave him any attention she didn't give August and the other hands. He knew Will had no cause to fire him—"unless he could read my mind," Julie had told his brother, "and the bastard wasn't that smart."

What Will had seen, that first summer, was that Julie was the good worker Martin Britt had said he was. Whether it was chinking the cabin, digging the well, or shaping sandstone for the house, Julie worked hard, faster and better than anyone else. In September, Will had hired him full time, and when Will brought the Herefords in during May of '66, Julie soon became his foreman.

Julie was struck by the notion of raising purebred stock, and he wanted to work with them. The bull had a pedigree, the first Julie had seen, and he argued from then on against the other hands who said the low-slung, red cattle with white faces were stupid, that face flies would blind them, that they wouldn't make it through the winter. He began to listen more carefully to what Fairchild said—that Herefords were good stock for an area that was growing because they produced such quantities of meat. So he agreed it made sense to build the little herd a shelter—even though the other men guffawed at it like a joke while they built a small shed open to the east just south of the bunkhouse in the south pasture.

A natural spring there provided plenty of water. Folks said it had never frozen or dried up, so they built down slope from it and didn't worry about well or pump. After a time, Julie also found that the purebreds were agreeable to work with, especially if you were used to running longhorns—which were skittish and could be downright dangerous if you weren't careful. "Them Herefords is plumb gentle," he'd argue. "They ain't hardly no trouble at all if you don't come up yellin' at 'em or goosin' 'em. You can just ease 'em along."

When Will saw Julie's patience and skill, especially with the cattle, he offered him the foreman's job at ten dollars a month, room and board—including a noon meal at the big house, clothes, horse, and tack. Julie figured permanent access to Annie was also, unbeknownst to Fairchild, a part of the arrangement, and he signed on willingly.

Julie had held his tongue, bided his time, and worked hard, but he didn't succeed with Annie. He tried everything he could think of, being late for dinner, being early for dinner, coming up unexpected in the morning or the afternoon or late evening, but she'd have help or a baby with her, and she just plain gave him no encouragement of any kind. He finally gave up and made his peace with Miss Ellie, but he never stopped looking at Annie and wanting her. It made him feel half mean towards her sometimes—and the children he ended up having to deal with, too.

They were all right as far as kids go, he knew, but he wasn't much of a hand with children, and these were always underfoot. He never knew a woman to keep her young ones so near to her all the time.

Julie thought the boy was smart, but he wasn't a smart aleck, Julie had to admit. When he was little, Julie would ask him innocent-like questions: whether he knew his colors and what color dress did his Mama have on today? What color nightdress did she have? Did he like his Mama to rock him? Did he help her when she was nursing the baby? But Julie never gained much satisfaction that way. For nearly eight years he put up with it until the Captain lit on him that summer in '73 with a pack of lies.

When he talked about it with Auggie, he said, "I don't reckon I should have been too surprised that he was a jealous son-of-a-bitch. They never did have no friends. Except for the Wilsons, I don't know who ever set foot in that fancy parlor.

"He wasn't no talker, either, except for tellin' people what to do. He must have been scared to death she'd set her eyes on some real man."

And though he didn't go back to Brittsville, he said anything he wanted to when the hands came into Abilene. He didn't say he'd had Annie, but he hinted that she might have been willing if things had been a little different. With no reason to doubt him, his friends added a detail here and a detail there until they had a nice story about meetings in the storm cave. Julie hoped it would get back to the doctor, and he liked to think about it himself. So it didn't take him long to return to Brittsville when he found out Fairchild was dead. He hoped Annie would be needing him in more ways than one.

It was about four weeks after the funeral when Annie found him at her door, a big smile on his tanned face, his hat in his hands. "Hello, Mrs. Annie," he said. "I reckon I'm the last person you ever expected to see at your door, but I heard about your loss, and I come to pay my respects."

Annie didn't think anything for a moment, then all of it flooded back over her. She was struck with embarrassment and maybe a tinge of fear that he stood there in front of her house. Her face flushed.

But just as quickly, she remembered that she never had cause for shame, and neither did Julie. She could see only his friendly, open face, and she felt happy to welcome him. Shifting Lydia to her hip and stepping aside, she said, "Well, for heaven's sake, Julie. It *is* a surprise to see you—and a nice one, too. Come in!"

"Is this your baby?" he asked right away. "I ain't seen her before," and he took Lydia out of Annie's arms and raised her high in the air.

"She's sure a pretty little thing," he said, tossing her and catching her, a little to his own surprise.

Lydia was giggling and kicking. Will played with her that way, and she loved it. Annie was flustered because she wasn't sure Julie would handle the child right, and she didn't want to embarrass him or end Lydia's fun. She could turn tyrant in an instant.

But then he caught her firmly and held her out to her mother. "Yes, ma'am," he said. "She's a right pretty little girl. She looks like you, Annie."

To her astonishment, Annie could feel tears starting. It seemed to be the way he said her name, without any irony or distance attached to it, and he managed to make it sound like music. She felt something sweet and admiring coming to her, and she hadn't been prepared for that.

She turned back toward the parlor, and he followed her. "I've come to offer my help, too, Annie, if you'll take it. I can't say there was any love lost between me and the doctor, but we learned how to farm and tend them Herefords together, and I reckon I'm someone who can do you some good right now, if you're willin'."

After all that had happened, and, worse, after all the gossip Will had caused when he fired Julie, Annie wasn't sure she should even talk to him. But the truth was another matter. The truth was that she wanted to talk to him. She knew full well how much she needed his help. Her conversations with Martin and Claude already showed her some of the complications. Annie was not very good with figures, but she was reasonably sure she owed money she didn't have, and she had no idea what to do about it.

She was also fretting about getting daily work done. Neighbors had tried to help with hay and the stock, but they couldn't do it forever, even if they knew what needed done, and the hands were, it seemed to Annie, working shorter days. They knew she didn't have ready cash to pay them, and she knew she couldn't expect them to work for nothing. She figured they would be leaving, and, again, she didn't know what to do. As she and Julie talked, she understood how much she needed his help, and she was much relieved to have him back.

"Julie," she said, "I don't know what to do first or if anything is being done right. If you want it, you've got your old job back right this minute," and they shook hands on it, both of them smiling.

As the days went on, he seemed to be an answer to questions she didn't know she had. He stepped right in to the farm work, and she knew he kept it going. "You got good men, Annie," he told her, "but they ain't too willin' to get things done without they got somebody to organize 'em. Seems like after I left, the Doctor, he seen to it himself pretty much, and now you ain't got nobody around to keep things movin'. They's a hay crop near ready, fences to mend, and cattle to separate."

She could see he was right, and she could feel the difference his presence made to the hands. Though two had left, August and Ray had stayed on, hopeful that Annie could pay them with fall sales of beef and wheat. Without a man there to manage, though, they wouldn't have stayed those extra months with no wages being paid. Julie encouraged them, and they gave him a chance.

By August, he had made the farm seem orderly and productive again, and he was also taking all his meals with the family. He was always cheerful, and Annie felt herself beginning to look forward to mealtime and their conversations about the work. He seemed willing to help her in every way, even with clearing the table and sometimes entertaining Lydia when the feisty little girl would permit it.

He started bringing Annie wildflowers again, and she remembered, with a changed sense of it, that he had brought them before. These times, she met his dark, eager eyes with her own, and her smile made him laugh out loud. "You always was the prettiest woman I ever seen, Annie," he said, and she didn't flush or try to hide her pleasure.

One September night after the girls were in bed and Edward was in Will's surgery reading, Julie came up behind her at the sink. She knew he was there. Her breath caught, and her head went right back against his shoulder as he kissed her neck and put his hands on her breasts.

"I love you, Annie," he said, and his lips touched her skin when he talked.

Then her head fell forward, and her shoulders moved against his chest.

"It's real simple for me," he said. "I love you, and I want you to be mine."

She couldn't breathe right at all. What she wanted was to turn and squeeze herself clear through him.

But she knew there was more than him and her to consider, and she knew she was the one who would have to do the considering. "Oh, Glory!" she heard herself saying. "This feels so good. I must be falling in love with you, too." And she covered his hands with hers so they'd stay where they were. "But we have to think. Are you asking me to marry you?"

He was silent for a moment, then he ran his teeth up the big muscle from her shoulder to her neck.

"Damn right I am, Annie," he said, breathing behind her ear, and he sounded as though he meant it.

"And the children?"

He seemed easy enough with the two little girls, but Edward and Tennessee hung back from him. Annie knew it was partly because he was where their Papa had been, and he couldn't begin to fill Will's place for them. That was to be expected. But she also remembered how Edward had disliked working with Julie, and she thought Edward understood why Will had fired him. She had talked some with them about Julie's coming back to help, but it was very hard, and Edward was not happy about it. She knew, as well, that it was much too soon. They needed more time to grieve for Will and to adjust to his absence.

But she did not. What she wanted was Julie—and some assurance from him that he would try to understand the older children's difficulties, that he wouldn't feel angry or try to force them. He needed to court them even if he didn't her. He said he saw what she was getting at.

"I know them younguns loved their daddy plenty. Mister Edward, especially. He wanted to be just like him, I think. I wouldn't never want to try to take his place with 'em, Annie. I would try to treat 'em fair and polite-like. And maybe I could help 'em learn a few things I know—like ropin' or shootin'. I ain't a total bust, you know."

She had to giggle when he said that; it was so plain and honest. And she did turn around to him then. She put both arms around his neck and kissed him good and proper. They were both trembling when they stepped apart.

"I have to tell you something," she said, shaking her head. She had remembered the baby.

He was a little shocked when Annie told him she was expecting another child, but he didn't falter much. "Well," he said. "I reckon one more won't make that much difference. It's quite a litter, Annie, and I ain't lyin' when I tell you babies scare the daylights outa me. But you're what I want, and I'll do my best by your children."

She knew he meant it. She thought he looked so bewildered and handsome all at once that she couldn't keep herself away from him.

Later, when Edward went upstairs, she and Julie moved back to the parlor. She closed the door behind them, and Julie turned to her. Clasping her hands in his, he raised them up gently and held them back against the door, lifting her breasts to him, pushing her up and back softly and slowly. He did everything slowly at first. "I want this to last forever, Annie," he whispered, teasing her with his lips.

But they couldn't manage that. They were both too eager, and soon they were on the floor. After a little while, he lay on his back, looked down at his quivering self, and smiled up at her. "Come on, Annie," he said. "Mount up."

He made them both laugh, and she didn't wait long to accept his invitation. Straddling him and taking him in her hands, she eased down on him. They were both moaning in whispers.

They tried to stay still again a little while, it was so fine, but they couldn't. It was too strong between them. Soon they rolled over, and Julie began to help her, never taking his eyes off hers. "You are so beautiful," he said. "Beautiful, beautiful, beautiful." He said it faster and harder as they strained together, and he stayed until she melted.

"Now it's my turn, you pretty little thing," he grinned at her. "I've been dreamin' of this for ten years, Annie."

She loved moving with him, feeling her insides pull him to her until he, like she, had to give way.

He stroked her face and kissed her eyes and nose. She ran her teeth along his jaw and fit her mouth over the lump in his neck. He tasted so good. It felt so good. She could hardly wait until they could do it again.

43

Julie liked everything there was about Annie—except her children, the endless work on her farm, which he found out had become his, and the debts. She made him glad to start the day with her smiles and kisses, and he liked it fine to walk barefoot on carpet or to snooze in the big, deep bed.

But Annie seemed to him like a jack-in-the-box. The sun wasn't any more than up when Lydia, who was three, would let out a howl: "Mama! Mamaaa!" From that distance, he thought she sounded like a cat you'd pinch the tail of good and hard. He could hear the other girls, especially Tennessee, shushing her and walking with her, singing to her, but Lydia wasn't about to shush until Annie got up to care for her.

And he hated the diapers.

"Lydia is hard to train," Annie told him, and he saw that she tried. But Lydia refused to use her little chair, and when she'd emerge from behind the rocker, smelling bad and yelling for someone to change her, he was repulsed and angry. How someone that size could run a household was beyond him. He thought she was a spoiled little hellion who kept them all in an uproar and who needed paddling about twenty times a day.

When he thought about the next one on its way, he could feel himself resenting it, too.

Every day started out the same, and Lydia didn't let up until she was in the bed between them. Sometimes even that didn't stop her. Close up, Julie decided she sounded like a hog caller, and after a while, he would get up and go chore without even a cup of coffee. He didn't like to think of her grown-up—or of all the years it would take to get her there. She was the prettiest little girl he had ever seen, but she was too mean-tempered and selfish for him to begin to like, and she was always right there between Annie and him.

The baby that was on its way was a different kind of problem. He had seen Annie big with the other children, too, but he wasn't living with her, then, always watching her grow bigger and finally too awkward to do what she wanted—which included making proper love to him. They managed to find different ways, and she'd had plenty of practice, he discovered. But later, he didn't like it if she couldn't, and after Narcissa was born, he didn't like all the milk. He'd heard some men say they liked making love to nursing mothers, but he wasn't one of them. Several times he thought of Ellie, but he didn't go to her. It was Annie he wanted, but he couldn't have her half as much as he needed or the way he liked.

After Narcissa's birth, Julie never thought of her as another reminder of Will. And she was a cute enough little girl. But he didn't have feelings for her the way Annie hoped he would. The older two he could talk to and joke around with some, and he didn't mind them—though he could tell they were more polite to him than they would have been had they liked him. Emily was usually off by herself. She could read when she was four, and he knew she was awfully smart. But they didn't pay much attention to one another. She did what she could with Lydia and the baby, but she and Julie went their own ways, which was fine with him.

The rest wasn't much better for him; in fact, it was worse. The work never let up, especially after Ray left, and Julie and August had all of it to do. Annie was worried about money from the time of Will's death, but Julie hadn't even considered having to pay off loans. He had always worked for wages, and he lived within his means, eating less if he lost at gambling, enjoying restaurant steaks and whiskey when he could. He'd never owned anything of value except his horse, and he had never been inside a land office or a bank. Now, faced with bills for doctor's tools he couldn't read the names of, for land, bathtubs, cattle and clothes, he realized that without daily earnings of the sort Will had made, he and Annie would never be able to make the payments.

"I didn't sign on for this," he said to himself, "paying somebody else's expenses when you don't know what they are and you don't like that somebody, and the son-of-a-bitch is dead anyhow."

But Annie was afraid, and he wanted to help her. He had said he would. So they found their way to where he least wanted to go, Martin Britt's office in the bank.

Martin had not yet spoken in great detail with Annie about Will's finances. At first, he had wanted to wait a decent time before laying out for her what he feared. Then when July Winkler had returned, he, like most others in town, faulted Annie, and he wanted to avoid her. The old gossip had started again, and people who had given Annie their sympathy and help after Will's death found it easy to revert to old thoughts about her being distant—or involved with Julie the way the doctor had suspected. The marriage worsened the matter. "It's too soon," many said. "They couldn't hardly wait for him to cool in his grave," others said.

Claire had tried to help Annie deal with it early on. "Annie," she had said, peeling potatoes while Annie fed Emily and Lydia, "it's likely none of my business, but having Julie around is makin' people talk some again, and I figure if you don't know about it, maybe you should."

"What do you mean, Claire?" Annie asked. She only knew she had stopped feeding Lydia because the little girl began whimpering. "What do you mean, 'People are talking again'?"

"Well, you know there was some rumors makin' their way around after Julie left. It was sudden, you know. And everybody knew he pretty much ran Will's farm. I heard it took two or three hands to replace him. So that give some substance to the talk.

"You know Claude and me, we didn't believe that at all, but, Annie, folks is funny. Sometimes I think they try to stir up things just to get themselves interested in livin'."

"So they are saying that now Julie's back he's in my bed, are they?"

Claire didn't look at Annie, but she nodded. "I don't know that anyone would blame you so much, Annie, if it wasn't so soon—or if they didn't think maybe Will had some cause earlier."

Annie felt such an anger rise in her—not at Claire, but at people who made up stories, then judged by them, people who took sides when they didn't have any notion of the truth, people who wanted her to fit their versions of her without paying any mind to what she wanted. Of course, that all got tangled up with what she knew they didn't know, what she couldn't explain. She finally just lay her head down on the table, tears rolling off her face, and she couldn't even help Liddy when she started banging the table and screaming for more.

Claire abandoned the potatoes and came to them. "There, there, child," she said, and to Annie, not Lydia.

Annie had to laugh a little at that, and when Claire understood, so did she. So she sat down and helped the girls while Annie went to the sink to finish the potatoes. Finally she found her voice.

"Well. It's true, Claire," Annie told her. "Julie *is* here, and I *do* love him. In fact, we're going to get married."

"It's awful quick after Will," Claire said.

"We know it's soon, and we know there'll be talk. But we can't help that. It's true that Julie has always loved me. Will was wrong to think there was anything between us, but it's true that Julie loved me."

"Nobody will believe it, Annie."

That stung Annie, but she felt stubborn and certain. "Then that's too bad," she said. "But we can't do anything about what other people think. We can't live our lives for them. I'm sick of living my life for somebody else.

"You know, Claire, that things weren't right between Will and me. I never said anything then, and I never will again. But you know that losing him isn't as awful for me as they think."

Claire was nodding, and Annie saw tears in her eyes, too.

"Of course it's too soon, and the children, Edward and Tennessee, anyway, are going to have a hard time with it. But, Claire, Julie loves me and wants to care for me. And I have strong feelings for him, too. Of course he's not Will, but...."

She didn't finish that out loud, but her heart did, "I don't want Will back." She went on. "And Claire, there's something else. I'm going to have another baby. I've got to have help."

Claire had looked astonished at that, and again she nodded.

"Julie knows how everything goes, Claire, and he can operate all the machinery. He can keep things up and going. I need him, and he's loved me forever. We're going to get married."

She said it the second time with more resolution.

Claire wiped the girls' faces, lifted them to the floor, and came over to Annie. "Child," she said, her arms around Annie who was dripping water on the floor. "You do what you think is right and proper. People will talk no matter what, but sooner or later, they'll likely get on around it. And no matter what, I'll always think of you as my own child."

But other people had been much less understanding, Martin Britt among them. He had refused to sort out all his feelings when Annie married Julie, but among them were anger with her and jealousy of her new husband. At Will's funeral and later, at the house when he had gone to talk with her and to get Will's papers, he had wanted to take her in his arms, just hold her and comfort her.

He had tried to tell himself that it was a fatherly interest and feeling because he knew he was at least twenty years her senior, and he knew he loved his wife. But he wasn't good at lying to himself, and when he later found himself being consciously attentive to Lizzie, he understood that he was in trouble. Then, before he could get those feelings straight, Julie had returned, and Martin had a whole new set of emotions to struggle with. This time he felt disbelief—that Annie had not turned to him the way he knew he wanted her to, that she had actually chosen a ne'er-do-well cowboy. And when he couldn't stop thinking of their being together, he discovered that he would like to squish Julie. He was sorry he had ever recommended him to Will. So by the time Annie and Julie finally walked into his office, he felt stiff and unpleasant.

Julie thought he looked like he had a poker up his ass, and the papers he kept shoving toward Julie, leaving Annie out of it as though she had no business there, made no sense to him. Later on, when he talked with Auggie about it, Julie, still astonished, said, "God-damn if it didn't turn out them bills *was* my responsibility! The way he saw it was that when I married Annie I took on her debts along with everything else. I ast him, 'How the hell am I supposed to pay off seven hunderd dollars? I ain't even had no wages since I come back here.'

"'Well,' he said, all proper and dignified-like. He wasn't even lookin' at me but at them damn papers. 'Sometimes when people rush into things, there can be repercussions.'

"That son-of-a-bitch."

Auggie nodded. "I'll bet he was a-crowin' inside because you was in trouble."

But Britt did give Julie a new loan. He put a larger mortgage on the house and said Julie could start payments after the wheat was threshed and he'd sold some cattle. But then he said, "This is a sizeable loan, though, and I'm not certain that extending it and adding in the interest to boot is ultimately going to help you."

Neither Julie nor Annie understood, and Julie finally had to ask.

"Well, I'm suggesting that perhaps the best solution to the immediate problem is not to continue the loan at this amount. If you were to deed back to the bank that last eighty Fairchild purchased, that would take care of much of this until the fall, and it would substantially reduce that payment." Then Britt finished with a recommendation that sounded more like an order to Julie. "My best advice would be to sell some of the pasture, also, and perhaps the new reaper. And you should not expect to hire any hands back. Frankly, I don't see how you can do anything else without the income Doctor Fairchild relied on when he entered into these obligations."

"Well, *frankly*," Julie said to himself, "I don't give a damn." He wasn't after a south eighty or a north forty. He wasn't in any competition. It seemed way too much for him, and he could hardly believe what he had gotten himself into.

But when he looked at Annie, scared and needful, her breasts rising and falling with her breath, he figured he had to try. When he signed the note, he was glad that, even though he couldn't keep right on the line, at least he didn't have to make an X in front of a man he thought was smirking at him.

Julie couldn't tell if Britt was helping them or robbing them, but at least it was settled, and he didn't have to sign for any more money. He told Annie he guessed they had less to pay for and less to lose, but neither one of them was sure they had done right. Julie figured it meant one thing for sure: they were not going to keep any heifers to try to increase the herd.

For him, the whole transaction went to show the real problem. He never did know the best thing to do. He was not a decision-maker. He never had been and never wanted to be. He realized that you need to be brought up to it or have some friends willing to help you out and talk things over. But he didn't know anything about families or farming, and it was clear to him that people weren't exactly falling over themselves to give him helpful hints.

It seemed to Julie that these papers and debts and signatures put a whole new complexion on his life with Annie, and he began to feel a new kind of fear. He didn't know how to sell land or a reaper, and, suddenly, without the boys to help Auggie and him, tending cows and farming didn't seem to be nearly enough. It was plenty of work, that was sure, but it wasn't enough. Nothing seemed to be enough. And not only did that take the fun out of almost everything, it made him feel a little sick to his stomach. He was worried for the first time in his life.

He did all he could. By the last of October, the wheat and oats were shocked and a nice hay crop was in. The cattle were fat, and they had nine calves. When the time came, he made that first payment, and for the moment, he felt some relief about it. He liked showing Martin Britt he had no reason to look down his nose at them.

But Julie felt worn down. Everything was up to him, him and Auggie—who actually didn't care about it one way or another. He was just as likely to leave the plow in the ground and take off to see the girls as he was to feed the horses.

Sometimes Julie would rather have gone with him than follow the damn mules back and forth, back and forth. He hated that. But they didn't have money to pay any other hands, so it was him or nobody. As long as it was good between him and Annie, he was willing to do his best. But when they couldn't be together and the children took her attention for everything from eating to reading to her making clothes for them, he got tired, tired and mad inside. Sometimes he and Auggie would come up for their noon meal, and Tennessee would be cooking for them. He wouldn't even get to see Annie until supper.

44

The following year in late summer, Annie first thought it was starting to rain, just a scattering of big drops before the late afternoon storm really broke. But then she heard Tennessee and Emily screaming, and she ran outside as fast as she could. The girls were striking at their faces and kicking, and the moment Annie stepped out the door, she began doing the same. Grasshoppers were everywhere, hitting her face like sleet, clinging to her hair and hands. She could feel them under her skirts on her legs. Actually, the air seemed to be full of snow. Like a huge, silver cloud, the hoppers were flying over with some few falling before the awful blizzard hit.

A single grasshopper is nothing, and these hoppers were very small. One of any insect is usually innocent enough. But thousands or millions at once—and they become monstrous. It's like a nightmare to see them and to hear them, let alone to feel them on you.

Almost before Annie could get the girls in the house, the ground was covered, and more and more hoppers were dropping like hail. She could hear them hitting the ground, the trees. Before her eyes, the yard became a crawling, chewing mass. The day darkened, and she could hear them clicking—everywhere.

Annie stripped the girls right there in the kitchen and set them to brushing the hoppers off one another or catching those that hopped or flew away. The girls couldn't open the door to throw the hoppers out without letting in a dozen more. Finally they began killing hoppers with their shoes, and the floor grew wet and ugly.

Annie didn't know what to do—or that she should try to do

anything—until Julie and August and Edward came riding up hard, yelling, "Come on! Come on! We've got to cover the garden. Bring quilts. Bring coats. Hurry up! Come on!"

"I can't, Mama," Tennessee pleaded. "I'm scared!"

"Of course not, Tennie. You don't have to. Go dress yourself and Emily. Tell stories. Try not to wake Lydia. Don't be afraid. It's just a lot of bugs. They can't hurt you."

But Annie wasn't sure of that, and she certainly didn't want to go back outside, herself. When she did, it was horrible. The ground and trees and buildings, everything was inches deep in the hoppers. Every step was soft and crunching. It sickened her to walk.

And covering the garden was like locking the fox in the chicken house. You could hear the chewing. Annie and the men straightway gave up.

Within two days, the hoppers had eaten everything, the corn, the potato vines, the beans, turnips. They ate the lettuce and cabbage first and the tomatoes last, but they ate everything. They ate the onions off below the ground. They ate the shocked grain, and they ate the watermelons, herbs and apples. They ate every leaf off every weed, every tree. They ate one another. Nothing was left except potatoes, and no one could stand to dig them because of the stink of rotting grasshoppers. Julie and Annie lost everything but the prairie grass, itself.

Of course, they weren't the only ones. Everybody in the area was grievously hurt, and some thought it was the hand of God punishing them. Many were so discouraged they were ready to leave.

Annie always believed that Martin Britt saved their town. He called for a general meeting, and he talked to the people, now numbering more than two hundred. He offered real help to keep them from being scared away.

"My friends," he said. "This is a terrible, terrible thing that has happened to us."

Annie saw for the first time that Britt was a powerful man. He had never seemed out of the ordinary to her before, but as he stood before the community, his strength and passion reached out to them and lifted them up, she felt. She was touched, and her fears lessened by the moment. She was a little surprised to think that this man was, in fact, their neighbor and, she felt strongly, their friend.

"The only thing I can think of that would be worse would be a fire or a tornado which would take our houses and maybe our lives, too. I know we're bent low."

The crowd hummed their agreement.

"But we can get through this. If we stick together and pledge to help one another, we can get through this. You know that we have worked together to carve this little town out of the wilderness. We have endured drought and Indians and ice storms. We must not fall victim to a bunch of inch-long vermin. We *will* not!"

He said it in such a way as to make some of them laugh a little, and he went on. "No, sir. We will not! We have all helped one another and newcomers in the past, and we will do it again, now. We are not dependent on the railroad or some Chicago corporation. We are a community, a town, not a bunch of strangers, not a bunch of individual, separate families without feelings for one another."

His eyes chanced to fall on Annie's face, and he felt a rush of pleasure and energy. He thought she looked as though she adored him, and he instantly forgave her everything. She became for him a kind of emblem of the needful assembled before him, and what he spoke took on an aura of love and gentleness they could nearly all feel.

"We have come here from all over—hundreds of miles, thousands of miles. We have shed blood here and buried our loved ones here. We will not leave them. We are like a family. We will not be broken up by a damned grasshopper."

More people sat up straighter, and some sent up a little cheer for Martin. He was right. Nobody wanted to leave. They were just scared and didn't know where to turn. He showed them.

"We'll start by taking stock of what we have—on the shelves of our kitchens and in our cellars—and we'll figure out what we've got to have to plant our crops, to take care of our animals, to get through the winter. Then the bank will make some long-term, no-interest loans, and we'll *get* what we've got to have.

"We can do this, ladies and gentlemen. We can do it by ourselves, if need be, and we will!"

Annie could actually see people relax and let themselves out a little. She did, and she reached for Julie's hand. He had not relaxed. "We already got a loan we can't pay off," he said. "What the hell are we gonna do with another'n?"

"Martin will help us, Julie," she said, and she felt confident it was so. "He wants us to stay."

"The hell he does," Julie muttered. "He'd like nothing better than to see us broke and him installed in that nice house he's took a new mortgage on."

She just squeezed Julie's hand, but he didn't squeeze hers back. Suddenly, she felt bad again.

It was too much for him, she knew. All of them—all the debt. He'd taken it on himself in a way she hadn't expected, and he'd worked harder than she thought he should to get the money for the payments. He would come in so tired and dirty she could hardly scrub him clean. He went to sleep, more than once, sitting in the warm water, his arms hanging down almost as copper as the tub.

But these hoppers. She and the men had to rake them into huge mounds and burn them. It was stinking, backbreaking labor.

Now, nobody wanted to buy their calves because nobody had feed for them or money to buy it. They managed to nearly give away some calves to neighbors for beef, but it wasn't enough for the cash they needed. They were forced to take out the new loans for seed and some grain for the animals. The governor had, after weeks, finally had it shipped in.

Then Julie had to plow and replant. It was an awful blow, and to his pride, too. Annie told him they could sell other land, try to ship the Herefords out. They could move to a different house and let Martin have theirs. She didn't care.

But he did. He especially liked those cattle, and he knew another house would be hard to find, even if he was willing to deed back theirs, which he wasn't. He did not want Martin Britt to have it. "Where the hell are the seven of us gonna light if we ain't here," he muttered at her.

Of course, she didn't know, but it seemed plain to her they weren't going to be in the big house much longer.

During the next weeks, he seemed to get more tired, and he was often cross with the children and Annie. He was never threatening like Will. But he was worn out and exasperated. It seemed to Annie as though he wanted to quarrel with everybody. Most of all, though, she thought he was quarreling with himself.

45

Julie finished eating first and rocked back in the kitchen chair. He knew Tennessee was watching him, disapproval in her eyes, so he belched as loudly as he could and rubbed his belly. A shiver ran through him, and he rubbed a little lower. "Jesus! I'm needin' me some."

"Why don't you and your little lady take the afternoon off," Auggie grinned. "I could stand makin' a visit down to Ellie's, myself."

Julie shrugged. "Hell, she's always got a kid hangin' on her."

Tennessee knew they were saying things they shouldn't, and she thought about leaving the room. But Emily and Lydia were there, too, and she was responsible for them. She felt angry that the men would talk like that not only in front of her but where the little girls could hear, too. She stared at Julie, not even realizing she was frowning, but feeling more dislike for him than usual.

He knew what she was thinking, and he felt just enough arousal and irritation of his own to want to keep it going a little. "What's the matter with you?" He rocked back. "You got a piece you wanna speak?"

Emily perked up at that. "Liddie and me know pieces we can speak!" Both of them were eager for the opportunity. Julie wasn't usually interested in listening to them.

"Do you now?" he laughed, and he cocked his head to one side. "What do you think, Auggie? Shall we hear their pieces? Well. Come on over here. Lydia, you set right up here on my lap, an' we'll hear little Miss Emily first. Then it'll be your turn."

Lydia wasn't often pleased to be held, but she did want to recite her poem, and Julie was making it fun. So she let him lift her, as he pushed back from the table, and turn her toward him.

She squirmed to sit sideways as Emily began, but he held her firmly and moved himself under her. Auggie saw his face come together.

"Jesus H. Christ, man," he laughed as Julie closed his eyes.

Auggie felt some twinges himself, and he picked up his horse whip and tapped his open palm.

Lydia knew only that she didn't like how she was being held or the prodding between her legs. Suddenly she didn't want to recite. She wanted down. "You stop that, Julie," she yelled at him, her black brows pulled together, her face red. "You put me down right now."

He didn't want to put her down, but he also didn't actually want this to continue. So he swung her to the floor, and as Emily started back to her chair, he felt just mean enough to stick one foot in front of her, tripping her to her hands and knees. Reaching in front of Lydia, he flipped Emily's dress up to expose her drawers. Winking at Auggie, he said, "Bet that'd taste like honey."

Emily knew better than to cry from the fall, but she pulled her dress down so hard she tore the skirt partly from the waist.

Tennessee sprang to her sisters, clutching them to her the way all women do. Her eyes were furious, but she was too frightened to speak.

Both men stood and looked at her, both aware of her as a cornered female.

But then Auggie turned away, going to the door, and Julie got himself in control. He knew, though, that the girl understood and could cause him trouble.

"Listen to me." He stood very tall over her, and she stepped back, the little girls moving with her. Emily was now crying silently. His voice was harsh. "If you know what's good for these younguns, you'll forget about this. Ain't nothin' happened anyhow. So you shut up about it."

Tennessee was very pale. She understood the threat. "I won't say anything, Julie," she said, directly and plainly. "There's no need to say anything to anybody. I won't. I promise I won't."

He tended to believe her. He could see her fear, and the promise reassured him. He knew Tennessee would not lie.

At the door, he looked back quickly. They had not moved. Tennessee only turned her head to watch him. "Not a damn word," he whispered, and she nodded agreement.

But Tennessee didn't hesitate. She watched the two mount up and head for the field, then she flew up the stairs to the bedroom where her mother sat, watching Sissie who had just gone to sleep, her lips like rose petals. Tennessee had dragged Emily and Lydia with her, both now wailing.

As Annie came to understand and folded her three oldest daughters into her, her insides went cold and drew together the way ice in cattle tracks pulls away from the sides that formed it. Imagining Julie entering the house, this room, Annie moaned and rushed to Sissie. Like Tennessee, she wanted only to flee. She had no doubt that Tennessee was truthful, and she had no thought of anything but her daughters' safety, their need to get away. She stopped for nothing. Seizing the baby, she ran from the house knowing only that she could not stay there another instant.

Claire could not make out what Annie was saying when she and her girls burst in the front door.

"Claire! Claire! Someone must get Edward! It's Emily! Julie! Julie...."

When Claire finally got her calm enough to talk so she could understand, she almost wished she hadn't.

Tennessee was the clearest headed. "He tripped Emily and said bad things," she said, her eyes filling. "And I think he was bothering Lydia, too. He wouldn't let her down. Then he talked mean to me. And August had a whip. I was afraid." She collapsed against Annie who already had Lydia and the baby in her arms. Emily just stood still, her head down and her chin full and dimpling.

It was a bad sight, Claire thought, a woman alone with so many little ones. Claire was scared for Annie that way more than because Julie had been after the girls. In her mind, nothing could be worse than for a woman to lose her man. And here, within two years, Annie was losing her second one.

Certainly Claire wasn't defending Julie, what he did. She knew it was a bad and frightful thing. But she also knew Annie needed him in the worst ways, and while she was crying and feeling sick over one mistake, Claire saw her walking cold and pale with her children big-bellied and big-eyed. She would need more help than Claude and

Claire could give her, and much of the rest of the town had never recovered from her marrying Julie in the first place. Claire didn't think Annie could hope for much charity in Brittsville.

With hugs and cold milk for the girls and as much calm as she could muster for Annie, Claire steadied them, but then Annie started worrying about Edward who had taken his lunch with him in the morning to go hunt white oak before working cattle with August and Julie in the afternoon.

"They're just a couple of silly cowhands, Annie," Claire told her. "They ain't meanin' that boy no harm. Now you know that. It's better we spend us some time here tryin' to discover what's best for you and the girls right now."

They set Tennessee to entertaining Emily and Lydia with some wooden blocks Claude had carved out for the Wilson children. Annie wouldn't even lay the baby down. "I've got to hang on to something, Claire," she chittered. She still acted like she was freezing.

"Why do you think you've got to leave your house?" Claire finally asked. "Seems more to me like he's the one trespassin'."

"I don't know. I don't know." Her tears started again. "I just couldn't stay there, Claire. The only thing I knew to do was run." She sniffled and buried her face in the baby. "And of course the only place I had to run was here."

Then she looked at Claire. "Oh, Claire. You're my only friend. Can you find it in your heart to let us stay with you tonight? Until I can see clearer? And maybe talk with Julie? Though I don't see how I...." And she was lost in tears again.

As the afternoon deepened, Claire discovered that Annie had no idea at all about what was hers or what could happen to the house and land. She didn't even know for certain about the conditions of the loans they had or whether her name was on any property deeds. Claire's own stomach told her how scared she was for Annie.

"Well, when Claude gets in, I'll have him fetch Edward over here, too. We can put you up a while, Annie. You'll have to sleep on pallets, but you'll all be together."

Annie reached her hand out to Claire.

"Maybe Claude or me can go with you to talk with Julie, if you've them kind of misgivins. I reckon it'll take Martin hisself to straighten out the property matter."

Annie was shaking her head yes, but she said, "Julie doesn't trust him. Will did, though, and I think I do. I know he never approved of Julie and me. He was awful stiff with us. But I think he'll be fair. I don't know what else we can do.

"But, oh, Claire. I felt so happy there for a while."

The day wore on, and Annie seemed to catch her breath and her stride some. Emily and Lydia were napping, and she was rocking Sissie. Little Tennessee sat at her feet between her and the babies.

"You'll never have to see him again, Tennessee," Annie told her.

Claire wished she wouldn't be that definite, but she was—as though she had some kind of control over it when Claire was sure she might as well have tried to hold a bronco with a piece of thread.

"You won't have to see him or talk with him. Don't you fret. He'll be no part of our lives from now on."

"Will he live in our house?"

Annie didn't hesitate very long. "No. I don't think so. I don't think any of us will be living there much longer, Tennie.

"Without your papa or Julie to help us, I don't think we'll be able to afford living there any more."

Tennessee's eyes grew huge. Her whole face was the question: "But where will we go?"

"I don't know, my darling. But I will find us a place. I promise you, Tennessee, I'll find a way. We will say here in Brittsville. We will be together. And July Winkler will never bother us again.

"I promise."

She sat back in the chair, straight and frowning, and she clutched Sissie against her shoulder, fitting her chin so tightly over the baby's neck Claire figured it would have taken Jehovah himself to snatch her away.

If Claire wasn't talking to her, Annie made every sweep of the rocker a picture of her hurting Julie somehow. Never before in her life had she wanted to hurt anything—surely not anyone. But she wanted to hurt him. She wanted to hit him, not with her hands but with a limb or a poker. She wanted to hurt him until he would plead with her to stop, until he would cry in pain. She couldn't keep her mind from making the pictures unless Claire talked to her or the girls needed something.

She also couldn't stop seeing what he had dared to do to her babies while she was upstairs worrying about him, helpless herself against all that she knew was going wrong, hating it so much that he couldn't laugh or make love like he wanted, wishing he didn't have to work so hard or worry about all of them when he'd never wanted anything but to be light-hearted and love her. She had been feeling sorry for him, even criticizing Edward and Tennessee in her heart because they weren't always accepting of him. And he was downstairs doing that to her girls.

The longer she rocked, the faster she rocked, and the more she wanted to hurt him. She could not understand, not ever, how God could let anything like that happen. She finally said to Claire, "If God isn't around when innocent children are being hurt, then I don't think He's around at all."

Claire's whole face fell, and she spoke right back: "Oh, Annie! Don't say such things. Course God's here. They ain't actually hurt, you see. God was protectin' them all the time."

But Annie had her doubts. Still she had to get herself in control when Edward came home. Once he understood why they were at Claire's, he was so angry Annie was afraid she would not be able to keep him from going after Julie.

Claude had met the men and Edward at the house after he'd come home for supper and found out what was happening, but he hadn't said anything except, "Annie and the girls are over at our place, Julie."

"Edward, your ma says for you to come on back with me."

He told Claire Julie hadn't asked a single question. He'd paled a little, Claude said, then he'd just gone on in.

Edward tried to find out what was wrong, but Claude wouldn't tell him. "I want you to talk with your ma, boy," was all he'd say. "She's the one that needs to explain to you."

When Edward turned red-faced and furious before Annie, she knew exactly what he was thinking. It was what she had been wanting the whole afternoon. But seeing it in him and realizing he might try to act on it, she had to go past her own anger and try to get him past his. "We're all right, my darling," she told him over and over.

He would take up Emily first, then Lydia, and pace with them in his arms far longer than they wanted. Emily would say, "Can I get down now, Eddie?" and he'd hold her closer.

"Dang it, Ederd, I want down right now," Lydia exploded. Her, he'd obey, then come back to Annie or Tennessee with more questions.

"Try not to think about him, Edward," Annie begged. "You can see that we're fine. If you go there, it can only mean trouble. He's bigger than you, and he's feeling mean and cornered. He's not worth getting hurt for."

Her heart pained when she said that, but she knew it had to be true. She could not understand, and she knew she would have to deal with her feelings before long. They were so confused. It was clear to her, though, that Julie had lost his place in their lives, and she wanted Edward to feel that, just to let Julie go.

"That worthless bastard," he finally said, his eyes tearing up again. "That worthless son-of-a-bitch."

Annie didn't like to hear him swear. She never had before, not when he meant it. She reached for his hand, and he grabbed hers and held it to his face. "He wasn't good enough for you, Mama," he sobbed. "He never was."

It was a long time before he was quiet enough for her to trust him to stay with them.

Later, as they lay on the pallets Claire fixed for them, when Tennessee had stopped asking questions about where they were going, when Narcissa lay still in Tennessee's arms, when Edward began his slow, deep breathing, when Emily relaxed her grip on Annie's hand and Lydia stopped tossing and twisting her hair and lay with one leg sprawled across Annie's stomach, then she could tell that she was no longer afraid of Julie, and she was past the need to hurt him back. Then she could finally try to think.

She wondered, first, if she had at last become what she had most feared before: the lost woman with the lost children. She didn't think so. She didn't feel like that. She felt as though she had her world around her and as though she would be strong enough to keep her children safe. She did not know how, and as she thought about it, she realized that she couldn't plan anything of that sort until she knew what she had left. She figured Claire was right about it; only Martin would be able to tell her. And somehow she was able to put that aside for this moment.

But she couldn't put Julie and herself aside just yet. She knew she never wanted to see him again, but she grieved for him anyway, not for him, perhaps, so much as for herself without him. She wanted to go back a day, six months, and feel his arms around her and to have him pet her and tell her she was what he most wanted in the world. He had become her comfort even though she had known he wasn't quite able to be. She went ahead and cried for a while.

A little later, she began to hear the house and its own talk as the wind blew against it. A dog barked, then another. The moon was orange. The hills beyond were black, she knew. Horses and cattle were safe there. She imagined she and the children would be, too, if they had to walk out over the land, under the stars.

Part IV: Annie Sherwood

"From me flows what you call time."
—Takematsu

46

For Martin, the most curious part of the whole affair was that she wanted her name back.

"Fairchild, you mean?"

"No, my own name. Sherwood."

"But, madam, ...Annie. Your children's name is Fairchild."

"But mine is not," she'd answered. "I want back the name I was born with."

He searched her face, hoping to find something to defend against, but he could not, so he looked down at her papers strewn in front of him. "It's highly unusual," he said.

"Divorce is unusual, it seems to me," she replied without hesitation. "Yet that is what I've got to do. And if I must divorce him and start over, I'd rather do it as my own self than with some borrowed name. If I have to look after myself, I might as well have the...the *debit* and the *credit* of it." She finished with a slight smile and gesture towards the papers spread between them.

He appreciated her little joke. This was not easy for either of them. He had expected anything but her strength, that and her insistence on her maiden name.

He had felt awkward when she came in, but she had helped him with her candor and her views of what she wanted, now this smile. He actually didn't know the law, but he assumed that, ultimately, a person could be called what they chose. He told her as much and added that she would probably need to confer with a lawyer.

"Will I have enough to pay a lawyer?"

Again, he wasn't sure, and as he looked at her, he felt, again, that he was more moved by her situation than he intended or wanted to be. Aware that she smelled like the prairie, he heard himself saying, "I rather think so. I'll look figures over very carefully for you. Then, if they permit, I'll put you in touch with an attorney in Abilene, a man I know and trust. He'll provide you good, honest service if this is what you are determined to do."

Again without hesitating, she said, "It is."

She surprised him; he confessed she did. She was so young, younger than his own daughter. But here she had come all this way from everything she knew. She had all these children. She had already had two husbands—the troubles and blessings of a lifetime, it seemed to him.

He had not spoken privately with her at his office before, and he half wished Claude had come with her. He'd accompanied her after Julie left, and she had been uneasy discussing the situation and what she needed to do about the loans. They hadn't talked long. Martin had already learned—along with everyone else in town—that she'd fled her house, accusing Julie Winkler of unseemly behavior. They all knew, too, that by the next morning he and his brother were gone.

He hadn't stolen a thing, Annie had said, her voice pained and anxious. "He took only what was his, clothes, his horse, his tack. He didn't take more than he brought with him," she insisted, "maybe not as much as he was entitled to, I don't know."

Martin hadn't known, either, though he was sure July would have no way to make payments on the loans and that, by default, he would soon enough have lost everything anyway. Julie had bitten off more than he could chew, Martin held, in trying to assume Will's debts—and his family. Then with the molesting. Well. Man-handling little girls was not what they stood for in his town. He imagined Winkler felt lucky to get out with his privates intact. And Martin didn't think he would turn up again any time soon to see if he had any property left.

Today, facing Annie alone, Martin was struck by the resolve that underlay all she said. Like Claire, Martin had not expected anything so clear from Annie, certainly nothing so strong. He had assumed that she would be flighty and inept. That was the character her reputation had taken on, that and seductive. But it wasn't how she seemed. She seemed to him as she always had, young, beautiful, and straightforward, and her manner helped him focus and gather the strength to lay the financial picture out before her — which he did not want to do. He had decided to recommend to her that she leave matters as they were for the moment. When the loans would be defaulted on, he explained, the mortgaged property would revert to the bank, then be sold as soon as possible to pay off the loans. She would have the use of her property until the notes became due.

"I guess that means we lose everything," Annie responded, almost as a question, but not really. He saw that she understood. She was looking directly at him, seeming very calm, but she was sitting straight-backed, too. "Julie was afraid of that," she added softly.

Feeling pulled to her, he suddenly wished he could just get rid of her. It would be safer for them both. As he glanced at her, he didn't doubt that a woman with her looks could soon have another husband and life if she chose. And he realized, just as quickly, that he'd rather she didn't. Yet he felt obliged to give her his best advice.

"I think," he said, not actually looking at her because he thought he might lose his way in her eyes, "I think you still have some property free. It looks to me as though you'll have fifteen or twenty acres around the bunkhouse out south. And some household goods have not been remortgaged. If Julie doesn't return to lay claim to them — and I don't think he'll be so bold — that much will effectively be yours." He hesitated a moment and added, "At least that would be my judgment."

For an instant he did look at her, and he found that it was a mistake. He made up his mind on the spot that the property *would* be hers, even if he had to absorb a loss, himself. "If you could sell that, Annie, it would then give you a small base to start fresh from." Then he pushed on to his suggestion that she leave. "You'll not likely want to stay here, I don't suppose. If you were to return to Tennessee or even move to Salina, a larger community, you might be, you would...."

He felt callous and manipulative knowing he was trying to help himself as well as her. "Well, a woman who looks like you isn't likely to stay single long, and you'd likely find more suitors in a larger town."

It was awkward, and he didn't like having said it.

She was quiet for a moment, apparently unaware of either his compliment or ambivalence. Then she said, "There is nothing for my children in Tennessee, even if I could manage the trip there alone. And as for another husband, I think not." She spoke very slowly and repeated, "I think not. I'll find my own way now." She did not sound angry or unkind. She sounded as though she knew what she meant and would not deviate from it, yet Annie was not conscious of having made any such decisions.

"But how will you live? What do you intend to do?" He thought his voice betrayed him, but again she did not respond to anything but his question.

"I'm not sure yet. But I'm young and strong. You say I have some pasture left—and the bunkhouse. We can live out there if necessary. With a little work, we can make it decent.

"I'll have a garden, some chickens, a cow. I've been poor before, you know. If we can make it through this winter, we can get through the rest."

In the next moment, they were both silent, he feeling suddenly happier than he had any right to, she, seeing a bit more clearly what she was deciding. Annie was the first to speak again.

"I don't think I'll sell anything," she said. "We didn't come all this way to wilt on the vine. You said as much yourself after the grasshoppers hit."

He remembered how she had looked sitting out there, her face lit up from within. He was surprised and very pleased that she had remembered, remembered and taken to heart what he had said.

"It was Will's dream to make this place thrive. We made five children to help it grow. It is what Will wanted for them. He said he'd had enough of death and destruction. He wanted to see things green and grow again. Will's buried here."

She spoke more and more quietly as though she was discovering what she thought as she said the words. "No. I don't think I'll sell, and I know I won't leave. I'd rather start over here. I can't say exactly how, but we will find a way. That much is clear to me."

He absolutely believed her, and he nodded approval. But his mind was going other directions, too.

She was right about the children. If they didn't die of starvation or diphtheria, they would become townspeople, needed and probably admired. They were nice youngsters, a good second generation Brittsville—and Kansas—needed. But he didn't think she had a notion what it would be like to live alone on a hillside in a bunkhouse—nursing one child and caring for two more under six, herself so small and with only the two older ones for help.

"It'll ruin you, Annie," he burst out. "Even if you survive, it will rob you of...." He was going to say "your youth and beauty," but he caught himself. "It's too hard," he finished.

She didn't flush or fidget. "I saw my mother cut up her last loaf of bread to feed a soldier who was too tired to eat it. We cared for men who had no faces or arms, and we dug their graves very nearly with only our hands. Survival is in my blood, Martin.

"You just tell me exactly what I have and what I don't. Then I'll know what I can use to find my way."

He sat back and looked at her without trying to disguise his admiration.

Her face was darkly tanned and slightly flushed with her emotion, and her eyes were sapphires, he thought, or cornflowers, maybe. They were dark blue. He thought of her as he had seen her ride in a dozen years ago, perched like a boy on that high-stepping chestnut mare but softly muscled and inviting, even then. Now she must be nearly thirty, and he remembered her in the black dress, hair up, strands blowing across her face, pale and strained that day. He remembered, too, how he had wanted to hold her.

The feeling came over him again as she met his gaze, equally frankly, but betraying no emotion beyond interest in what he would say. He cleared his throat, leaned forward, and found no words. So he shuffled the papers, waited, and came up with one idea. It occurred to him that his brother, a farmer and banker who lived near Salina, might well be interested in hiring young Edward to help on the farm. If Annie was determined to stay, perhaps that would assist her some.

She frowned a little, immediately worried about the separation. But she saw the logic, agreed, and thanked him for the favor, for all of his help.

Martin wrote Mancil a letter that afternoon explaining the situation and praising Edward's honesty, intelligence, and love of plants and animals. It wasn't a week before Mancil wrote back and said the boy would be welcome: "I'll pay him honest wages if he is as able as you say," he wrote, "and I'll make sure he continues his schooling right along with your nephews and nieces.

"Please convey my best regards to his mother. That's a sad story. Tell her I would be pleased to answer any questions she might have about her son's welfare and responsibilities while he is here."

Not long afterwards Annie moved out to the bunkhouse, and in a few days, Edward moved to Salina. He promised to send money home every month and to come visiting whenever he could.

He did both, to Martin's knowledge and pleasure. Martin felt well to have helped them a little and to have escaped for the moment what had felt to him like a schoolboy's declaration.

In her turn, Annie was encouraged by Martin's careful attention to what seemed impossible figures and legalities. She was glad to think that she and Will had been right to trust him. And she was warmed to feel that at least he, for one, wasn't holding the marriage to Julie against her.

"A bad, bad mistake," she told herself over and over as she tried to focus not on what was past but on what was immediately in front of them: moving to the south pasture.

Her letter home did not explain what she was about any better than her earlier ones had. She knew her mother could never properly understand what she was doing—either when she married Julie three months after Will's death—or divorced him not two years later. And Mary would certainly write—or have Mrs. Follett write for her—that Annie should come back to the Sequatchie Valley. They would find a way, Annie knew she would promise.

But in Annie's heart, she was convinced she was right to tell Martin she had nothing to return to. Her children knew from her stories every part of the Hollow Annie most loved, the granite rock, the waterfall steps, the tree bridges, the sound. Edward and Tennessee could remember her saying they would all go there one day. But she had stopped that before Emily was born. Her longing for the Hollow never ceased, but her need for it had quieted some, partly because the children had come so fast one upon the other, and partly because she learned to repress those feelings which always seemed to raise Will's ire and threats to separate her from her babies.

Though she never wrote Mary without expressing some hope that they would soon be seeing one another, in Tennessee or in Kansas, both of them knew it was only that, a hope, a precious and fragile sustenance that they managed to keep alive between them but could never actually plan for and say, "Then—now—it will come to pass." Too many other needs shoved the longing to one side, and gradually the habit of the words seemed to replace intentions. Of course, Mary had no money and would have been bewildered and lost trying to come west—even though the journey had become far easier, as Will had foreseen. But Annie's letters never quite invited her. Mary understood—although Annie wasn't clear about it—and assumed that underneath what the letters said lay questions a mother shouldn't ask a daughter.

So, after this divorce, they both again had to face their wish already deferred, denied, for more than a decade. What Annie didn't say or plan was foremost in both their minds as they read through her most recent letter: " ...so we will soon be fixing up the little bunkhouse Ma. It's something like our cabin used to be except that you can't hardly hear the spring and there aren't many trees around it."

That was a considerable understatement because no trees grew for more than two miles, clear to the creek that meandered through the Wilson and Mallincoat land—but not Annie's. Still, she praised the bunkhouse as solid and tight and the spring as the sweetest, freshest water around.

As for Julie and the move, she simply said, "I'm sorry to say it Ma, but he wasn't the man I thought he was and this is truly best for the children and me."

She emphasized how kind the Wilsons and Martin Britt had been and closed as she always did: "Be well Mama. Tell Billy hello for me. I hope to see you soon."

As was ever the case when she wrote or read letters, Annie wondered how it could be that you so often had to worry about putting any words at all on paper. They were hard to get right and more upsetting than mosquitoes if you made a mistake with them. For that reason, she didn't even try to explain the feelings she was having about guarding her children, making certain they were never hungry, never made afraid, never humiliated again.

She had taken her stand, even if unconsciously, that this was their place, their home. Even if it wasn't hers, it was theirs, and she intended to make certain it gave them what they had to have, no matter what she had to do—or miss: even returning, just once, to Tennessee.

47

Annie didn't mind leaving the house as much as she thought she would. She had felt a stranger there too many times to love it as her own—though, of course, she admired it. But it was very hard for the children, especially Emily and Tennessee. Edward was excited and anxious about going to Salina and didn't say much about the house although his anger with Julie still concerned Annie. The girls, though, hated to leave their pretty spool beds and their china dollies. Yet they had to, for these were included in Will's last note as collateral.

At the bunkhouse, Emily stood at the door, her little apron gathered in her hands. "It smells bad, Mama," she said, unwilling even to step over the threshold.

Actually, it smelled of smoke, cigarettes, mostly, and wood and leather. It wasn't offensive to Annie, but she understood. No aromas from perfume or fruit jellies or dill pickle canning or bread or cake baking had ever sweetened this wooden rectangle. Nothing softened it, either. Every angle was ninety degrees. The six windows were dirty and uncurtained. Six bunks, two on the back and each of the side walls, exaggerated all the hard, straight lines. A small, pine table and four sturdy chairs stood near a heating stove in the center of the room. Its long, black pipe was suspended by two wires and ran to the northeast corner, exiting there into a tin chimney that stuck above the roof. That round, crosswise stovepipe was all that stopped the eye from bouncing back and forth between the walls.

Annie's own heart fell a bit, but she could remember when her mother, father, her grandpa, Billy and she all lived in a cabin not much larger than this. That was five people, and three of them were grown. They had had to make do. So, now, did Annie and her family. "Wait until we bake cookies, my darling, and bring in the wash. It will be so different, so much better. You'll see."

"Where will we hang the wash, Mama?" Tennessee asked. "Where will we even *do* it?"

Annie hadn't thought of anything that practical yet. She only knew that—somehow—they would. Tennessee was thinking of the washhouse back in town with its own stove and tubs, so close to the outdoor well. She had never carried water from a branch or washed outdoors on a board or spread washing on bushes or in trees to dry. Here, unless Edward could build a line quickly, they would be spreading their wash on buffalo grass or across the backs of their chairs.

The bunkhouse roof was pitched in the center, and four strong beams crossed below it. Claude, Edward, and Jimmy Wilson worked for three long days to make a loft up there. Using lumber Claude gave them and from the bunks which they tore apart, they fashioned a false ceiling over about half the space above the east window and made a little ladder up to it. There, they laid the bunk mattresses Annie had spread in the sun on the hillside every day for the past week. Along the wall, they built a few shelves and hammered in nails to hang clothes on. If Annie crawled, she could move around to put linens on the mattresses.

She didn't exactly sell anything, but she did take out another loan on a few items that Will had paid for but that she couldn't take to the pasture house. She didn't expect to be able to pay it back. Martin said it would give her cash reserves, she thought he called it, to use as she needed. She didn't see him scratching his head over what he would do with a rectal thermometer and a cooling board.

Edward, Tennessee and Annie decided together what they wanted to try to move to the pasture house.

Of course, they would take Doll and Will's little buggy. She could pull the wagon, too, and they would need that to bring the firewood already cut and what they would gather at the creek. They would sell the Herefords but buy a milk cow. They would take a dozen of Tennessee's Leghorns, including Big Boy, the dominant rooster. They would take two straight-back chairs and one rocker, returning Claire's—along with her lamp and table which Annie had always kept. They would take the stove from the washhouse and use it for heating and cooking, selling the one in the bunkhouse.

They would take their clothes, the sewing machine, Annie's rag bag, Will's *Formulary,* and all the red lead and medicines he had left. They would leave his books, his surgical tools.

Edward had lingered over the books, but he finally said, "I'll never be a doctor, Mama. I like plants. I want to be a farmer."

They took the hatchet and axe and hammer, nails, and every piece of wood they could find, buckets, a washtub, dishes and kitchen flatware. They took gardening tools, splits, and Annie's froe and wedge. They took the heaviest blankets and all the canned food. They took a few toys for the children, including the dolls Annie had made them. She found some of the old, cracked gutta percha they'd bought in Kansas Town and brought that too along with the sewing tools she'd got to work with leather.

By the time they had piled all that in the middle of the bunkhouse, they hardly had room to turn around, and Annie wished they had an attic or shed, someplace to store what they weren't using. She determined then and there to buy some wood for a few more shelves and to hire a root cellar dug. It would work for a storm cave, too, but they had to be able to store lots of potatoes and turnips and onions. She couldn't even think yet of hay for the horse and cow, of their salt, of their grain. She couldn't think of where she and the children would put their drinking water or how they would wash their faces or find their way to the outhouse in a blizzard. She only knew that they were safe together, that she had her children beside her, that she had enough money to take care of what they had to have right then.

That first night as they lay in a tight little row in front of the open door—it was much too hot to sleep in their loft beds—she named over and over the people she was grateful to: always Claire and Claude, Jimmy, and Martin Britt who had made sure they had the pasture house and money for their needs. She remembered that it was Martin, personally, not the bank, who had given her the loan on the last items, and she didn't even care that he was the one, too, who would be taking over the payments on her house and moving there.

48

Annie had been mistaken to think the first winter would be the worst. It was by far the easiest. The children had good clothes and shoes that fit. They had all the food they had brought from the big house, and Annie had money to buy extras here and there. Claude had been willing to break the ground for their large garden, and though it was too late to plant much, she could buy seeds and sets. What probably helped most was that it was all so new to them. Every day brought something unexpected to do, to think about. How would the children get to school? Where would they keep the chickens? Would Beauty Bugle be able to keep coyotes and foxes away? Would the stove keep them warm? How would they fix a toilet seat small enough to convince Lydia she wasn't going to fall through?

The problems were endless, so they occupied the family enough to keep Annie from noticing how much they were eating, how the children were growing through their own clothes and their hand-me-downs, how very little they saw of anyone other than themselves. The bunkhouse was only a mile and a half or so from the Wilsons, but no road connected the families, only the horses' path Julie and the hands had worn between the bunkhouse and the big house. And now, almost no one rode or walked on it. Still neither Annie nor the girls paid attention to the isolation at first. They were too busy.

Tennessee became the gardener after Edward left, and little Emily took almost all the care of the horse and cow. Of course, Doll was a pet who would follow any of them anywhere, and Emily soon had the cow that tame, too. She named her Gretel and led her by a string around her horns.

One afternoon very shortly after they had settled in as well as they could, they were sitting outside in the east shade of the bunkhouse drinking some cool water Tennessee had brought them from the spring. She lifted her hair off her neck and said, "It's awful hot out on these hills. We need some shade trees."

They surely did. It was miserable inside the house. The windows were high and small, and even opened, they didn't seem to let in much air. Everyone stayed outside so much they had already worn the grass down. When they needed to rest, they moved to the shady side of the house in order to avoid the direct sun. There on the hillside, it seemed as though the heat came from the ground as well as the sky.

"I'm going to plant some trees," Tennessee suddenly announced. "I'll bring them from the creek. I'm going to start right now!" and she jumped up to go for a shovel and buckets.

Annie wasn't sure what to say to her. She was already hot and sweaty, and her mother was sure she would never be able to make trees grow around the house. The ground was so hard, and right under the topsoil was a layer of rocks. The hills were good pastureland, but Will had seen, years ago, that they weren't favorable to crops. Claude had had his own troubles turning the land for their garden. Annie didn't want Tennessee to work so hard at what she thought would just disappoint and discourage the girl.

"Tennie," she started. "I don't think we can make them grow up here. I'd love them, too, but this isn't Roarin' Holler!"

Tennessee understood immediately. She could, in her mind's eye, see the cool hills and trees in Tennessee as her mother had described them. "I know, Mama. I know we'll never have a place like that, but the spring is real close. I'll carry water to them. And not just trees. We have to have some hollyhocks and lilacs here, too. It won't be home if we don't have trees and flowers."

She was so determined Annie knew she would never convince her otherwise. So they all went with her, Emily walking with Lydia, Annie carrying Sissie on her shoulders like a little papoose in a sling she'd made for the baby. Tennessee and Annie carried the shovel and buckets. Annie decided to let Tennessee tell them what to do.

At first, she tried a cottonwood about four feet tall, but the root was much too deep for her or her mother to dig or pull up. Annie saw her frown. "We'll just have to get little, tiny ones," she decided, and they began their search.

Actually Lydia helped them most to locate the smallest trees, probably because she was so close to the ground. "A tree! A tree!" she'd yell, and she'd grab whatever she had found and pull back with all her strength.

"Oh, wait, honey!" Tennessee would run to her. "You've found one. You're a good girl. Now let Tennessee help you dig it up."

"I don't want help! No! No!" Lydia would insist. More than once she yanked on the little trees and fell backwards when she managed to strip the leaves off. After a while she was willing to let Tennessee or Annie dig around the trees to loosen and free them.

That first trip, they got seven trees, four cottonwoods, what turned out to be an elm, and a couple of oaks. They put them in the buckets, trying to keep lots of creek earth around the tiny roots.

The walk back was exhausting for all of them. Lydia was jealous of Sissie and wanted to ride on her mother's shoulders. So Emily carried Sissie on her back, and Annie hoisted Lydia to hers. They started with Annie carrying the shovel and one bucket and Tennessee the rest. Before they got far, the buckets became very heavy, and they had to stop often to rest. "We should have brought Doll and the wagon," Annie thought.

At one point, Tennessee said, "Let me try something, Mama. I remember something in my reader about how people can carry water on their shoulders. Let me see." She took the shovel and pulled a bucket over each end. "If they don't slip off, I think I can balance them across my shoulders, and it will be easier."

"Bless her dear heart," Annie thought as Tennessee trudged off ahead of them. "She's found the way to carry a double load."

Emily and Annie caught up and walked at each end of the shovel, pushing the buckets one way or the other if they slipped. And Tennessee carried them the rest of the way. Her face was red, and her hair was slick on her cheeks and neck, but she got her trees home. While Annie and the little girls went in to wash and begin supper, Tennessee labored to plant the trees. She dug holes and carried fourteen half-buckets of water from the spring, two for each tree. She began to grow her shade.

By October, Tennessee had planted over twenty trees around their house, and during the winter, she had at least ten oaks bursting through their shells, their long taproots making their way down through the soil in the Mason jars Tennessee lined up on all window sills. Even during warm days in winter, she carried water to her little forest. And in the spring, she replaced those few which had died. She also planted hollyhocks around the house—Claire gave her the seed as well as a tiny lilac bush she and Claude had ordered for the family.

That spring, when Annie was finally convinced that the trees would live in the rocky, hot soil, she tried to help Tennessee with the water.

"No, Mama," she protested. "You already have too much to do. I'll take care of my trees." And she did. Annie tried to help when she could, but Tennessee never failed to water them and pull the weeds and grass from around them. Everyone carried water to the garden, even Lydia—in a coffee pot, but Tennessee was the one who watered the trees.

Before she went to bed, after the evening chores and after Lydia and Sissie were asleep, when it was cooler, Tennessee carried water. Trip after trip after trip to the spring, two half-buckets at a time, she carried the water. She found a big limb, carved notches in the ends for the buckets, wrapped the middle in gunnysacks, and made a yoke to carry water to her trees.

She made her mother pray for rain.

That first spring, too, she hung a little set of wind chimes under the east eaves. Her father had given them to her when she was about five, and she had first put them over her bed here in the bunkhouse. They were colored glass, squares and rectangles, and if they struck just right, they made a high, ringing sound like fragile glasses touched softly together.

Tennessee danced to them. She was like a willow, graceful as she wove and bent to the ground, side to side, forwards, backwards as far as she could reach, her loosened hair sweeping the ground.

"I'm showing my trees what they have to learn," she giggled. After the hollyhocks bloomed, she braided them around her head and wrists and ankles, making complicated and lovely patterns as she danced. Sometimes she moved so quickly the flowers blurred into ribbons trailing her hands and feet. She would leap and whirl, her legs long and strong, or pause, nearly still, yet not at all still, her body and arms and legs intense but waiting, catching the sounds, showing her mother how sound looks.

Annie had never seen a ballet, only heard of them. But she knew no ballerina ever looked more beautiful than her Tennessee dancing in the moonlight, teaching her trees, as she said.

49

At the beginning, a few of the townspeople rode or drove out to bring the family something, usually a gift of food, eggs or a cake. Annie thought some had softened a bit in their feelings toward her once they saw how Julie had done — and once they realized that she would no longer have much of anything, let alone a fine house. But she wondered if others weren't just plain curious about what she had become. Nobody dared say it was their just desert, especially not about the children, but Annie thought some might feel that way, and Claire didn't disagree.

Martin Britt sometimes rode out to see if they were well. Occasionally he felt a little as Julie had when he could never find Annie alone. But he had to laugh at himself, too, because he didn't know what he would do if he did. He hated to see them cooped up like chickens in the tiny house, but curtains sprang up at the windows, the garden was well tended, and Annie showed him with pride the trees Tennessee was trying to grow. Annie had never been so brown and slim, he thought, and they seemed to be thriving as she had said they would.

Sometimes he would take some fresh beef or candy out, as much as he thought she would accept as a friendly gesture. He didn't often dismount because he felt it would be too risky. Annie seemed glad when he stopped by, but she was nearly always busy, and he was glad to have that as an excuse for not staying long. But he could not quite stop himself from needing to see her and hear her voice.

Even so, with his gifts and those of others — which dwindled after a month or so—they did not have all they needed, and the second summer they began to be hungry for meat. Annie had had Gretel's calf butchered in the fall, but it was too little to provide them much—even though Emily wouldn't eat a bite of it. To spare her as much as possible, John Johnson and his oldest boy had come on a cool school day in late October to slaughter Babe, as Emily called her. It saddened Annie, too, because all of them loved the calf, but they had to have the food.

They had good onions, beets, and potatoes, a little corn. The beans, peas, and turnips had done well. But they needed more. Annie had thought maybe they would be able to sell the calf, but they couldn't and she had no money left—though Edward sent what he could. They were needful. John would not take any of the meat for his and his boy's labor.

"Your first man saved our girl right after you come here, Mrs. Annie," he said, "and I don't want nothin' for this. No, ma'am. I'm pleased to return the favor." Of course, she was grateful to him beyond the saying.

Annie also wished they had friends. Sometimes she saw Kitty and Lucy, but not often, and when they did talk, something more separating than time seemed to be between them. Will and she had not been church-goers, and the people had felt that—for church gatherings were one of the most important kinds of community get-togethers.

And of course Julie and she weren't church-goers, either. Once she and the girls moved to the hill house, she didn't have the means to start. Or maybe she didn't have the desire. It seemed to her that god was far away from her and hers.

Annie loved Claire, and she was everlastingly thankful to Claude. Martin, too. She was thankful for the blessings she had for she was convinced she had blessings. But she didn't actually thank a god she could name. The little baby lying in the manger filled her with love sometimes, and the young man hanging on the cross in the cathedral filled her with sadness she never forgot. But neither of them seemed like god to her, and there didn't seem to be anything in between.

For her, the hills all stretched out to the ends of the earth and the animals making their way through the nights, the stars staying up there forever, all that seemed to her more like god, stronger than that little baby or that fine young man. She figured there might be a god behind the hills and stars, maybe sleeping in them as their guide had said. She supposed he could have created the earth. But if there was and he had, it didn't seem to have anything to do with her. So she just thanked the air around her, the space, she guessed, and let the children, the few friends she did have, and her memories warm her from the inside.

Then, when people did good things for her, like John butchering little Babe for free—and much later bringing back the calf hide all tanned and soft: "It'll be a fine lap robe for you in the buggy, Mrs. Annie," he said—they were extra and special blessings. She thanked John, not god, and the gratitude she felt brought tears to her eyes. He was embarrassed, and she was sorry for that, but she couldn't help it.

Still, body needs were more pressing than spirit needs, and after they had eaten all the beef Annie had put up, they didn't have enough that was substantial. There was nothing for it but that she had to start hunting. She knew she could. She could shoot a gun, and she could butcher deer and build snares. Billy and she had gone with their father and grandfather for years, and they had taught her the same as Billy.

But she didn't like to hunt, not then and not ever. She knew she had to just as she knew they had to slaughter Babe, but she hated it. If it had not been for the children, she probably wouldn't have done either unless she was starving.

Annie didn't have any trouble with the hunting itself until she had used all her bullets. Game was plentiful, and she could dress squirrels and rabbits, turkeys and raccoons easily enough. She shot only one deer. She had to wait so long for it to approach her tree that the children were desperate when she finally got back. All four of them were crying. Then, when they saw her, bloody from gutting the animal and half-carrying, half-dragging it to the house, so exhausted she could hardly crawl, they thought she was hurt, and they were scared nearly to death.

The venison was delicious and nourishing, but getting it was too much an ordeal for all of them, so from then on, Annie hunted only the smaller game—which was why she used the bullets so quickly. And she didn't have money for more. She had to snare from that time on.

Claire scolded Annie that she didn't send Edward to hunt when he visited and they had money for ammunition. But she didn't say more when Annie told her she thought killing was too terrible a thing for anyone to have to do. "Besides," Annie said, grinning a little to soften her disagreement, "I can shoot a thousand times better than he can, Claire."

During the second summer, in July of '80, Annie went early one morning to check snares she had set along the west creek not far from where Will died. As she was walking, she heard a strange bird cry somewhere behind her, and as she turned back toward the east to locate it, she beheld a sight that astonished her. At first, she didn't know what she was seeing. The prairie seemed to be sparkling and shimmering. It was as though it were frosted with ice, but here it was, hot July. The hillside was so beautiful she stood very quietly, feeling as though some benediction was spread before her.

It was spider webs, spider webs everywhere, millions of them, surely. They were all touched by dew and turned into what appeared to Annie as the finest glass. They hung like beaded threads between the tall, drying grasses or swayed like something in water in the branches of a small tree that had died and fallen there. They pulled big, green, fluffy foxtail toward one another and made them seem to bow. Shining with the dew, they looked prosperously fat, silky and solemn.

The whole place was alive with fragile and glittering ladders, tiny, flashing hammocks, and wheels—wheels of throbbing silver, wheels of spun glass, wheels covered in infinitesimally small sequins.

Annie thought of magic and the leprechauns her mother used to tell her about: little people working through the night, for this seemed a fairy land made of trembling mercury, and Annie knew no mortal could even think of such a thing.

She turned back toward the west, still hearing the bird, but now she saw no glistening world, only small brown spiders motionless at the centers of most of the webs—which were, themselves quite hard to see. For a moment, she got caught between imagining the spiders flying through darkness to weave death traps and seeing their webs as lace and crystal so fine they made her want to weep while she smiled.

She turned in a circle, trying to place the cry and wanting to see the wonder again. To the west and to her sides, she could see nothing but the usual lavender asters, the tall yellow sunflowers, the green foxtail and the buffalo grass. They were pretty in their own way, but not magical. She could believe she had been dreaming. But when she looked east again, there it was, the whole, blazing hillside that made her linger and feel blessed. She didn't frame words for it. She just felt joy.

But she couldn't place the sound, and as she searched, the sun rose, the dew dried, and the graced world disappeared. She kept looking for the webs, and sometimes she would see one or even walk into one and feel that sudden clinging threat she wanted away from. But the land was again familiar—and growing quickly hot, a little unfriendly. She finally located the bird cry, and as she set out for it, she thought of what she had just seen. She couldn't stop seeing it, actually, even as the sun rose and she walked into the webs, now mostly invisible. They clung to her face and arms, though, and felt like stray hairs. Her sweat helped catch them and stick them to her tighter. She didn't like that feeling of something leeched to her, and she brushed them off, rolling them into small gray strings that looked like insect egg cases. She thought of the vision she had been given, not five minutes before, and she wondered how anything so wondrous to see could feel so awful caught on you.

She guessed most things had that two-sidedness to them. Will did. Julie did. She wondered if she did. She could see it plainly in them, and she couldn't explain it in either of them. How could he touch her Liddie? How could any grown man do that to a baby—with her upstairs worrying about how to make it easier for him when everything seemed so hard and disappointing. She remembered that that was when Will used to be strongest and kindest, when everyone was discouraged and nothing seemed possible. That was when he took hold and tried so hard.

She wished she wouldn't think backwards all the time, but hard as it was, it was sometimes easier than to think about what was in front of her. Right now, she was hoping for a rabbit in a snare. She was hungry, and the thought of fried rabbit made her mouth water. She had to swallow like a dog. Sometimes she thought her ribs were grinding against her backbone, and dandelion greens weren't providing a very good cushion between them. Even so, she dreaded finding a rabbit. Sometimes it seemed harder to kill them than a possum or squirrel. She could never get a rabbit's screams out of her head.

She was caught between imagining the strong, salty taste and hearing the death cries, when she found herself very close to the birdcall. It was that loud, insistent squawking which tells you the bird's in trouble—and very young. It didn't hush when she drew near. Annie was not particularly fond of birds. Her mother usually had a canary, and Annie never liked to think of it, alone in the world, always separate from its kind. She figured canaries sang out of desperation, trying to connect with another, and they made her nervous, not happy the way they did Mary. So she wasn't glad to have to detour this morning to try to rescue some jay or robin. But she also couldn't ignore it. Something in her backbone wouldn't allow that. She continued toward the sound which was coming from a gooseberry thicket.

"Stickers, stickers, stickers!" she quarreled.

It turned out to be a little crow with a broken bone in its lower wing, and it was hung up in bindweed near the bushes. Part of Annie didn't want anything to do with it, but another part said, "Well, at least it's a scavenger and smart. It'll not really be another mouth to feed." And she pulled it out and cupped it in her hand. It became silent immediately, then Annie could feel its bill exploring her hands, and it began to make tiny, husky peeps, the way a baby chicken will.

She let her heart turn over, and she shook her head while she examined the bird for mites—which it didn't have. Then she held it under her chin. Her hair fell forward, and the little crow scampered over her shoulder and fell quiet, snuggling close to her neck covered by her hair. It went to sleep before Annie even knew it was content.

She didn't want it, but she recognized that it did change the day around for her. The spider webs weren't keeping her from walking the way the bindweed did the crow. Her wrist wasn't broken. And the bird was little and needful. She couldn't help but wonder what it would learn to do. And of course the children, hungry for company, would adore it. So she grabbed up her walking stick—which she also used to dispose of the animals she snared—put the crow in her apron pocket, went on to the creek, killed the rabbit, gutted it, fierce and definite in her work as she held tears back, and fed the crow the eyes and gouts of bloody muscle from the neck. Then she put the little bird back on her shoulder, its one wing hanging down with her hair, and it rode home there gurgling happily all the way.

The girls were as gleeful as Annie had ever seen them when they caught sight of the bird.

"Oh, Mama! A little bird!" "Birdie! Birdie! Birdie!" "Where will we keep it, Mama?"

Tennessee lifted it out of Annie's hands straight to her cheek, her eyes closed and her mouth opened in a silent laugh. She knew without being told what it liked. Lydia was bouncing and squealing. Emily looked a little uncertain, but she was already looking for some place to put the new arrival. She had a basket in one hand and a dishtowel in the other.

The girls were so happy. They were showing their mother again how much they lacked friends or toys or books, something to interest them. Sometimes she could feel their boredom. She could feel her own. And she couldn't always think of a way to end it. But this bird, a crow. It was like a new baby for them. They didn't know if it was a male or female, so they just called it Crow. They decided that, since it wasn't especially pretty, it was probably a boy.

The girls worried themselves sick about its wing, though it didn't seem to pain any. The bird could never fly, but it could run very fast, and soon it used its wings enough to get a foot or so off the ground. As time went on, it followed them everywhere, even up the ladder to the loft.

At the beginning, the girls worked together like a small army launched into a major food search. They brought everything from worms and crickets to weed seeds and flowers for the bird to try. They came close to tears over whose shoulder it would sit on, and they cleaned up after it without a word.

Annie made a little basket for it and put soft rags inside. The girls put a cottonwood branch in the southwest corner, hung the basket on it, and Crow moved in. It would hop up the branch, twig by twig, sit at the top and caw to everybody about everything, then climb in its basket and sleep.

It got so it would go to the person it wanted to be held or fed by. They would put it on a shoulder and head for the bug jar. It tried everything, but it preferred insects or whatever they were eating. It didn't like leaves, much to Lydia's disappointment, for they were easiest to come by. But it liked apples, potatoes, bread, and, most of all, any meat they could ever spare. It followed them to the spring, to the creek, to the outhouse. It made them laugh when it threw dirt all over itself or hopped madly across the floor after buttons, which it hid in the stove wood. It helped them relax and be gentle as it sat on their shoulders, running its beak up their head under their hair as though it were preening them. It was a sweet trickster, a comic crow Annie found in the bindweed that spider-web morning.

The rabbit hide was almost too small and thin-haired to bother with, but Annie knew she would never have enough skins. She was going to have to start making leather clothes for them soon. So after they ate every scrap of the creature, fried thick-crusted and salty, she scraped all the meat remnants off the skin for Crow and tacked the hide hair-side down onto a board. She covered it with alum, then leaned the board high against the house up among the other skins she was tanning—raccoon, squirrel, other rabbits, and a deer hide Claude had given her.

Shoes, leggings, scarves, mittens, hats, and capes hung there if Annie could muster the strength to make them.

50

The winter of 1881 was their hardest. Annie didn't know that the children were ever hungry, though she was. But they were often sick with colds, fevers, and they lacked spirit. They were all thin. They did not have what they needed to eat. And it was bitter cold. The days never seemed to warm. Even if the sun shone, afternoons were pale, as though they might shatter. The moon was so far away it looked like a frost crystal, and the earth seemed as though it would never bear again. The hills were snow-covered for weeks at a time.

Then in January, an ice storm struck. It started with rain and sleet early one morning, and by noon, when the three oldest girls got to the house after their teacher dismissed school, icicles were hanging off their boots and off Doll's whiskers and stomach hair. The children were warm under the calfskin robe and their deerskin capes, but they were very glad to be back at the house. "Even Doll slipped around, Mama," Emily reported. "We just walked her all the way."

"Emily wouldn't let me drive, Mama, even though I was in front."

Lydia was complaining. Her cheeks were bright red, and her eyes were flashing. She was so beautiful Annie's heart softened, but she wasn't any more pleasant than ever. She hated school and wanted to ride Doll by herself even if that meant her sisters had to walk. They frequently gave in to her, but this day, Annie was glad to see, they had not, and Doll had brought them all three safely and gently home.

By sunset, the sky had cleared, but it looked apple green and shrunken away, and huge icicles hung from the roof. Tennessee went with Emily to feed Doll and Gretel. They were the only animals left. Owls and coyotes had caught the chickens, and Bugle had apparently been prey to coyotes as well, but the large animals were still healthy.

"Mama, they're so cold," Emily said when the girls got back to the house. "And the wind has come up so hard from the northeast. They're in the shed, but they're humped up and shivering. Both of them are wet through and through. It's dangerous for them, Mama."

Emily knew about the creatures. She was a sturdy, sensible ten-year-old, and Annie trusted her judgment. If she was afraid for the animals, Annie knew she had better have a look, herself.

When she went out, she was surprised at how the temperature had fallen. And the wind was fierce and getting stronger all the time. It took her breath away, and she quickly pulled her muffler over her mouth and nose. Doll shied away from her touch but immediately hunkered up again, humping her back, lowering her head. It was very bad, and Annie caught Emily's fear for the animals. They were absolutely necessary to the family. Besides they were loved, and it seemed to Annie as it had to Emily that they were threatened by the wet and the cold and the cutting wind. She had to do something.

She made her way back to the house as quickly as she could and scurried up to the loft where they had stored the old gutta percha. When she got it down, she told the girls to spread it out as well as they could on the west side, then to move everything they could to the northeast corner, under the stove pipe.

"What are you going to do, Mama," Tennessee asked.

"We're going to have company tonight," Annie answered, trying not to let her worry show.

"Who's coming? Who's coming?" Lydia shrieked.

Crow caught the excitement and called from his branch, bobbing and weaving as though he were teasing a snake.

Emily's face became one big smile. "I know! I know!" she said quietly but with pure delight in her voice. "You're going to bring Gretel and Doll in, aren't you?"

"Horsie come in here?" Sissie asked, disbelieving and much less sure about it than her sisters. "Horsie too big."

Tennessee went to her rescue. "It's all right, baby," she said. "You and I will go to the loft and watch from there; all right? We can lie on the floor and peek over the edge to see what they are doing. Want to do that with Tennessee?" Sissie did—and so did Lydia as Emily and her mother led Doll and Gretel to the door.

293

They were not eager to come over the step, but once they seemed to understand, they walked right in. Annie had to pull Doll's head down, but she cooperated, and Tennessee was careful to talk to them all the while from the girls' perch in the loft so the animals knew where everyone was.

Crow was silenced for a moment, but he soon croaked and complained as he usually did, then he went to sleep in his basket.

Emily and Annie rubbed and rubbed and rubbed the animals, drying them as much as they could. Emily mixed them some oats in warm water, and finally they relaxed so much Gretel lay down, and Doll's head dropped.

"Mama, were you scared to bring them in?" Emily asked, and Annie had to admit that she was. She hadn't known how they would react to the smells and the sounds of wood burning in the stove or ice cracking on the roof. They were very big animals, and she had known they could do terrible damage to her little place if they became frightened.

But as the wind built and the night settled, Doll and Gretel slept. "I think they know we're helping them, don't you, Mama?"

She did.

After Emily fell asleep behind the stove, Annie sat on the floor between the horse and cow, her back against the wall near the water stand, just talking and singing to them through the late hours until the dawn. She had buckets ready, but neither of them dirtied during the whole night.

Their clean, fresh breaths and smells made her think of the beasts in the stable with the Christ child, and she felt all over again how they must have warmed him and his mother. Annie loved the story of Christ's being born among the animals and not in some golden palace which she believed would have been very cold, no matter how many fine fireplaces it might have had.

She looked up at Doll and at Gretel and thought how Claire would have scolded. But she felt such a relief to know they were safe this terrible night. Their hair glistened gold and white and brown in the moonlight, and their soft breathing was steady and big. They made Annie feel peaceful and safe, herself. Though she did not sleep, she was calm and happy sitting in her house with her horse and her cow and her bird and her girls.

51

Annie and the children were all right until about February. During the summer and fall, she had preserved lots of vegetables and what fruit she could, especially apples that the Wilsons let her pick—and gave her jars to can in—almost all their windfall, and gooseberries, so many gooseberries. Annie put up eighty quarts. Unless you have picked them and stemmed them and washed them and preserved them, you have no idea how many gooseberries eighty quarts are.

Annie had to walk the three miles to the thicket down on the creek. The Wilsons owned that land, and they went on the shares with Annie until they just didn't want any more and told her she could keep all she picked. Annie was convinced they only went on the shares in the first place so she could have the berries. She doubted they ever dreamed she would pick so many. Annie would pick the entire day. Using Tennessee's yoke, she could carry home all at once what she had collected because it was such a slow, stickery, hot business. She didn't have any boots, of course, but because of the snakes, she would wear the leather leggings she made for winter. They were very hot, and most of the snakes were cooling in the bushes, anyway, draped over branches.

Tennessee and Emily were wonders with the little girls, especially Sissie, for almost no one could ever please Lydia. Annie could not take them with her, and she had to go. That was the hardest part. They'd play all the games she had taught them and sing and make mud pies and dress the stiff elm dolls she had whittled for them in hollyhock or petunia skirts. Annie feared some to leave them, but she had no choice, and they were not afraid.

At night they would stem the berries. Mostly Annie did. Sometimes Tennessee would help, but she would often go to sleep, and the pan would slip off her lap. Annie would have to pick the berries up and wash them especially carefully. Sometimes even she would go to sleep, and the same thing happened to her.

Annie would usually leave about ten in the morning, pick all morning and afternoon, then come home to fix what supper she could and work with the berries later. This year, they had all gotten so sick of gooseberries: gooseberry pie, gooseberry jam, gooseberry dumplings. Still, it was food. But by February, almost everything was gone except a few potatoes and onions. There were four children. They were all growing. Annie just did not have enough to feed them. Without Edward's help, they wouldn't have had flour or sugar, even. Annie set many snares and small wooden traps, but she never provided enough meat.

She also hated to kill the creatures. She had to use her big stick, but she couldn't always dispatch them with one blow, and she longed for the rifle when she had to approach a frightened and helpless creature and beat it to death.

This winter she had worse luck than usual. More than once she found that the snares had been raided. She began to think the coyotes and badgers or owls must be having a hard time of it, too. But despite her pity for them, she felt some anger as though they were competitors for what she had to have. Once she found just the clean white tail of a rabbit near a snare, no other sign of struggle or death. Whatever was taking her catch was very hungry.

She left in the early mornings whenever Tennessee or Emily would be at home to sleep late and play with Sissie and try to play with Lydia. One such morning, she left before dawn in a heavy fog. Most often, despite everything, she enjoyed these walks. She always found something to interest her, so many sounds, or, as the sun rose, so many colors and shapes that were hidden during the other seasons. But on this morning, she could see almost nothing.

She was glad for her big stick because she felt a little uncertain, even in her stride. The world seemed foreign, all gray and black. Annie could see only a short distance in front of her. Of course, she had a path worn, so she knew where she was and where she was going. But it didn't seem that way. More than once she stopped and turned to look behind her. She could see nothing. She could hear nothing. The fog seemed to muffle sound as much as it obscured sight.

She continued on through the pasture until she reached a little gully, still about half a mile from the creek. On the side of the gully was some soft grass where she often stopped to sit and rest a moment, just sit and look and listen. When she got there this day, it seemed a small, friendly nook in a world grown otherwise strange, and she sank down into it with a sigh of relief. She even closed her eyes for a moment.

In the distance, dogs were barking. She heard the Wilson's spaniel and the Mallincoat's hounds. Somehow she didn't like to hear either this morning in the closed-in space. They sounded excited. The hounds even sounded as though they might be tracking. Annie heard a cow from somewhere bellow as though she was at bay. Annie guessed it was a cow. What an awful bugle it was, more like a wild animal. Cattle do that sometimes when they are frantic, she knew, and she hoped coyotes hadn't cornered a calf.

She realized that she was afraid. Her heart was pounding in her ears, and she felt hot. She tried to tell herself that she was being foolish, that under the fog lay the path and grasses she knew so well. But she was also thinking that, silly or not, this morning she was going directly back home without checking the snares.

Then, all of a sudden, Annie heard what sounded like a pack of frenzied dogs—coming right at her. She threw her arms up over her face and head, and she heard herself scream. Then she realized that the sounds were over her head. They were also in front of her and behind her. The barking was everywhere, but especially above, and it sounded completely mad. She was terrified, and she buried her face in her knees. Her hands were over her head, shielding it.

Finally and blessedly, she recognized the cries: geese! Annie was surrounded by a flock of geese that had lost their way in the fog. They were flying very low, apparently circling in their confusion, and they were honking wildly.

For about ten minutes she lay there in the grass, laughing at herself and wishing a goose would crash beside her. What a dinner they'd have then! Of course, that didn't happen, and after they had made their bewildered, circling way past, Annie went back home.

Later, though, she made a discovery that helped her catch a wonderful dinner and food for the next few days. What happened was that she returned in the late afternoon to check her snares. They were all empty, and she scolded herself saying that was what she deserved for having been such a coward in the morning. She started home again, very tired and very hungry.

The fog was lingering, but the sun was trying to shine, and the dappling effect was too beautiful not to admire for a few minutes. Annie snuggled down into her grass nest and looked up at the sky. From the north, she saw a line of geese. They were too high to hear, but they were especially splendid because the angle of the sun on them made their beating wings catch the rays in a great, glittering chain. They looked like a long strand of tinsel in the sky.

Then an odd thing happened. They disappeared into a cloud, and when they came out of it, or when it passed them, they were no longer in a line but in a kind of burst or bubble of golden sparkles. They formed a big ball of throbbing lights that made her catch her breath in pleasure.

As she watched them reform into a wedge, she understood what had happened much closer to earth that morning, and at just that time, Annie heard a turkey. She couldn't believe it, but over near the creek, in the direction of the Mallincoats, she heard a turkey. She didn't need to hear it twice to know what she would do. Hurrying back to the house as fast as she could run, she got her chicken catcher and two old ears of corn she had left. And away back to the creek she flew. By this time, it was nearing dusk, and Annie was afraid the turkey or turkeys would have gone back home to roost. But she could hear them as she approached the creek, and she took a moment to catch her breath and rub the ears hard against each other, shelling the corn into her muffler.

These turkeys had strayed much farther than usual. Annie didn't know if the fog had confused them, too, but they were a long way from home. Of course, she was now on the Mallincoat's land, and she felt more than a prick of conscience as she realized what she was doing. They were a well-to-do family and had plenty of cattle and chickens and turkeys. Still, she was going to steal from them. She frowned hard at herself, but she moved toward the turkeys anyway.

They weren't the least afraid of her though they eyed her as a stranger. When she threw the corn out for them, they pecked it up and moved toward her just as they had learned they should. She sat down and stretched the chicken catcher flat out on the ground, grasping the handle. One young tom ate the fastest, and Annie figured he would do just fine. She threw the grains closer and closer to the catcher, then just past it. Sure enough. He moved confidently to the corn. And she got him. He protested some, but in an instant she had him under her arm holding his feet in the other hand.

That turkey went through every stage a turkey could, from delicious baked to stew to turkey foot soup. And she finished him off as a feather duster.

52

Annie's spirits were raised even if her conscience was a little taken aback by the events of that day. She hadn't laughed so hard for such a long time. She hadn't seen anything so beautiful in even longer. And she'd never stolen anything before. She could tell herself that the Mallincoats were careless with their turkeys or that a coyote might well have killed that tom if she hadn't. But she knew what she had done and what it meant. It meant that they were going downhill at a time they needed more and more. She was going to have to manage differently if they were going to escape the fate of the lost women and children in her mother's songs, let alone become the pioneers Will planned them to be.

Though she was not systematic in her thinking, Annie saw more and more clearly the ironies of being a settler, of carving a place out of the wilderness, as Martin had said. Part of the reality was, in fact, the dream, the vision they all seemed to share, of staking a claim, working it until it prospered, and building a good future, a community of people who would know one another, help one another, become a family. It sounded so clean and fine. But part of the reality was also and unpredictably the people and the flow of events which had nothing to do with dreams or plans or even efforts. It was all far more random and dangerous than she had understood.

Annie thought of Will, of Julie, of herself, how nothing turned out to be what they had wanted. It would have been beyond the imagination of any of them to see her as she was, alone on a hillside with four children yet to raise. The daily was not the dream.

And only yesterday, Edward's letter had changed Annie's world around again. He had sent five dollars, as he did every month, but his note showed her that she shouldn't and couldn't continue to depend on him for that.

They had managed to make a kind of home out of the tiny space they had, and they had a routine to steady them. The oldest girls were able to go to school, and, except for Lydia, they were doing well. Lydia hated everything about it and everybody there. The five of them had pretty much learned what they needed and how to do with what they had. But they needed more, always more, everything from shoes and dresses for the girls to bullets for the rifle, and they could not nearly stretch Edward's money to cover everything. Now, as his letter explained, he was making plans for his own future, his own dreams. He wanted to go to college.

College!

Annie sat down when she read that. She had never once thought of such a thing.

"They'll take me right now, Mama," he wrote, "even though I'm only fifteen, because I can meet all their admissions requirements. You only have to be able to read and spell pretty well and do arithmetic up to percentages. Mr. Britt has been teaching me extra, and he says I'm a really good student, that I need to go on and study."

Annie sighed and read on.

"They have a program in horticulture and agriculture over at the college in Manhattan, Mama. It's just what I want to learn. I could study botany and chemistry. It's perfect for me."

Annie didn't know what all of the words meant until Emily looked them up in the dictionary at school. Then Annie could see exactly how important it was for Edward to have such an opportunity.

"Mr. Britt tells me he'll help me, and I'd have to work there, too. Everyone does. It's to help you learn how to do carpentry or gardening. They pay you for that, Mama. Imagine!"

"But you know, Mama, I want to pay as much myself as I can. I've been working at the mercantile here, too, and I can send you an extra dollar or two, I'm sure, but I'm trying to save a little every week, too. I call it my college fund! Mr. Britt showed me how to deposit it in the bank."

Annie knew how kind the Britts were to Edward. He was growing so tall so fast he wouldn't have been able to keep himself in clothes if it weren't for their help. They seemed to treat him like one of their family, and he had gone to school with their children from the beginning. He had written about how Josie and Rose reminded him of his sisters and made him homesick. And the boys, both a bit younger than Edward, were like his little brothers. It was clear to Annie that he was very fortunate, and she wanted to be able to tell him to keep all his earnings. But she couldn't do that yet. She didn't have any other income.

Yet, now that his future was changing, she knew hers had to as well. She was surprised, though, at how it was shaping. Of course, Edward was smart—like his father. And Emily was, too. But hardly any children went to college. Most didn't have a chance to go beyond the common course of the country schools, and lots didn't finish the eighth grade. Still, she thought, if any, why not hers? She just had to find a way. She saw how the daily reshaped the vision, how the dreams bowed to the moment.

Her children would, she had vowed, become secure, at home in this place. Now, out of the blue sky, that suddenly meant "college," a life necessity today when it wasn't even in her world yesterday.

"That's the way it is," she thought. "Something isn't, then it is. Or something is, then it isn't. There isn't a baby, then there is. And you don't know how you lived without it. Or you have a husband, and then you don't."

She didn't go on for she'd already reached that impasse a hundred times. In fact, she hadn't known how she would live without Will, then Julie, Will's dreams and urgency, Julie's comfort. But, of course, she had. Where she was now was nothing she or her men had envisioned, yet it was what she had laid her own claim to. She would change it as she had to, but her children's future was hers. That was her one certainty. Yet and still, she could hold to nothing absolute because of each day's power. You could not prepare for what might erupt even in your own head or body. It could be the unexpected and treacherous blow of fear or the equally unexpected and weakening flow of love, both of which made you want to enfold the child who would only be overwhelmed by your need. Or it was desire so strong you no longer felt your knuckles rubbing up and down the corrugated board while the water wet your dress to your elbows and breasts. No plan contained that. No dream.

All you could do was advance into it, day after day, sometimes surprised but mostly just determined that you will continue, that you will not give up. It wasn't that you couldn't; it was that you wouldn't. If you stayed, you would not quit. And if you had babies to carry along with you, you wouldn't care what you had to do as long as you were moving. Motion was the key, motion forward.

But here she was, Annie thought, at a standstill, or maybe worse, and she had to find a way to get started forward again. So one morning when Sissie was finally napping and the other girls were at school, Annie put one of the last sticks in the stove and sat down to try to think through it. The one necessity was money.

Annie thought first about selling Doll. So many people admired her, and Martin had always said he wanted a foal from her by a stallion of his choosing. It wasn't just her beauty. It was her speed. Martin and Will had raced a few times, and Doll could out-trot any horse Martin had. He had wanted to buy her then, but Will said he didn't think Annie would be agreeable, and, of course, she never was. Pet had not had Doll's spirit, and neither had her second and third foals which they had sold. After that, Annie had not had Doll bred again. Now she was maybe nineteen, and Annie used her for everything, field work, hauling wood. Even so, she was still a beauty, and Annie thought Martin might yet be interested in a foal. She also thought that if she could sell Doll and replace her with a sort of make-do horse, she might have as much as fifty dollars.

But that was Annie's head talking. In her heart, she was sick to think of it. Doll had been Annie's for more than half Annie's life. Next to her children, Doll was the most loved and perfect thing Annie had ever known. She didn't see how she could possibly sell the horse.

Still, they had butchered Emily's Babe. She knew life could be like that.

Annie thought some, too, about asking Martin's advice concerning what she might do. But the moment she had the thought, she remembered their conversation about her future, his disbelief that she would try to stay, then what she had seen as his pleasure when he knew she would. He'd helped her feel strength; she knew he wanted her to find a way. And he often brought them meat—which she hoped he didn't know how much they needed. For those same reasons, she didn't want to turn to him. It would embarrass her to have him see her stumble.

She thought about cleaning houses, but she had Sissie with her, always. She was a nice little girl, but she was only four, and she could not go with Annie into others' homes. Besides, Annie didn't actually know anyone in Brittsville who used hired help for housework.

She came to think of Mary cleaning, nursing, selling her baskets. For the first time Annie realized that her own mother must once have worried about money as she did now. It had been hard for her parents to take care of Billy and her. She had never known that. She could not remember their ever saying they were worried or that money was scarce. Making baskets was just something her mother and Annie did together. Then Mary would buy material for a new dress for Annie or trousers for Billy, or they'd get some flour or other supplies. But Annie had not realized it was necessary for Mary to work.

She felt encouraged instead of sad at her insight. She didn't want her children to think about being poor or to worry about how they would make do any more than she ever had. But she worried that they did, especially Lydia. Annie knew Emily had been hurt to her soul by losing Babe. In fact, after that, Annie wasn't sure she could stand it herself to butcher any more of the calves. When Claude had Gretel bred again for them, Annie had hoped she'd have a heifer and that they could find some way to keep it or to sell it for herd-building. If she had a little bull calf, Annie didn't know what she would do.

Still, it didn't seem to her that the rest of their lives was sad or worrisome for the girls. Sometimes they had lots of fun together, even if they were working. Plowing the garden and corn patch, they were like clowns part of the time. They would hitch Doll up, and Emily would walk ahead for her to follow. Then Tennessee and Annie would each hang on to a plow handle, pushing down as hard as they could. Sometimes they would tip over and fall down. Crow was usually following behind them eating grubs or worms, and he would jump around and squawk at them as though it were a game. They would all be laughing, and they would end the day looking black as Crow, but they did manage to plow nervous, shallow, little furrows. Lydia and Sissie would shout and laugh from the garden side—unless Lydia was pouting because she had to watch Sissie.

Or they would all go to the creek to pick up wood, and they'd have a picnic. Annie had made all the girls baskets just their size, and she would pack whatever surprises she could think of under their bread and jelly sandwiches—a new rag doll or a skinny elm branch doll complete with a new dress. They would give Doll oats in her basket, then make a mud slide down the creek bank into shallow water. All of them flew down it to see who could make the biggest splash. They would come home filthy but happy.

Sometimes Annie whittled whistles out of the elm branches, and the girls would blow on them or on flat grass and make more noise than the jays. She liked to play jokes: dangling over their faces a stove-blackened, cockleburr spider with long legs to wake them of a morning. They sang songs. Annie especially loved that. She would teach them what she knew, and the girls would sing their school songs to her. Annie was free to sing again whenever and whatever she pleased, and sing she did. "You're the singingest woman in the world, Mama," Tennessee would say.

Annie knew it made Tennessee and Emily feel safe to hear her. She had always felt the family was at peace when Sherwood sang to them or whistled. It was the same for her children. Tennessee and Emily would sit on the floor while Annie was rocking Narcissa or sewing and ask her to sing song after song after song.

They wept a thousand tears over "Tattoo On the Arm." The story was about a girl named Mary who flirted with two boys and tattooed her name on their arms. Then, at Gettysburg, one in blue and one in gray, Tom and Ned shot one another and fell into a single grave while Mary waited for them at home. The girls understood that their father and grandfather, their great-grandfather and uncle had all been in the war, and Annie saw that made the story special for them.

But they loved all the old songs. "The Indian Sacrifice" was another sad favorite. Bright Skies, a chief's young daughter, drew the lot to go over Niagara Falls. At the end, though, after she said a tearful farewell to her pony, her father went to her, then to his death with her. The girls would be sobbing long before Annie got to the last verse which went, "Oh, is there a father more grateful, who lives in the white race today? Or is there a daughter more faithful than Bright Skies who died to obey?"

"Oh, Mama!" Tennessee would ask, tears flooding her cheeks. "Why did they have to draw lots in the first place? Why did anybody have to die?" Annie didn't know. She just sang the song. But Emily asked their teacher about it, and the girls came home to tell their mother why such a sacrifice might come to be. "Sometimes you have to give some kind of gift to the gods, Mr. Geisendorfer says. He said that's the way you please them, and it makes the gods treat everybody better. It's like Jesus."

"It's a *scrapegoat*," Lydia said. And she was mad as a boiled owl when they laughed.

So Annie didn't think their life was all doom and gloom, even if it was hard. Only one matter much troubled her. Annie worried that her girls didn't seem to have good friends. They never stayed after school to play with anyone, and only Kitty and Claire's children came to visit at their house—and that, very infrequently.

Annie could understand it with Lydia, for she wasn't happy enough to make friends. In fact, Annie imagined that the children were scared of her, and rightly so. One day when she was wearing a shoe her mother had put a little wire in to hold the sole to the toe, she got mad at the Bogaart boy and kicked him in the shin. "It bled all over everything, Mama," Tennessee told Annie, handing her a note from the teacher, "and Mr. Geisendorfer tried to get Liddie to say she was sorry, but she wouldn't. He made her stand in the corner, but she wouldn't ever apologize. But then we felt so sorry for her it made us cry."

"Well, *I* didn't cry," Lydia announced, looking like a storm cloud. "And I'm *not* sorry."

She went straight to the loft and wouldn't come for supper, so Annie knew she was very upset. But she wouldn't say why. When Annie was finally able to find the privacy to ask her what happened, she turned her back and said, "I forget." And she never mentioned it again.

Mr. Geisendorfer's note was polite, but he had to inform Annie, he said, that Lydia was frequently uncooperative and unsocial. He wondered if Annie had any suggestions that would help him help her adapt better to school. "She's clearly an intelligent little girl," he wrote, "but she seems unwilling to try to work with me or the other children. I do not think punishment is in order, though I am often forced to correct her. Any assistance you could give me, Madam, would be greatly appreciated."

"Poor Mr. Geisendorfer," Annie laughed. She wished she *could* help him, but the truth was that Annie had started Lydia early at school in the hope that *he* could help her. So she knew Lydia would not have friends.

But Tennessee and Emily? They were sensitive and caring girls, and if ever anything made Annie feel anger toward the people she and Will had lived among, it was that few raised their children to include hers. Annie did not think it was because of how they lived. They had little, but it was as much as many had, more than some. The girls did not, though, have a father, and their mother hunted better than she cooked or kept house. Whatever it was, Annie believed she needed to help them be strong and able. It was all the more reason for her to find some way to earn money.

Annie struggled with one plan then another, sometimes getting lost in fantasies or imagined conversations, until Sissie woke up, and Annie had to feed her. She reached for an egg out of the egg basket, and suddenly it came to her. It was the most obvious and easy thing in the world, and she couldn't imagine why she hadn't thought of it in the beginning. Holding that egg way over her head, she burst out in a loud voice: "Baskets! I can make baskets!"

"Bastiks! Bastiks!" Sissie echoed. And Annie grabbed her up, covering her with kisses.

"Yes! Bastiks, darling!" This, Annie could do, and she knew how handy the baskets were. She had made a couple after Will and she moved, and Claire had always wanted some. Baskets! Of course! Of all things!

She could make egg baskets and potato baskets and clothesbaskets. She could make baskets for purses, baskets for dollies. She could make big, little, and all sizes in between. Baskets Annie could make with her eyes shut. "With a little luck," she thought, "I can sell one to every family in Brittsville!"

She immediately went for the washtub and set some splits to soak even while Sissie was whimpering for her dinner. "They won't make us millionaires," she thought, "but they will help us live a little better, and Edward can spend his money on college."

The first she made was for Claire, of course. Annie decided to weave her an all-purpose basket, one she could pack lunches in or gather fruit or vegetables or eggs in. Down in Tennessee, lots of mountain women made baskets, but valley people tended to like Mary's best because she used more splits, narrower ones, too, and she tapered the ends where they wove in behind the handles so the sides looked pretty—"Delicate," she said. She made the ribs and weaving splits different widths, too, starting with thin ones, less than a quarter of an inch, then gradually working up to some about a half inch across. She would use as many as thirty or forty ribs in her smaller baskets and maybe ninety weaving splits. "The test of a good basket," she once told Annie, "is if you can carry water in it from the branch to the cabin!"

Then she laughed and shook her head. "No, honey. That's not true. You can't do that. But I don't like to see much daylight through them. Good baskets are tight." So she and Annie wove them tight.

Mary also taught Annie to use broken glass to rub the splits smooth. They would look like the satin cows rub wood into. The glass would sometimes get too hot to hold, and gradually it would get smooth itself so they couldn't use it any more. When all the ends were secured and the shapes had emerged, Mary's baskets looked as though they had been picked, like fruits or nuts, that natural. Her baskets looked balanced and even everywhere—as striped gourds sometimes do. And when she dyed the weaving splits with weeds or nuts, then wove in strips that got wider toward the basket center, the ends looked like half the side of a big snail shell, all circling into itself in a perfect order. Mary made beautiful baskets. Annie wished she had even one of them.

She had Mary's in mind when she started Claire's, and she tried her hardest to do it just as her mother had. Two days later when she had finished it and she and Sissie had taken it over, Claire was delighted.

"I always wanted one of these, Annie," she laughed, turning it round and round. "This is the prettiest one. I love it!" Then she wanted to pay for it. "What is it worth, Annie?" she asked. "I'd be glad to pay you for it."

Annie wouldn't even listen to that. She knew she could never repay Claire for her love and help to the whole family. Some obligations can't even be spoken of. They've got to be lived up to. Annie's to Claire was like that, so Annie was proud just to give her something she liked. She did wonder, though, if Claire thought other people might be willing to buy them.

"Oh, my goodness, yes, child." Claire was beaming. "Anybody that's got the money. I know they'd be so handy. And they'll last forever, won't they?"

"If they don't stay wet or muddy, they will," Annie replied, all of a sudden feeling confirmed, as though she really might be able to do something people would pay for. "Claire, how can I let people know about them? How can they get to see them?"

"Well, why couldn't you make up two or three of 'em and take 'em over to the store? I'll bet Veryl would be glad to sell 'em for you, and he probly wouldn't want anything for the favor. He's a good person. How long would it take you to get some ready?"

Annie had quite a few splits from the previous fall, but not enough for many baskets, and she wasn't sure about gathering new wood in the winter. The splits might be brash.

But she wove three. One was for eggs, a little like a saddle so the eggs could be separated on both sides and with a low handle so you could fit the basket close over your arm and steady it on one side with your hand. Another was a potato basket. It was flatter on the bottom with wider splits, and it had handholds on both sides rather than a handle which would put too much strain on the weave.

Then she made a purse. She gave it an oval shape to fit nicely by your side. It had a tall, wide, oval handle for easy carrying and to let you lift the lid without taking the basket off your arm. The lid had a pretty weave straight across the middle, then bending out until little arcs formed at the ends. She tied it down on one side near the handle with a small blue ribbon, and even in her most critical view she thought it turned out nicely. It wasn't as pretty as Mary could make, but it had a very tight weave, and she thought it looked smooth and neat.

When she took them to the Mercantile, Veryl was very nice about displaying them. "These are just beautiful, Mrs. Annie," he told her. "I suspect I'll have to buy all three for my wife. But I'll make sure they stay here in the window for at least a couple of weeks. That'll let lots of people see them. I think they'll be real attractive to the ladies. Anybody wants one, I'll write their name down for you."

He and Annie agreed to ask seventy-five cents for the larger baskets and one dollar for the purse. It seemed like a lot to Annie, but Veryl told her he thought it was a fair price. "Don't you have several days work in them?" he asked.

She surely did, but she hadn't thought of that. By the time you counted hunting and cutting the trees, splitting them, rubbing the splits, making the frame and actually weaving the baskets, they all probably had six days work in them. She just hadn't thought of it that way.

Annie asked him how much he'd need to take care of selling them for her. He grinned and said, "With something this pretty on display, customers will come in just to see them. That'll be good for business. I don't want any pay for handling them, Mrs. Annie. Not a penny."

She straightway added Veryl to her list of people to be grateful to.

53

Annie knew Tennessee was sick, and she was worried. But she stayed in control until Tennessee told her she had drunk the castor oil.

Tennessee had been fretful for several days, feeling sick at her stomach and sore in her side, so Annie finally hitched Doll up and took the little girls with her to town to talk to the new doctor. Emily was scared to stay alone with Tennessee, but she knew her mother wouldn't be gone long, so she sat close to her sister, trying not to cry as she watched Tennessee moan and twist.

Annie had spent the basket money as fast as she made it, so she had almost nothing to buy medicine with. Besides, Claire had told her this man was a poor follow-up to Will. "He ain't no surgeon, Annie," she had said after she first visited him. "I ain't even convinced he's a real doctor. I sure don't want him handlin' me or mine."

But Annie had no other choice. For Tennessee, she had to try.

He was as Claire had described him, a leering and unclean old man who looked like a weasel, his yellow, chinless face all collapsing into his nose. Still he was the only one who might help.

He came much too close to Annie, and she could smell more than tobacco on him. But she stood as firmly as she could while he looked her over, and she tried not to flinch as he patted her shoulder. "Jiss give 'er a tablespoon or two of this here, Mrs. Sherwood," he whined. "She's probly jiss ate something that don't agree with 'er." He ran his hand down Annie's back to her waist. "Or mebbe she's comin' into her woman's time, now. How old is she, anyhow?"

Tennessee was thirteen, and she had had her menses for two years. She wasn't much bothered by them, and Annie didn't want to discuss her daughter's private life with a man she instantly knew was dirty and foolish. She was certain Tennessee's menses were not the problem, and she didn't want him even thinking about her that way. She moved away from his hand, and he rocked back on his heels.

Annie was very uneasy about the castor oil. Will had never liked to prescribe it even though everybody seemed to expect him to. He thought it could be dangerous. But she took it, more to get away from the persistent and slow-talking man than because she would give it to Tennessee. She knew she would have no help from him, and she was sorry she had left Tennessee to come. She wanted to get away from him, him and his fish and onion stink.

When she got back home, she didn't even mention the castor oil. She put cool cloths on Tennessee's head and changed her pillow to try to make her comfortable. Annie had made a little pallet in front of the door so Tennessee could catch any breeze, but she was very hot. She was in bad pain and so restless the linens were tangled before Annie could straighten them.

She could not tend to the little girls, so she told Emily to take them to Claire's and to see if they could stay with her. She was certain Claire would find a way to come.

Tennessee knew her mother had gone to see Doctor Sheffler, and it was terrible for Annie to tell her, finally, that he had had nothing for her. She saw the bottle sticking out of Annie's old basket purse, and she asked what it was.

"Oh, mercy, Tennessee. It's castor oil, and he sent it for you, but I don't think we should take any until we're sure what's making you sick. Your papa didn't like to give it to folks, you know, and he was a wonderful doctor."

"Better than old Doctor Sheffler?" she asked.

"Oh, yes! A thousand times better, Tennie."

She had loved her father so much Annie thought she might be calmed some to talk about him. "Remember how he'd admire your chicks and their eggs? How he'd always say they were the best and the prettiest of all the chickens?"

But Tennessee was too sick to talk.

Claire did come. When she saw how things were, she hurried back to send Claude for the doctor. She didn't ask Annie about it, or Annie would have said no. Annie begged her to comfort the girls as much as she could.

When Sheffler got there, of course he couldn't do anything except shake his head. Annie saw him look around their house. She moved aside as he tried to pat her arm, and she was relieved when he left them to themselves.

Annie finally had to go outdoors for a few minutes. When she came back in, Tennessee seemed even more breathless, and Annie could see the shine on her lips. "Tennie! Did you drink some castor oil?"

She nodded yes, but she was mostly just rolling her head. "When you were out," she gasped. "I took some. Oh, Mama. I hurt so bad."

Annie tried to stay calm for her, but she could not keep from crying, and she knew her whole world was coming down around her. She finally remembered the laudanum they had brought from Will's medicine chest. He had told her it was a good and a bad drug, that you had to be careful with it. She was furious with herself for not asking what that meant. She didn't even know if it had spoiled.

She gave Tennessee three tablespoons full, then another and finally another. She did all she knew, but it was nothing, and soon Tennessee was twisting like a dying animal. She was completely white, and her gentle eyes seemed to have gotten rounder and smaller. They looked hot and hard, like blue glass. She panted and screamed with pain. Annie knew then that it was appendicitis and that nothing would save her.

Annie never spoke to anyone about how hard Tennessee died. She knew no creature should ever have to suffer like that. Annie thought she could not bear to stay with Tennessee, but she could not bear to leave the room, either. She wanted to run, herself. She wanted to scream. But she had to sit beside this daughter she knew to be as fine a child as was ever born, and she had to watch it happen. For a time she feared she would do something violent, if not to Tennessee, then to herself. She wished for bullets. She even thought of the tree branch she killed the animals with. But she did not leave her girl.

Near the end, in the night, when Tennessee had gotten quiet and it seemed the pain was over, Annie ran outside, got on a chair, and took down the little glass wind chimes Tennessee loved so much and danced to. She brought the chimes in to her child, and in the stillness of that room, though she could hardly breathe, she held them over Tennessee and thought to blow on them. They made such a tiny, specific sound. Annie hoped it was right for Tennessee's spirit. And then she died.

That was all Annie knew for a long time.

Later, though she understood that it wasn't actually the medicine that took Tennessee, she wanted to kill that stupid man. She wanted to kill herself for ever taking the bottle, for not throwing it away, for being poor and not knowing what to do, for being alive when Tennessee was dead. She wanted to kill Will again for not being there to help them.

Then she had no more accusations, no more arguments, no more pleas to make. She just sat there looking at her child. But what crept into her vision was something that had horrified her once when she was a little girl in the meadow behind the cabin. It was a grasshopper, turned all over to a grisly pink, a cold, old bruise pink. It was impaled below its head on a locust thorn which was almost the same color as the hopper in the dead of winter. She had found a shrike's larder with a creature secured alive, Annie supposed, dying on a nail, to be eaten later when the bird wanted.

As she sat rigid beside her dead daughter, Annie felt the thorn enter her own flesh, and she thought again of Christ hanging from the golden cross. She felt fury rise in her heart that any god would be so arrogant and bullying and human-like it would ever want any sacrifice.

The Wilsons took care of everything. Without them, Annie did not know what would have happened. They cared for Emily and Liddy and little Sissie. They sent for Edward who came on the train with the Britts and their oldest daughter, Josie. Claude dug the grave out by Will's, and they got someone to speak for Tennessee. They arranged for the undertaker to lay her out there at Annie's house.

Annie could not do for her daughter as she had for her husband. She could not bear to look at the beautiful young woman's form lying stiff in the coffin which rested on two chairs. She could not stand to touch Tennessee without life or movement. She could not even comb her hair. They did it all, and they and the Britts pushed and led Annie through it as though she were some statue.

She knew she was poor comfort to her children. Edward carried

Sissie who, though she did not understand, kept asking for Tennessee. He walked beside Lydia who watched his face. She was sober and frowning but not given much to crying. She allowed him to pat her shoulder and touch her hair. Emily, like her mother, was stunned to silence. They held hands, but they did not talk. Annie had some sense that many people were at the funeral, and she felt the Britt's concern for Edward and her other children. Mostly, she felt cold and far away from all of it. Embraces made her feel even stiffer. Martin Britt was shaking as he held her briefly, and she believed herself to have become wood.

Afterwards, she would not let anyone be with her, and though they did not want to leave her alone at the pasture house, she was so insistent about it that eventually they did all go to Claire's and Martin's. She sat at her table the whole night.

The comfort she finally had was very strange, and she thought for a time that she had gone mad. Later, she knew she had not.

It began in even deeper horror, if such was possible. By herself in the house, Annie felt removed from everyone and everything, even her other children. It was as though she was in a pale, empty space where sounds or touch couldn't readily come. She felt dull and sick. But she began to talk to herself from that distance, and she said that she should work. She should do something. She should make some baskets, a basket. She realized that she had to do something to survive—in her mind and in her heart.

So when dawn broke, she untied the last of the splits, and she went to fetch her washtub to soak them in. She could not find it. She looked everywhere she could think, but she could not find it.

Finally, feeling hot and aching until she could no longer stand, she sat down on a rock out back of the house to look through Tennessee's trees down the hill a bit, just to rest and keep from falling down. And there, pretty much hidden in some tall weeds, she saw the tub with a board across it. Seeing it there was so peculiar that she got up, the fever gone instantly. She went cold and on guard as though she were facing a mad dog. She knew something was wrong—wrong or crazy—the way a person does when what is familiar and handy gets changed in a way you don't anticipate—like seeing the barns and fields all run together in gray that first real frost of the year. It doesn't feel natural. Neither did this.

What Annie found when she got there was Tennessee's blood.

Probably no one could explain how anybody could have let that happen, but they did. They drained Tennessee's blood into her mother's washtub, took it outside to a weed patch, and left it there.

That's what they did.

Annie stood for a long time looking at it as though she could not tell what it was. A part of her couldn't. Then she became so sick she thought she would faint, but she didn't. She bent double and vomited. She could not stop the retching. She didn't have much of anything in her stomach, and she heaved her insides until she finally fell down there by the tub while the sun rose higher and the gnats and flies circled.

It was probably the insects that forced her to recover herself some. She knew she had to dispose of it somehow. It was a hideous task, and in her deepest heart, she cursed any god that might be that any mother should have to do such a thing. Still she could not leave Tennessee's blood there for natural things to corrupt.

The tub seemed very heavy, perhaps because she was so weak. She could hardly lift the corner. But she did. And when she did, all of a sudden out from under the thin pink that had risen to the top came a stream of crimson which shone so boldly in the sun she was staggered all over again. It was as plush and elegant as Tennessee, and for the moment, it seemed to give her back.

Annie watched it spill out slowly there in the weeds, and the ground soaked it up very fast. The soil looked black and rich where it drained.

Suddenly she thought, "Why am I giving this to the weeds? Her trees! Her trees!"

In a kind of frenzy, she picked the tub up, very quickly yet very carefully. She found she could lift it easily, then, and she carried it, groaning and crying, toward the little cottonwoods and oaks that now surrounded the house. The motion jostled the blood back into its natural, heavy color, and it poured out like a fine red jewel the sun streaked with gold.

She tried to portion it so that every tree got the same—except for the lilac. It she gave the longest drink. Annie watched the crimson settle around the young trunks. She watched the earth blacken with Tennessee's own life blood, and somehow she was eased. She didn't know why exactly, but to see Tennessee's life and beauty enter the very ground the trees would grow from made her grant some circle to things. What comforted her most was that she didn't think it was from dust to dust as the minister had said. For Annie, it was from glory and dance to glory and dance.

After a while, she went to the stream where she washed and cleaned the tub then poured that water on the lilac, too. Finally, she set the splits to soak.

She went to the loft and got out her quilt rags. She found the crimson, sateen blouse Will got for her in St. Louis. It was still nearly like new. She cut it up, it and the black blouse and skirt she had now worn to two funerals. She cut them into strips and began piecing them together. The colors continued to calm her all that day and night as she hurried them into a quilt for Tennessee.

Of course, she didn't have enough to make the whole quilt crimson and black like the blood refreshing the earth, but she found pinks and reds, too, that she could use, and green for the trees Tennessee would become, and paisleys for the hills around them, and flowers for the hills of home she never saw.

Edward came to talk with his mother, and she found words to help him. He told her he thought he loved Josie, and Annie said she hoped he did and that Josie loved him back. He said he thought she did.

He asked if Annie wanted him to come back, and she said she did not. She wanted him to go to Manhattan and to marry Josie after he finished his courses. He was able to smile a little at her. He was a lovely, tall, black-haired boy who made her feel very proud.

After he left, she sewed for three more days until the quilt was finished and she could go to Claire's for her girls so they might continue the best they knew how.

54

Annie supposed that if people did not die of such wounds they either grow on through them as a tree does a horseshoe or they have a place inside that is always sore to touch. However it is, she believed they would have a vital part ruined or deformed. Yet because they do not die, because hunger and dirty clothes and birdsong go on, because they must sometimes laugh and always love, they go on, too.

In the weeks after Tennessee's death, Annie and her girls had to make a new routine, and it was very hard to do. In a way, Annie wished the summer was already over because that would have provided at least one kind of order for Emily and Lydia. But in another, they all had so much work to do, and because they also had to make up for what Tennessee had always done, that occupied them and helped them.

Emily was the first to go for the buckets to water Tennessee's trees. Annie hoped Lydia might herself think of it because she never wanted to do anything she was asked to. But she didn't. She was a tall, strong girl, eight years old, and she could have carried half-buckets the way Tennessee used to. But Lydia had to be asked and reminded, then reminded again. Still she put it off and sulked until Emily had finished.

"I'll carry water to the beans," Lydia said, and she did help with the garden. But the trees would have died without Emily.

Though some of them were three and four feet tall, they still needed care, especially during the hottest days, and Emily never failed them. She didn't say she was doing it for Tennessee, but Annie knew she was. Sometimes she would wander among them, just looking at them, and once she said, "I wish Tennie could hear the wind in her cottonwoods. It sounds like water."

They straightway discovered how much work Tennessee had done in the garden. Annie began to see that Tennessee had worked like an adult to weed and hoe and water and deworm. Annie had to spend twice as much time there now, and she was sorry she had not praised Tennessee enough.

Gradually they stopped looking and listening for her. Annie didn't put the wind chimes back up, and she and the girls finally became accustomed to that silence, too.

Annie found it hard to sing again, but Emily wanted it, so Annie sang, and Lydia listened, too, although she pretended not to. Within the month, Sissie stopped asking for her sister. Emily told the girls that Tennessee had gone to heaven with the angels, and Annie did not deny that. She had come to think her daughters would one day have to draw their own conclusions about such things, and if angels seemed comforting now, she didn't think it would harm them.

They had to go farther and farther along the creek to find white oaks Annie could make splits from. She wasn't sure she should cut them during the summer, but she had to. She marked those which might be ready in a year or two and chose those which were about four inches across.

They also gathered all the dead wood they could, trying to build up a woodpile to last through the winter. The wagon and buggy had never been protected from sun or rain, and years of exposure had taken their toll. So Annie and Emily stripped the seats and kickboard out of the buggy. Its wheels were tighter, and it was lighter for Doll to pull. They hauled wood on the frame making loads any man would have laughed at. Annie laid the larger branches on the bottom, of course, but she never thought to take a saw, and smaller branches went every direction. She braided and wove other twigs and broken limbs among the protruding branches, finally handing some up to Emily who had to perch, at risk of her own limbs, on top of the tall, precarious load that threatened to fall in any direction. Doll kept her ears turned to it as they lumbered home.

The trees Annie gathered were too green, but she managed to work with them and to make six baskets in July, including one large cradle-shaped clothesbasket with hand-holds on the sides. It was her own idea and the first basket that was not an imitation of Mary's.

Everything else had to be done, too, including gathering fruits and canning. They fished and picked berries together, but Annie went alone to hunt or snare game. One near-miracle was that Gretel had twin heifers in the spring, and they were able to sell one to John Johnson and the other to Claude. Annie had decided that whatever meat they ate would be wild game that had never learned to trust them. But they did have lots of good milk to drink and cream to make into butter. Sometimes they could sell a little of the cream or trade it for eggs. Nothing ever tasted better to them.

In early August Annie received a letter from Edward saying he was going to enroll in the agriculture curriculum of the land grant college in Manhattan. It would be a three-year course, he said, and he would study everything from trigonometry and English literature to botany and zoology. "I'm really looking forward to it, Mama," he wrote, "and you know something strange? The president of the college is a Doctor Fairchild! George T. Fairchild! Isn't that something? He's from some place back east. You don't suppose we're related, do you?"

Annie knew how much Edward needed some connection with his father. She was interested, too, of course, but she didn't think it would be anything more than a coincidence.

Later in the letter, Edward said something that surprised her even more. "Mama," he wrote, "Mr. Britt asked me a question the other day that I thought was real important. He wanted to know if you draw any pension from the government as the widow of a Civil War veteran. I didn't even know anything like that existed, did you? He said that if you didn't, you should write to Governor St. John in Topeka and inquire about it. Mama, you might be entitled to fifteen or twenty dollars a month! Wouldn't that be something? If I were you, I'd write right away, and if you want me to help you any with the letter, I will."

Annie stared at the words and reread them half a dozen times. It would be a fortune, and she could not believe it was possible. But she sent Emily and Lydia to the store that very day for some sheets of paper, and she began to write the letter in her head.

When the girls returned and Annie had to put the words on the paper, her heart misgave her. Writing anything was very hard for her, and she was a poor scribe, too. Emily could already write cursive, and hers would have been much neater, but Annie didn't want her to know what Annie thought she had to say, so she did it herself. Even with all the thinking, she didn't know what she should put in. She didn't even know much about Will's service. She knew he was a Union army surgeon who had served at Chickamauga and was discharged out of Chattanooga. She could say when and nearly where she and Will had married, and she could describe her present life and her need. She had to hope that would do.

When it came to the hard part, how much they needed the money, she almost couldn't write it. She stopped for two days, but then she finally said it. "We do not have any income except what I can make from baskets I weave," she wrote, "and it isn't enough for our food let alone grain for our horse and cow or shoes for the girls. We have a roof over our heads and the neighbors have been very kind to us so I reckon we are not the poorest of the poor. But since my husbands death we have lost nearly everything and I don't see what is to keep us from losing the rest if people don't buy my baskets. I thank you Sir for any help you can give us. Respectfully yours. Anna Sherwood."

This letter was very different from those Annie wrote her mother. Even those seemed mysterious to her. She wasn't much of a reader, and she could never quite understand how marks on a page could become words and have meanings and feelings attached to them. Yet she knew they did. Or they could work to cover up the real meanings and feelings. She had had considerable practice of that sort trying to help Mary understand what was happening to them without making her afraid or sad. But this letter Annie wanted to be full of feeling, and she couldn't tell if it was. Whichever way it went, these words were going to affect their lives profoundly. She wanted them to be exactly right, and she didn't know how to tell about that sort of thing. Finally, she folded the page very quickly and stuffed it into the envelope so she wouldn't have to look at the markings any more.

That letter changed how every day felt. The first ten days or so, Annie knew it was on its way and maybe in the governor's hands. That alone was intimidating and nearly inconceivable. During the next week, she knew he could be sending his reply. Those days made her nervous and eager. But after six weeks, she began to be afraid, and after two months, she gave up hope that she would ever hear from him. She felt abandoned somehow, even though nobody had promised her anything.

In September, Edward had moved to Manhattan and was very happy to be studying there. Annie received frequent letters from him. Early on, he wrote, "Mama, you'll never guess what. President Fairchild asked me to stay after the first class last Wednesday. I took this course in political economics just because he was teaching it, and he made my acquaintance right away. He asked me about my family and about Papa. Of course, I couldn't tell him much, and as far as we can figure out, our families aren't related. But it was fun to talk with him. He told me he'd be keeping his eye on me because Fairchilds are supposed to perform well. Mama, are you sure you don't know more about Papa's family? It is such a shame."

Annie was sorry not to be able to tell the children more about their father. They deserved to know if they had aunts or uncles. And she saw, every day, what their grandparents were missing. She had always told the girls and Edward as much as she could about her side, and Mary frequently sent them some little reminder on their birthdays. But there was no one from Will's side for them to connect with. It bothered all of them, and it bothered her. But there it was, and they couldn't do anything about it.

Annie did feel some guilt about one matter. She had long ago decided that she would not tell the children about Will's first family. He had never mentioned them to Edward or Tennessee, and it seemed to Annie that she should honor that. For her, it was all tied up with what made him sick, and she never saw any reason to go into it with the children. Once or twice, Edward started to ask about Will's drinking and why he would become so angry. And all of them wanted to know where he had come from and why they didn't know.

She could only find it in her heart to talk about what she had shared with him, mostly about his being a fine doctor and surgeon. She told them he had been saddened and depressed by all the wounds and deaths of the war, but that he had devoted his life to building a new country. That much was true, she knew, and they loved to hear it. It seemed to give them and what they did a special importance. And she told them about the trip north and west, the stagecoaches and steamboats and the wagon train, all the hard work Will had done, how much people had respected him. But she also told them that alcohol had hurt him and her. "Your father was a good man," she said, "but sometimes he drank too much, and that was hard on all of us." She tried to help them see that he drank because of what he kept inside, the sadness of the war and whatever it was that had separated him from his family, but she wasn't altogether truthful about which family that was.

They made up a thousand stories to try to explain the mystery. Sometimes it seemed a kind of game. But his lost past was forever a sadness to them and to Annie. She hoped what she didn't tell them didn't make it worse. And she always wondered, along with them, who it was she had made them with. Edward's letter brought it all back.

So did the letter she finally got from the Governor, long after she had stopped expecting any answer.

"Dear Madam," it began, and Annie sat right down. She had brought it all the way home from the store where Veryl had kept it for her, then fed Sissie and set bread to rise before she found courage to open the envelope.

"I am in receipt of your letter of September 19, 1881, requesting consideration for a pension as the widow of Captain Will Fairchild, GAR. I am pleased to inform you that upon receipt of the following information, I will forward your Declaration for Widow's Pension to the United States Pension Office for their determination of your status.

"Please send us the following: Proof of marriage to Captain Fairchild, Proof of your own identity, and Explanation of your name as it is different from his.

"Please be informed that written testimony from three adults who know you, preferably a parent, will satisfy the requirements for establishing your identity.

"Believe me, madam,

"Your obedient servant,

"J. P. St. John,

"Governor of the Great State of Kansas."

Well!

Annie discovered that her hands had sweated clear through the paper, and she was panting. What a surprise it was, even to have a letter from such a person. She was so excited she couldn't collect her thoughts. But then, when she could, she wondered what she would do to answer those questions. She knew she could get people to say who she was. That was all right. And she could explain her name, though all of a sudden she wondered if marrying Julie or taking back her own name would make a difference. Maybe her status was "divorced woman" and not "widow." And maybe they would think poorly of her because she was divorced. Lots of people did. She did, herself, a little, sometimes.

But what was hardest was proving she was married to Will. They had signed papers that day. She remembered the shining red wood of the desktop. But who the judge was, she did not remember. She could recall the priest, Father Corbet, who refused to marry them, but not the justice who did. And she didn't know the street or number. She didn't remember that Will took any papers with him. It gave her such a bad feeling. It was like being in that dress store again and having the woman know Will was neither her father nor her husband.

Annie decided that only Martin could help her. He knew more than anyone else in Brittsville about legal matters, and he was one of the three people she intended to ask to identify her, him, Claire, and Mr. Johnson.

When she strode through the office door that day, she was sweaty, windblown, and harried. She refused to wear bonnets—"They are too hot," she told Claire who had offered to make her one—and her face was as brown as her hands. Some gray strands made her hair shine, even tangled, and she was so intense on what she was about that energy seemed to flow out from her. She had ridden Doll in bareback, and she smelled like horse and dust. Martin felt assailed by her.

She moved straight to his desk and sat down facing him. "I have a problem," she said, without actually greeting him, "and I hope you can help me."

Trying to focus on what she was saying, he smiled at her. He was forever trying to find ways to help her, and here she was, finally sitting before him, asking. He smiled a little, and asked what he could do.

Annie liked Martin and trusted him, but now that she was facing him and forced to talk about herself and Will, she discovered she didn't quite want to. Some part of her hesitated.

He sensed the change and tried to make it simple. "Annie," he said, gently, "surely you must know by now that I would do anything in the world for you I could."

324

But she was too concentrated on herself to hear what was behind the words. She was encouraged to speak, though, so she did, finishing her explanation with, "...so I don't know how to give him what proof he wants, and I thought maybe you would know what to do."

It had not been easy for her to speak of being married in St. Louis with no family or friends attending, married by a stranger to a stranger. She didn't say any of that, of course, but she didn't have to. He knew she was from Tennessee, that she and Will must have come upriver together before they were married. Just those facts revealed much more than she wanted known, and she understood he could guess they were fleeing, running. She found herself saying, "My mother liked Will and agreed to our marriage. She was always sorry it couldn't be there in Pikeville." But then she knew she had hinted at trouble, again, and she grew flustered and silent.

He didn't care any more about how she and Will had met, and he was only curious about—not actually interested in—the story they had made before he met them. He knew haste and difficulty would be part of it. Their empty wagon and the differences in their ages and manner declared all that. But he no longer wanted to hear it.

Annie, though, he cared for. He could not help it. He had never thought a man could love two women at once, but he had long ago found that he did. Lizzie was his chosen, his friend and beloved companion. She amused him and pleased him and loved him back. He knew that and was secure with it.

But there was Annie, anyway, pretty, fresh, and dear to him. He knew she excited him, but it was deeper than that. Something about her pulled him. Once he thought it was her flesh; then he thought it was her helplessness; then he thought it was her spirit. Since Tennessee's funeral when he had felt his own helplessness before her grief, he didn't think about the whys so much. He only knew he was drawn.

But it was not simple for him. While he wanted Annie and wanted to be with her, he also did not want the involvement, the betrayal of Lizzie and their children, his town. He didn't want the whole mess of it. Still, smelling Annie, seeing her, hearing her, his senses full of her, he didn't know what he was going to do.

Finally realizing that her voice had stopped and that he had not actually caught what she had said, he looked into her face and saw her frowning. He could remember where she had started but not where she had left off. Taking a chance, he reached for her hand.

She was surprised, but she didn't draw back. He was her friend.

Turning her palm up, he touched the calluses. Then, when he closed her hand in his, he saw her broken, not altogether clean nails, small, old scars, fresh scratches. "I know it's hard for you, Annie," he found himself saying, while he forced down his need to kiss the marks of her labor. "But you are finding a way. You said you would, and you have; you are. We all see that."

He grasped her hand in both of his, then released it, and she looked steadily at him. "I don't quite know how to advise you. I think the best thing to do is write the governor exactly what you've told me. Lots of times, papers get lost. The governor, of all people, should know what to do. Trust him and see."

Then Martin sat back, uneasy and moved, and Annie rushed out thanking him although she wasn't sure why.

She finally sent St. John what he asked for about who she was and her name, but she had to explain that she couldn't prove she and Will were ever married. She felt so humiliated she would never have sent the letter if it hadn't been for the children. This time, she was sure she would never hear back from him. In the meantime, winter set in, and they had to continue to try to live on the few dollars she earned with her baskets. She had told Edward they no longer needed his help, and she was determined that they would not.

She did write her mother to tell Mary she, too, might want to write the pension office, but Annie wasn't hopeful for her, either.

55

In November, early on a Saturday morning when Emily and Lydia could help Sissie if she awakened, Annie went to check her snares. Crow had followed for about a mile, but then he wanted on her shoulder. She supposed his feet were cold because it had snowed some, and puddles of water were frozen hard. He snuggled into her skunk skin muffler. It was a beautiful day.

The tall grasses were covered with light snow, every foxtail looking like a string of tiny, white chrysanthemums. Devil's claws had softened into crystal tongs, and burst seedpods cradled snow as though they were warming it. All this world seemed delicate and clean, and Annie felt eased. No matter what people did, the hills and trees looked unmoved, untouched, unsoiled by anger or mistakes. It restored her to walk where nothing welcomed or noticed her yet all gave her the assurance of strength and order that she needed.

At the edge of the creek in the shallows, small reeds stuck up from the ice instead of the water, but just above the surface, the wind and currents and dropping temperature had worked together to produce what looked to Annie to be beyond imagination or explanation. Around nearly every reed, maybe a half-inch above the ice, moisture had slowly and perfectly formed into little crystal shells and bells, tulips and lily pads, even tutus—all sorts of the most intricate and unexpected shapes, all glistening in rainbow colors.

Annie stood quietly to admire it for just a moment. She knew she mustn't linger. An animal might still be alive and struggling, and she put its need above her pleasure. Still such beauties were gifts she knew she ought not pass by. Sometimes she felt that her soul depended on them. They didn't take away the savage business she was about, but they seemed to balance it a little.

All of a sudden, she heard a sound which made her stiffen. Every hair on her arms and neck stood up under the heavy animal skins. She did not breathe as the combination of screech and caw hit her. She did not know if it was animal or human, but it seemed to her a sound the tortured might make. Crow shivered and pushed even closer to her. She covered him with her hand, and they both remained absolutely still while this cry pierced them.

Then it changed and became a kind of chant, an Indian song. A woman was singing. And at that moment, Annie remembered stories of the wailing woman, the wandering woman, the crazy Indian woman who haunted creeks to the south looking, the stories said, for her dead son. Annie's heart stopped, then she felt it falter and leap as the sounds changed to sobbing and moans worse than the old-country keening Mary had tried to tell her about.

Around the bend, near but hidden from Annie's sight, a woman chanted in Cheyenne an elegy for her child:

> I, Snow Bird, search in the brown grass for my son,
> For his deer-foot or his bones.
> He is dead, they have told me.
> They shot him in his head, they have told me.
> They found him where he crawled.
> Seven moons after Dull Knife led him into foolish battle
> They found him where he had crawled,
> Into a cave, they said.
> It was not a cave.
> It was a hollow in the creek's bank.
> He had dug it with his hands. I can see it.
> I can see his bleeding nails.
> He could not move his leg, shattered in the hopeless battle.
> He had crawled many miles on his elbows,
> Dragging himself like a deer with broken spine.
> He had lived thirteen winters.
> He had not touched the white women.
> Dull Knife told them that.

He had not touched any woman.
But they gave him a third eye.
One said, "No! He is only a boy!"
But the other's long rifle spoke,
And my son would never stand to sing his death song.
They cannot tell me where he is.
I walk to find where he crawled.
I walk and walk, sing my grief.
I look for a trace.
I caw for the black crow that came for him
To guide him to the spirit world.
I, Snow Bird, am not a crazy woman as they say.
I am a mother sick with hunger for her son.
I search; I sing. I weep; I caw.
There is nothing else.

Annie stood like a tree and tried to gather her wits, but she felt dazed by more than fear in remembering how Dull Knife and his band had raped and mutilated dozens of people in those last raids.

The sounds went through themselves again, a trail of anguish and mourning that brought Tennessee instantly to her heart and chilled her there. She felt a bond with the grieving woman. The stories said that she kept looking for her son, fleeing from the Cheyenne reservation year after year until the law stopped sending her back. Settlers had killed him, wounding him at the homestead where the band had ravaged and killed the woman and her two daughters, then trailing him for a week before they found him by a creek and shot him.

Surely he deserved to die, Annie thought. Yet, this was his mother.

The voice didn't seem to be nearing or receding, so Annie bent low and crept toward it. Something was pulling her toward the grieving woman. Annie couldn't keep her moccasins from crunching in the snow, and the woman heard Annie before they spied one another.

Snow-Bird stopped her chanting-cawing-keening, and Annie stepped around the little bend that separated them. She was holding her killing stick like a club, and her first glimpse of Snow-Bird showed Annie that she was holding a hatchet the same way. But Annie seemed to have lost her fear, and when she saw that the Indian woman was sitting, she, too, sat, without approaching any closer. She faced the creek more than Snow-Bird who did not take her eyes off Annie, though Annie had the sense that she was not looking so directly at Annie as she was at Crow. He had hopped on top of Annie's head when she sat down.

Annie didn't look straight at Snow-Bird, either, but she could tell that the woman was so thin she was all eyes. And she was sweating even though it was very cold. Of course, she could be afraid, Annie thought, still feeling shaken, herself. And though the woman didn't offer to get up or make any gesture of threat, she still had the hatchet raised.

Very slowly, Annie laid her stick down then pulled her muffler away from her face so Snow-Bird could see Annie was a woman who intended her no harm. They sat that way for a minute or two, then Annie remembered that she had brought a small hunk of bread with her. She had to take off her mitten and stand to reach under her cape for it, and when she did, she could see the woman tighten again. But Annie moved slowly, and when she brought out the bread, the woman's eyes were stark as she looked at it.

Annie took it to her, and she put the hatchet down to accept it. Still, though, she stared at Crow. Her eyes seemed fixed on him. Even as she bolted down the bread, she watched him.

Annie took Crow onto her hand, but such fear came into the woman's face that Annie put him back on her shoulder, away from Snow-Bird. He was quarreling a little for he wanted to share the bread, but he was suspicious of all strangers, so Annie knew he would not go to the woman. Annie was surprised that she seemed afraid of him.

After Snow-Bird had eaten the bread, Annie didn't know what to do, so she nodded several times and backed away. Annie found that she wanted to touch Snow-Bird, maybe pat her hand or stroke her face. But, of course, she could not. Annie also couldn't stop her tears. She didn't know whom they were for, the wandering woman, Annie's own self, their dead children. But something in her had to weep. She tried to hide her face in the muffler, but she thought the woman saw.

When she had backed nearly to her stick, Annie turned away to pick it up, then she started to go on by in the direction of her snares. Crow turned to look behind them, and in a moment he was back on

Annie's head, dancing and clicking and menacing with his wings. The woman was following.

Annie stood still, watching her make her way behind them. She was limping so badly she was nearly dragging her right leg, but she seemed determined to come with them. Annie waited, and when Snow-Bird stopped a few feet from them, Annie extended her walking stick, nodding her head despite Crow's loud warnings. Snow-Bird handed Annie the hatchet, nodding herself, always staring at Crow, and Annie turned again, walking much more slowly so Snow-Bird could keep up.

When Annie took the rabbit out of the first snare, she hoped the woman would understand what she and Crow were doing. She used the hatchet to kill the rabbit, and Crow hopped down for his usual banquet. Annie saw the woman back away from him.

Annie got a rabbit in each snare, and Snow-Bird offered to clean the last one. She had the wickedest looking knife Annie ever saw. When Annie started home, Snow-Bird was right behind her though at a respectful distance from Crow.

56

Sissie named the woman Bright-Skies although Annie knew it was the least likely name in the world for this woman and although Lydia protested that Bright-Skies was dead and only in a song, anyway. The woman did not understand their argument, that or anything else Annie or the girls said. They could gesture to her, to communicate eating or drinking, but that was all.

The girls acted thunderstruck when she first came in, and even though Annie asked them not to stare, they could not help themselves. To be honest, neither could Annie when she thought the woman would not notice. She was very weak, and her clothes were filthy.

Annie began by having her sit at the table while Annie fried all three rabbits. She also fixed some green beans and gravy to eat over bread. When the girls came to the table, Annie passed round a wet cloth and told them to wipe their hands and faces right there.

"Why do we have to do this, Mama?" It was Lydia. "We are not dirty, and we never do it this way."

Annie was glad the woman—Bright-Skies, they all began calling her—could not understand what Lydia said. She certainly understood about washing, though, and when Annie gave her her own cloth, she used it vigorously on her face, her neck, her ears, even her hair a little, then her hands. She seemed to enjoy it, and they nodded to one another.

The children saw that and started nodding, too.

"Why are we doing this?" Sissy asked, nearly making herself dizzy.

"We are trying to be nice, Sissie," Emily said, very low and calm, not looking at anyone. So Sissie spent most of the meal nodding her head every which way even when she was chewing—which combination seemed to confuse her and certainly made her unsteady.

But Annie wasn't sure their guest noticed. She was too hungry. Annie could see that she was trying not to eat everything at once, but she could not slow down, not until she had finished one whole plateful.

"Is she starving, Mama?" Lydia asked.

Annie nodded yes—which sent Sissie off into a new round of nods, and all that saved them embarrassment was that Bright-Skies— as Annie now thought her—was more concerned with Crow than with them.

As the day went on, Annie could see how tired and sick the woman was, and Annie decided that if all of them were to be comfortable, they would have to start by being clean. She also wanted to see what was the matter with Bright Skies' leg.

So they got down some of the old gutta percha and put the wash tub on it in front of the stove—as they always did at bath time. "I'm not taking any bath," Lydia protested. "I'm not dirty."

But her mother insisted. "Get ready for a bath, my darlins," she said. "Everybody! We have to show Bright-Skies how we do it here. She needs to wash, and she needs a change of clothes, too. We have to help her. Sissie, you're the littlest, so you go first!"

Despite their complaints, Emily and Annie scrubbed the little girls all over and got them dried and dressed in fresh clothes. Then Emily jumped in with only a little warm water added. Sissie and Lydia went to sit beside Bright-Skies who was dividing her attention between them and Crow—who always got excited at bath time.

Emily and Annie sang a song or two as Emily scrubbed, then Annie washed her brown hair. She jumped out and, like the little girls, ran over in front of the stove to dry off and dress. Annie had had to go for more water while Emily bathed, and Bright-Skies had seemed to understand. She stayed with the girls while Annie brought in two bucketsful from the spring. When that started to heat, Annie went for more. Then it was her turn.

All three of the girls helped their mother wash her back and arms, and they giggled when she pretended to have soap in her eyes or to shiver. By the time she had finished, she hoped Bright-Skies would be ready—and willing, too.

Annie laid out her largest nightgown for the woman and a heavy shawl she had knitted, then she motioned for Bright-Skies to take her turn with mostly clean, warm water. She was very shy, but she wanted the bath, and slowly she disrobed and stood in the tub. The wound in the calf of her leg frightened Annie. It was four inches long, badly infected, swollen and red. Bright-Skies had great difficulty trying to sit partly because of the pain and partly because she was so tall, so she knelt in the tub. She was willing for Emily and Annie to help her, and when they rinsed her hair, it was beautiful and long and black. She smoothed it back, and Emily grinned at her and said, "Beautiful. Very beautiful," gently touching the shining strands.

Bright-Skies caught Emily's hand and leaned her cheek into it for the briefest moment, then her eyes went back to Crow. She had faced him the entire time.

Annie helped her stand, and with a clean cloth, she made a motion to wash the wound. But Bright-Skies caught Annie's hand in a different way and herself pushed the warm, wet rag against the blazing cut. Annie could see that it agonized her, so she gave her a towel, helped her step out, and led her to the stove.

The girls poured out her bath water and wiped off the gutta percha while their mother helped her put on the gown. She was a large-boned woman, and even though she was very thin, the gown was hardly ample enough. But she was clean, and she pulled the soft shawl close up to her face.

Annie knew such a wound had to have some attention. The best she had was the Nuremburg Plaster she always kept on hand. It had the strongest drawing power of any medicine Will knew, he had often said, and it was easy to make. Annie was never without it. So while Lydia and Sissie took turns standing in a chair behind Bright-Skies and combing and braiding her hair, which she didn't seem to mind, Annie went for the plaster. It smelled like cloves and was pleasant to touch, cooling and smooth. When Annie handed Bright-Skies the jar and had her smell it, then showed her, on Annie's own arm, what she should do, she did not hesitate. Though it hurt her, she smoothed the mixture thickly the length of the wound, and when she handed the jar back to Annie, she smiled for the only time. Annie wrapped the leg in what was about her last clean cloth, and in a little while, when she had fixed a pallet for Bright-Skies behind the stove, the woman at last fell into a deep, deep sleep.

All that afternoon, Annie sat at the table where Bright-Skies could see her. She had the feeling that if the woman awakened and got frightened, she could do more damage than Doll and Gretel might have.

Very late, she did awaken, and Annie put her furs around Bright-Skies and helped her go outdoors. When they came back in, Annie fixed her some warm milk, and they redressed her wound. The cloth was already yellow from the infection the plaster had drawn. Annie gently washed the cut. This time Bright-Skies permitted the kindness. Then she put the plaster on a second time, and again Annie wrapped the leg.

The last thing Annie did that night was heat more water and wash all the cloths they had used—and the woman's clothing. Annie hung it over the gutta percha on a line stretched between the walls.

She hoped it would be sunny and above freezing the next day so they could do the towels and her and the girls' clothes.

57

You are the crow,
Cunning black bird of the spirit world
Come again to wait for death.
You ride on her head,
Little woman made big by skins of animals.
You sit above them
In your tree,
In your house.
You sleep in a basket
In your tree.

They feed you first
From their own dishes.
You are the crow,
Spirit of the dead,
Waiting again in your earth home.

Late one night after Bright-Skies had been with them for five days, her voice awakened Annie. She quickly got up and looked over the loft edge and, there in the shadows of moonlight, she saw the woman standing by Crow's tree. She seemed to be chanting again, but Annie didn't hear any tones that frightened or hurt her, so she knew this was different.

She was somewhat concerned for Crow because she knew Bright-Skies feared him. When they played with him, she always went to the farthest corner, so they were careful to keep him away from her. He seemed to understand, for he never offered to go to her, and he always made his alerting sounds and raised his wings if she accidentally came closer than he wanted her to.

As Annie watched and listened now, she could see that Bright-Skies had roused him in his basket-nest. He was looking at her and clicking, but he wasn't actually up.

> I did not think to find you here,
> Black bird of the spirit world.
> But I know you,
> Even in this house of the blue-eyed woman.
> I understand you.
> In my sleep you have revealed to me
> What I longed to know.
> Now I thank you,
> Clever bird of the death god.
> I give you this gift,
> My father's gift to me,
> With the golden eagle
> Which flies
> Beyond seeing,
> Beyond hearing.
> I thank you.
> Now I will go back,
> North over the cold hills,
> Away from the creeks I have followed,
> Back to my people.
> I will leave the lonely trail
> Which will never lead to Deer Legs.
> He is not here.
> You showed him to me
> Wrapped in the great white cloud
> Beyond the eagle's flight.
> He is safe where you left him.
> I cannot go there. It is not my time.
> I have come too soon and too late.
> I have walked around time, around the rim.

I could not fall in. It is not my time.
It was his time. It was not mine.
Thank you, spirit bird.
And thank you, great spirit.
Now I will go north.
I will wait for you there,
Black bird of the gods.

As Annie watched, she saw that Bright-Skies was dressed in her own clothes and that her skins and leather pouch and hatchet were all beside her. Annie knew she was preparing to leave, and her first thought was to try to stop her. But as Annie watched and listened, she started to feel differently. Bright-Skies had her own way and her own purpose, Annie understood. She could never help this woman find her answers. If she thought she had to go, and in the night, Annie could not interrupt her.

After a long time, the woman stopped her song and stood like a soldier at attention. Then very slowly, she bowed to Crow. It looked like part of a ceremony to Annie, who pulled back into the darkness so she would not be seen and watched, with her breath held, while Bright-Skies raised her hand to the basket. She seemed to slip something into the nest.

Crow sat still and stopped clicking.

She stepped back and bowed again, very low. Then she turned her back, put on her furs, and, with a long look around the house and up toward the loft, she opened the door and left. Annie could see her through the window by the table, a tall, dark shape walking quickly into the white hills.

Annie sat at the table the rest of the night, cross-legged in a chair, feeling lonesome, bent under skins with the fire low. She felt no more tension, no more need to try to see a soul in someone's eyes, no more curiosity. She was the only adult again. Nothing showed that the Indian woman had been there except her pallet and the jar of Nuremburg Plaster which she had left beside it. Annie sat without a light, half hoping the woman would return but certain that she would not.

At dawn, when Crow started rustling, Annie decided to see what her guest had put in his basket. He murmured to Annie as she put her hand under him, felt around, and located a hard, round object.

It felt like a large button. Taking it to the window, she discovered that it was a coin which shone bright in the early light. Quickly Annie lit a candle and moved to the table to examine the piece. In disbelief, she turned it over and over, letting the candlelight warm an eagle on one side, its wings spread out over a shield of stars and stripes, on the other, the head of a woman surrounded by thirteen gold stars. Below the head was a date: 1853. Below the eagle was printed "TWENTY D."

It was a twenty dollar gold piece.

"Oh, Bright-Skies!" Annie cried out loud as she clutched it to her breast then her lips and visualized flour, sugar, salt and chickens, for she was immediately determined to try them again come spring.

She saw shoes for Lydia, material to make dresses, shirts, trousers, and underclothes. She saw repairs for the roof, a new awl, two needles and threads of all colors, buttons, bullets, and grain for the animals. She saw savings for Emily's schooling, okra, dill, cucumbers and beets. She saw so much she knew she'd have to start all over again and make a list of what they needed most, starting with bees' wax, red lead, and cloves for more plaster.

It was a gift beyond gifts.

Annie could not imagine how Bright-Skies had come by the coin or why she had not used it for herself when she was so hungry and needful, why she had given it to Crow. Then Annie wondered if the woman had even known what it was, and Annie was struck to think that she actually had intended it for Crow. Annie could not understand, not then and not ever. But she decided that if Bright-Skies wanted what was best for Crow, then she wanted what was best for his family, and Annie thanked her from her heart.

Then she sliced off a big piece of bread and warmed some water to put on it. She sprinkled cricket parts and rolly-pollies over it for Crow's breakfast. Then she picked up his oiled cloth, took him outside, and put him in the top branches of one of Tennessee's cottonwoods while she went to the root cellar for milk, butter, and apples. The girls awakened to fried apples, warm bread and milk, good treats to take their attention away from the new vacant place at their table.

When Emily and Lydia left for school, riding Doll and carrying her noon oats, Emily said, "I miss Bright-Skies, Mama. Don't you?"

With her hand clenched around the coin in her apron pocket, Annie nodded. "Yes, my darling. I miss her very much."

Sissie stood beside her mother, solemnly nodding in all directions.

58

It came to Annie in a dream that she should sell Nuremburg Plaster. She was dressed like Bright-Skies, and she pulled a little yellow peddler's cart like Mr. Lerner's. Hers had FAIRCHILD'S WONDER PLASTER in a circle on the sides. People were crowded around, throwing coins, pleading for the miracle medicine. Annie had a thousand jars of it. Lydia held the crowd back with a whip, and Sissie collected the money and handed out little blue and brown jars of the clove salve.

When she awakened, surprised to be in a dark loft with her sleeping girls, Annie thought a long time about the dream. She finally decided that it made sense. The plaster was an excellent medication. Annie remembered what it had just done for Bright-Skies, and she knew it was something people would want. She didn't doubt that she could sell it if she could get enough supplies to make it. That very morning, she bundled the girls onto the buggy frame, dropped Emily and Lydia off at school, and drove with Sissie to the Mercantile.

Veryl had sold four more baskets, and with that money, Annie ordered the little salve jars and ingredients for the plaster. "You make it up, Mrs. Annie, and I'll sell it right here for you," Veryl said. "Your baskets have brought me plenty of customers."

But something in Annie wanted to make it a matter of business rather than friendship, so they talked about that. Annie didn't know what was fair or proper, but she finally asked if he thought ten percent of the profit would be all right.

"Well, I reckon that would be fine, Mrs. Annie," he said, "but I'm not sure how to figure it."

"I'm not either, Veryl, but Emily will know. I'll have her write it up for us if that will do."

By the first of December, Annie had made up thirty jars for a cost of about two dollars. If she could get fifty cents a jar, Emily told her, she would need to give Veryl $1.30 for selling them, leaving her more than $11. So well before Christmas, Annie took in her plaster and two more baskets. Emily had lettered strips of paper with "NUREMBURG PLASTER from the recipe of Will Fairchild, M. D." They pasted the strips onto the little jars which looked pretty and smelled even better. Veryl said he would give Annie a five-dollar advance, he called it, for he was confident the products would all sell.

With that, Annie bought Sissie a doll with its own dress, Lydia a comb, brush and mirror, and Emily a blue dress from the store. She bought denim pants for Edward, chocolate to make everyone fudge, and a big slice of beautiful white cheese Mr. Lerner had sold Veryl. She left a new order with him for three dollars' worth of supplies for more plaster. That left her with about nothing, but they would all have presents for Christmas, and she would have enough to make more than forty jars next time. Brittsville was receiving new families all the time, now, and Annie was sure her wares would eventually sell. She also intended for Mancil and Edward to take some plaster to Salina and Manhattan.

In February, just before Sissie's birthday, Veryl rode out to their house with a letter from Washington, D. C. "It looked real official, Annie," he said, "and I knew you'd been looking for a letter. So I just ran it on out here for you."

Annie had given up, once again, ever hearing about the pension, so she was very surprised—and as quickly upset, for she didn't like to remember what she had had to say in her last letter. She thanked Veryl and asked if he'd like some tea, but he said he had to get right back to the store. "That last batch of plaster's nearly sold out," he told her, "and the baskets are long gone, so get me some more as soon as you can. Here's the last of your share, Annie," he said, and he handed her three dollars for the last plaster and baskets. They both laughed, then Annie went in to read the letter.

"Dear Madam," it began. The seal was raised and shiny.

"It is my pleasure to inform you that, the estimable Governor St. John of Kansas having sent me documents supporting your declaration for a widow's pension, we have decided favorably."

As she usually did with letters, Annie had to sit down.

"We have considered the identifications provided by your three neighbors, citizens Wilson, Britt, and Johnson, as testimony to your being common-law wife of Captain Will Fairchild with whom you lived from 1865 until his death in 1876."

Annie felt sick to her stomach at being called a common-law wife. She didn't want to read any further. But of course she had to.

"You may expect to receive a cheque each month in the amount of $12.50. This is a lifetime benefit, Madam, and we trust that it will in some small way acknowledge the debt these United States owe to your late husband.

"I am, Madam,

"Your obedient servant, etc."

Annie sat there an hour, she supposed, or until Sissie needed help. Annie was making a new kind of list in her head, new for her, anyway, a kind of financial list. If she could actually plan on twelve dollars a month from the government, she should be able to provide for her family without help from anyone. And if she could continue selling baskets and the plaster, maybe in Beloit or Abilene or even Lawrence or Topeka, she might make another ten dollars or so. Maybe, she thought, her insides slowly falling back into place, maybe she would never again feel desperate in that way.

But she hated the letter. She never wanted the children to see it. She wanted to destroy it, but she worried about some mistake which she might need the letter to remedy. So she got down Will's old *Formulary* and put the letter in the middle.

"Someday," she told herself, "I will have great pleasure burning that blamed thing."

Once again she saw Bright-Skies putting the gold coin in Crow's nest, and once again she thanked her. "You were the start of our good fortune," Annie said into the air between them.

59

In the spring, Mr. Lerner paid them a visit. He came every year and always to their great pleasure. He looked grizzled and a little formal with his long, gray beard and black suit, maybe something like Will in the one picture they had of him. But his eyes and smile were always warm. He was the kind of person you wanted to stand close to, Annie thought, and she didn't know how to explain that. But once in a while, Annie realized, you find someone you know would never hurt you or, even more, you know you would like to have beside you if you had to meet God. Annie and the girls all trusted him and made over him, even Lydia. Yelling and giggling, they had left the garden when they saw him coming.

Annie had been baking bread in the Dutch oven over an open fire. As always, Crow had helped her fan the kindling, and he had got a little too close, as he sometimes did, so he was cooling his feathers, really, and quarreling for all he was worth in the top of the nearest cottonwood. He redoubled his efforts when Mr. Lerner drove up. They hadn't recognized him coming up the trail because he was driving a handsome, little, blood bay gelding who pulled a neat, brown wagon shaped like a box. "Lerner's Traveling Mercantile" was printed on the sides and front.

Mr. Lerner had always come to their house even though they had rarely been able to buy anything. He would give the children candy, anyway, and he would talk with Annie and drink a cup of tea. Sometimes he would hold the baby. Once he dried dishes, and another time, he chopped wood. But his best gift to Annie was a sense

344

of calm and courage. She liked him very much and was always happy to see him.

After the girls had explored his wagon—it was like a little store and house combined with a place for his mattress and a tiny cook-stove—and chosen a treat, which they could actually pay for this time—they went inside with Annie and him to enjoy some fresh bread. Emily brought milk, cold from the spring, and they all ate hot bread with butter and wild plum jelly.

"This is real delight for me, Mrs. Annie," he said—with a heavy accent and a smile clear across his face.

"And for us, Mr. Lerner," she told him. He liked the bread and jelly so much Annie wrapped part of the loaf for him in a clean, white cloth and set it aside with a jar of jelly. "This is for you later," she said.

"You are very kind," he nodded, as though he had never given them anything.

Lydia and Sissie had pulled their chairs close to his. They watched every move he made and touched his beard, his hands—which were rough and freckled with age spots. They seemed to feel about him much as Annie did.

"They have no grand-papa," he said, smiling at them.

Annie nodded. "I worry about being out here, never seeing anyone we belong to. I don't mean out here," and Annie looked around the house. "I mean out here in Kansas when my mother is in Tennessee. It's a shame not to have family close."

For a moment, Annie was embarrassed, for she wasn't thinking about him, and she had never known a person apparently so far from everyone he loved as Mr. Lerner was—unless it had been Will. But Emily went on and sort of hid her mother's stumble. "We don't know where Papa's family is," she said.

"Is true?" he asked, and they all nodded.

"We know he spent some part of his boyhood in Philadelphia," Annie said, "and that he saw the ocean in New York. But that is all. So the children have no knowledge of any relatives on that side. And of course they have never seen my mother. And she and my brother Billy are all I have left, since the war. My brother never married, so he stays with Ma, but we haven't seen one another in seventeen, eighteen years. That part is very hard."

"Yes. Very sad," he agreed.

He didn't say anything about his own family, and Annie was glad the children didn't ask. She thought he looked so sad they were silenced. Even Lydia reached out to pat his shoulder. He was more alone than they were.

A little later, he asked Annie about the baskets and Nuremburg Plaster he had seen in Veryl's store. He thought they were excellent products, he said, and he wondered if he could take some with him to try to sell on the road.

"I go every place, you know. Next year, I will stop to tell you how they do!"

It seemed a fine idea to Annie, and she set about gathering up baskets she had recently made. She had six of assorted shapes and sizes and a new purse. It was striped in red and black, and she had thought of Tennessee all the time she wove it. It was very special to her.

"Is remarkable," he said, running his fingers over the splits.

Annie was surprised to feel tears coming. It was as though he understood. He handed it back to her without even asking about taking it to sell.

When he explained to Annie how he wanted to handle the business, she was surprised again. He wanted to pay her the "retail price," he called it, a little more than Veryl charged. Then he would try to sell the products for slightly more. "We test and see," he laughed. "Maybe next time we do it another way," and he counted out the money.

Sissie had been listening to him very carefully, and she finally had to ask. "Why do you talk that way?"

"Because I am old Jew who don't know any better," he laughed, and lifted her high in his arms. All the girls were wrapped around his legs when he tried to walk to his wagon.

He hung the baskets on a rope along the wall inside the little house. Annie thought of her clothesline and wondered if that was his. He lined up the twenty jars of plaster in a pretty box with bright designs all over it.

As he climbed up into the driver's seat, he cast an eye over the trees. All of them leaned to the northeast ahead of the southwest wind. Most of them were taller than the wagon, and Crow was on one tiptop branch.

"Her trees do good," he said quietly, and his eyes met Annie's as they frowned and said goodbye.

60

When Mr. Lerner left that day, Annie still had two dollars from her second pension check with the expectation of twelve more in a few days. As spring yielded to summer, the check came each month around the fifteenth, and now she had received five. Three were curled in a sugar bowl along with some money she had received from Veryl. She smoothed the papers frequently, looking at them as though they were a new, unexpected pet. Already she had bought everything she thought they had to have, then some pure luxuries such as store dresses for Lydia and Emily and a new bridle for Doll. She had even sent money to Edward, but he had sent it back to her saying he was able to get along. Annie could not quite admit that their good fortune was real.

It was strange for her to look for such a monthly event. She was much more accustomed to waiting for the full moon to plant by or preparing for her menses or those of her daughters. Emily, like Tennessee, began when she was eleven. And Lydia was growing up faster than either of them. Sometimes Annie wanted to hold them down, push them in. She saw that they were moving toward their futures far faster than she could ever be ready for. And lately she had begun to think that because the girls had no hope for money or valuables from their parents, they, like Edward, would have to be educated. Unless they married someone who could provide for them, they would have to provide for themselves, and though they were sweet and pretty—with the exception of Lydia who was sulky and beautiful—boys were sensible. Penniless women, even sweet and

347

pretty, are less desirable than their plainer sisters who can bring husbands ready cash, as Martin called it, or livestock and land. Annie's girls would be penniless, she thought. So she had to provide them something else.

She decided that unless the family was hungry or sick, they would live as they could from what they grew or earned, and the pension check would go into a college fund for the girls.

First, though, she had to fix the chicken coop to make it stronger and to separate the young ones. She had cobbled together a little shed, herself, mostly from what she could find at the dump outside of town and what she could tear out of the old wagon.

Annie wasn't much of a carpenter, and she imagined how her father would laugh at what she came up with. She had to laugh at it, herself. It was mostly a frame covered with rags, small skins, some of the oiled cloth, and covers off the buggy seats. The only actual wall was to the north where Annie balanced some short, wide boards in between and on top of each other and tried to secure them with wires and a broken buggy shaft. She had never before had enough nails, and now that she did, she couldn't find much to nail anything to. Some of the rags were just tucked in or under or between wood of a dozen different lengths and widths. Rocks weighted down some strips. But Annie had found some slatted canvas, and she was determined to add it to the south side and roof. Any wind to speak of would whip away some part of her mosaic shed, and she figured that, in a real storm, what chickens didn't blow away or drown would be scared to death if she didn't do something. So she was wrestling with the canvas, trying to fasten it down at least here and there when Martin came riding in from the west.

He had not talked much with Annie since she asked for his help with the pension letter, and he had tried not to let those details of her private life lead him to think more or differently about her. What he wanted was to befriend her as he could and place her securely to one side of his heart and mind so he could go on without creating chaos in everyone's life.

On this day, he had decided to hunt, and he had three turkeys, one of which he intended to give her. As he approached the bunkhouse, he could see Annie standing on the buggy frame and straining to pull the canvas up to the roof of her old chicken house. In spite of himself, he had to chuckle at the sight, and as he jumped off his horse to help, he saw Annie grinning back at him.

"What in the world are you doing?" he called.

"Well, Martin," she replied, "I'm making fruit salad," and together they laughed while he worked alongside her to spread the canvas up and over.

"How will you keep it up here," he asked, and she pointed to some rocks she'd collected.

"We'll weight it down," she said. "You hold it up there, and I'll hand the rocks to you. It's rickety, but it'll give these chicks some kind of protection—unless it falls down and squishes them all!"

It seemed like a game to him. He could hardly believe the little shack would do anything other than spread over the hill in a good wind, but he dutifully placed the rocks around the edges of the canvas. He could see the outline of the frame beneath, and he was careful not to lean hard on it. "You're a wonder, Annie," he said down to her, and she laughed.

He wanted to ask her if she was well, how she was managing without Tennessee, if the checks were enough for them. But he didn't want her face to change. He had so rarely heard her laugh. "Could you use a turkey?" he asked, turning back to his horse.

She saw the big birds hanging behind his saddle, and she was suddenly very happy. For a moment, she wanted to tell him about catching the Mallincoat's gobbler, but she thought better of it. She wasn't that desperate now, and she'd as soon he would never know she was. "Oh, Glory!" she laughed. "Those are fine turkeys, and we can do one justice. It's very kind of you to think of us," she finished, and started to take it from him.

"He's heavy, Annie," he said. "Let me carry him for you," and together they started toward the chopping block east of the house where Annie had rigged her tripod to hold her Dutch oven or one of the mess pots she and Will had bought. She had dug a pit there and built a rock wall to the southwest. It was where she would heat water to scald the turkey. As they emerged from Tennessee's trees, Doll nickered from east of the spring where she was tethered, and Martin was glad to have something to divert his attention from Annie's shoulders and neck.

"She's as beautiful as ever, isn't she?" he said. "How old is she, now?"

Annie supposed she was somewhere near nineteen, maybe twenty.

"You still don't want to sell her, I guess?" He was smiling.

"I honestly thought of it not long ago," she admitted. "But I just don't think I could stand it. And maybe I don't need to now," she finished, her voice expressing some disbelief in what she was saying. "I was thinking, though, if you still wanted a foal from her, I'd be willing to have her bred again—if we could find the right stallion."

Martin was immediately interested. "I'd sure like to have a foal from her, Annie. She's one of the best horses I ever saw.

"You know, there's an Arabian standing in Salina. He has her color, and he's built like a spring. Mancil has used him, and he's got some good foals. If we could bring them together, we might get something fine."

Martin was talking faster all the time, and Annie caught some of his enthusiasm.

"Would you take her to Salina?"

They discussed it for a half hour or more, two people loving horses, and they finally decided that Martin would pony Doll to the stallion in November so she'd foal in late September or October of the next year. Annie would keep Doll until spring of '83, then they would move her to Martin's barn and lots where he would keep her until the foal was weaned. Annie would have her back in the late spring of '84. They agreed to decide together when the foal was on the ground if they wanted to breed Doll back. Martin would feed and care for Doll, pay Annie fifty dollars for her use, and loan her a horse while Doll was gone. Annie and the girls could see Doll any time they wanted.

The next day, when Annie asked him to help her set up an account in the bank, he felt for the first time that Annie might, in fact, be able to stay and—not prosper, maybe, but—survive. He said as much, adding how greatly he admired her strength.

"I don't think I could do what you do, Annie, make such sacrifices, get along the way you do."

He had explained to her that if she could save regularly, say six dollars a month, she would have over a hundred dollars for Emily to start college with in three years. Then she could start Lydia's fund, then Sissie's. But he hadn't thought that possible, and after seeing her chicken house, he couldn't recommend it.

"You deserve that money, yourself, Annie," he insisted. "It's hard on you to work as you do and live on next to nothing. The pension is yours, and you should use it to make your life a little easier."

But he saw her back straighten.

"What I want is for my girls to have a decent life, to be able to help themselves if they must. Poor girls have to be at somebody's mercy, and that's not the way it's going to be for mine, not if I can help it."

He heard the iron in her voice, and he decided it was time to cease and desist. "You've done fine by them so far, Annie, and I reckon you can make up your own mind now, too.

"It's your money and your life. I'm not about to try to tell you how to live it."

Annie never forgot how what he said made her feel: " Your money...your life."

She had known it before, of course, but to have someone else—Martin Britt—affirm what she herself could sometimes only half see, that made her feel suddenly tall and wise.

She laughed out loud. "It *is*, isn't it?

"It *is* my money, my life, my decision."

She never felt stronger. She jumped up and stuck out her hand, as she had yesterday. "Thank you, Martin—for all you do for me."

As he rose and accepted her hand, a little surprised, she added, "And thank you for that lovely turkey, too. We must have eaten half of it last night."

When she left, he felt as though a small whirlwind had just blown through.

Martin let Annie choose the replacement horse from his little herd, and in late October, they made the switch. Annie left her beauty there and took home a gentle, slightly crow-footed, older gelding which Martin said would let the girls ride triple or pull the plow for them. His name was Tornado.

"My oldest girl named him when he was a colt," Martin laughed. "I think she was hoping for a little more than she got."

After riding him half a mile and never getting him out of a walk, Annie had to agree. Still when the girls got back from school, they straightway set about making him their new pet. "He's not very handsome," Lydia observed, with special attention to what hung between his hind legs. "But maybe we'll get to have a little baby horse, too, some day," Emily answered. She was like Annie about horses. And somewhere inside, Annie echoed Emily's hope—that they would, indeed, have one of Doll's foals.

That was not to be, however. When the filly was born, there were complications no one could stop. The foal was splendid, very like her dam. But within hours, Doll began to sweat and tremble and try to lie down. Martin sent a buggy for Annie, and by the time she got there, they had the filly drinking from a bottle. She had nursed some, so that was good. But Doll was hopeless. When Annie couldn't force her to walk anymore and she lay moaning in pain, Annie told Martin it was time. He had her shot.

He asked if Annie wanted the foal, and she shook her head no. When she could talk, she told him she would like to try to buy a granddaughter for Emily some day, if that was possible.

"Consider it done," he said, then asked if he could drive Annie home. They rode in silence for a little while, then he asked if he could pay for Doll. "She wouldn't be dead, Annie, if I hadn't wanted the foal so bad."

But Annie knew that wasn't right. She remembered who made the offer, and she thought perhaps she should return his fifty dollars for use of the mare. He wouldn't hear of it. She asked if she could buy Tornado because she had to have a horse.

"God, Annie. You can have him. He's not worth selling. If you feed him and care for him, he's yours."

He turned to her and saw that she was weeping. Pulling the horse up, he put his arms around her whispering, "Let me hold you, Annie. Let me just hold you."

Rubbing his cheek in her hair, he murmured over and over, "I'm sorry, Annie. I'm so sorry. Dear, dear Annie."

For a moment she felt and loved his strength, the smell of him, most of all, the pure comfort of a man's arms. But then she felt him tremble, and she instantly pulled away, careful not to look up to see what was in his face. She rubbed her eyes and shook her head. "I'm all right. I'll be all right."

So it was that Doll gave them Magnolia but took another part of Annie's heart away.

And so it was that Annie decided she must be her own consolation.

61

In April of 1885, Edward and Josie were married, and preparations for the wedding threw Annie and the three girls into a tizzy. The girls squealed and danced in a circle until Crow got so distressed he wore himself out threatening them and finally squeezed down in his basket sulking. They would get new clothes. They would ride on a train. They would stay overnight at Mancil Britt's home in Salina.

Annie didn't know what to do first, so Claire, who would also be going, brought her Sears Catalogue and came to help.

Money wasn't the worry it once was. Annie had managed to save almost $120 for Emily, and she still had the $50 Martin had given her for Doll. So she knew they could buy what they had to. She hoped she wouldn't have to go into either account, but she had refigured money enough times to come to see that this savings business didn't always go the way a person planned.

Her main worry was making the clothes. She was much better sewing skins together than she was frills. She could copy what Veryl had in his store or what the girls could describe to her, but she didn't like using the sewing machine, and if anyone had ever looked closely at her hand-work, they'd have discovered that she didn't do anything very fine. Her stitches were long and practical, and they covered lots of territory. But they didn't tend to hold very well, and they certainly weren't pretty. She decided she would do what she could and ask Claire to help with the impossible.

After days of deciding and undeciding, the girls finally chose the dresses they liked best, then Annie ordered plenty of material to make the frocks and new underwear and nightgowns. She was grateful it was springtime so they didn't need new coats. While she cut out the dresses and sewed and sewed and sewed—disliking every moment of it—the girls took over readying the garden spot, and Emily cooked their meals while Lydia and Sissie did dishes and dusting. Lydia did her best not to be quarrelsome for a change.

In her turn, Annie tried to prepare them for what they might run into—the people and the party after the wedding. But she didn't know, herself, what to expect, and all she could think of was what Mary had once told her. So before they left, Annie lined them up and told them to mind their manners the very best they could think to. "And if you aren't sure what to do, just be kind," she added. "Ma said that would pretty nearly always be all right, and I think it will."

Lydia shook her head in disbelief, but Emily and Sissie nodded their thanks.

Annie had fashioned for Emily, fourteen, tall, and brown, a cream-colored dress with puffed sleeves and a long skirt. Her stockings were cream to match her dress, and her shoes were spotless white, shining leather. "No single last shoes for my girls," Annie had laughed to herself.

Lydia was radiant in a pale blue blouse and long tan skirt cut slim with diagonal peach and blue stripes. She wore her hair up, as her mother sometimes did, and no one who looked at her could force their eyes to move on quickly. Narcissa, eight and brown like Emily, wore a little pink dress with a full, ruffled skirt. She had new shoes, too, and her own wrist corsage of tiny pink and cream paper roses Annie had made. Annie herself wore a light gray dress cut like the old black skirt and blouse. It was high-necked with a soft round collar, and she had added red accents in the buttons, a flower at the throat, and her red and black basket purse. Her shoes were shining black.

When they were joined at the depot by Martin and his family, the Wilsons and all their children, Annie was happy to see that, if she were a stranger looking at her girls, she would think they must be a delight and joy to whomever was lucky enough to call them daughters.

Annie sat with Claire and Lizzie while the men and children clustered themselves on the hard benches. She was glad not to be near Martin, and as she talked more with Lizzie, who was kind, direct, and funny, she felt immense relief that she had not made another bad mistake the night Doll died.

Hettie Britt, Josie's mother, was a fluttering woman, everywhere at once, and more nervous about hosting Annie and her family than she was about the wedding. She was actually very glad Josie had "got" Edward, as she had written her twin, Hattie, in Boston. "He is the most gorgeous boy—well, young man—inside and out. He has the blackest hair and the fairest skin I ever saw on a boy. I'll bet his mother hated it when his whiskers started."

Then she had tried to describe Annie. The only time they had met was at Tennessee's funeral, and Hettie had been brought to silence, if not by the circumstances then by Annie and her house. She had found Annie beautifully dressed in her old-fashioned, black blouse and skirt, even if they were a little large for her. And Hettie thought the costume set off Annie's eyes and hair, streaked white and black and pinned loosely on top of her head. In fact, Annie had seemed all eyes to Hettie, and she felt drawn to her. But, as she wrote her sister, "I didn't know what to say or do. Part of it was what had happened to little Tennessee. I felt so awful for Annie, and there simply weren't any words. She was so sick and unresponsive. I wasn't even sure she knew who we were, Hattie. She really could not talk. She seemed completely unaware of herself—or of us. She just wasn't quite there.

"And then I couldn't reconcile how she looked with what I had imagined when Edward told us that she hunted and butchered animals—then tanned skins and plowed fields. It was hard to believe, she seemed so fragile that day.

"I remembered his saying that she wouldn't let him hunt because she thought he shouldn't have to kill anything. But he said she could hit a squirrel at twenty paces and I guessed that was a pretty long ways. Mancil said it was a hell of a long ways! But at the funeral it seemed impossible that she could ever be that strong or, well, tough. Yet, I saw the skins on the side of their house!

"And the house!

"Hattie, I couldn't have stood it, to move from Martin's place to that single room out there in the hills. And she had to. I'll swear, she made me feel like I was pampered and lazy—and I'm not. You know that. And I know that was just me. I don't think she thought much about me one way or another."

Hettie's letters had gone to considerable lengths to share how proud Edward was when Annie's baskets and plaster began to sell well in

Salina and Ellsworth and other towns. And she added, "If you run out of the Nuremburg, let me know, and I'll send some as soon as a new batch gets in," for Hettie had been buying it for everyone she knew.

She did not feel useless in comparison to Annie, but she did not know what to expect when the family would arrive for the wedding, and she couldn't calm herself until she actually saw them coming up the walk, lovely, summery-looking—just like everyone else—all except Lydia whom Hettie could not stop admiring. Then she was able to let Josie and Edward and the wedding preoccupy her.

Edward, who was a year younger than Josie, had decided to remain in college one extra year. Josie, red-haired, ringleted, and as boisterous as Edward was ebony, ivory and serious, had laughed and declared she needed that time to be half-ready to marry anybody so smart and solemn. Edward had also decided not to remain at the college to teach—as Doctor Fairchild urged. He preferred, he said, to help his father-in-law on the farms.

"There isn't even a decision to make," he had told them. "I love Josie, and I love you. I want to be here. Then, too, it's closer to Mama, and she'll be needing me more in time."

If he hadn't already won their hearts, that declaration would have. They began to help plan Josie and Edward's new house, and no one was happier than Hettie. After the wedding weekend, she was also delighted with Annie, and she wrote Hattie dozens of pages.

"One of the dearest things that happened was when Annie saw Mancil's old guitar—which he hasn't played since we were married, and he didn't hardly play it then. She asked if we'd mind if she tried it. Of course, we didn't. Well, you can't imagine, Hattie. She began to sing, and she sounded like an angel. Such a low, beautiful voice she has. It was so lovely we all wished she'd have sung at the wedding.

"She said the strings hurt her fingers because she didn't have any calluses. But then she looked at all the calluses on her hands, and she started laughing and said, 'Well, I guess I just don't have them in the right places anymore!' She's charming, Hattie!

"And after a while, she turned to Josie with a big smile and sang 'I Dream of Jeannie.' Only she sang it 'I Dream of Josie with the Bright Red Hair,' and we all laughed. It was a good joke. But then we all listened, for it was the prettiest thing you've ever heard.

"I'm afraid young Mancil was smitten with Lydia before the two days were out, and I fear for his heart. Edward has always told us Lydia is difficult, and I could see, at least a little, what he means. She did not laugh and join in with the others. She was not impolite, I don't mean. But she was not exactly agreeable, either. She holds herself in reserve, somehow.

"Poor little Mannie. He was turning himself positively inside out to please her, and she looked at him as though he were a mildly interesting toad! Such a beauty she is!

"What astonished me more than anything was the gift they gave the children. It is a beautiful, decorative, green basket Annie made. It's squarish with a wide weave and flared in a circle at the top. It is just full of her marvelous paper flowers—roses, carnations, and fern. Then in an envelope was a check for $50. Imagine!

"In a note Emily had written, 'We all love you so much. Use this to buy something pretty.' Then they had all signed their names: Emily, Lydia, Sissie, and Mother.

"Edward couldn't even speak, and I thought for sure he was going to cry.

"She laughed out loud and said, 'Your banking family is teaching me some new tricks, Edward. I have some accounts now, too, you see, and one is called "Weddings"!'

"We all had such a wonderful time we hated to see them go, but the train trip home was only their second, and they were excited about it. Besides, Annie said they had to get home to take care of their crow.

"They keep a live crow on a tree branch in the house! I can't imagine. Edward says it's like a watch-dog and actually helps Annie build fires. —I don't ask!!!

"Mancil came to the coach, of course, to see them off, and he was carrying something behind his back. 'What have you got, Mancil,' I asked him. With a little grin, he brought around the guitar and handed it to Annie. 'If you'll permit me, Annie, this needs to go home with you,' he said. 'I'd be very pleased if you'd take it.'

"She smiled so big. 'You know, I've been wanting a guitar for twenty years,' she said! 'I just love to play it. It will give me so much pleasure.' She just beamed. And she took it so happily without a word about how he shouldn't or she couldn't. She made us all feel really good, the way you want to, you know...."

62

Emily decided to go to college for two years even though she wanted to teach in the county schools. "Edward explained it to me," she told her mother. "The curriculum doesn't actually have anything that can help me in a direct way, but I think I can learn what will be useful to me. I'd like to learn to play the piano. That would be fun for me and the children. And studying some science and literature seems very interesting to me, Mama."

"You'll meet lots of interesting boys, too," Lydia interrupted, and Emily dropped her head and flushed.

Annie thought there never would be anyone for Emily but Andrew Geisendorfer—who had taught her and her sisters for several years, dear, sweet Andrew who was himself only twenty-six. Even after Emily had learned all there was for him to teach her in the county courses, he tutored her in Latin and gave her books of history and poetry to read, novels, too. They ate dinner together every day to talk about what she had read, and she helped him with the beginning students each year.

"They'll be cuter than Mr. Geisendorfer ever was," Lydia persisted. She was only thirteen, but she was already womanly, and she was merciless teasing Emily about their teacher. She had seen it as quickly as Annie had the June Saturday a year before when Andrew had ridden out to bring Emily a book to read, *The Scarlet Letter*. Emily had been carrying water to the garden, using Tennessee's old yoke, and he snatched it off her shoulders and ran back and forth to the spring until she had to stop him. Then they sat together in the shade of one of the cottonwoods reading and talking and laughing.

"He loves her, doesn't he?" Lydia asked, sitting on the table and watching them through the window. She turned around to Annie. "Mama, that's stupid. He's her teacher, for God's sake."

"Don't swear, Lydia," Annie said, her own insides a little uneasy as she granted the love part of what Lydia said.

"He's too old for her, isn't he?"

But Annie wasn't sure about that any more. "Sometimes those things don't matter so much, you know."

"I think it's stupid…. And he's not the least bit handsome."

"Well. Sometimes those things don't matter so much either, Lydia. Not everybody can be as handsome or pretty as you are."

At that, Lydia frowned at Annie, jumped off the table, and started outdoors.

"Lydia!" Annie called her sharply enough to stop her. "You go on about your own business, now. Don't bother Emily and Mr. Geisendorfer. And don't you tease her, either."

But she might as well have talked to the wind because before the hour was over, Annie saw Lydia sitting on the ground in front of them, then Emily came in and ran to the loft, and Andrew left. Later Lydia sashayed in, arch and self-satisfied.

It had been that way ever since.

Now Emily calmed herself and said, "I don't want to meet a bunch of boys, Lydia, though I'm sure that's hard for you to believe. I want to learn more." She looked at her mother before she went on. "Mr. Geisendorfer thinks it would be a good thing to do, Mama—just for two years. Then I'll be able to handle the older boys better."

Lydia giggled, and Emily frowned and went on.

"They can be awfully troublesome sometimes, you know.

"Then I'll present myself for the third grade certificate and teach a couple of years before I go for the second and first. I want to score highly, Mama, and the study will help me. I want to take math, science, history and economics, too. I'll take everything I can. That will help me know what to study later, too, on my own.

"Do you think we can manage it, Mama?"

Annie thought so. She had continued to save all she could although the basket and plaster sales had tapered off, and Mr. Lerner had not returned for two summers. Still, she had more than a hundred and ninety dollars for Emily, and she was very glad to be able to tell her that.

Lydia was furious with both of them. "How come she gets all that money, and we have to live out here and wear animal skins for coats? It's not fair, Mama," she shouted, and she ran from them out-of-doors.

It was the first time any of the children had spoken openly about how the family lived or how their mother managed. Although Annie understood perfectly well that Lydia could flare up and say unkind things she later regretted, Annie also realized that, in this moment, Lydia had spoken from her heart. And it was about more than jealousy of Emily. Annie's face must have registered what she felt, for Emily jumped to her and hugged her tightly.

"Mama! Don't you listen to what Liddie says. You've done more for us than anyone else ever could have. Don't you feel bad! Don't you ever feel bad about us." She dried Annie's eyes with her apron, then they put their foreheads together and laughed at themselves.

Lydia didn't come back in until after dark. She also didn't do her share of the chores.

Annie knew it would serve no purpose to tell her that her own savings would start the moment Emily left for school, that Annie was saving for each in her turn. Annie knew Lydia was an impatient and needful girl, and she did not understand her stormy daughter. She didn't think she could have satisfied Lydia if she had been able to give her everything, but sometimes she wished she could try it, just once.

In the meantime, she and Emily and Sissie continued to plan for Emily's departure. At the table, Sissie would sit as close as she could to Emily, Emily's arm around her as they thought what it would be like for her in Manhattan and for them on the hillside without her.

Lydia never joined them.

63

One bright October morning—the kind Mary used to say looked like scraps of paper colored by a child—Annie went outside to fix Crow a new branch up into his tree. He didn't need much, just a long piece of wood wedged snugly against the trunk so he could walk up and hop onto the lowest branches. But every couple of years or so, she would have to change the stick, for the trees were growing tall. It had already been nine years since Tennessee planted them. Most of them were giving pleasant shade, and of course Annie never felt it without thanking her Tennessee. She no sooner got the stick steadied than up it Crow ran, scampering to the very top of the tree where he glistened in the sun like a big black iris and preened and cawed as though he owned the world.

Annie turned the chickens out while she could watch them. From the beginning, she had treated these chickens differently. She wouldn't let herself or anyone else make pets of them. She intended them for meat—if she or Lydia or Sissie had to have it—and definitely for eggs, so she tried to keep the old chicken house standing to protect them.

The chickens still didn't have any real roosts or nests, but she wove some sticks together for them to climb up and sleep on, and she put some wheat straw around for them to lay eggs in. She was looking the shed over to see what most needed her attention when Crow began to click his warning. Annie looked up the trail, and there came someone dressed in black and hunkered down in an old buggy pulled by a horse that looked a little like Tornado. It was Mr. Lerner.

He hadn't been by for a long time, and she was very glad to see him, but she became anxious right away. He had almost nothing with him, and he looked terrible. His eyes and cheeks were sunken, and he was ill-shaven. Worst of all, his ears were wrong, wrinkled somehow, and Mary always said that was a sign of death.

He smiled to see Annie, though, and let her help him step down. She forgot about the chickens and took him right inside. She had some gooseberry pie and fresh cream for it, and he ate a big piece, smacking his lips over it and telling her how fine it was. But something was very wrong, and Annie was scared for him.

He asked about all the children and about her, as he always did. He was especially happy about Edward and Josie's new boy. "Mancil Joseph. Is good name," he said, and smiled into his tea. He was also very pleased that Emily had decided to study at college even though it didn't seem practical to most people. Claire and Claude had tried and tried to get Annie to change her mind.

"Goodness gracious, Annie," Claire said, her face flaming. "Emily can teach if she wants to without all that extra expense. It don't make sense. And she'll just get married anyhow, you know." She was positively mad at her best friend.

But not Mr. Lerner. "It is good. Men. Women. No matter. She should learn and learn. Is good inside, no matter what she do. I am very happy for her—and that she has such a mother to encourage her."

Everything in Annie said that he was right, not Claire.

He noticed that they had lots of canned vegetables and fruits, and he was glad they were doing well.

"And you, Mr. Lerner? How are you?" Annie asked him, and she went ahead and put her hand over his.

For a time, he said nothing. She thought he could not. It was his son, he finally managed, a man who raised cattle and goats and made cheese near Manhattan. "Is where I get cheese to sell," he said, and Annie nodded. She remembered how delicious it was. "They run him away," he said, his hands shaking until she finally took his tea from him.

What had happened was that one night his son's barn had been burned, his barn and four of his cows. Six others—and his goats—were saved. That was bad enough, but the madmen also threw stones through the windows of his home with notes threatening him and his family.

"They don't want no Jews," he said, raising his eyes to Annie's. "We go back to New York, back to that place." He looked out and up. "Not so much sky in New York.

"And no Crow." He chuckled a little when he said that, but his frown stayed, and they were both silent a long time.

Annie didn't have words to fit anything as wrong as this seemed to her to be. Whatever she could think to say would sound to the side, somehow. All she knew to do was pat his hand. But here they were again, these feelings and acts of anger, of hatred, a kind of lynching like that she had heard of when she was a girl, the sort of thing they fought the war over.

She thought of Will moving out here because of his hopes for a better place. She thought of Melva moving on north for the same reason.

"Is New York better?" she asked.

He shrugged. "No. No. Is same."

And suddenly she understood. There was no better place. There couldn't be. All of it was inside the people, themselves, her, Will, Mr. Lerner—and those who hated. It wasn't outside in the air or the horses or the trees. It was in the people.

He looked over at her and went on with his own thought: "Only more of us in New York. We don't need nobody else back there."

"But I need you here!" Annie heard herself crying. "I need you. I need Melva. What could you possibly do—or your son—that people don't want you here? What is in us that we have to destroy anything that is the littlest bit different?"

He patted her hand and tightened his lips.

"It's not fair," she said. "It's like Tennessee's death. It's not fair."

"Maybe is God's will," he said softly.

But Annie insisted. "I don't think god has anything to do with it. It has to do with us, what we're afraid of or what we're too ignorant to deal with.

"Tennessee died because Will wasn't there to help her live, and I didn't know how. Melva had to move because people wouldn't help her and her family the way they did mine. And you have to go where you don't want to because people who preach love and forgiveness behave like savages."

She thought of Bright-Skies. "And people who are supposed to be savages give help to strangers."

The more she talked, the more confused she felt, and she was more angry than she had been since Tennessee died.

"People keep looking for miracles from god. Or they do terrible things or they watch other people do terrible things, and they say that it's god's will. They say god understands the truth and helps those who suffer. But the suffering goes on and on. If god is there, he's not helping anybody. It's like us sitting down beside an old dog caught in a bear trap and saying to him, 'I understand your pain.' That doesn't help the dog. What you've got to do is get him out! No! I don't think god has anything to do with it. We're the ones. We're the ones." Her face was as stormy as Lydia's.

Mr. Lerner stood and patted her shoulder. He took their cups to the wash-basin and came back to her.

"Maybe is God's will, Annie," he said very gently. "Maybe we are truly free and must become what we know is good and right.

"Maybe is awful struggle all must make. Maybe is God's great gift to us: we must choose to do what is good when that is hardest to do.

"Maybe is not God who can take dog from trap. Maybe is us who must learn not to make trap in first place."

He leaned down and kissed her hair. "Anyway, my Annie. So long as there is people like you, we have chance to learn what we must."

Then he had to go. They both knew he would not come back that way.

He gave her a few dollars, from the last of her baskets and plaster he had sold, he said. She did not want to take the money, but he insisted, saying that it was part of the profit he had made.

"But that wasn't our agreement," she reminded him.

"Is new agreement," he laughed.

Then he told her what she already knew. Most of the people who were going to buy her wares already had, and she should not expect to sell nearly the quantities she had at first.

She understood. That was the way it was in Brittsville, and in Salina and Abilene. Newcomers would buy, if they could, and people would replace the plaster as they used it, but the "start up market," as Edward called it, was gone. It was serious for Annie because it meant she had to live more and more off the pension checks. It was enough, especially because only three were left at the house, and she had milk and eggs and chickens. But she couldn't save for Lydia as she had for Emily, and her "Doll" and "Weddings" accounts had stopped growing altogether.

Yet nothing seemed serious beside her knowledge that she was saying a last goodbye to someone she loved. When he left, she stood there clutching the money and feeling something like her mother must have the morning she held Will's sword in front of her and watched them out of sight.

64

It seemed to Annie that she been thinking of her mother ever since Mr. Lerner left. This was the first time they had not heard from her—or from Mrs. Tollett who wrote letters for her—some time around Christmas. Annie was worried.

The last they had heard was in November. Mary said she was fine, just a little older and a little tireder. "But who isn't?" she'd asked. Billy was well. It was cold. Her knees hurt. She was proud of the children. She longed to see Annie.

In the twenty-three years separating them, Annie had forty-six letters about like that one, two a year, every year for all that time, two letters and birthday remembrances for the children. Like her mother, Annie knew what the letters didn't tell. She understood the years of walking, making splits, hoeing, killing copperheads, aching, wanting, aging, waiting. Annie supposed she knew her mother's days nearly as well as she knew her own.

She just couldn't see Mary's face.

So when Veryl brought Billy's telegram that Mary had died on January 8, Annie was shocked but not greatly surprised. She sat with the paper in her hand, wondering why something with those words on it did not burn her fingers, wondering if Mary had suffered, wondering if she had known what was happening, wondering what her eyes last looked upon.

Annie had to ask again what a life is and why it matters so. But she knew exactly what a mother is.

She felt older by half and closer to Mary than she ever had before. She let the tears fall and wished she were out on the hills at night with the stars above her and the coyotes howling.

65

After two years in Manhattan, Emily came home in May, as she had before, but again only for a visit. Like Edward, she had done so well the President urged her to stay as his assistant in the political economy class, and she intended to return a third year.

"He wants me to study lots more, Mama. He says I should study for a doctor's degree! Me, Mama! He says I have one of the best minds he's ever encountered. Those were his very words, Mama!"

Annie had always known Emily was a smart child. Will had recognized it, too. And she was glad for Emily to go to college. But this was far beyond anything Annie had thought of, and she didn't know what to think or say.

"But I don't think I want to do that, study for the doctor's degree." Emily was sitting at the table, drinking coffee from her old tin cup, looking up at Crow. "I'm not sure I need to do that.

"I can always read and learn what I want to know. I don't think I need more teachers for that, now, though I know I can always write to Doctor Fairchild if I need to. I just want books, and Andrew says he'll help me get those."

She smiled as she thought of him. She had gone to visit the school the very day she got home, and since then, they had spent hours walking together, reading, talking. Emily took up her old chores for the interval, and Andrew helped her. While they hoed or pulled weeds, they talked about everything from Herman Melville to whether women should vote.

Annie could see what good friends they were, and she knew they would be good life partners, too. They made her feel happy the way

Edward and Josie did. She was very glad for them, and she expected every day that Emily would tell her they wanted to marry. Annie thought this would be the time.

But Emily's expression changed, and her voice took on an edge. "You know, Mama, that if Andrew and I were to marry, I could not teach?" Annie sat still, looking carefully at Emily's face. It showed anger.

"It's an unwritten law, you know. They will only hire unmarried women—to teach in the lower grades."

Annie may have known it, but she had never given it any thought. She frowned, too.

"Andrew is free to marry and teach, but I am not. They say they don't want the children to see a married woman working outside the home. It would be a bad example, they say, demeaning to the image of wife and homemaker.

"What I really think is that they don't want the children to see a pregnant woman in front of the class." She laughed in scorn. "That might make them have impure thoughts, and it would be a bad example of a *teacher*—someone apparently devoted to learning—which they apparently think means *sexless*."

Annie was very surprised at what Emily was saying. Her face grew darker and grimmer as she went on.

"You tell me, Mama, if that is fair. We can't marry else we'll be bad teachers—as if being in the family way were somehow unclean. And we can't teach else we'll be bad wives. It's insane, Mama. It doesn't make any sense at all. And people like Martin Britt and Claude Wilson—even Andrew—maybe even Papa—the leaders of the town, the school board—they make those rules. We can vote here in Brittsville for who we want on the school board, but it doesn't make any difference for they're all men and always look at such things the same way.

"I hate it, Mama. To tell you the truth, that's the real reason I'm going back to school another year. Doctor Fairchild told me that Susan B. Anthony comes out here—well, out to Lawrence and Topeka—nearly every year, and he is taking some of his advanced students to meet her in the spring. He knows her personally, Mama. He graduated from Oberlin College—which has always worked for women's rights.

"He says that our future is in the hands of people like her—and young women like me. He says that I've got to work for change. I want to do that, Mama."

All Annie could think to ask was, "Who is Susan Anthony?"

And after she found out, all she could think to ask was, "What about Andrew?"

Emily rubbed her fingers around the rim of the cup and shook her head. "I don't know, Mama. I don't know what we are going to do." Almost together they rose to go to the garden, and Emily spoke no more of what Annie halfway feared as feminist and outlandish ideas.

Then in June, Emily asked if she could use the rest of her money to buy one of Magnolia's foals. "I'll get paid for helping Doctor Fairchild next year, you know, and if you'll take care of the filly this year, I'll send you two dollars a month for grain and extras. Then the next year I can drive her and have my own way to get around."

"Do you think you can afford to buy one of those horses?" Annie asked her.

"If I don't have enough, I'll ask Mr. Britt for a loan and pay it off on a longer term. He knows I'm a good risk," she laughed.

But she didn't have to do that because Annie could help her with the $54 in her "Doll" account.

They spent the rest of the summer playing with a wonderful yearling, a chestnut filly Emily called Athens. Annie thought it was a peculiar name for a horse, but Emily said Greece was the birthplace of western civilization, and this horse would be the beginning of her herd.

"You're going to breed horses?" Annie asked, astonished again at Emily's way of thinking.

"Yes, ma'am." Then she grinned at Annie, "With a little help from my mother, I am!"

And there was no help her mother would rather give. Annie didn't think Athens was quite as elegant as Doll had been—and apparently Martin didn't, either, else he wouldn't have sold her—but she looked much like her grandmother, except for a wider blaze. And she was a very sweet filly who loved to be with them and was willing as could be. Emily bought some small rope, and with that she made a halter and long reins. They were soon driving Athens everywhere although, of course, they didn't ask her to pull anything more than a good-sized log.

In early September, before Emily went back to Manhattan, she and Annie, Lydia and Sissie all went with Andrew into Brittsville to a little harvest celebration the town held every year. This year was special because, in addition to the exhibition of new machinery and tools, in addition to tables showing ladies' fine quilting and crocheting, in addition to the stalls for barbecued beef and pork sandwiches and marvelous cakes and pies and lemonade and tea, this fair had a merry-go-round.

They could hear the calliope and the hissing steam well before they got to town, and they were a long time making their way through the crowd to see the dancing horses with their red, flaring nostrils and floating manes. Annie believed that, if she had never seen Doll and Athens, she would have thought these the most beautiful creatures in the world.

Sissie, who was a little timid around large animals, was wide-eyed at these, and like every other child there, she immediately started begging for a ride.

"We're all going to ride," Andrew declared, "and it's my treat. Four rides apiece," he told the ticket man, and handed him a dollar.

Delighted with their black and red and brown prancing beauties, they allowed Andrew to lift them up, side-saddle, all nice and proper, Annie riding beside Sissie, Andrew standing in front between Emily and Lydia, to "steady them should they start to fall," he said. Up and down, round and round their horses took them, and they laughed and waved at people watching.

Emily was on the inside horse, and she had to look back over her shoulder to talk to Andrew. Mostly she just smiled and peeked at him once in a while. But Lydia was facing him, and she seemed very talkative. Annie saw her lean toward him over and over again to get his attention. As one ride stopped and another began, Annie saw his face lose the open, cheerful look it always had and take on an expression that seemed like pain. Lydia finally stopped talking then, and she rode silently above him, looking from him to Emily to the horse and back to him, her blue eyes flashing and her hand occasionally dropping to his shoulder as though to balance herself.

66

Another strange vision came to Annie in a dream in April after Mary's death. She could see her mother walking on the mountain, not far from her Grandpa's cabin. It was May, the green time Mary most loved. She was just reaching for the laurel. Annie could see freckles on her arm and hand—which surprised her, and she thought, "Ma's skin was so white." Then the land was burned, all the flowers gone, the trees become black snags, and Annie was there, but her mother was not. She ran through the ashes, and they rose into the air all around her, choking her, and she coughed and screamed out, "Ma! Ma! Mary Sherwood! Mary Elizabeth Sherwood!"

It was that which woke Annie. When she called out Mary's name, which she didn't remember ever having said before, she saw it at the same time: MARY ELIZABETH SHERWOOD, all written out in a bookish way. It was on metal, brass, Annie thought, like that on Will's old kit.

And below, in a big square under glass was a wreath of flowers. They weren't real flowers. Annie couldn't tell what they were made of. They weren't all Tennessee flowers, either, it didn't seem. She could recognize roses and daisies and lilies-of-the-valley. There was lots of fern. The rest she wasn't sure about.

They formed a circle around a poem. It began:

> If we are slow forgetting
> It is because....

But when she was fully awake, she couldn't remember the rest of it. She could see it in neat lines one after the other, the second one set in some as in their old hymnals. But she couldn't make them out. She knew she had read it all before she awakened, and it was for Mary, but Annie couldn't remember it no matter how hard she tried.

She felt dazed when she got up, a little dizzy and tired as though she had not slept. Her heart was jumping some, but she was used to that and paid it no attention. She was preoccupied with the vision. No matter what she did, having a bite of bread and milk, fixing the girls' dinners, she had before her eyes the picture of that square full of flowers below Mary's name, then the sight of her arm, then the desolation.

It was late in the morning when Annie finally figured out that she was seeing her mother's grave marker. That bewildered her. She had never "seen things," and she couldn't make out why she was seeing this now. It made her nervous, and she couldn't concentrate on what she was supposed to be doing. She hadn't any more than realized what she was seeing than she began wondering where the marker might be. She couldn't see in her mind's eye any background for it, so she couldn't tell if it was no place at all or if it was down in the bend of Roaring Hollow where the old rock markers—most without any names on them—stuck about half-way up out of the ground and huddled together under the trees like a little flock of sheep. Her father and grandfather's were among them. She couldn't imagine what she'd seen as being there, yet she knew it was her mother's and should be. She decided to think of it beside Sherwood's right there in that bend.

Once she'd done that, Annie could see the oaks and hackberries hovering over it, and she was sure that's where Mary was. She could imagine the green and cool bend with the branch running just below it, flowing over rocks, sounding like cattle when they eat hay. It was where they had always knelt to cup water in their hands to drink or splash over their faces. It was always fresh. When Annie could see and feel that, it took away some of the hot, rough air that lingered in her throat from the dream.

Annie finally went out to the old rocker under Tennessee's front cottonwood, and she thought about the tombstone while the sun rose, moved west, and started down. Crow jumped on her shoulder and ran his beak into her hair, but she paid him no mind, and he finally hopped up his stick to his branch where he quarreled at her and begged until even he got tired and dozed. Lydia and Sissie came and went, but she told them she was just tired, and they honored that.

Her insides were unquiet. It was as though she had forgotten something important, and she couldn't rest until she remembered it—or as though she had lost something she had to have, and she had to go over every square inch of the house to find it. She just sat there, but her stomach wound tighter, and she felt miserable.

Then, just as the sun comes through the fog, it came to her that she was going to make this tombstone for her mother. She was startled, but it seemed to her that the moment she latched on to that insight, she stopped thinking about the dream and even, in a way, about Mary's death. All her attention got focused on trying to figure out how such a thing could be made, and she was eased.

She got after the flowers first, maybe because she had made them from paper all her life, and she was more comfortable trying to think of them. Even so, she had no idea how to make these particular ones. They couldn't be paper because it wasn't strong enough. These flowers would require something else, but she could not think what it might be. And she didn't even know what some of them were.

And the letters! Annie got down the old *Formulary* to study letters and for a moment felt happy to remember the nice blaze the pension letter had made. But she had never looked at printed words before to see how the separate parts were put together. She soon realized that she had never made anything like these at Hickory Grove School—or any place else, for that matter, in what she had written down herself.

The g and a letters were totally different, and so were the capitals. All those little bars and lines in the W and M made them look like bird feathers or fallen trees to Annie. She studied and studied them, then got a pencil and a piece of blank paper out of the back of the *Formulary* to try to copy the letters she knew were in the poem. Hers ran up and down and shook like letters little children make. She felt more upset about ever getting them shaped even and right than she did about figuring out the poem they'd have to make.

Whether it was shelling corn for the chickens or milking Gretel's Girl or hoeing or canning, Annie could think of hardly anything else besides the marker. Wherever she looked, she seemed to be searching for a place to begin, something which would reveal the marker's insides to her. The one thing she could do was practice making letters, and she did that on every old scrap of paper she could find—which wasn't many. She traced over her best ones until she pushed her pencil through the paper.

One morning Annie started to break the water to do the wash, and she found she was running low on lye. When she tapped the tin against the side of the tub, the tin dented. She held it in front of her for a second, then she pushed against the side with her thumb. It gave. Forgetting all about the wash and not really planning anything, she went in search of some scissors.

They worked. Although it was hard to do, she found that she could puncture the side and cut the tin. She removed the top and bottom, then cut straight up the seam. Spread out on the table, the tin was like a piece of stiff, sharp paper, and Annie knew what she would make the flowers from.

With all the spring and summer work, she couldn't spend much time experimenting with the tin or the letters, and Lydia and Sissie were less than enthusiastic, anyway. For their lives, they couldn't see what she was up to, and from the beginning, they scolded. Sissie quarreled at Annie for making tin slivers that were forever getting in their feet, and Lydia complained at her for running all over the country "begging," as she put it, for tin cans.

"My God, Mother!" she said. "What will people think when they see you with a gunny sack over your shoulder at the dump digging through other people's trash?"

They both said, "You can't make a tombstone for Grandma. You just can't up and do a thing like that."

And Lydia added her usual, "That's really stupid, Mother."

When Emily was there, she mostly observed and stayed silent. It seemed impossible and strange to her, but she wanted to wait and see what Annie would come up with.

The other girls were indignant, though. Part of Annie understood. But the rest of her knew that it would take more than their worries about other people's opinions to keep her from doing this thing which pushed so hard at her.

However, much later, she did come to wonder if she had allowed herself to be too distracted by it at a time when Lydia perhaps needed her most. She never excused herself by thinking Lydia wouldn't have listened anyway. Annie believed forever that she should have tried harder and acted more wisely on what she saw at the fair: Lydia's manner with Andrew on the merry-go-round, that very instant when Annie feared Andrew was lost to Emily.

She couldn't imagine that Lydia had a serious thought in her head about him. She had always abused him to Emily as ugly and gawky and old, though he was none of those. But it was all too clear to Annie that night that he had a thought in his head about Lydia. Annie was distressed, and she faulted Lydia for being such a careless flirt. Still, Annie was unsure about Emily's intentions, and she didn't know how to intervene even if she thought she should, which she didn't.

Annie knew Andrew was too honorable a young man to court sisters, and because Lydia, at fourteen, was still his student, even if she did flirt with him, Annie didn't think he would break that trust. She concluded that he would not be calling at their house any more, and she was very sorry about it.

Emily had gone back to Manhattan the next week. She had not mentioned saying goodbye to Andrew, and Annie couldn't tell whether she knew. She seemed preoccupied and very quiet, but Annie thought that could be because she had made her decision to return to school and prepare for a life as a teacher—which could also mean without Andrew.

Annie didn't think she should ask.

Lydia was no more forthcoming. Annie noticed no changes in her behavior. She was no more pleasant than ever, and her grades were still very poor. Andrew continued to write dutiful comments and corrections on her papers, asking her to reread certain pages in her texts, to write misspelled words twenty times, to try to learn the parts of a sentence. But while Sissie often brought home a reader to practice with or asked Annie for help with arithmetic, nothing Lydia did at home ever suggested that she was in school.

She spent a good deal of time studying her reflection in darkened windows, creating her own dresses when Annie would buy material, and nagging her mother to let her have some money from the account she now knew was begun for her. She wanted to go to Salina to stay with Josie and Edward.

"I could help with their baby. I could do housework for them. Mama, it's so boring here. I hate it."

But Annie wouldn't agree to any of that. "Lydia, you don't like to do housework, and you ignore babies. What makes you think you wouldn't be bored there, too?"

She pouted and sulked, but Annie was unmoved. Lydia was not going to Edward's house.

What concerned Annie most was that she didn't know where Lydia could ever go—or what she could ever do. She was a good seamstress, but she didn't like sewing. If she hadn't been vain, she never would have touched a needle. When Annie tried to talk with her, she would grow silent or angry with her mother for criticizing her, which, of course, Annie never intended. Annie loved her very much and told her so, but that was in no way enough for Lydia.

It was Sissie who told Annie in the spring that Lydia and Andrew always ate their sandwiches together at noon. And sometimes Sissie walked home alone, telling her mother that Andrew was helping Lydia with some lesson or another. Still Annie did not think anything would come of it. She knew Lydia did not care for him, and she never believed he would deceive himself into thinking he cared for her, however beautiful he found her.

But Emily did not come to Brittsville that summer after her third year. She was going to work for the superintendent of county schools in Manhattan to help revise the curriculum of the eight grades. If Annie could keep Athens until late September, she wrote, she would come then to collect the horse and move to Meridan to take up her first teaching post. And it was not until Annie tried to call the girls for morning chores—just after the harvest fair—that she realized they were gone, Lydia and Andrew. Sissie came down from the loft, but Lydia did not.

Annie remembered that she had gotten up in the night, but she had said she had to go outdoors, and Annie had fallen asleep again. She didn't know Lydia had not come back. Even in the morning, she didn't know. Later, when she went to call Lydia, she saw the rolled up blanket in the bed. Lydia had apparently taken out some of her things in Annie's old carpetbag before they ever went to bed. She left with that and all the Nuremburg Plaster her mother had recently made, twenty jars. Annie supposed she intended to sell it.

Sissie and her mother sat at the table facing one another, their voices filled with tears, and tried to understand it. "Mama, she just laughed at him when we walked home. She said he was a silly man who didn't understand anything that wasn't in a book."

Annie had to smile just a bit. It was very clear to her that Andrew was about to learn a great deal that wasn't in his books. Still, she could not explain to Sissie or herself, not then and not ever, how Lydia could be so bold, how she could be so cruel, to them, to Emily, even to Andrew, how this could ever have happened.

Annie went through the motions of the day, the week, but she found no answers. It is one thing to lose a daughter, to feel your heart go into the ground with her, and to go on living with that awful certainty. But it is altogether different when your girl runs away, even with a man like Andrew. Annie knew Lydia would never stay with him. She knew that even if Andrew did not. Lydia did not want him. She wanted out, out and away. But to what? That was the horror of it for Annie—never to know, always to imagine, never to be able to put it in place. It would never end.

Everyone knew what had happened almost as quickly as Annie and Sissie did because Andrew was not there to begin the school year, and Lydia was gone, too. Annie believed everyone also understood that they would go far, far away to try to avoid their shame. People were as kind as they could be, and Claire tried to comfort the two of them—and later Edward. Lydia was so beautiful, she said, and Andrew so nice a man. They would make their way. They would write in time.

But there was no comfort in what Annie saw and thought: Andrew had not been honorable, and Lydia's beauty did not cover a good heart. Annie loved her beyond the saying, and she felt stabbed in her own heart. But she knew they were gone from her, from everyone. And there was nothing she could do, no place to search, no one to help. Nothing. She just had to sit and let it hit her.

When Emily came for Athens, the school board tried to hire her. But she would not break her word or her contract, she said, and she prepared to move to Meridan. She had ordered a small buggy and harness, and within a week, Athens was working well for her.

"I am not bitter, Mama," she told Annie as she drank her coffee while Annie had her tea that last morning. "I knew from his letters that Andrew's feelings were changed somehow. I suspected it was Lydia. They have made a terrible mistake, and I think I love him still. But I'll get over my anger with them, and it's partly my own fault for not knowing what to do and for not being definite with Andrew. I could not expect him to wait forever.

"Sometimes people can't help themselves as much as we think they should," she added quietly. "I'm not trying to be a martyr, Mama, but sometimes that's how I see my life: trying to get others to help themselves—more as they should."

She laughed just a little. "And it appears to me I've got my work cut out for me!"

67

During the years Annie worked on the marker, Claire must have announced a hundred times that she had never seen anything like it. She was pained herself even to think of it, but she was always in awe of it. She said to Claude, "Claude, she ain't takin' proper care—of herself or that girl she's got left. She's all the time hunkered there in the middle of the floor or out by that stump she drug up to kill chickens on. She's all the time cuttin' or whackin' on them tin cans. An' you know, she's made a plumb pest of herself, beggin' for 'em at every door, and she's asked all us women to save 'em for her, especially lye tins which she says is the best."

Claude had his own story, and it substantiated everything Claire said. He had seen Annie out at the ravine where everybody dumped trash. "I took them old wheels and busted up barrels out there," he said, "and there she was, teeterin' up atop that trash heap, pokin' around with a stick taller than she was.

"What you doin' there, Annie?" Claude said he'd asked her.

"Hello, Claude," she called back, just as cheerful as if she was picking flowers. "Bet I'm the biggest rat you'll see here today."

He laughed back at her and asked again, "'What in the world *are* you lookin' for, Annie?"

"I don't rightly know," she told him, then she chuckled and added, "But I can usually tell it when I spot it."

Claude went ahead to unload the wagon with Annie standing there watching him, and she said, "Claude, I'm looking for tin cans, tin cans and writing paper—anything I can cut up or write on."

He saw that she had a kind of tote sack over her shoulder, an old burlap bag with a red shoulder strap of sorts sewed on to it. He could see it had some bulges in it. "Claire told me you was tryin' to make some flowers out of tin."

"That's right. I am. Look here."

She held up her hands then, and Claude was shocked.

"Claire," he said, "they was all cut to pieces. She had cuts and iodine and bandages on ever' blamed finger! She said she wasn't very good at it yet, so while she healed up from one bout with it, she'd go out and hunt for more tin. She said she was wishin' she'd find her a pair of tin cutters out there. She said her scissors don't work very good." Shaking his head in disbelief, he finished, "She's tryin' to cut tin with plain scissors. Couldn't no man do that."

That was when Claire asked him if *they* had any tinsnips. She figured that if they did and if they didn't have any present use for them, she could take them over to Annie's and have a fresh look at the wreath she was making. Claire had collected a few tins, too. If Annie was searching through the town trash, she would be glad to have them.

When Claire arrived at Annie's door, she was nearly struck dumb. She found it impossible to comprehend what Annie was doing with the tins. The kitchen table was covered with what Annie called petals, different-sized, shining squares. Some of them were cut into a shape like a rose petal that was flattened out, and they all had a tiny strip of tin running down from the bottom like a little tail.

"I'm afraid the worst is yet to come," Annie had grinned at Claire, shaking her head at the mess and looking at her hands. "I know I can do it because I've made one rose already, but it's awful hard. I need some tools to work with, and I'm so cut up right now I can't make any more for a while." She laughed out loud and held up her foot with a shoe on it. "Look, Claire. I can't even go barefoot anymore, the floor and yard are so full of tin slivers!

"Sissie has fits all over me, and we have to watch Crow like hawks. He wants to hide all the pieces in the stove-wood, and I'm afraid he'll eat something he shouldn't."

She seemed cheerful to Claire, but she had dark circles under her eyes, and her hands were mangled. "I'm sorry for this mess, but you know how I am once I get started on something. I can't rightly think of much else."

"Let me see the one you finished," Claire said.

"It's right over here," and Annie picked up a big tin flower from the shelf over her washstand. "Of course, it's not painted yet. I'll have to dip them. But you can see how nice and tight the pieces make up."

What she showed Claire was a cabbage rose. It was in full bloom and looked to be about five inches wide. The outside petals curved around, their tops smoothed over backwards and down as naturally as those on a live rose. They curled around circle after circle of petals, the inside ones nearly straight. Even though it was still shining tin, Claire swore to Annie that it looked soft. It invited her touch, but another look at Annie's hands helped her change her mind about that.

"It has thirty-eight separate petals, Claire," Annie said softly, as though she herself felt genuine admiration for it.

"It's a beautiful thing, Annie," Claire declared, and she meant it. "I think I'll go the rest of my life without ever seein' anything like that rose. It's purely beautiful."

Then Claire asked, "Where did you ever see such a flower? I'm sure I never did."

"Well—it's the main flower in that dream I told you about. But I remember it, too, from a book one of my old teachers showed us. It'll be a kind of pink color. That wasn't in the book, but it's how I saw it. I love the shape, don't you?"

Claire did, and she said again that she thought the flower was wondrous. She was quieter than usual. "How in the world do you do it, Annie. How can you get the petals to curve like that?"

"You have to do it in stages. Here, I'll show you. Once you get them cut out, you build the blossom from the inside out, and you use this little copper wire to tighten the petals together by these bottom strips."

They sat down at the table. Claire couldn't keep herself from brushing the seat carefully when Annie couldn't see. Then Annie picked up one of the larger petal shapes and an old tin cup she had.

"I need different shapes for the curving. Sometimes I use a spoon or one of these rocks I've broken down into a shape I want. But here. See? You can press the tops of the petals down around the handle of the cup. You see?" She used the side of her scissors to press the tin down, and she moved the flat piece into different positions to make the curve deeper. It seemed to change the shape of the petal some, too.

Claire was not a person who could make things, and what Annie was doing seemed astonishing to her, miraculous. She was pleased to tell Annie so.

"I know it must seem peculiar for a grown woman to be doing such a thing, but I'll swear, Claire, it's got power over me." She was pushing the petal against the side of the cup, now, curving it just the tiniest bit. "See? This will be one of the biggest, outside ones." But then she broke one of her cuts open, and the blood dripped on the tin. "Oh, Glory! There I go again!" She was impatient and wiped her hand on her apron. The fresh stripe crossed dozens of others dried dark there.

It was then Claire finally remembered to give her the tinsnips. They were big and clumsy, but Annie grabbed them up and gave Claire a hug. "Oh, Claire! You've no idea how much these will help me. *They're* going to be the miracle."

Claire immediately began wondering what other tools Annie needed. Before she left, she invited Annie to come by the house to see what else Claude had that might be useful to her. Claire figured she could find a way to convince him that what Annie was doing was so fine they ought to help her even if it did seem crazy and her garden was too small.

68

Sissy suffered most because of the tombstone. She told her children she couldn't remember how many years they had to eat in between paint cans and petals—or how many slivers they had to dig out of their feet. "It messed up my girlhood," she would declare, "and I resented it. It's a wonder we didn't die of lockjaw!"

She was pretty sure it was what killed Crow, and on grouchy days, she'd say that was one good thing to come of it. But she never left the story there. She would soften it some. "Oh! I don't actually mean that. Mama loved that damned old bird, and he *was* company, I admit. But he belonged outside. Mama wouldn't hear of it, but that's where he belonged. And if he'd been out there, he wouldn't have eaten the tin slivers and sliced up his insides. At least that's what I figure happened. Mama said there was blood in his last droppings. But maybe he died of old age. I don't know. She found him in his basket. He just didn't get up one morning.

"She cried, and I helped her bury him out under his favorite tree where she liked to rock and watch him. I wasn't so sad about it, though, I have to tell you. All the time Isaac came to see me, there that crow was, hopping around over our feet or on the chairs or on Isaac's shoulders and head. He knew better than to try mine! Isaac just laughed, but it embarrassed me.

"And as if Crow wasn't enough, we had to traipse around all the junk Mama hauled in for the tombstone.

"That tombstone!

"Only it wasn't a tombstone. There wasn't any tomb and there wasn't any stone. And if there had been, we didn't know where Grandma was buried, and we didn't have a snowball's chance of getting it to Tennessee. It was just the craziest scheme I ever heard of."

Maybe because she was Lydia's younger sister—or maybe because she was the youngest child—or maybe because she grew up in a house with a tree in the corner, a crow in the tree, and a tombstone every place else, Sissie became a practical woman. She lowered her sights on Isaac Bogaart when she was fourteen and he was a big, strong boy who had already finished county school. He seemed wise and steady to her, and she had as many designs on him as he did her, only he didn't know it. He helped her get through the hard years after Lydia left and when her mother was possessed by the tombstone. He told her she should be patient with Annie.

"She's had a lot of sadness, Narcissa," he would say, his big, green eyes as gentle as a baby's, she thought. "If it pleases her, just let it be. She sure isn't hurting anybody."

And Sissie tried. She dusted what surfaces were safe, swept out between the floor-boards with the broom sideways to try to get the slivers out, milked cows to the rhythm of Annie's hammer flattening tins on the chopping block, pulled weeds and watered the garden— using Tornado to carry the buckets, though— and did her best to be helpful to her mother.

In her turn, Annie devoted herself to Sissie, at least in her own mind. She took care of the chickens, of Crow, of the horse and cow. She baked, prepared the chickens they ate, for she never wanted Sissie to have to stretch a chicken's neck through the nails and chop off a head—though Sissie was matter-of-fact about it as Isaac's wife and homemaker—and did all the wash for both of them. Annie never stopped working, and she never stopped trying to see what Sissie wanted or needed.

She wasn't a scholar like Emily and Edward; that was clear to Annie as she tried, occasionally, to help Sissie with her reading. She didn't seem to hanker for clothes the way Lydia did, although she could sew as well and occasionally made dresses for both herself and Annie.

What Sissie wanted was Isaac.

Annie could see that it was mutual, and she was glad for both of them. He was a sturdy, hard-working boy, sometimes helpful even to Annie when she was plowing the garden or trying to straighten up her chicken house one more time. He was always welcome.

But the tombstone had to be done, too. Crow was still her lucky bird, and she still wore her skunk skin muffler. For Annie, those were facts Sissie and Isaac would have to deal with. And she continued to work at her vision as regularly as she fed Gretchen, their latest cow.

Sissie remembered best how her mother made the lilies-of-the-valley. She couldn't remember who—probably Claire—but she believed someone must have given Annie some tools because she knew no money would have been spent to buy punches or a chisel, and Sissie remembered that Annie had both.

What she would do was cut out a small square of tin, then punch it down into the nut off a bolt. She'd take it out then cut down the tube to separate the petals. Finally she would bend them back, round them down, cut off the excess tin, and there they were, perfect little blossoms.

Sissie didn't remember how Annie made the other flowers, the coreopsis, or the leaves, but she could see they were all exactly right, too, the stamens and pistils rising right out of the rough little centers, the petals as yellow as the sun or as white as wild plum blossoms. The roses were dusky pink, nearly like a dove's breast. And the leaves had veins you could touch as well as you could see. They were perfect in every way Sissie's realistic eye could tell, a big wreath of bright and gentle flowers tied at the sides with two, big, soft, white, tin bows.

Sissie did see that what Annie was making was very pretty, and Sissie knew it meant the world to her mother. "But good lord!" she thought. "Enough is enough."

Still the work continued. Annie found a lot of tins in the trash. She also found a roll of wallpaper—from the Mallincoat house, she suspected. That roof got blown off while they were finishing the upstairs bedrooms. This paper had been very beautiful, dark green, like silk. But it was sodden and ruined when Annie got to it. She figured she could spread it out and dry it, though, and when she did, it gave her all the writing paper she needed, more than enough practice space for the letters she was forever struggling to make.

Best of all, she found a chicken incubator, a little, zinc Trusty just the size she wanted. All she needed to do was find a way to fit a glass over it and build it a frame of some kind. It was exactly what she needed, she realized the moment she saw it.

It was heavy, but she was afraid to leave it to go get Tornado. She feared someone else would take it. She imagined, at the same time, that she was being foolish, but it was such a treasure for her she couldn't convince herself that not many people would be looking for a worn-out chicken incubator. It wouldn't go in her sack, and she couldn't drag it, but she managed to squat down and get it up on her head. She padded under it with her sack and steadied it with one hand, swinging the other out to balance herself and her load. She reminded herself of the Negro washerwomen from Pikeville. They carried wash and water and sticks, everything but babies, on their heads. Annie decided that a person's neck is pretty strong.

It took a long time for her to make the lines she put behind the wreath. She had found a nice, old barrel-head at the dump, and she was going to put the poem on it, then attach the wreath, then put the whole thing in the bottom of the incubator. She intended that to stand vertically and become the central focus of the marker—as she imagined it. She would have to find some way to make it stand up and to protect it, but she simply worked at what was in front of her. She usually found a way to make things come out if she could get started. But the poem. That was a different matter. It wasn't something she could just figure out or stumble across. It was words, and they always did plague her.

Annie never did think she got it quite right, not the lines or the shapes of the letters. When she finally stepped back from what she had copied onto the barrel-head, even after she had drawn faint pencil lines across the dusty pink she had painted it, after she had tried her hardest to follow the lines and make the letters perfect, even then she could readily see that the first lines were smaller and closer together than the others. She just wasn't good at that kind of thing.

The first four lines sounded better to her than the last ones, too. She thought that might be because she got most of a couple of them from her dream—to help her get started right. The other two had come to her unexpectedly one night when she was watching the sun go down after she had fed the chickens.

The sun and moon always pleased Annie because they were the same as in Tennessee, and she could remember looking at them with Sherwood and Mary and Billy, especially when they would gather on the stoop to sing or just to be quiet together. Kansas and Tennessee were never the same, but the sun and moon were, and she liked to watch them not only for themselves but for the memories, what they helped her see again.

This particular evening, as the shadows lengthened beside the trees and made the old shed and her chicken coop look more off-balance than usual, a little mysterious, the sun turned the sky red and gold and pink and lavender before the blues began and darkened. Annie had a tired and peaceful feeling, a little sad because that time of evening always makes you want to be home, and she didn't rightly have one. And the lines came to her naturally and steadily:

> If we are slow forgetting,
>   It is because the sun
> Has such old ways of setting
>   When evening chores are done.

She felt comfortable with that. She knew it to be true. But it wasn't enough, and nothing else came to her, not that night, not for days.

She finally just had to sit down and wrestle the words out of nothing, and she didn't have the same easy feeling about them:

> Somewhere in Eternity
>   Beyond the primrose west
> We know your trials are over
>   Your troubled spirit rests.

For one thing, her mother was east, not west. For another, Annie didn't think Mary's spirit was troubled. But once a thing like that got in her mind, she couldn't seem to get rid of it. And once she wrote it down, it wouldn't budge, no matter what she tried. She decided, finally, that the verses were at least half true. Mary was in eternity, and her trials were over. Annie reckoned that was good enough for poetry, so she quit.

She practiced it over a hundred times and drew straight lines to write on, then penciled the verses on the wood. She still had to double back the next to last line because she hadn't planned it just right and didn't see that until it was too late.

Then, to top it all off, after she had darkened all the letters, finished all the little dots and bars and flat lines they were capped by or stood on, after she had completed the whole thing and taken a deep breath and let it out slowly, when she finally stepped back from what she had done, years of work, at least, a big mistake just jumped out at her.

"Oh, Glory!" she exploded. "I've left the r out of forgetting!"

She penciled it in the best she could, just above and between the o and the g, and it was the best letter of any of them. But it was a clear mistake. "Wouldn't you know it?" she quarreled at herself, flaming mad. "It's going to be like a wart on your nose—the very first thing anybody sees—and forever."

69

Edward agreed with Sissie. He couldn't see any way in the world to set that old incubator up over a grave, even saying they could get it to Tennessee and then find where their grandmother was laid to rest. But Annie was set on it.

Edward had visited her every six months or so, and he had seen the marker grow in pieces and patches. But he and Josie were both astonished at what she had done when they drove out to the house from town and saw the work assembled.

They had gone up to Brittsville with the older children and their third baby, Edward Claude, purposely to take Annie a glass for the marker. But they had stayed at the hotel because it was just easier for everybody. For one thing, though little Joseph and Annie J. were sweet as could be, at eight and four they were a handful. Josie was always scared they would fall out of the loft if they slept up there. Frankly, Edward was, too. That was one reason they had wanted to add on a bedroom for Annie back of the house. But she wouldn't hear of it.

Then, too, Sissie had been complaining for years about their mother and her project. "Now that I'm about to get married and move out," she had written, "it's finished. And if you don't come and help get a glass over it, Mama will leave it in the center of the room forever. Our grandchildren will have to walk around it!"

Sissie also warned them not to let their babies crawl on the floor or go barefoot. "They'll be cut to pieces on tin slivers," she insisted. "We still find them all the time!" When Edward laughed, she said, "Well, don't tell me I didn't warn you." So he and Josie decided the hotel would be safer as well as simpler.

But when they saw what Annie had completed, all their smiles and irony faded before it. Edward looked at Josie, and her eyes were full. It was as beautiful a thing as he ever hoped to see, and he knew Josie felt the same. The flowers looked as though Annie had just picked them, natural, bright, and fresh. But at the same time, the whole effect was very strange. Edward had the sense of being near something that had its own mystery, its own soul. It made him feel full in the chest, and not just because it was his mother's hard work and naked heart there in front of him. It moved him so deeply he had to catch his breath, and he could only hug Annie and tell her it was wonderful.

But that didn't solve any of the problems it created.

"I haven't decided how to stand it up the way I want it," she said, "and I don't know how to get it there. But those things will come to me if I give them time."

She didn't seem especially interested in how Edward fixed the glass and frame. He supposed she knew he would do his best to make it tight and secure. She had baked the children tiny pies which had about three cherries apiece in them, and she, Joseph, and Annie J. were having a tea party with a set of little blue and white dishes she'd gotten, including tea pot and sugar bowl. Then she rocked the baby and sang to him the way she had to all of her children.

Edward couldn't stand that, so he meandered outside with the older children and told them about how their aunt Tennessee had brought all the trees up from the creek—and about Doll and Crow. He had fixed a swing for them in one of the oaks, and they played in that for a while. He saw that Annie had some morning glories started on the wire he had fixed for her. He saw that her chicken house was as awful as ever and Tornado's shed nearly as bad.

But she had plenty of chickens, and these cows looked healthy and were obviously good milkers. The new buggy they'd got her looked fine, and so did the new filly she was training for Emily. Sand, this one was, for some writer, Annie said Emily had said. Annie loved her. Edward thought the reason Emily took up horses was to help their mother find a new Doll. "This Sand may be the one," she had written.

When he was fairly sure Annie had stopped singing and he

wouldn't be in any more danger of crying, he and the children went back in. Annie gave little Claude to Josie, and she came to examine Edward's work on her tombstone.

She gave it a considerable study, then she said, "Well. It's not just how I see it, but it's all right for now. I think that's all we can do for the time being. I've worked at it and around it for so long I'll feel a little lonesome when it's gone."

She ran the back of her hand over the glass, all around the wreath, then she said, "Let's take it up to the loft. I've got some old painted canvas up there we can wrap it in to protect it if the roof leaks. We need to get it out of here," she finished. "It's not natural to carry on your life around a grave marker."

As Edward eased it up the ladder, following Annie who had gone ahead to find the canvas, he saw Sissie roll her eyes up and heave a big sigh of relief. As far as he knew, his mother never saw it again.

70

Sissie and Isaac's wedding wasn't anything like Edward and Josie's, but Annie thought it was just as wonderful and even more fun. They had a big dance in his father's barn, and everybody in Brittsville and the surrounding territory was invited. Most of them came.

Annie made the newlyweds three beautiful baskets with fifty dollars in each one. Sissie hadn't gone to college and hadn't known Annie was saving for her. As Sissie saw it, Isaac just wouldn't abandon her. He saw her through Crow and the tombstone and Lydia and all her own silliness in between.

As a girl, she had been surprised that he would want anything to do with her or hers after Lydia had been so hateful to him. To his dying day, he bore the scar where she kicked him. Then she ran off with Andrew—to Sissie's enduring shame. But Isaac never held anything like that against her or her family. In fact, well before they married, he told Sissie he was the instigator of the quarrel with Lydia.

"I reckon I deserved what she gave me," he said. "I was botherin' her, and of course she always did have plenty of spunk, even as a little thing. I hate to admit it to you, Sissie," he said, "for it was a bad thing I said. I was just a thoughtless kid and didn't know any better. Well. I reckon I did too know better, but I was feelin' ornery, I guess, for I made a comment about your mama. I'd just heard it some place and repeated it to get Liddie's goat. I told her I guessed her mama wasn't any better than she should be, marryin' a second man before her first was cold in the grave.

"Damn! She hauled off and let me have it before the words was hardly out of my mouth. Served me right, too. I hadn't oughta of been spoutin' off like that. I always did feel bad about it even though I never got around to apologizin' to Liddie."

Sissie told him then and there than he never needed to feel bad about it again, for he had made it up to all of them a thousand times.

After they had married and got set up on a nice farm adjoining his parents', he did many more favors for Annie. He and Edward finally persuaded her to let them build on a bedroom in back so she wouldn't have to climb up the ladder to the loft any more. Gradually that became a place for the children to play once they were old enough, Sissy's four and Edward's surviving three. And they fixed her an indoor bathroom with an enameled tub and a pretty commode. They dug a deep, deep well and put a pump just by the house so she didn't have to carry water so far. She would never let them put in running water or electricity, but it wasn't because they weren't willing.

"I just don't need it," she told them, "and I don't want it!" They knew she meant what she said.

Emily bought her an oak ice box after she became superintendent of schools, and Edward bought her a good heating stove so she didn't have the old wash-stove in the middle of the room. Finally, at long last, she bought herself some pretty rugs and a handy, two-burner, cook-stove.

Isaac and Sissie wanted her to come live with them, but she wouldn't hear of it. "I've got too much to take care of out here," she would say, and Sissie supposed she did, in her mind, anyway. By this time, she had a fourth or fifth generation Gretel. They were always Gretel or Gretchen or Gertrude. She had her own mare, Delight, only Annie called her Della. She had her chickens, lots of chickens, for after the children were all gone, she wouldn't eat them anymore or sell them to be killed.

And she had a half-coyote dog that guarded the chickens day and night: Dick. He was the biggest reason she wouldn't move to Sissie's. She knew Sissie would never tolerate a coyote in the house. Then, too, Annie's chickens would have to mix with theirs, and she thought that was a problem. "The horses and cows would learn to get along together," she said, "but chickens are funny. Yours would pick some of mine to death, for sure, and that would be a shame. And I can't part with Dick."

So that was that.

Over the years, Sissie and her family visited Annie two or three times a week, and Annie loved the babies to pieces. But they never could get her to stay even overnight in Brittsville.

71

Annie knew she was growing much weaker. It seemed to her it was happening a little faster than she wanted it to, but then, she thought, nobody asked her permission. Sometimes she was just too tired to stay awake, and lying down was such a relief. It was her heart; she could tell that. Sometimes it would jump and race, and she would sit and wait for that to pass. It didn't hurt except down her arms and in her back, but she didn't have enough breath to sing or even dust very much.

To tell the truth, the dusting didn't bother her, for she never did tend to her house as she thought she should have. But she knew the children wouldn't mind anymore, not even Sissie. Emily was coming Saturday, and she would straighten things and make sure the ice box had enough food for the next week.

"Dear, dear Emily," Annie thought. She was so proud of her and looked forward to voting right beside her one day when she would finally have helped get women that right. But she could never quite get used to her driving a Ford car instead of her chestnut team.

Then she thought of Doll. "My Doll! How beautiful she was!" Annie could see the world separating around Doll's ears. They pointed it out to her—-what interested or worried the eager little mare—unless Annie would say, "Easy, beauty. It's all right, girl." Then she would turn one ear back to Annie to show she had heard or to find out what Annie wanted her to do next.

For a moment, Annie thought her arms were up around the horse's neck and she was smelling Doll's sweet, warm breast. But then as quickly she was not, and Della seemed to be nickering to her.

Emily understood horses, too.

When Annie got up, she felt dizzy and more tired than if she had just delivered a baby. She sat back down on the bed. She only wanted to lie there. But then she thought she heard Crow begging, and the sun was bright, so she gave it her best try and managed to shuffle around and dress.

She was very surprised to see how Crow looked. He was white as a rabbit's tail. But he was acting as he always did, standing up on a chair back, stretching his neck out, positively screeching at her, impatient as ever. Suddenly feeling mad as could be that he was giving her orders from her own chair, she quarreled back, "You be still right now, Crow."

She thought she sounded like Lydia. For a fleeting moment, Annie could see her there, stormy-faced and livid. She'd have chased him to the top of the cottonwood. Annie caught the edge of the table as the old pain for her daughter came back. She never felt it so strongly, and she thought it might kill her this time. But it didn't, and Annie heard herself saying Lydia's words the same as always: "Please be safe. Be well," before she headed on to the stove to stir up the fire and fix Crow's breakfast.

There weren't any scraps, and she couldn't find the bug jar, so she mixed up some bread and a little milk gravy. She couldn't breathe right at all, and she couldn't stand up straight, so she made a double batch. She figured that would last him until Saturday if need be. Then Emily would know what to do for him and Dick and the others. They could make their way in the meantime.

She thought she managed to pick up his oiled cloth, then Crow, turned to pearl, followed her on outside, quarreling every step of the way like a noisy, old floor-board.

The morning glories were a vision, a whole curtain of evening sky hanging there on the screen her dear Edward had put up for her. She pulled the rocker a little deeper into the shade and watched Crow.

She thought of Sissie, how indignant she was to have a crow in the house—and not even in a cage.

"Mama! He craps on things," she would scold, and Annie knew it was true. Sometimes he did. It didn't seem to bother her so much, but she understood how Sissie might be embarrassed.

"I'm scared to bring a friend here," she would say, "for fear that danged old bird will do his duty right in their lap. Mama, it's not clean!"

And Annie supposed it wasn't.

But sweet Isaac came anyway.

Crow hadn't had a branch to climb up for years, but he seemed to be in the tree just the same. He looked so strange, like alabaster. Annie could hardly believe it was him, but there he sat on his limb, cleaning his beak, then his feathers, all the time keeping up a steady conversation with her.

Sissie didn't remember how he had tried to help her.

Annie seemed to remember burying a bird.

The tree was big, and the breeze was picking up so the leaves sounded like water, a stream. Annie could close her eyes and hear the pasture spring—or even Roaring Hollow when it was low. But she concentrated on the pasture spring. Water always comforted her.

She was so tired she kept dozing off.

Dick came and licked her hand then stretched out by her chair.

Annie thought she was dreaming a lot—Tennessee, red-faced and determined, bringing water to the trees, dancing to the wind chimes, herself become a willow; Mary, reaching for the laurel. Annie saw Will touch Edward's face.

Once she woke to hear a jay arguing with Crow who had his wings out like a silver aeroplane, the one bent at the end. He was advancing down the limb. The jay quit the premises.

Annie remembered how Bright-Skies was afraid of him.

Dick looked up at her for some reason, then yawned and went back to sleep.

She was so easy. "It feels like home," she thought, with a small, comfortable surprise that she wasn't thinking of Walden's Ridge but of this very place, this spot by the blue flowers and the green trees and the gray boards of her house. She reached out to Tennessee's big cottonwood and pressed her fingers deep into the cracks of the bark.

After a while she could see the snow cradles and crystal tongs, a Ferris wheel of spun and spinning glass, and a golden explosion in the sky. Geese honked, very distant. Then tiny ice bells rang out sweetly, clearly.

From the center of a tulip cloud, ruby petals or thick, unsteady, crimson jewels all tinged with gold floated down, lingering, molten....

The tree felt solid under her hand, not like far-away and pale, dappled oaks in Roaring Hollow.

"I'd rather be here," she thought she heard herself say.

Epilogue

In 1892, William J. Sherwood donated to the Pikeville Historical Society a sword and sash once belonging to Union Army Captain Will Fairchild. These items were later given to the state historical society in Chattanooga, Tennessee, where they are catalogued and await exhibition space.

According to the *Kansas City Times* of August, 1890, a July Winkler was stabbed to death outside Annie Chambers' brothel at Third and Wyandotte.

Neither Andrew Geisendorfer nor Lydia Fairchild was ever again heard from.

In 1977, the Clendening Library of Historical Medicine of the Kansas University Medical Center received an anonymous donation of a cherry wood amputation kit made in 1855 by the Snowden Company of Philadelphia. Though well used, it had no name engraved on the brass nameplate.

The known descendants of Will and Annie Fairchild include a Kansas state senator, an astronaut, two physicians, four bankers, a reporter for CNN news, a poet, a county agent, and generations of farmers, teachers, 4-H leaders, and other productive citizens.

Emily Fairchild became one of the most respected teachers and school superintendents in the state of Kansas. After sixty-one years of devotion to her profession, she was honored by Delta Kappa Gamma, the national education society, with tributes from many of those whose lives she had touched. Some recalled how she used her fine horses to break snowdrifts and bring medicines to those struck by influenza. Some recall how she gave food or money to desperate families. Others spoke of how much she demanded of them in their studies. Her unfailing spirit was perhaps best captured by one of her students who wrote a poem for her including these verses:

> Would God grant you a favor
> In keeping with your grace,
> I think He'd mold a platter
> And on it fondly place
>
> A thousand precious jewels,
> Each one a fortune, yea,
> For you would have such pleasure
> Just giving them away.
>
> And when the dish was empty,
> You'd ponder—as of old:
> "Now who would be the happiest
> To have this piece of gold?"
>   —Leta Collins
> (Reprinted with permission from
>   the author.)

In 1996, an antiques dealer in Dyersville, Iowa, sold a large, roll-top desk to one Bruce Hennessey who, when examining it, found in a locked drawer marriage documents for Will Fairchild and Anna Sherwood. Discharge papers from the Union Army and several children's drawings by Edward, Tennessee, Emily, and Lydia were among other items found there.

When Anna Sherwood died, her estate was valued at $1720, excluding a savings account in the name of Lydia Claire Fairchild which was then valued at $312.

Tennessee's quilt remains in the possession of Edward's descendants, currently William C. Fairchild, M. D., and his wife, who keep with it Edward's narration of the circumstances in which it was created.

In the Parrish cemetery outside of Pikeville, a cedar more than seventy feet tall shades and protects the grave of Narcissa Fairchild and infant son.

In July, 2000, Anna Bessinger, great-great granddaughter of Anna Sherwood, donated a grave marker and a red and black striped basket purse, both created by Anna Sherwood, to the Mitchell County Historical Society Museum in Beloit, Kansas.

Together with her mother, husband, and children, she also placed a stone for Mary E. Sherwood along the Roaring Hollow branch near Pikeville, Tennessee, and wrote the following poem for Anna Sherwood—whose husband, family myth says, would never allow her to return there.

> We're going in for you, Annie Elizabeth Sherwood.
> We're cruising into the Sequatchie.
> We're climbing up the Ridge.
> We know about the branch,
> And we're headed for the Hollow
> Where wind roars through hickory and oak.
>
> We're going in for you.
> We can't save you from that strange-eyed man,
> But I'm here to tell you
> That when he bedded you and bedded you and bedded you,
> There was issue other than pain—
> And the five you knew—
> And we will take you with us for centuries.
>
> We're going to your very hill
> In the heart of Walden's Ridge,
> And we'll stomp on any copperhead
> That tries to scare us from your great, flat rock
> Where we'll stand and yell into the wind
> And into the water
> And into the tree roots
> And into the sky
> And into the snakes' very eyes:

"I've come back,
You blessed hills,
I've come back.
A part of me is back."

—This he could not see.
This he could not stop.—

"I'm back, my Tennessee,
I'm home."

The End

Printed in the United States
43587LVS00004B/40